Something She Can Feel

Also by Grace Octavia

PLAYING HARD TO GET

HIS FIRST WIFE

TAKE HER MAN

Published by Kensington Publishing Corporation

Something She Can Feel

GRACE OCTAVIA

KENSINGTON PUBLISHING CORP.
http://www.kensingtonbooks.com

DAFINA BOOKS are published by

Kensington Publishing Corp.
119 West 40th Street
New York, NY 10018

All Kensington Titles, Imprints, and Distributed Lines are available at special quantity discounts for bulk purchases for sales promotions, premiums, fund-raising, and educational or institutional use. Special book excerpts or customized printings can also be created to fit specific needs. For details, write or phone the office of the Kensington special sales manager: Kensington Publishing Corp., 119 West 40th Street, New York, NY 10018, attn: Special Sales Department, Phone: 1-800-221-2647.

ISBN-13: 978-0-7582-4564-7
ISBN-10: 0-7582-4564-6

First trade paperback printing: July 2009
First mass market printing: October 2011

10 9 8 7 6 5 4 3 2 1

Printed in the United States of America

For every sister woman who has ever had to
break free of the suffocating strongholds
others' trajectories have built in her life.
Get free.

TO YOU: AN ACKNOWLEDGMENT

When I was twenty years old, I walked into an office at Henry Holt & Company to begin an editorial internship with a stranger who said she liked my get-up-and-go attitude as we worked on a project over the phone. This stranger, I would soon learn, was Tracy "Boss Lady" Sherrod, my first real boss, who would later become my mentor, career advisor, coach, corrector, agent, and good friend. As we have worked together in those capacities (some all at once) over the last twelve years, I have learned so much about what it means to put in work and expect the best.

Looking back at thirty-two, I recall one thing Tracy always said to me when I was in my early twenties and still had the belief that all I needed to be happy in life was a good husband and a good job. Laughing heartily at my little goings-on, she and her friend Beverly would always say, "Wait until you get into your thirties. None of this stuff you're going through will matter. You'll have a better understanding of who you are." They'd walk off down the hallways at the office or into the busy New York streets, shaking their natural hair behind them as they continued into more serious conversation, and I'd say, "What do they know?"

Now, on the eve of my thirty-third birthday, my "Jesus year" (see Natasha Trethewey's poem "Miscegenation"), I know that those martini sipping sister women knew a lot. This thirties thing and coming to a realization about who and what I am has been so real to me and in this short time, I'm confident in saying that I've blossomed into more of a woman than I could've imagined. What's more, I've done it on my own; I've sacrificed, taken chances, been very afraid, sometimes a victim, but always victorious in the end.

I recall all of this to bring to light what I hope readers will get out of reading Journey's story in this little, hopeful novel, which in many ways is simply a study of one person coming to a realization about her life—it isn't working! It's a bildungsroman about a grown, black woman who thought all she needed was a good man and a good job to be someone. And who learned, in some odd ways, that there's got to be more.

That said, this book, *Something She Can Feel*, was written to acknowledge the journeys that all sister women have taken simply trying to see a true mirror image of themselves in a world that can be so hard on womenfolk.

In writing it, I first acknowledge the female spirit, the giver of life and hope in God, for inspiring this work and giving me the talent to bring it to life. To all of the sister women who have come before me—from my grandmother Julia Reid to my good-mother Jaimie Riley-Reid, thank you for believing in my dreams, supporting my vision, and having the courage to live in the world. To my sister peers, who are going through what I'm going through—you see the light at the end of the tunnel. Go on and get you some freedom! To the ladies at Kensington, who have worked with great patience and care with me on this project, *Essence*, *Black*

Expressions, *Romantic Times*, all of the dedicated book club leaders, book reviewers, conference organizers, writers and readers—this women's fiction thing has great power. It's for us and mostly organized by us. Let's continue to interface and grow.

Lastly, to my little sister girls—know that your dreams are your own, and whatever you want to be, *be* even better and bigger than that. Always search for something *you can feel* in your heart and in your soul first. The rest is trivial pursuit.

You treat me so much better than him.
And if I was sane, there'd be no competition.
But I'm in love with someone else.

—Jazmin Sullivan
"I'm In Love With Another Man"

Prologue: DOA

June 22, 2008
Ghana, West Africa

There was a click. There was a bang.

And then everything behind me went frozen. Dead.

My arms reached out toward the man falling to the ground in front of me. My heart stopped beating. The only sounds in the room were the bracelets clanking on my wrists and the thump the stranger's head made as it bounced hard against the barroom floor. I stood above him, frozen in place, and my throat felt tight and grainy. I couldn't breathe. Couldn't think of what to do next. This was the closest I'd ever been to someone so near death, and the farthest I'd ever been from home.

When it was done, when it seemed that I and everyone else in the backroom was sure the thing was over, time flickered from being a still, silent thing to something real, something moving, quick and sneaky. This was no picture. No fiction. Not a part of the love song I'd written in my notebook. It was the real thing. What in the hell was I doing there?

I gasped.

I heard the sound of a woman, who I thought was one of the waitresses, screaming, a glass hitting the floor, men rising to their feet.

The little air I had left in my gut was forced out when an arm belted itself around my stomach. It was Dame pulling me out of the backroom, across the narrow dance floor, toward the door. I could see the gun, pointed up now, in his other hand.

"He's dead. Oh-oh, my God, he's dead," I said, falling out of the bar behind Dame. The street was empty and we rushed, one behind the other, to hide behind an old van parked a ways down. "You killed him," I said.

I turned and tried to stop to look at Dame. I wanted to see his eyes, so I could know that we both knew what was going on, what had happened in just seconds.

Minutes earlier, we'd been laughing with the stranger in the red shirt and tan hat. His skin was the color and shine of oil. He hovered above our table, his teeth and eyes perfectly white and glowing in the dim light. He'd smiled wide when I told him that since we'd been in Ghana, Dame's already shadowy skin had tanned to the color of midnight and my once-permed hair had sweated out into a moist, perfect Afro. We were two lovers, mismatched and careless in the middle of a strange place, drunk from liquor that had no label and from heat that made my reality a blissful haze.

"We have to go," Dame said, tossing me back around before I could get a look at his eyes. "They'll kill us, if they catch us."

My heart sank. I heard wrestling and shouting coming from up the street. I craned my neck around the back of the van to see the bar emptying out. People were pointing in different directions along the dirt road and speaking a language I didn't know.

"Go," Dame said, his hand pressed hard at my back. A strong wind pushed my hair into my eyes and I struggled to see.

We hustled fast, in silence now, to the car, which seemed so far away. One of my bracelets popped and the wooden beads—red, black, and green, spelling out my name in rude, hand-painted white letters—scattered J-O-U-R-N-E-Y everywhere.

"Get everything. Everything," Dame growled after he'd kicked in the door to our hotel room. "I'm calling Benji. We going back to Accra right now."

He paced the floor, flipping his cell phone open and closed as I sat motionless in the space I'd found in the middle of the bed. Dame was in a rage. Moving his body around heavily, deliberately like a boxer.

I didn't know what would happen next. I had to think. I needed to pray.

With my purse still on my shoulder, I looked around. Everything was the same. The same as it was when we'd left the room that morning. My sea-colored sarong was on the floor. His sneakers were next to the nightstand. Outside, the black night above the beach was awaiting our nightly walk. It was still Kumasi. But everything was different.

I closed my eyes to pray for clarity. For forgiveness. For the man's soul. For Dame's soul. For anything I could think of. Just in that one second. To try to understand. But all I could hear was *bang. Bang. Bang.*

"This shit ain't working," I heard Dame say. I opened my eyes and looked up to see him looking at the phone and then at me. "Journey," Dame called, walking to me, "what you doing? We got to go."

"I—I . . ." I wanted to say something, but I kept remembering the blood seeping out of the tiny holes in the man's stomach as he landed at my feet.

"J," Dame said softly, bending down in front of me at the foot of the bed. "We don't have time for you to get all nervous now. We got to get out of here. You saw those people. They gonna come for us."

I watched as he tried to soften his eyes to persuade me. But I could not be moved. The man I was in love with just took someone's life. Or was he a man at all? Had I just been lying to myself all these weeks? Was everyone else right about Dame?

"You didn't have to do that," I said.

"Fuck!" Dame got up and turned his back.

"If you'd just let Benji come with us . . . everything would've been . . ." I got up and followed him as he rushed to the closet.

"Fine?" He looked at me as he pulled out our suitcases. "You said you wanted me to yourself."

"Yeah," I cried, "but I didn't think anything like this would happen."

"What do you think the bodyguards are for, J? You ain't with some random nigga. Everywhere I go, some fool comes up to test me," he said, frustrated. He threw the bags onto the bed and then began clumsily tossing things from the floor inside of them.

"But you still didn't have to do that. You shot that man."

"He pulled out a gun. He would've killed both of us."

"It was just on the table. He didn't say he was going to use it. He just wanted your watch." I looked down at the circle of diamonds and platinum hanging heavy and oversized from his wrist. Suddenly it seemed incredibly out of place.

"So, I was supposed to give it to him and then he was just gonna let us walk out of there? It don't work like that."

"I don't know," I said. "But I know that you didn't have to let things get out of control."

"Look, I ain't no country nigga that's about to have some fool that ain't even pointed a gun at me take my shit. He took the gun out first. He should've used it first. I ain't no pussy and if you want a pussy, I believe you got one at home waiting on you."

"Don't bring him into this."

"Well, that's what you wanted, right?" Dame stopped again and looked at me, his dark eyes seemingly looking right through me. "Me to talk it out and shit? Give that motherfucker my watch and then buy him dinner? Drinks on me? Right?" He turned to me and through his shirt I could see beads of sweat swelling across his tattoo-covered skin. A picture of Mary and Jesus on his stomach; a cross etched over his chest; his grandmother's name on his right arm; the entire continent of Africa across his back, the northernmost tip near his left ear and the southernmost by his rear. He was all strength. His muscles moved in consistent, solid shapes when he took a single step. Massive and strong. I once loved this. But now he seemed larger than anything I could handle. Almost dangerous. He snatched the bag from the bed and turned around, nearly hitting me with it.

"I just don't understand you."

"Understand me?" He threw the bag down angrily and hurried over to me, grabbing my arms and pushing me up against the wall. A vein twitched in his right temple. I saw the devil in him suddenly, pulsing in erratic red threads in his eyes. He wasn't even thinking. Pressed against me, I could feel his heart thumping madly, faster than the seconds that ran by. "Don't try to fucking understand me. I told you not to." His voice was hard and distant. "I ain't that man. I ain't him. I ain't . . ." He shoved me against the wall again and pushed away from me. "Shit," he shouted, turning away and balling up his fists, punching at the air in anger. "I knew this would happen if I brought you here. You don't belong here."

"What?" Still up against the wall and afraid to move, I began to cry. Now my heart was thumping and twitching in fear. I struggled to breathe. "Now I don't belong here? What about everything you said?"

"Look"—he turned and came back to me—"I ain't trying to be understood. I ain't that motherfucker. I'm from the street. All I know how to do is live. Stay alive." Spit gathered at the sides of his mouth and tears glossed his eyes, but in his rage not one would fall. "I'm an animal." He swung at the wall to the right of my head and his fist went right through to the other side. He pulled his hand out of the wall and blood dripped to the floor. "I'm a fucking king. No one in the world understands me. Not supposed to."

"Oh, my God, what did you do?" I said. I tried to grab his arm, but he pushed me to the floor.

"Take the car and go," he said, his voice now void of any emotion. He reached into his pocket, pulled out the car keys and threw them to the floor beside me. "Go back to Accra and get on the first plane back to Alabama. Get as far away from me as you can."

"But, Dame," I said, picking up the keys and fighting to see him through the tears in my eyes. He wasn't thinking. "They're gonna come for you."

He looked at me hard and just before a single tear fell from his right eye, calm and clear as the waves outside the door, he whispered, "Go," and walked out.

Journey . . . Just Living

June 23, 2008
Sunrise

My father lied to me. Love does hurt. In fact, sometimes, love can hurt so badly it burns your insides fast and heartless like the blue part of a flame. Now I'd known this for a long time. I'd seen that blue flame in my mother's eyes when my father didn't come home from Bible study some nights, even heard it in the cutting cries of my best friend when the love of her life hurt her and let her down again and again, so hard all she could do was weep. But I'd never felt it for myself. Never been there, out on the flame, burning and ready to die for something I'd loved with all of my living heart. I'd been safe from it all. In the incubator my life had built around me. Until that morning. The morning after Dame left me alone on the floor of a hotel room in the middle of nowhere in the world. Through the blue-black night, I'd found my way out of Kumasi and to the airport just as the sun rose in the sky. After spending every nickel I'd had on each of the plastic cards in my wallet to get on a plane home, I was standing outside on the tarmac of the runway waiting to board a plane back to the United States.

Flicking the ticket in my hand back and forth to create some coolness in the already humid morning heat, I felt a sinking in my insides I'd never known. Hours ago I had everything I ever wanted. Freedom. Music. And true love. Out of my incubator, I'd convinced myself that was all I needed from the world to survive. I'd risked everything for that. Walked away from my whole life. And now it was all gone. Just like that. I was going home. Alone. Hopeless. And feeling like a complete fool. My mother was right. I was thirty-three years old and playing with my life like I was a child.

I kept running through everything that had happened. Dame's hand on my thigh. The man sitting at our table. The watch. The gun. The bang. The fight. It wasn't real. I wanted so badly to hate Dame for everything that had gone wrong. For leaving me. But the Dame from last night wasn't the Dame I knew. Wasn't the Dame I loved. And standing there in that line, hurt from everything else in the world, my heart felt pain because I really wanted him to come chase after me. To at least apologize. Even I knew that was crazy. But it was true. Hidden in my heart, it was true. And I kept peeking over my shoulder to see if he'd appear. Lord, I prayed he'd come running. To make this all right. To make me not seem so crazy for turning my back on my life—my family, my friends, my world, my husband—for him. Foolish. But I looked and looked and he never came.

* * *

"Mother Africa will wait for you to return. Don't worry," a voice announced behind me as I looked out of the window after boarding the plane. I turned to see a slender, dark brown man, dressed in a navy blue business suit seated next to me in the aisle. He was handsome and I could tell by his accent that he was Ghanaian.

"I hope so," I said weakly and praying he would just leave me with my thoughts. I didn't feel like talking. I looked back at the gate door outside of the window.

"Oh, I see this all of the time—people crying as they lift off. Thinking this lovely place will just disappear. Just die. But no worries. Your mother is stronger than time. She has a secret and she is the only continent that can survive a living death. She'll survive forever. She'll always be here for you." He sounded eloquent and melancholy, like a poet. Through the corner of my eye I saw him ease back in his seat and put on his seatbelt as the flight attendant walked by.

"You must fly a lot then," I said.

"More than I'd like to. But it comes with the job." He extended his hand to shake mine. "Kweku Emmanuel Onyeche, attorney at law."

"Journey De-. . . Cash. And I'm . . . just . . . living."

It takes over sixteen hours to get to the United States from Ghana—and that doesn't include the layover. When I first got on the plane on the way over to Ghana with Dame, I wasn't even worried about the time. Others had Sudoku and laptops and DVDS and iPods, anything to keep them busy. All I had was my hand in Dame's and a smile plastered on my face. We'd laugh and joke and touch the whole way and even when we slept, we'd still be together. It seemed then that was all that mattered.

Now I was two hours into my return flight and with only my mind to occupy me, I was feeling restless and burdened by my sadness. A baby, who'd been wailing during takeoff, probably because of the air pressure building up, had finally been calmed and the flight attendants were busy serving drinks in the aisles, so I couldn't get up to walk around. Kweku, who I could tell was a bit older than me by his graying, distinguished side burns, was reading a magazine and clearly avoiding a stack of papers he'd set on the seat tray in front of him. I looked out of the window at the blueness surrounding the plane and thought of Dame. Of our song.

"I am worried about what people will say," I heard Kweku say. I turned to see him still looking at his magazine, so I didn't say anything. Perhaps he was reading aloud. "I wonder what they will say if I let you return to the U.S., looking so sad, 'Journey Cash . . . just living.' "

"I stopped caring about what people had to say a long time ago," I said, looking back to the endless blueness.

"Point taken. But this is my homeland we're talking about here. And I can't have them thinking it was Ghana that gave you such a sad face. So I'm thinking, 'Kweku, how do you get rid of this sad face to ensure the positive image of your country?' Ah! I must cheer up this pretty girl." He wagged his index finger in my face knowingly and we both laughed. "Now I could turn on my lethal charm and romance her like any true Ghanaian man would . . . but something tells me that perhaps it is not the attention of a man she needs." He tilted his head toward me for a response.

"No," I said with sadness infiltrating even this single syllable.

"So . . . then I think, perhaps it is an ear she needs."

"No, not that either."

He slid the magazine onto the pile of papers and folded his arms across his chest as we sat there in what seemed an unexpected silence. A man seated behind me began coughing and wrestled to clear his throat.

"Look," I started, "I've been through some crazy stuff and now I just want to go ho—" I couldn't finish the sentence. My voice splintered and I knew not to keep talking or I'd begin to cry.

"Easy," he said calmly. And when he moved to pat my knee, I could smell jasmine and oak. It was soft, yet masculine, a familiar scent I'd gathered in sniffs surrounding most of the well-to-do men I'd met in Ghana.

"I just—" I whispered. "I can't." I felt hot blood rushing to my face.

He patted my hand gently to stop.

"We have a long time together. And nowhere to go. So we might as well talk. Now, I could talk about myself, but my life is all contracts and reports." He pointed to the pile. "It would bore you to death. At least it did my last wife."

"She left you?" His tangent calmed me.

"No, she died. Literally . . . was listening to one of my stories from work one day and just died."

I wanted to laugh, but the solemn look on his face

was so serious. And I didn't know if he was kidding or not.

"Just fooling with you," he said finally and we both laughed. "But I am making a point. No one wants to hear about my life."

"Fine, but I don't know if I'm ready to talk about what happened."

"Well, maybe you don't have to. If you don't want to talk about what's wrong now . . . maybe start with when everything was right."

"Right . . . my life . . . when everything was right?" I exhaled and looked at him. Even in my gloom, pictures, moments came and I felt silly for even pulling them toward me. I had no clue who the man was sitting next to me. But something about him relaxed me. His confidence, the sincerity in his voice. He had the patience of my grandfather in his eyes and somehow I felt I could trust him. I had to trust somebody. I looked at the time. More than twelve hours to go. "Are you serious?" I was feeling weakened and wanting to embrace anything that would quiet my sadness. If just for a moment.

"Yes! Start wherever you like. When times were good—great." He looked off as if he was imagining me doing something fun. Dancing. Canoeing. Camping. "Before any of this thing that's troubling you even began."

"But that was a long time ago."

"If we have nothing, we have time," Kweku said, pushing back his seat to relax. "And if we run out of subjects, I guess we'll talk about . . . the contracts."

"Funny," I said, looking to the other side of the plane and wondering where I could begin to tell my story to this stranger. "Well," I began, "and I still don't know why I'm telling you this . . . but"—I took a deep breath—"if I had to start with when everything seemed good—great, I'd have to begin with my wedding."

PART ONE

Hear

Chapter One

July 7, 2007
Tuscaloosa, AL

I'd been nervous most of the morning before the wedding. Still wondering if I'd made the right decision. Evan was the only man I'd ever dated—we'd been together since the third grade. I loved him, and he loved me, and everybody loved us together. And coming from where I'm from, that was supposed to be enough to last a lifetime. Everyone, including Evan, expected us to get married right after college. But I wasn't so certain. I thought that just maybe there was more to see and do and that, well, perhaps Evan wasn't it for me. He was the perfect man. Good to me. And I loved him dearly. But something in my throat stopped me from saying, "yes." So against everyone's wishes, I made Evan wait ten years before I agreed to walk down the aisle, so I could be really sure. And I was for a while.

But when I woke up the morning of the wedding, something in my gut said that something else was missing. It was screaming and tossing inside of me like a banshee. But then my mother came to me wearing her pink bathrobe and rollers all over her head and told me this was normal. A case of the "cold feet" she'd had at her own wedding. We prayed together, both of our hands on her grandmother's Bible, and she reminded me of everything I loved about the man who was waiting breathlessly to be my husband.

Evan had done a lot of growing since he was a pudgy-faced, yellow boy with acne and chicken legs chasing me around the town when we were kids. Once his face slimmed and testosterone thickened his muscles, every girl from our street to Birmingham was asking so-and-so for the who-and-what about Evan DeLong. By the time we began freshman year at the University of Alabama, even I had to admit that Evan was easily the most handsome boy on campus. His face had the kind of refined charm that made him the perfect escort to the cotillion, the man on whose arm you wanted to be seen. But he only wanted me—the girl who everyone said looked like his sister. My Alabamian roots drew back to the days when African slaves, Choctaw Indians, and poor white Irishmen often married, and I was a few shades lighter than Evan's sandy-colored skin. I had brown hair that was streaked the color of corn during Alabama's long, hot summers, and despite a voluptuous size 18 frame, Evan and I did look a lot alike with our perfectly nana-pinched noses and clear, light brown eyes. My mother said it was because, like her and Daddy, we were around each other too much as children.

With those memories of who Evan was and the honorable, distinguished leader he'd become, my mother assured and reassured me, laced me up in the corseted, princess-styled gown we'd shipped from Milan, patted me on the back and held my hand until I walked down the aisle, whispered "I do," and Evan slid the shiny, platinum wedding band on my finger. Even then, I turned to look to her tearful, honey-colored eyes for certainty and waited for the thought of "something else" to fade.

And then it did.

The reception was at a refurbished twenties mansion at the end of a long, winding road on the outskirts of Tuscaloosa. Evan and I'd found it one day during a "get lost" drive when we were just teenagers. After jumping out of his first car—a silver, hand-me-down Mustang—and walking around a bit, we fell in love with the stately white columns and romantic, oil-burning light fixtures that led to the front door. We dreamed of one day living in that house; however, when it went up for sale just before we got engaged, we knew we couldn't afford it—I was a music teacher and Evan had just assumed a position as superintendent of the local school system. But Evan decided we should try to have a little piece of it and he got the real estate agent to let us use the five acres in the backyard to set up a tent for our wedding reception. With weeping willows and a still lake in the background, it was the ideal Southern setting for our new beginning together. The tent was draped in cream roses and silk ties; soft white lights and candles brightened every surface.

We arrived hand in hand, sitting atop the backseat of a fire engine red, convertible, 500 Series Mercedes-Benz. My dream car. It was brand new and Evan had somehow talked Sam Meeks down at the local dealership into letting us borrow the car so we could make what he'd called our "grand entrance as husband and wife" at the reception. "A car under the tent?" I asked when Evan told me his plan.

"It'll be fabulous. Don't worry," he said with his eyes sparkling. He loved attention.

So after the "I dos" and vows, and my daddy giving his blessing, we were riding into the reception, sitting at the back of that pretty red car, and waving at 350 seated guests like we were king and queen of the prom again. Evan clutched my hand and I looked to him to see him grinning and looking at me the way he always did.

"Do you remember what I told you when you said you would marry me?" Evan asked, his hand still holding mine as we rode slowly in the car on a path through the middle of a wide ring of tables. Everyone was waving and smiling at us as the DJ called our names and played a sweet Ray Charles song my mother selected for our arrival.

"What?" I asked.

"I told you," he began as his cousin Lenny stopped the car in the middle of the circle. He turned to me and looked into my eyes softly. "—that I'd give you the world."

Before I could say anything, the DJ stopped the song and began speaking to the guests.

"Now, I know everyone's excited that our couple has joined us, but please remain seated, because the groom has something he wants to say to his new bride."

Everyone began cheering and I looked at Evan, unsure of what was going on. We'd said our vows at the church. I certainly hadn't been prepared to say anything else. The DJ rushed over and handed Evan the microphone and with his usual charisma during such happy occasions, Evan jumped up and helped me out of the car.

"Now," he said into the microphone when we were standing beside each other next to the car, "I was just reminding my wife—"

When he said "wife," all 350 of our guests began to cheer wildly and even I felt myself blushing.

"That's right . . . my *wife,*" he went on. "I was reminding my *wife* that when she agreed to marry me, I said I'd give her the world. If nothing, I'm a man of my word! And I intend to do just that. So, Mrs. Journey *DeLong,* I have something I want you to know."

"Yes," I said shyly. Evan wasn't big on surprises. He was a planner and he seldom planned anything I didn't know about.

"He's pregnant!" my younger brother, Justin, hollered and everyone laughed.

"No, that's coming though . . ." Evan said playfully. "But seriously. Journey, you know that dream car you always wanted?"

"What?" I asked. "You mean—"

"Yeah, that car right there." He pointed to the pretty red car. "Well, darling, you don't need to dream about it anymore."

"What?" I shrieked this time.

A steady mix of "wow" and "ohh" came rising from the tables around us. I turned around to see my parents looking on arm in arm. My dad gave me a quick thumbs-up.

"What?" I cried in disbelief this time. "What?"

"Yes, it's yours." Evan smiled, and we hugged tightly.

"I love you so much," I whispered into his ear. "How did you—"

"Wait, y'all," Evan said into the microphone as people continued to applaud. "There's more . . ."

"More?" my best friend and maid of honor, Billie, shouted. "I hope there's a car for me!"

"Are you ready for this?" Evan asked me, holding the microphone behind his back with one hand and using the other to hold me. His eyes were now intent and serious.

"What is it?"

"There's a house in front of this tent," he whispered. "Eight bedrooms, ten bathrooms, a three-car garage—"

"No—" I broke loose from his embrace and looked at him, covering my mouth with my hands.

"And a master suite with a walk-in closet," he went on, "that now has every item of your clothing inside."

"Evan," I said happily as I began to cry. "We can't . . . we can't—" The indecisiveness I felt earlier was fading fast. I was Cinderella at the ball right there in that moment.

"No such thing." He placed his finger over my mouth before I could finish and handed me the microphone. "You tell them this one."

"He bought the house. He bought the house," I said, keeping my eyes on Evan. I couldn't believe it. I felt like I was living a fairy tale. And if I'd been looking for something when I woke up that morning, now I had everything. The perfect husband. The perfect house. The perfect car. What else could I ask for? Right?

Chapter Two

April 19, 2008

For the first few months of our marriage, I was above the clouds. Somewhere out in the cosmos, starring in a novel, living every day happily ever after. I was in love with being in love and sometimes I had to remind myself of how I felt just hours before I got married. I'd look at my ring and thank God my mother was there to prop me up. Our marriage was everything Evan had promised and as we decorated our house, hosted parties, went to church, and just settled into our life, I knew for sure I'd made the right decision. Other people were fighting and some were even breaking up, but Evan seemed to only want our lives to be perfect. And it was.

With Evan's new position in the school district, our recent nuptials, the house, and the pretty red car that seemed to get attention wherever we went, Evan and I had grown into a kind of celebrity couple in Tuscaloosa. People smiled when we walked into the grocery store, sent us expensive gifts and cards during the holidays, and we were on the invite lists of every event in town. We didn't even have to save spaces at the Alabama tailgates that season; other people held them for us.

Evan, brimming with pride at the kind of stature he'd sought since we were young, relished in the attention—committed himself to memorizing the names of all the important people we'd cross paths with each day, meticulously answered each holiday card and gift with a quick thank-you note boasting a picture of us sitting beside the fireplace in our mansion, and extended his arm to lead me into rooms filled with people as we continued to make our "grand entrances." While he was often over the top, this was just Evan. He was a true Southern gentleman—strong and gallant; full of honor and always wanting to exceed expectations. At times, it seemed like to him our life was a sitcom where he played the doting husband and I was the overjoyed wife. He was never angry and seldom raised his voice. One day, I pointed out that we never talked about anything that was serious, upsetting, or confrontational. I wanted to discuss what was happening in the world, who we really were, where we were going. Big stuff that I hadn't even thought of. To challenge and be challenged. To see outside of our little world into the big world in ways that would make us love where we were from that much more. Not planning my family's annual "Roll Tide" homecoming tailgate where we'd do our screaming duet of Lynyrd Skynyrd's "Sweet Home Alabama" and what red was *actually* crimson and what crimson was *actually* red. To this, Evan grinned and, after kissing me on the forehead, said I should be happy we didn't need to argue over stuff on the nightly news. He did that all day at work and didn't want to come home to it. We were happy and safe from all of that. This was a good thing.

While I was just as excited by the idea of happiness and living a carefree life, sometimes it felt so unreal that I wanted to scream and just argue about something. Anything I could bring up. It felt childish, but I wanted to prove that we were alive and not just these perfect robots. But I always failed. I'd jab about the laundry piling up and Evan would smile and call for the housekeeper. I'd complain that we needed to spend more time together and he'd clear his calendar for the day. It was wonderful. Amazing. But as we neared our one-year anniversary, I started to feel like I was suffocating. Caught in a tumbling storm of happiness and contentment with my life that made me feel like I was more dead than alive. I felt the need for *something* again, and just as they had before, both my mother and Evan seemed to have their own ideas about what that something was . . .

"When you gonna have a baby?" Opal Ivers, a student in my fourth-period chorus section asked abruptly one Friday as I waited to begin class. Opal was a petite, brown-skinned girl, who might have been pretty if she'd gotten braces when she was younger, but now her teeth were bucked and seemed to part comically with each passing week. The kids had a habit of teasing her, but that didn't stop Opal. She loved being the center of attention and took their laughs as encouragement.

Sitting at my desk behind the shaky piano I dared not ever use, as not one key was in tune, I frowned and dismissed the bold girl's question with my eyes, but she was reading my mind. In what had become a habit of late, Evan had hinted about a baby over breakfast just that morning. He'd pointed out that I was about to turn thirty-three that Sunday and that my own mother kept saying it was time. "My mama said a married woman got to have a baby," Opal went on. "That's why you get married in the first place. Your husband rich, too!"

"Opal," I started as the room continued to fill up with faces, "not all women want to have children . . . or can. And as far as my having a baby, that's private."

While I did want children, I just wasn't sure if it was time for me to take that step in my life. Yes, like Opal and her mother had pointed out, I was married and had a wonderful husband and home, but I still had other things to figure out. That, and not to mention, there was a school full of other babies that needed my attention.

The bell rang and a few stragglers came rushing in without apologizing—as I would never have done when I was in high school. But a lot had changed since then.

Last to arrive as usual was Zenobia Hamilton, a mother and second-year sophomore whose child's father—a second-year senior—was expecting another baby this summer with Patrice, another one of my students (luckily, she was in first period). Zenobia walked into the room with an air of marked carelessness; her feet were angled at a lazy ninety degrees and her lips were turned under into a nasty frown. Her short hair was undone and standing all over her head as if she'd just rolled out of the bed and onto the school bus.

"Ms. Hamilton," I said, signaling for her to come to my desk. I unbuttoned my suit jacket and slid it onto the chair behind me.

"Ummm-hum?" She was trying her best to communicate attitude in her voice. She rolled her eyes and balanced her weight on one of her ducked feet. This kind of unnecessary and unwarranted anger so early in the day used to perplex me eight years ago when I started teaching at Black Warrior, but now I'd figured out that mistreating me and mistreating their education, which for most of the students in the poorest school in the county pretty much made up the only structure they had in their day, was simply how they dealt with the emotional minefields that had been titled their life. Zenobia knew she was wrong for most of the things she did, but being bad and stepping out of line was the only thing she thought she could control. If I was fifteen, poor, and had a child with a high school student who was now expecting another baby with my classmate, I might be duck-walking and rolling my eyes, too.

"First, it's, 'Yes, Mrs. DeLong—' "

"*Yes, Mrs. DeLong,*" she said under her breath, repeating my words with no trace of sincerity.

"And second, what's wrong with your hair?"

"I ain't felt like combing it today."

"But you knew you had to come to school, didn't you?"

"Yeah, but my mama took my braids out last night and then my auntie ain't come over to braid it."

"Personal situation aside—what's the rule about hair grooming at the school?" I asked. The classroom grew quieter with each exchange. I didn't want to embarrass her, but the hair was really standing up high and now that she'd mentioned that she'd just taken out braids, I noticed that it hadn't been combed out and drifts of dandruff cradled her balding edges.

"I know the rule. We can't come to school without our hair combed."

"You know I have to send you to the office."

"It ain't my fault," she said. "I told my mama my auntie wasn't coming. She took my mama's money and went to smoke it."

It seemed every student knew what she was talking about—some had drug addictions of their own—and it was no longer a hidden Southern secret, not something these children felt they should be ashamed of. Zenobia hadn't lowered her voice.

"Ms. Hamilton," I whispered, leading her to the door. "I can't allow you to sit in my classroom with your hair like that."

"I know." She crossed her arms and shifted her weight again.

"Then, if you know, why would you—" I stopped myself. I could hear my voice becoming frustrated. "Just go to the bathroom and comb it. Put it in a ponytail or something and—"

"My hair don't fit in no ponytail. I ain't got no gel . . . no weave."

"Well, just comb it down and come back."

She sucked her teeth and flicked a red, wide-toothed comb out of her back pocket. One she could've used hours ago.

"Fine," she snarled. "I'll be back." She turned and waddled through the doorway and as she exited, I saw the promise of a firm belly imprinting the edges of her oversized T-shirt. I closed my eyes for three short seconds to say a little prayer of "no" and "God, please, no" over the pudge before turning back to the students.

"Let's do a quick warm up and then we'll pick back up where we left off on Thursday with 'Swing

Low'—we have only five more weeks to get this perfect for graduation," I said, looking up at the other students in front of me. Some were other Zenobias, others were coming close, and fewer, Opal included, were fighting their best to escape it. The rest simply hadn't come to school.

On cue, they groaned and rolled their brown eyes as if they'd thought there was some chance I wouldn't require them to sing—in chorus. Send them all home for not having combed their hair. Zippers unzipped and song sheets rustled as they were taken out to be held in front of the faces of the few kids who still had their copies or needed the words.

"Swing Low, Sweet Chariot" was the traditional spiritual the choir had sung at every graduation since Black Warrior was founded for Negro students in the early 1900s.

"Let's go." I walked to the organ I'd placed in front of the old piano.

Hum.

Hum.

Hum.

Hummmm.

I keyed and sang each note for all of the sections to warm them up and just as they did whenever I sang in class, the students relaxed in their seats and looked on like babies being soothed to sleep by a lullaby. They requested the notes again and again and finally, I laughed and said it was time for them to sing.

"But we want you to sing," Opal whined, and I shook my head no. But I was used to this. I'd grown up being a soloist in the choir at my father's church and my mother always bragged that I had the voice of an angel. I wasn't that confident, but when I was just a little girl, I realized that my singing could do things. My father would push me to the microphone and I'd sing nervously, watching as people fell to their knees and got saved right in front of me. Grown men and women would crawl on the floor and sing along with me, crying and praying, some speaking in tongues.

Hum.

Hum.

Hum.

Hummmm.

The sopranos. The tenors. The baritones. The altos. They sent waves of vibrating sounds through the oval-shaped room as I keyed the notes through the short warm up. Suddenly, the room went from dull and tired to a soothing rainbow of sound. The echoes from each group bounced around the room in a tide of confidence and calm.

Zenobia had come back, and we went on, charging at "Swing Low" so hard that it seemed as if the spirits of our ancestors, who rested on the very plantation that the school was built upon, were singing along. The children could feel this energy. All of them. And it came through in their voices. They were forgetting the past with song and living just in the moment in the wonder that we could sound as one. Right now, who they were and where they were from really didn't matter. When class ended, they would walk out and return to the world; but for now, singing and "Swing Low" held their spirits captive. In that moment, I was winning.

"Wow," Billie exclaimed, her face appearing and reappearing in the waves of a sea of students rushing out of the room when the bell rang. My best friend since she stopped Angie Martin from beating me up on the school yard in second grade, Billie taught language arts at Black Warrior. "They sounded really good. I heard them all the way down the hall."

"Thank you." I sat down at my desk and sighed. "Let's hope they sound that way at graduation."

"Oh, they will. They always do. Anyway, let's go get some lunch. I need to get out of here."

"You know I can't do that," I said, reaching for the running sneakers beneath my desk.

"You're working out today . . . again? This is five days in a row. This is getting out of control."

"Don't be mad at me because I'm actually *keeping* my grown lady New Year's resolution," I said, and Billie rolled her eyes at my reminder of our New Year's pact. At my parents' annual New Year's Day breakfast that year, Billie and I sat stuffed and sleepy in my parents' den, talking about how fast time was flying by. It seemed that only days ago, we were twenty-one and just graduating from college—making plans neither of us would keep and feeling like the rest of our lives were in front of us. And then, just in a quick snap of time, we'd awoken and found ourselves grown up and feeling like the rest of our lives had already happened. The maps had been laid out and we were just biding our time at work and in the mall. We groaned and complained that we were too young to be so old. We weren't in our forties, fifties, or sixties. We were in our thirties! And that was supposed to be the new twenties! So, why did we feel so . . . over? Not young enough to hang out in the new nightclubs downtown, but not old enough to play bingo in the basement of the VFW either. Then Billie came up with an idea—we had to make "grown lady" resolutions. We had to set up three goals for ourselves for the new year and not let another year pass us by without moving on them. Billie's grown lady resolutions came quick—letting go of her tumultuous relationship with Clyde and finally dating other men, going back to school to get her master's, and getting a new car—she'd been driving the same red Eclipse since college. My resolutions took a little longer. I just didn't know what I wanted. But finally, I decided that I wanted to start to travel—to see the world beyond the South, to start writing songs again, and to lose all of the extra weight I was carrying around.

"I'm just walking around the track outside for an hour." I added, "You should come, too."

"But it's Friday!"

"And?"

"And . . . it's your birthday weekend. You'll be thirty-three on Sunday." She sat down in the chair next to my desk and whimpered helplessly. "We need to start celebrating now."

"Celebrating what? It's just another year."

"You're one year growner!"

"Growner?"

"More grown . . . whatever." She flipped her hand at me.

"Okay, English teacher."

"Just . . . why don't you seem excited? Not even a little bit?"

"I'm excited," I said, hearing the lack of enthusiasm in my voice.

"Then come eat with me, pleeeeassee," she begged.

"But I have to walk today. I promised myself. I have to do something with these bad boys by summer." I pointed to the round hips that seemed to be stretching my size eighteen slacks into the next cut. "I'm not trying to be the Southern cliché of a black woman—in the church, singing . . . and big."

"Please, J. You know the brothers love those country curves."

"Not Evan."

"Well, *the* Mr. Evan Deeee-Long is a different breed. Everybody has to be picture perfect around him—since he wants to be the first black president of the universe—"

"Well, Obama's already on the way!" I said and we both laughed.

"Exactly. But I say, bump perfection . . . when there's a tasty sandwich shop waiting to feed us. Come on, girl!" She grinned and waved her hands rhythmically in front of my face to entice me.

"That's easy for you to say; you're a size 6," I said, laughing as I slid off my shoes and began putting on the sneakers. One of the smartest, boldest people I'd ever known, Billie was the kind of pretty girl other pretty girls hated to walk into a party with. For her, beauty was something she didn't have to work at. Billie's chestnut skin, doe eyes, and slender cheeks made her an eyeful even when she was asleep—and I lived with her for four years in college at Alabama, so I knew.

"Size doesn't matter when no one's there to look at it," she said, her voice sinking. "Sometimes, I feel like I could be a size 2 or 202 and that fool still wouldn't notice."

In high school, Billie was voted "Best Looking," and we expected some Prince Charming from New York or Atlanta to come swooping down to see her beauty and take her far away from Tuscaloosa. But she had other plans. The love of her heart, Clyde Pierce, wasn't from New York or Atlanta and he'd sworn long ago that he wasn't ever leaving his father's land. He graduated from Stillman College the year before we left the University of Alabama and took a job teaching gym and coaching the varsity football team at Black Warrior. No one was surprised when Billie signed up for a teaching job the following year—even though she was a finance major.

"Oh, Billie, don't bring up Clyde. I thought you were finally moving on . . . remember?" I said.

"I know, but it's hard to have his shit just all up in my face like this, you know?" She leaned her elbow on the desk and rested her chin in the palm of her hand.

As coach of the football team, Clyde had been enjoying his own form of celebrity in Tuscaloosa. And for years, he'd had a long line of fans linked up behind Billie. The biggest problem he had was crowd control—especially with the other female teachers at the school. But Billie loved even the sweat that bubbled on Clyde's brow, and while she usually wrote off his philandering and slipping in and out of janitorial closets as rumors, the last chitchat hit her like a bucket of his sweat in her face. Nearly a ringer for a younger Billie, the new physics teacher, Ms. Lindsey, was twenty-one, petite, and so cute the senior class voted to have her put on the list for their "Best Looking." Last year, when word spread around the "grown people senior class"—that's what we called the faculty—that Roscoe the janitor caught Clyde and Ms. Lindsey in his storage closet, giggling like teenagers . . . and naked, Billie broke it off and she'd dedicated herself to finding a good man ever since. I was happy that she'd had the strength to move on, but also thrown off by the fact that unlike every time before, it seemed that this time the breakup was final. And not from Billie's position either. Unlike the others, Clyde seemed serious about Ms. Lindsey. He paraded her around town, and sometimes I caught him looking at her the same way he'd looked at Billie when she was twenty-one and vibrant, her mind not caught up in the desires of a grown woman looking for a husband and family. This, of course, I never told Billie.

"How's the Internet dating thing going?" I asked, trying to change the subject from Clyde.

"It's great." She perked up suddenly. "In fact, do you remember the guy I've been writing? Mustafa?"

"Mustafa?"

"Yeah, the hot Nigerian man? We've been chatting for like a month. Anyway, he's coming to visit me this weekend."

"Visit you? Did you check him out? Are you sure he's not a part of some credit card scam or trying to marry you so he can get a green card? Did he ask you to transfer money into an account? I saw an e-mail about that."

While I'd accepted the fact that the chances of Billie meeting a single man above the age of twenty-five in Tuscaloosa was nil, and that next to driving to Birmingham every weekend, the Internet provided the next best way for her to fulfill her grown lady resolution, I was still a bit nervous about the men she'd been meeting online.

"Don't be so closed-minded, J. You know better. Mustafa is a good man. He has his own business and money. He's single. No kids. Lives alone," she rattled off but something in her voice was so rehearsed. I just couldn't figure out what it was. "He has it going on. And with the shortage of good men over here in the States, a sister had to expand her options to the Motherland." She started doing a ridiculous African dance and we both laughed.

"I'm just saying—he's coming here to see you? All the way from Africa? Does he know anything about Tuscaloosa? This isn't exactly a melting pot."

"Well, he has a little extra money and neither of us wants to wait . . . so, we figured . . . why not? We're grown."

"That's a good attitude, I guess," I said, running out of questions. "At least you know he's real and not some kid in Wisconsin with braces and a humpback."

"And I'm bringing him to church, so you guys can meet him."

"Bringing him to church?" I repeated. This was a serious "don't" for a single woman in the South. Bringing a man to church came with too many complications, including aunties assuming you two were getting married now (and saying prayers out loud over that very thing) and other single women trying to steal him away before the service was over. "This seems pretty serious." I stood up and began walking toward the door in my sneakers.

"I hope so. I want to get married, too! Get me a mansion and a Muuu-say-deess, Mrs. DeeeeLong," she teased.

"You're so funny." I laughed.

"So, I guess I won't see you until Sunday, then," Billie sighed, walking out of the classroom behind me.

"You know Evan has all these plans."

"Dang, I thought I'd at least get some time for girls' day at the mall. We need to get you some new clothes."

"New clothes? What's wrong with my clothes? I look fine." I looked down at my tan suit.

"Girl, it's time to step away from those two-piece sales at Belk," she said, eyeing me. "You look like you're going to church everywhere we go. Work—suit . . . picnic—suit . . . I think you wore a suit last week when we met up for dinner."

"I like my suits," I declared, laughing at her little list. "And I can't fit the itty-bitty teenager clothes you wear. I'm too big for that."

"First, you're not that big. And second, haven't you seen one Ashley Stewart?" she asked. "Thick girls are dressing divas now, too."

"I know, but I'm not trying on that stuff. I'll look silly."

"Don't knock it til you tried it!" She sucked her teeth slyly.

"Well, I'll have to 'try it' some other time. Because, like I said, this weekend, I'll be wearing *my suit* to hang out with *my husband*."

"Evan. Evan. Evan."

"Hater." I laughed. "I'll see you Sunday. We're having dinner at my parents' house after church, so you can come celebrate with me there."

"Will do, Ms. Journey. Will do. Ohh . . . What do you think Evan got you this year? I know it's something amazing. Evan knows how to give a gift." She rubbed her hands together in anticipation.

"I already got my gift."

"What?"

"My Juliet," I replied. "Last week, Evan finally had a contractor come out to the house to cut the Juliet balcony into the side wall of the bedroom. Now I can look out into the sky as I fall asleep. See the moon.

It's like I'm sleeping outside. You know I always wanted to do that."

"Now that's good living, ain't it?" she said as we both imagined the Alabamian star show I'd been enjoying beside my bed each night.

"It is. It sure is."

As I walked around the track, sweating fiercely beneath the lunchtime sun with the track team and a gym class running what seemed like light speeds ahead of me, I thought of what Billie had said about me not being excited about my birthday. I hadn't realized how passive I was being. She was right. I wasn't exactly running toward it—not the way I'd raced with cuddly kitten-clad calendars tacked up on my bedroom wall like posters for my thirteenth, sixteenth, eighteenth, and even twenty-first birthdays. Then, I was unable to be contained, felt free by the turn in time. My hips spread and swayed, my stance and step became more confident and in my heart, I believed the next year would be better, simply because I was older.

But the older I got, the more I learned that being older only meant less freedom, less spread and sway, and more of an acceptance that things were probably not going to change. It was flat-out hard to be excited about that. I supposed Billie and I were trying to avoid this feeling by making our resolutions to slow things down a bit, but so far, little was happening. On an impulse, I'd applied for my passport and carried it with me everywhere I went, just hoping that having it with me would help me plan my trip to anywhere sometime. But Evan was too busy with work and I couldn't go alone, so the thing just collected dust at the bottom of my purse. And it had company there, too—right next to the passport was the empty pad I'd bought to write all of my new songs in . . . whenever or wherever I was inspired by something. So far, I hadn't been inspired and, therefore, I hadn't written a single word beyond "Please Return To" and "Journey." The only thing I had going for me on that resolution list was my weight loss. I lost a few pounds over the months and if I wanted to keep them off, I had to keep on walking. Lunch could wait.

Chapter Three

Exodus 13:17. That's what Sunday is like for me at my father's brainchild of a church, Greater Prophet House. In the Bible, that's when God leads Moses and the Israelites out of Egypt through a desert road that leads to the mouth of the Red Sea. The Egyptians are coming up behind, and then old Moses lifts his staff and the entire sea cooperates, opening up a pathway for the fearful people to pass through safely.

In magnitude and magnificence, "The House," as everyone calls it, couldn't sit in the shadows of the Red Sea, but it was certainly getting there. The church my father, *the* Reverend Dr. Jethro Cash, started with just four members (my mother, older brother Jethro Jr, me, and my Nana Jessie) was now ministering to 20,000. Over thirty-one years, I watched from the front pew in my Sunday clothes and patent leather Mary Janes as my father's beard grayed and the choir loft grew from my mother holding a microphone with her gloved hands to a competition-ready chorus of 1,600 singers in seventeen choirs. Behind me, the pews bustled and busted out of control as we outgrew three sanctuaries, the second of which we marked with the birth of my rambunctious baby brother, Justin, and finally ended up in "The Big House"—a huge dome of pews that seemed to stretch out to the sky. It had seating for 25,000 and always filled up—even the overflow auditorium had additional overflow space. While the expected logistical chaos and traffic nightmare that was required to get worshippers into the sanctuary to hear the sermon was despised by everyone in the city from the mayor to my own mother, my father said he wouldn't stop adding on to the House until he had enough seats to make Bryant-Denny Stadium's 92,138 seats look like a pigpen—only instead of the Crimson Tide, we'd be "cheering for the Lord." And that was a big calling, because in our town, people christened their own babies in the name of the Tide.

Now as many screaming babies, casket-sharp men, and women in sun-shading church hats and nylons as there were in the House, when Evan and I got there, the bulging sea of people seemed to subside as we made our way to wherever my parents' orders were taking me. The people didn't turn their backs or walk in silence in another direction. Instead, they smiled and waved in the familial, responsible way people tend to look at preachers' kids they've watched grow up.

By the time we made our way to our seats, my cheeks were red from countless sweet kisses from church mothers and deaconesses. Evan's arms were weighed down with shiny gift bags, and his hands were filled with cards. Against Billie's wishes, I was wearing a teal and black pantsuit that hid the curves I didn't want to be seen and Evan complemented me in a black suit with a teal bowtie and handkerchief. I always told him we didn't need to match quite so much, but he loved doing it on special occasions. He said it looked better in pictures.

Around us, the church was coming alive with preparation. There were teleprompters and flat-screen TVs. A section for the hearing impaired and blind. The quiet room with the long windows toward the back where they took the women with the white prayer hats who'd gotten the Holy Ghost and needed to be rested. Dressed in their long red and black robes, the choir assembled on the bleachers, the band was in the pit, and the noble deacons and immaculate ushers were lining up and organizing the maze of rows like the officers had done to the cars outside. From where I was sitting, the House looked like it was preparing a crowd for the kickoff at a championship football game. While I'd known or brushed shoulders with most of the people inside, in the rows in front of me, their faces bled into a crowd of expectant onlookers. Worshippers who came to see something happen.

"Hallelujah," I heard my father's voice boom through the sound system before he walked onto the altar. "This is the day the Lord has made. Let us rejoice and be glad in it."

While I'd heard that voice and even those same words a million times before, I smiled at the familiarity and like everyone else, I stood up as my mother and father walked into the sanctuary, flanked by the assistant pastor Jack Newsome, a random circle of deacons, and the church secretaries.

Just as they did every Sunday, the band struck up the tune and the choir began to sing the words my father had just uttered. The praise dancers, girls and boys with happy, brown faces dressed in angel costumes, glided down the aisles, carrying colorful streamers, waving them on beat to our singing. The place came alive with people singing and holding their hands up and out in joy for the moment.

My mother turned beet red when she saw me. Breaking ranks with the procession, she dashed toward me with her arms extended.

"Yes, Lord," she cried, pulling me into her center. She added a drawl at the end of all of her words. And her sweet voice was decidedly and unapologetically Southern. "Thought you'd moved to Mexico."

"No, Mama," I said.

"Well, I called you last night, at 12 a.m. on the nose. Had to wish my only baby girl a happy birthday."

"I saw, but I was sleeping," I tried, shouting over the voices around us.

"No time for your mama? Not even on the day I gave birth to you." She grinned and hugged my brother Jethro Jr, who was standing beside me.

Jr was only five years older than me, but he assumed all of the righteous dignity of a Buddhist monk—even when he wasn't being righteous or dignified. He was a good-looking man with skin lighter than mine—almost like the insides of my hands—and serious, thick eyebrows. But like my father, what was most striking about my big brother was his size. At 6 feet 7 inches and 275 pounds, he and my father almost had to be leaders, because everyone had to look up to them. Jr, of course, ran with this. He'd served as the church's ministerial director since his senior year of college, and fought endlessly with Jack Newsome over who'd take my father's place when and *if* he ever retired.

While Jr looked like my father, my mother looked like someone had taken a video recording of me and pressed fast forward. She had skin the color of mozzarella cheese and eyes that were amber in the shade of my grandmother's front porch, but then lit up like fiery embers when the sun hit them. She was lovely to look at, pretty in the kind of way that reminded people in the South of how ironic it was that something so beautiful could come from the ugly things that happened during what they now called with an intentional drawl, "a long time ago."

"Little Journey made it to the Lord's house," my father said, making his way up to me from behind my mother. "And now a father can rest."

We hugged and people around us beamed at the sight. It was the family's tradition to hug in front of the congregation and sit together. It proved that our family was still close and leading the church. Even when we were all mad at each other and ready to draw blood, we did this because it was what was best for the church.

"Hey, Daddy," I said, nestling my head into his massive chest. While I was three, maybe four times the size I was when I had my first memories of resting my head there, he still seemed larger and more solid than anything in my world. Jethro Sr had his flaws, but being a good father to me and my brothers wasn't one of them. Yeah, he could be pushy and controlling, but he was there and when he gathered me and my bleeding knee, cut elbow, or hurt feelings up into his arms, I believed anything he said and knew the pain would go away with just one of Daddy's magical kisses. He was what people were speaking of when they said "he's a good father." Daddy loved his family, his church, and God. Over the years, I'd seen many men try to be him. Some were successful—they'd gone out and started their own churches in Huntsville and Mobile. And many more failed. Looking at my two brothers, I knew that neither outcome was easy.

Jack Newsome went through church news and greeted the visitors and church sons as we took our seats. Daddy and Mama sat in the first seats with the visiting sons and Newsome's seat beside them. In the next row, I sat beside Evan, Jr and his wife, May, Nana Jessie, and the heads of the largest ministries. Last in the row was the empty seat. It belonged to my younger brother, Justin. While he'd moved to Atlanta to go to an art school, which (according to paperwork my mother kept away from my father) he'd de-enrolled from after one semester, my father insisted that we leave a seat open for him in case he returned. Justin was always kind of an outsider—both in our family and in Tuscaloosa. He was sensitive, didn't really like to wrestle and compete the same way Jr did. He preferred to sit in the house and gossip with me, play with dolls and help me pick out their outfits. By the time he was in high school, he had a kind of sway to his step that led to the rumors swirling around him to grow from "he's soft" to "he's gay." It bothered him a lot. He always swore it wasn't true and even pointed to girls he liked, but inside I felt otherwise and thought he just didn't know it yet. Our upbringing hadn't left him space to know it. When he said he was moving to Atlanta, I secretly prayed

Justin would find himself—gay or not gay. I dared not tell anyone, but it really didn't matter to me. I just wanted him to be happy.

Billie always said that from her seat, my family looked like the happiest black people she'd ever seen. People talked about us. They watched as Jr tapped my father on the back and they shared a laugh. Loved it when my mother's face lit up every Sunday when she walked in the doors and saw me. And they thought Evan and I looked like we'd have perfect "pretty" babies. But it was what they weren't talking about in our presence that made us not so perfect. At the top of that list was Justin's absence and my father's indiscretions.

"I'm humbled, church," my father said after finally making his way to the altar with my mother by his side. "Every year, on this day, at this time, I'm humbled . . . because I'm reminded that I'm a daddy. . . . Not just a father or dad—my sons call me 'Dad,' you know? But a 'Daddy.' And there ain't but one person in this whole, big world that calls me that," he continued. "My baby girl. Now, I expect only the other 'daddys' in the room to understand what I'm talking about. It's a beautiful thing, you hear? When you have the love of a daughter. Nothing else in the world compares to how she looks at you. To how she holds on to you. To how it feels when she calls out to you, and you know that everyone knows that if nobody can't stop her from crying, her daddy can."

"Pastor ain't never lied!" a man cried from the front, standing up with his daughter in his arms. I looked a few rows ahead of him to see Newsome's mother, Sister Iris Newsome, being escorted to her seat in the front row by one of the ushers. She smiled toward Jack and through the corner of my eye, I saw Jr shift in his seat and whisper something to May.

"Now, Journey, you may have someone new to kiss your boo-boos and pay your bills," Daddy went on, looking at me as everyone laughed at his usual humor. "Evan, you'd better be paying her bills!" He squinted his eyes as Evan laughed and kissed me on the cheek. "But today, on your birthday, your daddy wants you to know that he's always gonna be here. You can be grown. You can even be gone. But you got only one daddy. And I have only one Journey. I love you. Happy Birthday!"

"Thank you, Daddy," I mouthed and then blew him a kiss.

"I promised myself I wouldn't cry," my mother said, taking the microphone. She'd been saying that for years, but I'd never seen that woman miss an opportunity to cry in public. She wiped a tear from her eye. "It's only once every few years that your birthday falls on the same day of the week. And whenever it's a Sunday, as a child of God, I like to make reason of it." Her voice turned strong and she looked out into the crowd with focus. While my mother taught elementary school for many years when I was young, she now led the women's ministry and served as the CEO of our church's women's center downtown. It took a while and a lot of nerve for her to finally take up a leadership role in the church. While most people loved her, there were some detractors—a constituency of five or so women who'd been linked or linked themselves to my father through nasty gossip and church chatter over the years. It always seemed like some woman who'd refused to leave the church was claiming my father was her man and leaving my mother. And while it hurt her deeply and I could see the distrust building in her eyes, he never left us and the rumors always eventually subsided. While I knew much of what people—mostly lonely and desperate women who'd turned from worshipping with him to actually worshipping my father—said was untrue, like my mother, I knew some had to be otherwise. And whenever we walked into a room, I felt her doubt and anxiety as she wondered who'd been in the company of her husband. But that anxiety had long faded and my father was growing too tired to fill up his calendar. So my mother grew stronger with her new attention and with that came her Word at the pulpit. Which everyone seemed to love.

"Today, my daughter celebrates her thirty-third birthday on a Sunday. Those of you who know your Word know that this is her Jesus year."

Daddy shook his head and the older people began to clap.

"The Bible lets us know that our Savior died at the age of thirty-three," she went on. "Now, I'm not saying this to bring you down. We don't need tears today. But when you really think about it, no one should be crying anyway. Because the day Jesus died also marks the day we were given eternal life. Something was renewed that day on Calvary. Yes, Lord. Something was reborn."

"Amen!" May said, standing up and clutching her Bible in its red leather case.

"And it was grace. It was glory. It was the opportunity to rectify your life through the blood!"

My mother jumped back from the altar and bounced on one leg as my father held her up.

"And when you—church and Journey—reach

your thirty-third year of life, you have to remember that," she said. "Remember that sacrifice and take stock!" She turned and looked at me as the sun came shelling through the skylight at the top of the dome and caught the embers in her eyes, the golden streaks in her hair. "Take stock and see what you've given, what you've done, what you've sacrificed, and know where you're going. Appreciate your life and the fact that you're still here, because Jesus knew that He wouldn't see a thirty-fourth birthday."

"Hallelujah!" More people began to stand up and the band began to play the soft notes of a song I used to sing lead for when I led the choir years ago, "It's Your Time."

"Know that anything is possible, baby," my mother said, waving for me to come to the altar. "It's your time."

I rushed to her side and hugged her more tightly than I had before. I'd woken up that morning without so much of a thought of what the day was supposed to be. What it meant. It was just another birthday, but for some reason I knew that I really needed to hear what she was saying to me.

"Sing, Journey," she said, handing me the microphone. "You know your mother loves to hear your singing."

I took the microphone and looked out into the crowd, my eyes bumping up against smiling and expectant faces, lights glaring from cameras and teleprompters.

I opened my mouth to sing but I couldn't. I couldn't do it. I couldn't sing. It was like a gob of glue was stuck in the bottom of my throat and nothing came out. Not a sound. I looked to my parents in panic and I stepped away from the altar. "Thank you," I said into the microphone and held it out to my father.

"She's choked up. It's okay, baby," my father said, taking the microphone. "It's okay, baby." He sent a nervous glare to the choir and Ashley Davis, who'd taken my spot in the lead when I left the choir, jumped up to catch ahold of the note.

Chapter Four

"*Here comes the preacher's kid; look at her shoes,"* Billie sang as Evan and I made our way back to the car after the service. Aside from accepting a few gifts from people passing by and greeting others, we didn't talk about what happened in the church. I didn't want to. I wasn't even sure what to say. Maybe I was choked up with all of the attention or maybe it was because I hadn't been up there in front of the congregation in months since I'd left the choir. Either way, it didn't feel right.

Billie's voice cracked on the possibility of every single note in her ditty. She was leaning against the passenger door where she always waited for me and Evan after church. A few steps away from her stood a tall, dark-skinned man, who was dressed in a distinctive, black suit. Even though Evan and I were still a few feet away, the man filled the suit out in such a way that I could tell that beneath the fabric was a solid, toned body. As we got a bit closer, I spied that in addition to having a handsome body, he also had a handsome face. A clean, close haircut framed an angular face with full lips and dark, masculine eyes. He stepped toward Billie and she stood up, sliding her arm around his waist and snuggling into his side.

"Who is that?" Evan demanded.

"I think it's her friend visiting from Nigeria."

"Africa?"

"Just be nice," I whispered to him before we approached.

"Thirty-three and older than me," Billie said, breaking away from the man and hugging me.

"I'll never be older than you, old lady," I said. "We're still counting gray hairs . . . and not years?"

"Very funny."

Evan and the man shook hands and I heard him say, "Mustafa," in an unyielding and defined voice that echoed *some* African nation. As they greeted one another, Billie and I exchanged quick, secretive glances that only two women who'd shared jokes their entire lives could understand. My glance said, *He's handsome, but who is he?* and Billie's glance said, *I know, girl.* We then regained our composure and turned back to the men.

"Journey, I'd like you to meet my dear friend," Billie said, trying to sound formal and as if she hadn't lost her cool. "Mustafa Serenge. He's from Nigeria."

"Most wonderful to meet you," Mustafa said, taking my hand and bowing down to kiss it. When he looked into my eyes, I saw that Mustafa was actually beyond handsome. He was striking—in the way that those *Ebony* male models were who always came to town with the fashion shows. Evan, who was a few inches shorter than Mustafa, recoils and looked on baffled like the other women who were walking by and stealing glances at the dark and lovely stranger.

"Oh," I said, knowing my face had turned red. "Well . . . it's a pleasure." I glanced at Billie again. My eyes said, *Where did this man come from?* Mustafa didn't look like he'd come from anyone's Internet dating site. More like someone's dreams.

Billie simply smiled and I knew I had no reason to be surprised. This sort of episode was perfectly in line with the drama filled arc of her life. Since she wore her grandmother's 44DD bra to second grade show-and-tell, I knew Billie to be the type to show up cloaked in the unexpected. That's why we'd been so close. It seemed that whenever I wanted to act out and just really be myself, Billie was right there, waiting to be my accomplice. Now, I wondered what I was signing up for.

"Your father is a holy man. You should be very proud," Mustafa said.

"Why, thank you," I replied, trying to sound as dignified as he did. "Did you enjoy the service?"

"It was fulfilling. I have much to share with my Christian brothers and sisters in Nigeria."

"Wonderful. I hope you'll be joining us for dinner at my parents' house this evening."

"We wouldn't miss it," Billie jumped in all giddy as she swung from Mustafa's huge arm like a little girl. "Mustafa will be here for three weeks, so we're making sure he sees everything . . . and everyone."

"Three weeks?" I repeated. "That's a long time. Don't you have to work, Mustafa?" Billie glared at me, but I ignored her.

"I am on holiday from my work," he said, obviously flustered, and I even heard a break in his voice.

"I closed my office, so I could be with my African violet."

Billie giggled and rubbed his arm.

"African violet?" Evan rolled his eyes and I nudged him hard.

"Well, we look forward to seeing you two later, then," I said, as Evan stepped away to open the car door.

"No, we look forward to it!" Billie cheered.

"Who was that?" Evan asked as we pulled off, still waving at Billie and Mustafa.

"Mustafa."

"I gathered," he said drily. "But what's he doing here?"

"I guess he's Billie's new boyfriend." I shrugged my shoulders to defend my best friend against whatever Evan was thinking about Mustafa, even though I was probably thinking the same thing. But I couldn't admit it. Evan had little patience where Billie was concerned. Through suggestion and snide remarks, it was clear he wanted to classify Billie as "wild," just like everyone else. But I knew that he knew this wasn't true. Evan was just offended that Billie was the other ear I had a hold of. The two always disagreed and Evan often suggested I get "more like-minded" friends. This made me wonder what exactly he thought was in my mind.

"Wait until Clyde gets an eyeful of this."

"Well, Clyde's moved on with Ms. Lindsey, so why can't she?"

Evan looked at me vacantly.

"We're not talking about what people should do. We're talking about Clyde and Billie. I hope that woman ain't trying to start something. Brought some fool over here from God knows where to start something."

"Start something? What are you talking about? If anything, Clyde's the one who started something. He's been starting something for years."

"Exactly," he said. "Billie should know his card by now."

"So she should just accept it and do nothing? Be single for the rest of her life as she puts up with his crap?"

"Again, we're not talking about what people should do."

Billie was squeezing my right hand. Hard. We were standing beside each other in a circle with everyone around the dining room table, holding hands as my father blessed the heap of food in the middle. While my mother alternated between two cooks during the week, so she could keep up with both my father's and her schedule, on most Sundays, she, Nana Jessie, May, and I made Sunday dinner together. "Got to learn the old way," Nana Jessie would say to May and me as she rolled and cut bags of collard greens and made biscuits from scratch with a precision that belied her age.

My parents lived in a gated estate that they'd planned room by room together. It was a gorgeous home, nearly twice the size of mine and Evan's, that had been featured three times in *Southern Living*. The editors simply never had enough space to capture all of the rooms my mother had specially designed herself.

About five minutes into the prayer, as my father

started praying for the homeless people in Tuscaloosa and the grandchildren he didn't have, Billie started squeezing my hand just as she'd done during my father's long prayers when we were children and she'd stayed for Sunday dinner. Then I'd really want to focus, to be prayerful and thankful for everything he'd mention, but sometimes it seemed the longer his prayer got, the farther my mind would drift. Most times, I felt guilty for not being able to "meditate on the Word" the way he and Jr seemed to be able to do. But the older I got, I realized that, like everyone else at the table, I was just hungry.

I was trying my best not to laugh at Billie's tight grip, but as I held it in, my body began to shake a bit. Evan, who was on my left, yanked my hand. Still listening to my father, I opened my eyes to see Evan frowning at me. Next to him was my father, his head low and nodding reflectively with each word, my mother, Nana Jessie, Jr, May, and Mustafa, who was next to Billie.

"Stop," Evan mouthed angrily.

I frowned back and rolled my eyes playfully at my father, who was now actually repeating a part of his sermon.

"Amen," my mother said suddenly during one of his pauses. "Amen and hallelujah."

"Amen," we all said quickly, opening our eyes and smiling at my father to reassure him we were prayed up sufficiently enough to eat.

A crease between his brow, he eyeballed each of us hard and slow as he always did and then looked to my mother.

"Amen," he said, resolved. "Let's eat."

Everyone relaxed and we sat down and began passing the large platters of Nana's macaroni and cheese and collard greens around like it was Thanksgiving. I watched as Jr eyed everything May put on her plate and scowled at him when he snatched a biscuit right from her hand. May, who was brown-skinned and had peach-shaped features and a sweet smile that immediately warmed everyone she came in contact with, had been taking fertility pills so she and Jr could finally have their first child after ten years of marriage. Over the last three years, her once petite frame had picked up more than fifty pounds and a face full of acne. But there was still no baby. It wasn't necessary to spend more than ten minutes with her and Jr to see that this and her new appearance was taking its toll on their marriage. He seldom even looked at her, and when he did, it was most certainly to say something nasty.

"You need to say no to the carbs, too," he said to me, laughing with Evan as I frowned at him for taking the biscuit.

"I don't see six packs on the two of you either." I reached and grabbed a second biscuit in protest—I'd regret that later. But my little demonstration was completely necessary. May was the most saved and sanctified person I knew. She knew her Bible better than most pastors and often spent hours in prayer. Because she was always trying to preserve her peaceful and angelic demeanor, she was often railroaded by Jr's antics. Her only ally at most dinner tables, I usually picked up the boxing gloves on her behalf.

"You two stop it," my mother said.

"There's nothing wrong with a woman with a little meat on her," Billie said, wiggling delightfully in her seat beside Mustafa. "They like big women in Nigeria. Don't they, Mustafa?"

"Yes. The queen must have fertile hips," Mustafa

said confidently and everyone looked up from their plates and at him. Jr's fork fell to the table, May leaned in to be sure she could catch every word, Nana Jessie's glasses were slid to the tip of her nose as she peeked over the brim to get a closer look. Even the crystal pyramids hanging from the chandelier over the table seemed to sparkle right on Mustafa.

While I'd explained everything I knew about the situation with Mustafa and Billie before the two got to the house, my family just wasn't the sort of crowd I could spring surprises on—at Sunday dinner, no less. We'd hosted many guests, some from as far away as Ireland and another minister who always came for Easter from Australia. But still, the Cashes weren't exactly the United Nations when it came to non-Southerners. And this non-Southerner happened to be with Billie, who my father swore was just out in the world, sleeping around with everyone since she wasn't married and thirty-two. Naturally, they'd been waiting to dig into Mustafa and he'd presented the perfect starting point for their inquisition.

"Fertile?" my father asked.

"Yes," Mustafa went on, "so she can give her husband many sons."

"Oh, you don't have to worry about that with Billie over there. She ain't the motherly type," Evan said. "Are you, Billie?"

"Yes, I am!" Billie cut her eyes at Evan. "I'm just looking for the right man. And I think I found him."

She and Mustafa linked hands on top of the table.

"How lovely," my mother said politely as she put more ham on my father's plate. "Mustafa, I hope you enjoyed worshipping with us today."

"It was quite moving, Mrs. Cash. It was—"

"Yes, that was a wonderful sermon, Dad," Evan cut Mustafa off, his voice effortlessly reverent.

"Amen," Nana Jessie agreed.

"Sure was," my mother added. "And it would've been better if Journey would've sung." She looked to me. "What happened?"

"I don't know. I just froze. I've been tired lately."

"I remember when you used to sing at church and the pews would fill up," my mother continued. "And I was so proud. Seemed like people got just as much out of your singing as they did the Word. Like the Holy Ghost was standing right next to you."

"Thank you, Mama."

"Don't thank your mother," my father said. "You thank God by using your gift. You can't do that if you don't sing—won't sing in the choir no more? You going to stop coming to church next?"

"I never said that. I'm just . . . busy with the school."

"Please," Jr said. "Those kids don't need more singing. They need some old-fashioned whipping. There's no parenting happening at home. Spare the rod—"

"—spoil the child," my father finished his sentence.

"Now, if the parents did more at home," Jr went on, "they wouldn't be in such bad shape. They got the Bloods and Crips and I heard they even got some gay sex parties there, too."

"Really?" May clutched her chest.

"Well . . . they're dealing with a lot," Evan said, his coolness lifted. With the new job, he became defensive whenever someone brought up something bad about Black Warrior.

"My Lord!" May bowed her head and began to

pray silently. I rested my elbows on the table and shook my head. All this in thirty minutes.

"I remember when children acted like children," Nana Jessie said. "Down here in the South, they listened to grown folks. Called them ma'am and sir and there wasn't none of this fighting going on."

"And that was because they got a whupping if they did," my father added. "Now they just let the kids run wild."

"It's not all bad," Billie said. "We have some success stories. Like that rapper Dame. I saw him on the cover of *Rolling Stone* at the grocery store the other day. He had on boxers and LOST painted on top of a cross on his chest. It was hot." She fanned herself playfully.

"The one with all the tattoos?" my mother asked.

"What you know about that, Mama?" Jr jumped in and we all looked at my mother surprised.

"I'm a Christian—not blind," she said. "No woman I know could've missed that cover in line at the grocery store. You can hardly ever get out of the store without seeing him on the cover of some magazine. And he never has a shirt on."

The men looked to the rest of us, but we just diverted our eyes. My mother was right. Dame was the big buzz. While I didn't listen to much hip-hop, I couldn't check out at the grocery store or even watch the news without seeing his face. He was bigmouthed and always in the news, shirtless and sweaty, his wild dreadlocks hanging over his shoulders like a lion's mane as he invaded the covers of magazines with headlines like "Crush the World" or "Take Over." In the tabloids, he was making love to married Hollywood stars and bed-hopping in London and Dublin. He had a clothing line, a beverage company and, as

I'd heard one of my students mention, a sneaker deal. All of the kids at the school wanted to emulate him because he was from Tuscaloosa. In fact, he'd gone to Black Warrior and was one of my former students. But still I wasn't so sure he was the best role model. The one song of his I'd listened to was about sex and drugs. Nothing unique. The kids needed much more than that.

"So you women all crazy about some rapper?" my father asked in the silence.

"He's not just some rapper. He's sold millions of albums and he got six Grammys last year," Billie insisted. "And he's from here."

"Tuscaloosa?"

"Yes, Dad," I said.

"Who are his people?" he quizzed.

"The girls at the clinic say he's one of those Simpsons from Hay Court," my mother said.

"Oh, he's from out there? I should've known," my father said, going into one of his speeches about how rap was ruining the black community and the world at the same time. He detested any form of rap music and refused to allow the kids to listen to even gospel rap at the church.

"Journey had him in her class," Billie said when he was done.

"You did?" My father looked at me as if I'd done something wrong.

"That was seven years ago when I first started teaching. He just sat in the back. He dropped out halfway through the year." Dame, whose real name was Damien Mitchell, joined the choir with two of his friends, but instead of singing, they mostly sat in the back of the classroom acting up and Dame would often write in a notebook. Because he was clearly the leader of the pack, I'd approach him sometimes, telling him that he was going to fail and that just sitting in the room didn't mean he was present. He'd promise to do better, but I knew he wouldn't change. He was a charmer—nice to look at, cocky, but very kind. The sort of boy the girls couldn't stop looking at and the boys wanted to follow. Those kinds seldom changed.

"So, y'all at my table bragging about some high school dropout, who's poisoning our kids with trash-talking set to music?" my father said. "He isn't doing anything but bringing down the community. Probably the reason the school is in such bad shape now."

"Well, not exactly, Dad," Evan said. "He's actually trying to give back."

"What?" I asked.

"He's been talking about coming to Black Warrior and donating some money to the school. We're trying to get a date together right now. Could be as soon as the week after next."

"You didn't tell me about that."

"It could still fall through," Evan said. "He's coming off of his promo tour and getting ready for a world tour later this year. I didn't want to speak before anything was confirmed. He's trying to get BET on board."

"Well, you can pump blood money into that school if you want," my father said. "It won't make things better."

"Oh, Jethro," my mother tried correcting him, "what do you want the boy to do? Give back or not? If the school needs money, they should take it. Just imagine if all these basketball players and football players and rappers all went back to their hometowns and gave away money. Look, let's not ruin Journey's birthday dinner talking about this. We should just discuss positive things."

"Thank you, Mama," I said, not knowing I'd want her to take that back in ten short seconds.

"Fine with me," my father said, turning to focus on me. "When are you and Evan going to give me a grandbaby?" he asked. "You're thirty-three. You don't want to wait until your eggs dry up."

"Dad—how could you even say something like that? Look, my *eggs* aren't going anywhere," I said, avoiding looking in May's direction. I hated it when he said things like that in front of her. "I'm fine."

"Well, what's the holdup?" he continued. "You got a husband, a good job, a home. . . . Do you need something else?"

Everyone at the table stopped eating and looked at me. Even Evan. He'd been working on me about this for a while now. It had turned into a regular argument and once it was clear that I hadn't made a decision and wouldn't stop taking the birth control pill until I did, he simply stopped having sex with me. He'd been claiming he was tired, but I suspected he was just trying to punish me by controlling me in some other way.

"It's not about what I need. I just want to do some other things in my life before I have a baby. I mean, I want to travel. I'm thirty-three and I've never used my passport."

"Well, you should've thought about that when you were younger," my father said.

"Where you want to go? Spring break in Cancun or something?" Jr laughed.

"You two back off," my mother said. "Journey, if

this is about travel, why can't you and Evan just take a trip together. You can go somewhere special before you have the baby."

"That's not what—" I tried, but Evan cut me off.

"We've actually been talking about having a baby." Evan slid his hand on top of mine on the table. Everyone got quiet. "Maybe this summer."

"Wonderful!" my mother shouted as if she hadn't heard anything I'd said and only Evan's words counted.

"Really?" May looked at me glumly.

"That's not what I said," I murmured to Evan. "I said we'd *talk* about it this summer."

"Oh, I'll have to start collecting squares for a quilt," Nana Jessie said. "I can cut some of my mama's old dresses."

"That'll be good luck for her," my mother cheered. "Oh . . . a girl, a baby girl. Finally another girl in the family."

"Who said it's going to be a girl? I never even said I was going to—" I tried, but this time my father cut me off.

"Ain't gonna be no girl. It's bad luck for the first baby to be a girl. Got to be a boy to pass on that blood line." He nodded to a smiling Evan and then glanced disapprovingly at Jr.

"Yes, sir," Evan said proudly, poking out his chest like my father.

"Now, after the boy, then you two can go right on and have a girl quickly," my father went on. "Don't wait like me and your mother did with you. Had you and Jr too far apart. That's why you don't get along. Have them back to back."

I kicked Billie beneath the table. Along with my father's long prayers, she'd seen this too many times at the dinner table—me entangled in the vector of my family's trajectory planning. Usually, Jr just went along with the plan; I took the approach of holding out until they changed the subject; Justin just ran away. As everyone else continued to eat and sip on their iced tea merrily with the thought of my two children, I looked to the tenth chair in the dining room set, empty and tucked away beside the china cabinet, and thought of Justin. Sometimes it seemed like he was the lucky one.

"So, I guess my baby sister's going to beat me," Jr said, walking me and Evan to the door after May and I'd helped my mother clean the kitchen. Billie and Mustafa left early to give Nana Jessie a ride home and my father departed with a plate he was taking to Mother Oliver, who'd been on our shut-in list at the church for years.

"I'll go get the car," Evan said, rushing out ahead of me.

"Beat you at what?" I asked Jr.

"Having a baby."

"That's still to be decided."

"Children are great. A blessing to any family."

"What do you know about it?" I asked. "You sound like you have one."

"Journey," he said, looking off, "just do it. Stop being so stubborn."

"Stubborn? You make it sound like I'm buying a car."

"You never could commit to anything."

"I can commit to not listening to you."

Jr had a way of twisting what seemed like human

concern into the platform for an insult. I had to fight back or be slaughtered.

"Journey, I'm not trying to argue with you," he said, opening the front door and gesturing for me to step outside. Evan was already sitting in the car at the head of the oval driveway that parted before the front door. "I wanted to talk to you."

"What's up?" I asked, already knowing what he was about to bring up. Whenever Jr did take time to talk to me—and it was rare—it was either to say something bad about Justin or bring up my taking over the entertainment ministry at the church. Besides the children's ministry, which Jack ran, the entertainment ministry was the biggest department at the church. Newly formed, it included dance, our visual arts direction, theater, the orchestra, the marching band, all of the choirs, and the biggest deal at the church since my father announced he was considering a move to television—audio and visual production. When all of the smaller ministries were organized under the umbrella of entertainment, my father instructed Jr to appoint a salaried director. The six-figure position would be the seventh of its kind at the church. Included were Jr's leadership of all of the ministerial directors, my mother's position as the executive officer of the women's clinic, the church's executive director who presided over all financial matters, and Jack, who doubled as assistant pastor and director of the children's ministry.

"I think it's time for you to come be with us," Jr said. "You know I still have that position open and waiting for you."

"We talked about this before." I stepped down to

the bottom step. "I'm at the school . . . I love what I do."

"Would you stop being selfish and think about your family . . . our legacy? This is your father's church. We can't entrust such a big role at the House to an outsider. Someone not in the family. There's too much at stake for us to do that again."

"Outsiders? Are you still angry about Jack? Is this about him?"

Jack had been a pebble in Jr's shoe for some time. Our father appointed him as assistant pastor and when he put him in a fully salaried position over the children's ministry—with equal pay to Jr—my brother took it as a personal attack. Suddenly, Jack couldn't be trusted and Jr was waiting for him to mess up.

"Don't bring that nigga up in front of my father's house." Jr raised his voice in a way that wasn't at all normal—even for him. I'd pushed a button; that was clear. I just didn't know which one.

"Look, I don't see why you think I'd be better for the job than anyone else. I have no training. No experience. I've been teaching all of my life. I don't know how to do anything else."

"You grew up in that church. You and I know what the people want. That's all it takes," he pleaded as we stood next to the car. "And we can pay for you to go to graduate school again—get an MBA this time."

"It's a big undertaking."

"You ever think maybe you got more to offer the world than just teaching some badass kids how to sing? Like maybe there was something else out there for you?"

In true Jethro, Jr style, he was tunneling into me

now. Digging so deep that his insults rang with a kind of honesty that made me second-guess my own feelings.

"Your place is in the church, Journey," he added. "Don't forget it."

Chapter Five

The ride home from my dinner celebration was so quiet that I could hear the loose gravel on the road skeet beneath the tires and pop up against the bottom of the car as Evan and I drove along. The grainy bursts reminded me of the hits I'd been taking all evening at my birthday celebration.

I was no fool. I knew Jr was just trying to twist up my thoughts to get his way, but I kept thinking maybe in his errors there was something correct. Maybe he was right. Maybe I couldn't sing because I hadn't been singing. Not outside of my classroom. Then I started thinking about why I'd left the choir in the first place. I said I wanted to focus on my students. It was true, but really, right before I left, I just kept feeling like I'd done everything I could do for the choir. It had been twenty years. I was ready to move on. But to what? Shifting things around in my purse, my eyes went from the empty passport to the empty notepad.

Even thinking I could make up the next step hadn't helped me find one.

It might've helped if I could talk to someone about these questions that were pitching against my brain, but Billie was so busy getting over Clyde and sometimes talking to my mother seemed impossible—she was so caught up in the things she wanted for my life. Then there was my perfect husband—the other person I was taking hits from all night, who was sitting next to me in silence.

I was still reeling from what he told my parents at dinner and I had nothing to say to him.

Evan hadn't necessarily been in rare form. His desire to be in the good favor of my father usually led to him agreeing with my father's constant hovering and dictation over my life. But he'd had some nerve twisting my words in front of my parents and making it seem as if we'd discussed and agreed to something he knew full well I said I needed more time with.

By the time we neared our house and Evan turned onto the dark, winding half-mile road that led to the driveway, I realized that my silence wasn't being refuted. In fact, it was becoming clear that Evan wasn't speaking to me either. As we swung into the driveway, I noticed that he hadn't turned on the radio, opened the windows, or even let down the top—as he usually did during these warmer spring nights. Disgusted that he could be playing upset when I was the one with reason to be on edge, I rolled my eyes and looked to him as he turned off the car. His face was tight and dismissive. He saw my glare, but he only slid the key from the ignition and opened his door, letting out an exaggerated groan.

"Okay, then," I said, still sitting in my seat as I waited for him to dare not come open my door. I was ready to fight. Not only had he discounted my feelings, but now he had the nerve to downplay my position by having his own. This was typical Evan. In any situation, he had to be the center of attention. Even the attention he gave on his own seemed to come with a price tag.

I sat and watched as he walked slowly and methodically from his door and then over to mine, taking his time as if helping me had now become a chore.

"So, you didn't want to open the door for me?" I asked.

"Don't start," he said gruffly. "I just want to get in the house and go to bed. I don't want to argue."

He slammed the door behind me and headed quickly toward the house. I knew what he was doing. He wanted to let my anger roll away in the middle of the night and then wake up in the morning cheery-faced and smiling, as if nothing had happened. Like my brother and any other man who ever tried to close a conversation by saying, "I don't want to argue," he meant he wanted to avoid a confrontation and quietly get his way. But it was too late for that. My birthday had already been ruined and I was ready to fight.

"I want to talk about what happened."

"Journey, I'm tired and if I was slow opening your door, I'm sorry."

"You know that's not what I'm talking about. I'm talking about how you acted in front of my parents," I blurted out, charging behind him into the house. "You spoke for me like . . . like . . . it's the Middle Ages or something."

"Don't overreact. No one was trying to speak for you. I was just answering their questions." His voice sounded more pained and stressed with each word.

He was trying to make developing an explanation for my questions seem like work, so I would appear more ridiculous. Like I was being irrational.

"Don't patronize me. You know what I mean, Evan. You know I never said I was ready to have a baby. I said we could talk about it this summer. Not go ahead and get pregnant. That's a big step. We need to figure it out."

"A big step? Figure it out?" His voice grew loud and echoed up and down the stairs in the middle of the vestibule. "Do you see this?" He raised his hands and turned around, looking at the house. "Do you see our lives? We're married. Are you going somewhere? Do you plan on going somewhere? What do you think is out there? Somebody else? Something better?" He walked over to me and stared into my eyes. "'Cause I know ain't no man gonna love you like I can. I'm not going anywhere and if you're not"—he put his arms around my waist—"there's nothing else to figure out. Let's not fight about it."

I heard everything Evan was saying and it made perfect sense, but I wanted more time and I couldn't find another way of explaining it to him.

"It's more than that," I said.

Evan dropped his hands and turned his back to me. He was quiet and he raised his hand to wipe his face.

"What more do you want from me?" he asked, his voice helpless and broken. "I'm a good husband. A good provider." He turned to face me. "I come home every night. I don't cheat on you. Never have. Not in twenty-five years. *Never.*" He came closer and I could see tears in his eyes. "I haven't tried to do anything but love you and make you happy. Provide a life for us. I waited ten years just to be your husband. I promised you I'd give you everything and you have it. Why can't you just do this for me?"

He looked at me and as we stood there quietly, motionless, I watched as his chest just sank in. Seemingly crushed, he slowly pulled off his tie and walked up the spiral staircase to our bedroom.

Lying in bed beside Evan, his back twisted tight and his face pointed away from me, I struggled hard to keep my position. But I was hurting now. The anger inside of me began to lessen as I suffered Evan's pain. My feelings aside, I knew Evan was a good man. He was right. He was a great husband and I didn't want to hurt him.

From my side of our king-sized, four-poster bed, my thoughts drifted to the beginning of my relationship with Evan. Before the pressure and everybody's opinions. Before we could even imagine sleeping in a bed together, in a house that was our own, in a town that we'd sworn was too small to ever consider for forever.

He'd asked me to be his girlfriend in the third grade.

"Just be my girl until Anne Toomer moves back here in the summer," he'd begged, splitting a little piece of Mary Jane candy with me at the river behind my daddy's first church where they used to baptize people. *"You gonna give me candy everyday?"* I asked, unsure of what a girlfriend was anyway. *"My mama says ain't no chil'en supposed to have sweets every day,"* he responded. I sighed and then he gave me the other half of the Mary Jane. *"I guess I can disobey her though . . .*

for you Journey Lynn Cash." I ate Evan's piece, Anne Toomer never came back to Alabama and we've been together ever since.

He'd been my best friend. Twenty-five years. That had to count for something. I could trace nearly every smiling moment of my life back to him. And while this knowledge—that I'd only realized a few years ago—both annoyed and stunned me at the same time, it was comfortable and Evan's presence alone always made me feel connected to something. He wasn't perfect, but I loved him.

Being a mother wouldn't be a bad thing I supposed. I thought of how much joy my brothers and I brought to my parents' lives, the fact that May couldn't even have children, and Zenobia, a girl with the rest of her life ahead of her, had one she couldn't even take care of. Suddenly, laying next to my husband, my feelings seemed selfish. I was scared of something Zenobia went running toward and May dreamed of. Opal's mother was right. It was the next step.

"I'm sorry," I said softly, not knowing if Evan was still awake.

He exhaled and rolled over onto his back.

"I didn't want to fight," he said.

"I know," I said.

"I don't know what came over me at dinner. I'm just so excited. I can't wait to be a father." He looked at me sadly. "But if you want to wait. . . . I guess we can talk about it this summer."

"No," I said, remembering his sweet face out by the river that afternoon. "You're right. Maybe it's time. I don't know what I'm waiting for. We'd be great parents." I thought of seeing another pudgy, yellow face like his walking around and smiled.

"You just made me the happiest man in the world,"

he said, sitting up and letting the sheet fall from his naked chest. Evan never worked out, but after years of doing work for his father's moving company when we were teenagers, he had a naturally powerful build. In the moonlight coming in from the French doors of our bedroom, I could see the muscles in his pecs tighten as he bent down to kiss me. His lips were soft, his kiss forceful, as it always was when we made love.

"Wait," he said, pulling away from me.

He pushed me onto my back and slid his arms between my arms and my body, opening my legs with his and then lowered himself toward me. His kissing became more passionate and he moved his hips in a way that made my body grow hot. As he pulled my nightgown over my head, I caressed his penis and kissed his chest.

"I love you," he said, sliding off his boxers. "I love you so much." He came down and pressed himself into me. I quickly wrapped my legs around him and kissed him on the neck.

"I love you, too."

Chapter Six

"Fight!" I heard someone holler from out in the hallway in what seemed like seconds after the fourth-period bell rang and my students were hustling out the door. I'd just slid my purse over my shoulder and was heading to the conference room for an emergency Wednesday lunch meeting the principal, Mr. Williams, had announced via a red slip in our mailboxes on Tuesday afternoon.

"Oh, no," I said, dropping the bag quickly and putting it back into my locking drawer. I'd broken up many fights—it came with the job nowadays—but somehow, each one had its own set of complications. The new ones sometimes included weapons and students so bold they weren't afraid to hit teachers—knock them over the head for trying to break up the fight. We'd gotten security guards into the school to deal with these kinds of issues, but still, the teachers were expected to respond initially. This presented me with another set of worries, because even though

I loved the Lord, I wasn't sure how I'd react if one of the children put their hands on me. *Help me, Holy Ghost!*

The students still left in the room, bumping into each other like blind bees, began to push to see what was going on outside.

"Fight!" someone yelled again as I tried to make my way through the tight throng. Outside of the door and in the center of a chaotic circle of violence-thirsty students was Zenobia and Patrice locked up chest to chest.

"You stupid-ass bitch," Zenobia shouted, twisting herself and somehow getting Patrice around and into a headlock. Patrice's belly poked out far and unprotected, a stretch appearing naked beneath her tight T-shirt. She shook and wrestled to get away, but, rushing in, I could see that Zenobia had a tight hold. "He don't fucking love you," Zenobia went on. "He ain't gonna ever love you."

"Break it up," I screamed, trying to force my way between them. "Someone call security! Security! Security," I hollered, knowing it would be a minute before they made it to the back of the building where the music room was located. As I attempted to pry Zenobia's hands from around Patrice's throat, I saw that Patrice was turning red and probably losing air.

"Let her go. She pregnant," one of the boys yelled.

"Let her go, Zenobia," I said. "You don't want to do this."

"She came over here fucking with me," Zenobia snarled. "I was minding my business."

"Let her go!"

One of the boys jumped in and tried to help me get the girls apart and when he did, I took a hold of Zenobia to restrain her, but Patrice came swinging and nearly hit my head. She landed a punch right in Zenobia's face.

"You want some, bitch?" Patrice yelled and I jumped back, thinking maybe she was talking to me.

Zenobia got away from me and charged Patrice, swinging her arms wildly. The entire crowd swayed with each step they took. Everything was moving so fast that I was afraid to get into it. Two boys finally grabbed Patrice again and I seized Zenobia with another student.

"Take her to the office," I screamed, out of breath.

"Fuck that! Let that bitch go. I'll drop that load for her! She don't want to see me!" Zenobia was still rapping, even as I pulled her toward my classroom.

"And Mike don't want you. He don't want your stanky pussy no way," Patrice cried.

"Get her to the office," I said again to the boys. "And the rest of you, go to the cafeteria."

When I finally got Zenobia into my room and seated at my desk, I realized that one of my earrings had fallen out in the tussle and my bun was hanging loose.

"What was that?" I asked, standing in front of Zenobia at the desk. She was still hot and looking like she wanted to race out of the room and find Patrice. If she had, she might've made it. I was worn out.

"I just told you," she said. "She came over here to fight me. I was just leaving class and she came up in my face . . . man, fuck this . . ." She kicked my desk.

"Zenobia, don't you dare use that language in here," I hollered. She just looked away and didn't say anything. "Now, it doesn't matter who attacked whom." I swiveled the chair around toward me. "That girl is pregnant. If you hurt her, you'd be arrested. Do you understand that?"

"Well, she'd be arrested, too . . . for hitting me." Zenobia's voice dented and she slackened a bit in the seat.

"What's that supposed to mean?" I asked and suddenly I remembered the little pouch I'd noticed beneath Zenobia's shirt the week before.

"You know what it mean."

"You're pregnant?"

She didn't say anything. She just looked down at the floor and shrugged her shoulders.

"Oh, Zenobia." I got up and closed the door. "How did this. . . . What happened? You just had a baby." I stopped and looked at her. "Is it Michael's?"

"Yes," she said. "I ain't no ho."

"You're still seeing him? Even after he got Patrice pregnant?"

Disturbed, I sat down on top of the desk beside Zenobia.

Mr. Gentry, one of the security guards, burst into the room.

"What's going on?" he asked with his hands clutching the weapons strapped to either side of his hips. "You been fighting?" He walked over to Zenobia. She kept her head bowed and focused on her knees. Her big talk had gone with the crowd. "Wild girl. You always in trouble."

"It was a fight," I said. "One student is in the office and . . . I'll bring Zenobia down in a second. She needs to cool down."

"You sure?" he asked. "This one's evil as a snake."

"Yeah, I'll walk her down. Don't worry."

"Okay," he said, looking at me doubtfully as he

inched away. "I'm going to be waiting at the end of the hall in case something happens."

"Great."

When Mr. Gentry walked out and I was alone with Zenobia again, I didn't know what to say. I was so disappointed. Zenobia wasn't the best student. But she was smart and if she'd just lose some of the anger she had, she could actually graduate from high school and maybe one day support herself and her baby. This was saying a lot at a high school where fifty percent of our students either didn't graduate or receive a standard high school diploma.

"How did you get into this, Zenobia?" I asked finally. "You already know what it's like to have a baby. It's not easy."

"I can't let her just take him," she said, looking at the door. "She having a boy. He wanted a boy."

"So you got pregnant to keep Michael?"

"No, it ain't like that. I love him."

"But, Zenobia, he's sleeping with other girls. And is he taking care of your first child?"

"He be with Mikayla," she said. "He loves her. And we was talking about getting a place too. But he gonna have to pay for Patrice's baby. Her mama gonna take him to court soon as he get a job. She told him."

"That's not just Patrice's baby. It's his too. Look, what are you going to do now?" I asked. "Have you told your mother?"

"No. She gonna kill me. Tried to the first time." Zenobia bent over in her seat and started crying.

"You have to tell her," I said, massaging her back as she cried, "so you two can come up with a plan together."

"Why did he have to get Patrice pregnant? He so stupid. She told him she was gonna do it."

"You can't think about what everybody else is doing; you have to focus on what's best for you and your baby," I said. "And you start by telling your mother."

"I can't," she said. "I can't tell her."

"We're just waiting on Ms. Davis and then we'll get started," Mr. Williams said, sitting at the head of the table in our conference room, surrounded by chatting teachers and administrators. "I think Superintendent DeLong will be running a bit late"—he looked down at his watch—"so, we'll get started without him." A former art teacher who'd been promoted to principal after the last No Child Left Behind sweep came through our school and led to all of the administrators being fired due to low test scores, Williams maintained little respect from the staff and most times it seemed we were just tolerating his leadership. He was a short, sunken-in, yellow man, who always looked lost and boyish in the suits he wore. If it wasn't for his balding head and graying beard, visitors would think he was a student and trample right past him. He wasn't the type of person you'd expect to see leading one of the most troubled schools in the state, but as Evan said, there wasn't exactly a list of people signing up for the low-paying, high-pressure position. So, he was it.

As we sat and waited for Ms. Davis, I noticed an attractive, dark-skinned woman sitting beside Mr. Williams. I'd never seen her before and I knew she wasn't from Tuscaloosa because she was wearing a sharp, tailored wine-colored suit that I was certain could be found nowhere in the state. I wondered if she was from the government, No Child Left Behind again, and she was coming to fire everyone or, worse, shut down the school altogether.

"Sorry, y'all," Billie said, running into the room with the look of a tardy student on her face. "I had tutorial." She looked around the room; her eyes, which were filled with anger she'd managed to conceal with her voice, nearly set Clyde on fire when she saw him sitting in the back of the room, two suspicious chairs down from Ms. Lindsey. I coughed to get her attention and keep her from going back there—as everyone but Clyde and Ms. Lindsey had hoped—and signaled that there was an empty seat next to me. Billie had been doing a fine job of parading Mustafa around every place in town in just two days. And as I suspected, most of these places were frequented by Clyde. But against lady lovebird's best wishes, he had yet to be in the right place at the right time.

"Thank you, Ms. Davis," Mr. Williams said as Billie sat down. "Now I know no one is happy about this meeting, and we all want to get to lunch, but it's necessary."

"Don't tell me we don't have a speaker for graduation again this year," Ms. Anderson, the history teacher, said. Everyone groaned at the thought. "We ain't got but a lick to go."

"No, no . . ." Mr. Williams said. "Let's not try to guess what the matter is. And also, it's a good thing."

"Good," Ms. Anderson replied, "because I don't need somebody's uncle to go up there and put me to sleep again."

People started laughing and the meeting was off to growing into an example of how it was equally difficult to manage adult teachers and young students.

We too had prom queens, class clowns, gossip girls, a class president, and even a jock with the new girl making out in the back. We even separated ourselves like the kids: the school someone went to, the fraternity or sorority they pledged, the side of town they grew up on made the difference between close friends and associates, best friends and working enemies. The only difference between us and the students was age and the fact that we preferred to call each other "Mr." and "Mrs."—and even that could be done without being totally polite.

"Well, we could just have Reverend Cash speak since his daughter works here. . . . I mean, if he has time," *Ms.* Angie Martin, the chemistry teacher, and my former elementary school enemy, said trying to sound helpful, but really more hateful. After our run-in in elementary school, she'd become even more sour on me in high school when Evan refused to make out with her in the boys' locker room. Things only got worse when I went to Alabama and she went to Stillman and we pledged different sororities. Ms. Martin—Angie—was purely nasty to me and she had a circle of grown-up girls to help her out.

"No, as I said," Mr. Williams went on, sounding a bit annoyed now—he was losing control, "we don't need a speaker. I called this meeting for two reasons. And in order to get things going before DeLong gets here, I'll just start by introducing the person next to me, who most of you probably don't know."

He gestured toward the strange woman from out of town and everyone got quiet, eager to discover who the new face was.

"This is Ms. Kayla Kenley. She's here to take over Ms. Oliver's biology class while Ms. Oliver is out on maternity leave. Ms. Kenley is a graduate of New York University. She's taught science at the Math and Science Academy in Manhattan and while she mostly teaches teachers now in the education program at Columbia University, we're lucky enough to have her for the last few weeks of the school year. We hope she'll leave an indelible impression on our students and pray she'll join us next year, as Ms. Oliver will still be out for a few weeks. Let's welcome her."

Everyone clapped and Ms. Kenley smiled accordingly, saying a few friendly words as Evan slipped into the room behind her.

"Oh, the man of the hour," Mr. Williams said, his face brightening when he noticed Evan behind him. "You're right on time."

"Mr. Williams," Evan said, imposing his stately voice and public demeanor. "Everyone." He waved quickly toward the middle of the room, but to no one in general. He looked in my direction and nodded at a few people seated around me, and then finally at me, smiling and winking quickly. We noticed a long time ago when Evan first got into office that in contrast to his mostly white colleagues downtown, our being married wasn't looked upon too positively by people at the school. Some argued favoritism, others put out rumors saying I made more than the principal, and many people blamed me for the fact that the school wasn't getting more money, claiming I should be able to convince Evan to get more funds into the system and directed at Black Warrior High. It was a barrel of ugly crabbiness, and to avoid it, Evan decided to keep things very simple in front of people.

"First, I want to thank you all for taking time out of your lunch break to meet with me. And second, I want to praise all of you personally for the fine job you've been doing, working with our students this year," Evan said. "I know it's not an easy job, and I want you to know that your district supports you. Thank all of you. Go on and give yourselves a round of applause." He smiled and led a mediocre, yet spirited, wave of claps.

"Now," Evan went on, "I'll be quick with my reason for having Mr. Williams assemble you all today. I know everyone wants to get to lunch." He paused and a few people snickered, but there were no outbursts as there had been with Mr. Williams. "I've been having some discussions with a former student of Black Warrior, a Mr. Damien Mitchell, who the world knows as Dame—and I know many of you have taught him. Basically, he's interested in coming to the school and bringing a crew from BET with him."

"Dame is bringing BET here? To Tuscaloosa?" Ms. Lindsey called from the back of the room like one of the students.

"*Whore,*" Billie blurted out while coughing to cover up her outburst.

"Yes," Evan responded to Ms. Lindsey. "Apparently, BET has a show where it features a day in the life of an artist. They're doing an episode featuring Dame and he'd like to bring the crew to our school—to Black Warrior High School—next Tuesday."

"Next Tuesday?" Ms. Lindsey shrieked, touching her hair as if she was already planning a full makeover. "That's less than a week away."

"I'm sorry . . . but who's this Dame?" one of the older faculty members interrupted.

"He's a rapper," Ms. Lindsey added enthusiastically, shaking enough in her seat so that her breasts bounced from one side to the other. "He's been number one on the charts since his new album, *The Same Dame*, dropped two months ago."

"Is that heifer a rap groupie? Video ho?" Billie whispered to me, but the secretary sitting next to me heard her. I was sure that remark would soon get around the school.

"Well, it seems that those high sales have served him well," Evan said, "because when he comes, he's presenting us with a check for one million dollars in front of the whole school."

"A million?" Billie asked. "To Black Warrior?"

I looked on stunned. Nearly immediately, I, along with everyone else, looked around the outdated, pale green conference room that hadn't changed in one way since my own father called the building "school." It was as if the mention alone of "one million dollars" in a room of desperate, tired teachers could make the place just change. The walls—pale green with speckled black and white nothingness—would become bright and clean; the table—an old oak, pitted and picked mass between us—would be mahogany; and instead of beat-up folding chairs, we'd be in leather swivels that turned and turned and comforted us as we taught the next generation of leaders. I could see, just as clearly as the woman next to me, but as I looked, I wondered what price we'd pay to get the pretty stuff. As my father always said, "Some things that are free cost you."

"Yes, you all heard me right! He's giving us a million dollars and he wants to present it to"—Evan suddenly looked toward me—"his favorite music teacher, Mrs. DeLong."

"Me?" I asked.

"Yes. He asked for you specifically. He wants you

to give the tour of the school with the camera crew and accept the check in front of the student body."

All eyes went from the walls, the table, the chairs, to me, falling around me like dominoes. Evan gave the rest of the details to a room of open mouths and internal thoughts so heavy I could hear them in their silence. I could even hear my father miles away: "Beware of those who don't sing for the Lord."

"You know he probably suggested Dame visit his wife's classroom," I heard one of the teachers in Ms. Martin's circle say when I walked past after the meeting.

"She ain't even a real teacher," another said. "Music—shit, I can teach that."

"Let her tell it, she's a damn college professor."

This exchange was just loud enough for me to hear, but low enough so that if I asked what the problem was, they'd all look at me like I was crazy. I didn't bother to turn around. I'd faced these kinds of comments in barrels behind me and also to my face. When I was much younger, I'd tried to make women like Ms. Martin and the others like me. But it was no use and after teaching and policing all morning, my feet were hurting and my big toe was threatening a revolt through the top of my gray leather heels.

"We certainly can find positive things to do with that money," I heard Mr. Williams say to Ms. Kenley and Evan when I reached the front of the room where they were still standing.

Evan was in the middle of excusing himself. He shook both of their hands very quickly and then nodded at me.

"I'll see you later," Evan said evenly.

"Sure," I replied, while I'd just rushed to the front to speak to him about Dame.

"Ms. Kenley, I want you to meet Mrs. DeLong," Mr. Williams said when Evan departed with a few teachers hoping to talk to him following closely behind. "She's Dr. DeLong's wife."

"Great to meet you," she said as we shook hands.

"My pleasure," I replied. "How are you settling into Alabama?"

"I'm fine. Just trying to get used to this heat. Got my hair all crazy-looking."

Another group of teachers came over and pulled Mr. Williams to the side.

"Oh, just let it go. Put it in a bun." I pointed to my hair.

"Good advice," she said.

"Hey, Ms. Davis and I normally go out to eat after work on Wednesdays. You're welcome to join us tonight. Nothing big. Just a local place a lot of teachers go to on hump night."

"That actually sounds great. My dinner date is working late tonight," she said. "Now, I hope you don't mind if I have a few drinks. I know I'm in the South now and you all are supposed to be Southern belles."

"Well, I don't know much about drinking," I said, amused by her assumption about Southern women, "but I can tell you, if you're looking for some fierce drinking competition, you sit down at a bar next to a 'Southern belle.' "

We both laughed and walked out of the conference room together.

When we stepped into the hallway, I could see Billie and Clyde a few steps down talking. His body was pressed against the wall with one knee up toward Billie and she was standing in the middle of the hallway with her hands on her hips. Her head shook from side to side as she spoke. In the dim light the sun sent through the window at the head of the hallway, their shadows could have been fifteen or fifty-five. The argument was the same—someone had done something and the other person was upset. Both Ms. Kenley and I stopped. There was no need to explain the situation.

"You're taking some African dude all over town. I heard you even took him to my brother's barbershop yesterday," I heard Clyde say loudly and agitated.

"He's not *some* African dude. His name is Mustafa and he needed a haircut," she said. "And what I do with him is none of your business." One of her hands fell from her hip. "You lost the right to that information a long time ago."

"So you love him?"

"Why don't you ask your little girlfriend if I love him? She seems to know everything else. Better yet, don't ask her a damn thing about me, because I don't want my name in her mouth."

"Jesus, Billie," he said. "Why do you play so many games?"

"Games?" She flicked her hand at him. "Games are for children. I believe your girlfriend knows about games." Billie flung her head around to seal her reading of Clyde and turned toward Ms. Kenley and me as she charged down the hall.

"There's one of our Southern belles now," I said.

Chapter Seven

"So everyone comes here?" Ms. Kenley, who'd I'd started calling Kayla, said, looking around the dining room floor of Wilhagens at clusters of teachers leaning into the mouths of emptying glasses as they sipped from skinny black straws. Like the other teachers, Billie and I ate dinner at Wilhagens most Wednesdays. It gave us a chance to decompress and, most recently, rag on Ms. Lindsey and Clyde. But most weeks, we just complained about work and the kids—who was bad, who was worse, and who we wanted so dearly to choke.

And it wasn't because we hated teaching. There were good days when we got their rolling eyes to stop and shine. But the energy it took to even out those times called for dinner and a martini (or two—for Billie).

"Best hole-in-the-wall in town," I said, pushing away from the table.

"Best cheap drinks in town." Billie raised her glass. "Notice all of the poor teachers in here!"

We took a quick visual survey of all of the tables on the dining room floor. They were filled with teachers, laughing and drinking merrily as if tomorrow wouldn't come in just a few short hours. Way in the back near the bathroom was where Angie Martin sat with her cackling crew of idiots at their normal table. When I first got there and rushed to the back to go to the bathroom, I heard one of them say, "There's Ms. Tuscaloosa herself! I wonder where her tiara is?" and they all laughed. And just as I opened the bathroom door, I heard Angie mention, "If only she knew her life wasn't as perfect as she thinks." At first it bothered me, as I wondered what she was talking about, but then I remembered what Billie always called them—Big Little Girls, meaning they were grown women who still played school-yard games. We had a lot of those in our town. They were unhappily married and happily evil to other people. And I wasn't going to fall victim to their crap.

"I see," Kayla said, looking around at everyone. "It looks like the entire staff is here. Aren't there other bars to go to?"

"If Tuscaloosa has anything, we have lots of bars. It's a basic requirement during football season," I said.

"Roll Tide, baby!" Billie hollered and Kayla nearly jumped out of her seat. I laughed and thought she'd have to get used to that in Alabama territory.

"But you can't beat two-for-one martinis at Wilhagens on Wednesday night," I said, still laughing.

"And they sure make them strong!" Kayla looked at her glass.

"But, Mrs. DeeeLong here, she can't partake."

"Yes, I can. . . . I just can't overdo it." I pushed my empty glass of iced tea to the center of the table. I'd skipped my one martini for the night, but hadn't told Billie why yet.

"Why?" Kayla asked.

"It's just a small-town thing," I replied.

"If certain people see Journey drinking, they'll go reporting all over town how she's a drunkard and living life on the edge," Billie added dramatically. "A life of sin!"

"My father's a pastor."

"Of the biggest church in Alabama," Billie chimed in.

"Oh, a preacher's kid!" Kayla said.

"Yep, a PK," Billie continued. "And we have to be careful how Ms. Journey represents herself in public. She could hardly sip a glass of wine until she turned twenty-five without it being in the church newsletter . . . and a part of her daddy's sermon."

"Really? That must be difficult, living under a constant spotlight like that."

I looked down at Kayla's black stilettos, hanging sexily from her feet where her naked, brown legs were swung out from beneath the table and crossed in a way I'd learned never to do. I bet she had red toenails inside those shoes and red shoes just like the ones she was wearing in her closet at home. And that no one had ever told Kayla that this was the sign of a "wild woman." While these admonitions were now outdated and certainly overturned, having heard them time and again throughout my childhood made me do a double take each time I saw a red toenail, red shoes, or hoseless brown legs flung out from beneath the secrecy of a dinner table—even when they were my own.

"You get used to it. I'm so used to it, I hardly know any other way to live," I said, thinking of how country and old-timey I must've seemed to her. Thirty-three and caring what other people thought of how much I drank? But this was how things were done with my family . . . with my community. Image was everything. I was a Cash. I was a DeLong. And new times or not, everywhere I went, that went with me. Now being a PK wasn't easy. I always had eyes on me—eyes that judged and tended to hold me in a higher regard than it did other kids. Unlike other PKs I knew (including Jr), I fought not to let the trappings of other people's ideas rule my life or add to my circumstances. When I was just eight years old and discovered that Nana Jessie had Krazy-glued the clothes onto my Barbie and Ken dolls—for fear I'd ever see them naked—I decided that I had to discover the world on my own. I'd soon see that that was easier said than done.

"What do you do to really enjoy yourself?" Kayla asked.

"Oh, we find ways," Billie said mischievously.

"Yeah, Billie's been quite the understanding friend," I said, petting her hand playfully on the table.

"Not like Ms. May," Billie jumped in. "She's good and saved."

"Who's that?" Kayla asked.

"That's my sister-in-law," I responded. "She's a bit of a holy roller."

"Jesus was her first boyfriend." Billie giggled.

"You laugh, but he must've been, for her to put up with my brother!"

"Yeah, I saw her on Monday night at the gas station. She looked so sad," Billie said.

"Really? You didn't tell me."

"I forgot all about it. Mustafa and I were filling up and she pulled up and got out of the car."

"Was she alone?"

"Yes. And I called her name, but she just kept on walking. So I didn't say anything. I figured she must've been coming from Monday night Bible study or something."

"You guys have Monday night Bible study here?" Kayla asked.

"Please, we have Bible study every night around here," Billie said. "We study the Bible so much down here that some pastors just be adding their own chapters. Talking about what Martin Luther King, Jr., did in the New Testament."

"Stop playing," I said, slapping Billie with my napkin as we all laughed. "But enough about us. What about you? What brings you to Tuscaloosa? And I know it wasn't to come teach at Black Warrior."

"Love," Kayla answered as if she'd anticipated my question.

"Love?" Billie and I said together.

"Love in Tuscaloosa?" Billie added. "Is he fifteen or fifty-nine?"

"No," she laughed.

"Well, you must've left him in New York City with the Prada, because there are no single men down here," Billie revealed.

"Who is it?" I asked.

"His name is Richard. Richard Holder."

"Holder?" I repeated, running through faces and names in my head.

"Little Dickie?" Billie jumped in, taking her third martini from the waitress.

"Yeah. You two know him?"

"Know him?" we said again together as our eyes widened and we looked from Kayla to one another in amazement.

"Girl, please, Tuscaloosa's the size of a squirrel's nuts. Of course we *know* him," Billie said matter-of-factly but with a hint of a question surrounding the word "know." Not only was Richard a traffic cop that led the way for me to the church every Sunday, but Little Dickie was also newly divorced from his wife of fifteen years. Without speaking, I knew that both Billie and I were wondering if the Kayla Kenley sipping blue liquor out of the martini glass at our table was the woman behind the rumored e-mails that split them up.

"I met him three months ago when I was up in Birmingham at my aunt's funeral," Kayla said to eyes that I'm sure were wide and still on her. "I'd never been there before and he was in town for the day. He showed me everything there was to see. I fell in love with the place . . . and then him. And here I am."

"Here you are . . ." Billie said, kicking me under the table and making the glasses shake so that Kayla knew what was happening.

"I know . . . I know," she started. "He's just gotten a divorce, and you two probably think I'm the Wicked Witch of the West. But the whole thing wasn't my idea. Richard was in Birmingham, trying to figure out a way to tell his wife it was over. Before we knew that we were anything more than a tour guide and a passenger, he told me that the whole marriage had been arranged." Kayla looked up at the ceiling fan above our table, her head tossing almost unnoticeably with each turn and I could tell that the blue liquor was probably getting to her and making her tell more than she should, but I wasn't about to stop her.

"He got her pregnant on prom night and her father and his father said they had to get married, so Richard did it. Only she miscarried a few days after the wedding. He stayed anyway, thinking it was what a man should do. But after fifteen years of living with someone he wasn't in love with, he wanted out. He just had to tell her . . ."

"Damn! That has got to be the saddest shit I've ever heard. More sad than hungry kids in Ethiopia and Hurricane Katrina combined. . . . Damn!"

"Shut up, Billie," I said.

"No, she's right. It is sad. But the one thing happy that came from it is us."

"But you have to be scared," I said. "You left your whole life behind to move down here to be with a man who could be on the rebound?"

"Journey Lynn! Do you have to suck the life out of every dream?" Billie hollered, slamming her fist on the table jokingly. "Kayla, do you have a stun gun, because I need to put her down?"

We all laughed, but I was serious. Even if Richard knew he didn't love Deena, how could he know he loved Kayla in just three months?

"I know it sounds crazy," Kayla said. "But not as crazy as it feels when I'm not with Richard. And even less crazy than it feels when I'm with him. So I figured I might as well do the least crazy thing and just move. I tried not to do it this fast. But he kept begging me to come. Said I didn't have to work or anything. 'Leave everything behind,' he kept saying. And he had me wrapped around his finger with that Southern talk of his. These Southern men are something else. Strong and sweet. Real men, who just want to take care of you and love you. They don't make men like that up North anymore."

"Oh, please," Billie said with her voice as dry and bitter as mustard. "Stay a while!"

"I wanted to be with Richard so badly that I just woke up one day and packed my bags," Kayla went on.

"But what if it doesn't work?" I asked.

"You know, I don't think I even care. I'm thirty-four. I know how to pack my bags when I'm ready to go. I haven't even sublet my apartment yet—you don't let go of New York real estate. I'm in love, but I'm not crazy. I told Richard I need a marriage certificate before I do that. I'm a big girl. . . . I mean, haven't you ever felt this way? Like in love and like you were willing to do anything for it? Just to feel it?"

"Girl, you're preaching to the choir up in here," Billie shouted, high-fiving Kayla over the table.

"It's like nothing else matters. Just you and him—that's how it is with me and Richard."

"Yeah, I felt that way about someone once, too. Only thing was half the women in Tuscaloosa feel the same way about him," Billie cut in, her eyes averted and sad. "Linda!" she called to the waitress, "I need another martini!"

Standing by the bar, Linda shook her head no and held up her hands like she was managing a steering wheel.

"What about you, Journey? I'm sure you feel that way about your husband," Kayla said to me.

"Yes, I love Evan. But I just. . . . I'd never do anything that crazy."

"You know, I think love should be crazy. Like that should be a basic requirement," Kayla said. "That love should make you feel something. Like in those songs Luther used to sing—just yearn for somebody to come home. And feel sick if they don't. Love should be crazy like that."

"Jalapeno pepper beneath your tongue crazy," Billie announced.

"Headless chicken crazy!" Kayla added and I couldn't help but chuckle.

"Bobby and Whitney crazy!" Billie topped it off, slapping her hand on the table.

"Hell, yeah, that's it right there. Bobby and Whitney crazy love," Kayla said emphatically.

"What?" I asked.

"Yeah, you know, imagine how she must've felt when his ghetto behind came sniffing around her skirt? She had it going on. Probably had princes and sheiks and all that after her, but no, Bobby stepped in and laid it down," Billie joked.

"Yes, he did!"

"So this is about sex?" I asked.

"No. We're talking about love." Kayla's voice filled with passion. "About how he probably made her feel so free, she thought she was probably going to explode if she didn't have him. She turned her back on everybody to be with him."

"Now that's crazy love," Billie added.

"But it was also cracky love," I added, and they both laughed.

"Good point," Kayla said, still laughing. "I guess there's a thin line between the two."

"I'll pass then," I said.

"So, what kind of love do you and your husband have?" Kayla asked casually and I had no response.

We had love. Just love. No adjectives. I'd never even thought to define it. It was just always there. And anything I could think to say—deep, true, real—sounded cliché and textbook in the face of crazy and even cracky. Anyone could have deep, true, real love. I wanted to say I had more. "I didn't mean to pry," Kayla added, looking concerned.

"No, you're not prying. I just never thought I had to define the kind of love we had."

"Anglerfish!" Billie said randomly, as if she'd just returned mentally to the table.

"What?" Kayla and I asked.

"I was trying to remember what Evan's mother used to call you two when we were in high school. She called you two anglerfish."

"Anglerfish?" Kayla said.

"Yes!"

"You remember that?" I asked.

"The female anglerfish uses a light on the top of her head to attract food," Billie started.

"A real light?" Kayla asked.

"No, it's just a collection of bacteria, but deep underwater it shines really bright like a light," Billie went on. "Anyway, the male anglerfish is like forty times smaller than the female and when he sees the light, he becomes hypnotized and just like her food, he just swims straight to the light. And when he gets to the female, the male bites into the side of her body and doesn't let go."

"Oh, I can't believe you're telling her this foolishness," I said.

"And the craziest part is that he doesn't even have his own guts, so he just continues to chew into her skin until he becomes a part of her. He becomes a little knob hanging on the side of her body, disappearing into the female. Giving up his whole life for her. For a long time scientists didn't even know male angler-fish existed. They thought the bumps on the females were just growths."

"That sounds pretty gross." Kayla frowned.

"Don't listen to her," I said.

"It wasn't me. That was Mrs. DeLong. Even she could see how much Evan loved you. He's the one who's crazy in love!"

"My husband and I have a great relationship," I said to Kayla. "Evan's mother was right. He can be very giving when it comes to me, but there's nothing wrong with having a man at home who loves you."

"You can say that again!" Kayla cheered.

Evan was sitting in the living room when I walked in the door. Still dressed in his work clothes, he sat back in one of the cozy chairs by the fireplace with a bottle of beer in his hand.

"Well, hello," I said, setting down my keys and purse on a huge oak table that sat in the middle of the foyer before the living room.

"Hey!" He jerked and turned to me quickly, making it clear he didn't know I'd walked in.

"You okay?" I asked as I walked toward him. We hardly ever sat in the living room unless we had company.

"Yes. I was just sitting here admiring my big house and waiting for my lovely wife to come home." He grinned and motioned for me to come and sit on his lap.

"Oh, don't try to flatter me, Mr. DeLong."

"What? Why can't a man just admire his life? His

wife. His home. His baby on the way—" He tickled my stomach as I sat down.

"I guess that's perfectly innocent. So, you've been sitting in here all night?" I said, laughing. "You haven't even taken off your work clothes."

"No. I just got in about thirty minutes ago. I was in a meeting with the school attorneys and then I met with Mr. Williams about those scholarships. Everything ran over, so I'm just getting home." I could tell he was exhausted. Evan got like this sometimes. He'd work himself until he was literally turning blue at his temples from the pressure.

"Have you eaten?"

"No . . . I'm fine."

"Evan, I told you not to do that. It's not healthy," I said, rubbing his temples.

"There was just a lot to do. I have to get ready for this thing with Dame and you know the white folks are nervous about having a rapper come to the school."

"You're kidding me."

"Yeah. There's all this stuff about image and what the other districts will think," he said.

"I don't think Black Warrior needs to worry about image. Besides, we need the money. I'm sure they understand that."

"It's hard to understand people needing money when you have it and you've had it for a long time. They think the kids are just lazy. And the teachers aren't doing their jobs. And with me standing over the whole thing, it's so easy for them to say, 'And they have a black man leading the ship.' " He sighed and took a sip of his beer. "It's just a lot of crap, but I have to play their game until I make it to the top." He paused and looked at me. "That's why I'm glad you'll be there."

"What do you mean?"

"I'm gonna play this thing with Dame from a distance. Take a few photos and get out of the way. The last thing I need is for him to get into some trouble down the road and it comes back to me. They'll use it to bury me when I run for office." Evan sliced at the air with the side of his hand with each point he made. He always did this when he was nervous. He'd been considering a run for mayor for years.

"So you want me to play babysitter? Is that the real reason I was selected to accept the check?"

"No, he really did request you. Called me himself."

"Hmm," I murmured, shrugging my shoulders. "I'm not happy about being in pictures with him either. What will people say about me?"

"Nobody's looking at you, sweetie."

I narrowed my eyes at Evan.

"No, baby," he said, laughing. "I didn't mean it like that. . . . I meant it more like, more people will be looking at me. I'm not asking you to sleep with the boy. I just want you to take a check from him."

I folded my arms and turned away from him.

"Oh, baby," Evan pleaded playfully. "Now, I was just sitting in here thinking about how beautiful and fine and funny and brilliant and wonderful and sexy and—" He stopped and kissed me on the back.

"What, you ran out of words already?" I said, poking my lip out farther.

"No. When I said, 'sexy,' I just remembered what you look like naked," he said between kisses.

"Evan." I giggled and turned around, swatting him with my hand. Evan seldom made direct passes at me.

"Sexy," Evan said again. He put down his beer and grabbed my hand. His voice turned deep and suggestive. He traced the imprint of my nipple beneath my shirt with his tongue and moved his hand down toward the hem of my skirt. He slid his hand between my thighs, scratching at my leg a bit.

"Now, tell me, sexy, did you take your pill today?" Evan asked, looking into my eyes dreamily.

"No," I whispered.

He groaned and began to kiss me more deeply, as if he was afraid of getting caught. I cupped the back of his head and grabbed some of the loose curls at the nape of his neck, pulling his face closer to mine. That's when Evan opened his mouth wider and began clawing at the insides of my thighs, tearing my stockings and then my panties, too. He undid my blouse, and gently tugged at my breasts with his mouth as he kept his eyes locked on mine.

"Take my pants off," he whispered as he moved from one breast to the other.

I stood up and teased him, slowly opening his buckle and then his button, and then unzipping his pants.

"Oh, shit," Evan cried and knocked the beer to the floor. Neither of us reached for it.

He bent down and kissed me again, stroking my thighs as he worked my skirt up around my hips. He moved so quickly, so forcefully that I was out of breath when he picked me up and tried to carry me to the bedroom. We made it there . . . eventually.

We laid beneath the sheets, shoulder to shoulder, our mouths wide open, our bodies breathless. Our love-making had lasted more than two hours and by the time we'd finally ended up in the bed, it was after midnight and the moon was peeking into our bedroom like never before. Probably at us. Because we'd never had sex like that before. And I'd had sex enough with Evan to know the range. This time was different. I felt like Evan was putting his whole self into me. He'd stop and start again, coming at me harder and harder and each time his fiery passion echoed throughout my body, vibrating so deeply, the energy exhausted me.

"You okay?" He sounded like I had earlier.

"Yeah," I said, still trying to catch my breath. "That was a lot." I turned to him, grinning and kissing his shoulder.

"It was. I don't know what happened."

"Don't apologize," I purred. "You've never been like that before."

"I think it was the idea of making a baby . . . it really got me excited." He smiled and kissed me on the nose.

"That's had you excited every night this week," I teased.

"Did you really stop taking the pill?" he asked.

"Yes."

Chapter Eight

I was convinced I was pregnant. My period wasn't late, I wasn't vomiting and in contrast to the other symptoms listed on the long list of Web sites I'd visited, I wasn't experiencing breast tenderness, cramping, or weight gain. But I just knew. It was like I felt a light spinning in my belly, and with each hour that drifted past, I was sure that the fizzing tickling me after lunch or the extra trip to the bathroom was my new baby letting me know our time together had begun.

All this and it hadn't even been a week since my birthday. I knew it was a long shot, but I'd stopped taking the pill and Evan and I had been having sex every night. While months before we would meet between the sheets and he'd complain that he was too tired, now he was holding his arms around my body tightly and making passionate love to me until we could do nothing else but go to sleep. He was smiling and tracing circles on my stomach most nights. And watching him glow, I grew more excited at the thought of being a mother. I was still nervous, but it was easier to look forward to something the world seemed to want for me.

I needed confirmation, of course. And while I was a grown woman with health benefits and a gynecologist I'd been seeing for fifteen years, I felt funny about requesting a pregnancy test. Dr. Maple, who I called Aunt Maple, was everyone's gynecologist. Visiting her office was like going to a sorority social, where I was certain to share old magazines with friends from high school, college, church, and the grocery store. We all knew and loved her and had our baby pictures tacked to the walls of her office. Although I was seldom excited to step in to see her for my annual, I was never nervous. Evan and I did have sex before we got married—long before we got married, but we'd always practiced safe sex, so an unplanned pregnancy or STD was never written on the list of concerns when I checked in at the nurses' station. If I got pregnant now, it would be celebrated, but I didn't want it to be front-page news. I wanted to avoid whispers in the office or the knowing smile on Aunt Maple's face as she announced the news to me. And I certainly didn't want her to share the information with my mother, who was sure to then hit the ball right out of the park long before I was ready to run the bases.

All of this amounted to my being horrified about getting tested at Aunt Maple's office.

Scanning the shelves at the drugstore on Saturday afternoon as Evan played golf with my dad, it became clear that this "knowing" wasn't going to come easily. There were hundreds of pregnancy tests—some for early response, immediate response, and even easy response. I just wanted any response, so I bought all of them. I hid the little boxes deep in the bottom of my basket, concealing them with a set of cheap T-shirts, a picture frame, nail polish remover, and a copy of the *Rolling Stone* magazine with a sweaty Dame on the cover.

As I made my way to the front of the line, smiling at a few familiar faces and turning around to be sure none were too familiar or close, I thought of the other ways I could've gotten the test—Billie, mail order, sent Evan—and then, as I tipped my sunny-day glasses, I thought of how ridiculous it was that I'd felt a need to stash the tests in the first place. It was my first time buying pregnancy tests, but I was a married woman. An adult. Thirty-three years old. Not some teenager sneaking around to hide a bump beneath her sweatshirt. When I got to the front, I just dumped the things on the counter, tired of playing into my own episode of *Desperate Church Wives* and starring as the neurotic daughter in *The Preacher's Kid.*

The cashier, a pretty Asian girl with glossy lips and too much eyeliner, looked down at what had to be seven or so tests and then looked back up at me.

"Everybody does the same thing," she said.

"Really?" I asked, taking off my shades.

"Yes, ma'am."

As she scanned the boxes and began dropping them into a bag, I felt more confident and looked down into my purse for my wallet. An eerie chill swept through my body and I thought maybe I'd left my wallet in the car, but I dug a bit deeper and fished it out from beneath my cell phone and the feeling quickly dissipated. Yet, as I handed the girl my check card, it returned.

"Journey?" my mother said, poking her head right over my shoulder.

"Mama." I looked at the cashier and she rolled the bag up quickly like she'd been in this situation before.

"I knew that was you right when I turned the corner," my mother said as I turned to face her.

"Yeah, I just stopped in—" I slid my wallet back into my purse and picked up my bags.

"What you got?"

"Nothing, really. Just some . . ."

She tugged at one of the bags and I snatched it back abruptly.

"Journey?" She looked up at me in disbelief. "Did you just snatch the bag?"

"It's just some things for Evan, Mama. Nothing."

"Oh, you should've told me. You know I work two blocks away from the drugstore. I could've picked it up and it would've given me a reason to visit my favorite two people." She smiled and combed my hair into place with her fingers.

"Thanks, Mama. But it's okay."

"Well, what did he need?"

I was sure this trade sounded silly to anyone else, but to my mother, at least when it came to my life, a conversation could be culled from anything. How long I kept meat in the freezer. If I used color-safe or regular bleach. The flowers we were expecting to bloom in the front yard in the spring and when was the best time to have them planted. If Evan and I had tried the new, organic toothpaste she'd bought us. . . . The nuances of our lives were of utmost priority to her and I knew if I kept trying to snatch the bag away, she'd grow more and more suspicious and only keep tugging. I had to get her mind off the bag quickly.

"Mama," I said enthusiastically as she ogled the bags—probably tapping into the X-ray vision she'd developed bringing up three children. I slid the bags behind me and tried to think of something she'd be so happy to hear that she'd lose focus. "Let's go to lunch!"

"Lunch?" she repeated, straightening up. "Now? I'm working. You know I'm at the clinic on Saturdays."

"Yes. But I want to spend time with you."

"But I have to pick up the prescriptions for some of the women at the clinic, and then I was supposed to have a business meeting." She ground her teeth in frustration. I was just happy to see she wasn't looking at the bag anymore.

"Oh, I understand," I said. I was off the hook. "Maybe another day."

"No," she said suddenly. "I should spend some time with you. I'll pick up the prescriptions and have Lisa cancel my meeting, so I can have lunch with my baby girl."

"No, Mama, I didn't mean for you to—"

"No way I'm missing the chance to spend private time with you," she said, cutting me off. "It's done. Let's meet at Harry's at 1 p.m."

"Great," I said between clenched teeth. "Harry's at 1 p.m."

"Wonderful," she said. "I can't wait."

Daddy was talking expansion again. Adding a few thousand seats more to the House, building a secondary education tutorial center and buying another twenty acres of land from the family that owned a farm behind the church's campus. My mother looked exhausted just talking about it. She twirled the tomato soup around in the bowl in front of her and reminded me of how he'd promised the last expansions would be final and that he was thinking of retiring in five years.

"There's no way he's retiring in five years if we add more seats to the House," she said. "Then we'll have to get more members to fill those seats and he's the only one who can draw them in. We'd have to get people driving in from Birmingham to keep the money right."

She frowned and her cheeks pinched back. It was the same look I discovered on her face when we moved into our second church, when we built the church bookstore, and then the credit union. I knew this was really bothering her because she never talked to me about things concerning my father. She'd just smile and in her eyes I could see that something was wrong. But if I pushed, she'd deny everything.

"What's Jr saying about it?"

"You know your brother. He's all for it. He says with the services being televised nationally after the summer, we'll attract more people anyway. Says we need to be prepared." She leaned into the table and breathed out deeply. "You know I've always supported your father and I love serving God, but sometimes I wonder how we can know people are getting the Message—really getting the Word—when we can't see most of them. We have deacons and sisters and greeters touching our members. I remember when I could touch each one myself. I could really be there when they needed me. I could stand outside the church with you in my arms and greet everyone as they walked into our church. Now it's impossible to make a personal connection. Sometimes that makes me miss that little church."

"Mama, the Message is still the same," I said. "The Word doesn't change. I guess we all just have to adjust."

Looking forlorn, she leaned back in her chair and nodded slowly in agreement.

"But if you can't take it, you have to tell Daddy."

"I've been trying to tell your father to cut the hair growing on the tops of his ears for forty years—you think he's going to listen to me about a church?"

"But this is your life, too. You have rights."

"I know. But when I signed up for this thing, marrying your father, I knew I'd have to share him . . ." —she paused—"with the church. The pastor's wife is never selfish." She spooned the soup and then looked up at me, a refreshed smile now on her face, but thin tears in her eyes. "So, tell me, how are things with Evan?"

"We're fine," I said. "Just doing what we do." I knew better than to tell her about the fizzing in my stomach.

"Your father tells me that Evan's really considering running for mayor next year."

"He's still getting some things in order. If we get the right backing, I think he's going to try."

"That'll be something, won't it? A black man in the mayor's office in Tuscaloosa and one in the White House in Washington, D.C." She matched my grin with a hearty laugh.

"Let's not speak too soon."

The waitress slid our bill onto the table as my mother looked off reminiscently.

"I remember a South where none of this was possible. But it's good to see you young people changing things. Chasing your dreams," she said.

"Yeah, I'm still trying to figure out mine."

"What do you mean?" she asked, putting cash onto the table.

"Nothing," I said, regretting my slip. I didn't want to become the topic of conversation. And I was already late meeting Billie at my house so I could take the test.

"No, really. Tell me," she pushed.

"It's nothing, Mama. I just wonder sometimes what I'm doing with my life," I blurted. "Jr is begging me to come work at the church. Daddy wants me in the choir. The kids need me at the school. Evan wants me at home. And I have no idea what I want. I know I love teaching, but I don't know if I want to do that forever. It's like you said at church the other week, I'm thirty-three and I feel like I should have all this figured out by now."

"Dear, I told you that so you could see the blessing that your life is and move ahead in that peace," she said. "You know your father picked out your name, and sometimes I think we cursed you with it. Because, forever, you've been trying to find somewhere to go when your life is right here." She pat me on the hand and smiled meaningfully. "I'm not saying you need to just accept whatever life gives you, but you must have the wisdom to know when you have a good thing going."

"I know, Mama. But sometimes I wonder if a good thing is enough to make a life on. Like maybe there's somewhere else for me to be. Something else for me to have." I thought of Kayla and how she just packed up her life and moved South to chase love. I wished I had that kind of passion for anything.

"No, listen to me. Some people search the planet looking for something to fill them up, never happy with anything. But in the end, they realize that everything they needed was right in front of them. They wouldn't notice it only because they thought they could find something better." She sat back and laughed. "When I was young and we were trying to go into town to just sit at white restaurants like this one and order a soda, we had a little joke. We'd ask if the apples in a black yard were better than those in a white yard. We always said the white ones were better. Bigger. Sweeter. But really, they just seemed better because we'd never had them . . . and when we did have them, we'd fought so hard to get them that they just seemed better, bigger, and sweeter. But you know, after you have five of those apples, you realize that they're all the same. In fact, those black apples are better because they came from your yard."

We got up and walked to the door and I tried to make reason of what she'd said. My mother always had a way of making everything sound so easy.

"Now I don't remember fighting over apples at all," she added. "The joke was really about the way people see things."

We stopped in the doorway and she turned to look at me, her honey eyes soft and calm.

"Your life is what you perceive it to be, Journey. If you want to be happy, you will be. If you don't want to be happy, you won't. It's that simple. You have a good life. You just have to take time to look at it," she finished, rummaging in her purse as we both searched for our keys before walking out of the air-conditioned opening.

"Oh, no," she said, peering down in the bag. "I think I left my keys on the table."

"You sure?" I asked.

"I had to."

"Don't worry. I'll get them."

"You don't have to," she offered when I'd already turned to retrieve the keys.

As I headed back toward the door, I noticed my mother standing outside talking to Deacon Gresham—one of my parents' childhood friends who'd been with the church forever. He was a handsome man, one whose good looks hadn't faded with gray hair and a cane-assisted step. Deacon Gresham was always sharply dressed and wearing or carrying a hat to match his handkerchief-donned jackets. A retired attorney, his wife of forty years had died a little over a year ago and he'd become the choice chatter of my mother's circle. Grandmothers and some great-grandmothers, they sounded like teenagers when they plotted over dessert as to who'd get with Deacon Gresham.

I could see that his face looked stressed, his jaw was tight, and he hadn't smiled. He looked at me and then shifted his eyes very sternly back to my mother. She turned to me, shooting a blank stare, as he said something and then walked away.

"You found the keys," my mother said, smiling nimbly when I came out.

"Yeah, they were on the table." I handed her the keys and looked down the street to see the back of Deacon Gresham. "Why didn't he stay to say hello?"

"Oh, Journey, I don't think he saw you."

"He looked right at me."

"We were," she started slowly, "supposed to have lunch."

"I thought you said you canceled a business meeting."

"We just meet for lunch sometimes. He's still very sad about Emma, so we talk about old times."

"Okay, but I just don't understand why he walked off like that." I looked back down the street. He was gone now. "Anyway, I'd better get going. I have to meet Billie." I looked at my watch.

"Give her my love," my mother said, asking not one more question about where we were meeting or what we were doing. This was more than a rarity, but a welcomed departure I was in no position to question.

"Okay," I said quickly.

We traded pleasant kisses and departed.

In the car ride home to meet Billie and take the pregnancy tests, the discussion I had with my mother reverberated throughout my mind. Here, I'd signed up to start a new life and it seemed I had no clue how I fit into my own. Now how was that? How was I thirty-three and so unsure about everything around me? I wanted to put on my high-heel shoes, click around confidently like Kayla, chasing love and life like I knew exactly where I wanted to be. When I was a teenager, I dreamed of being bold like that. Of just doing what I wanted to do and not caring about what other people thought. But at some point, I just went numb and accepted less from myself.

"That's how life's lined up," Jr said to me when I was sitting in the passenger seat of his car after he'd been sent to get me from a party in shack town my parents specifically told me I couldn't attend when I was fourteen. Billie was in the backseat and we both had our arms folded over our chests, angry at the world that he'd barged in and embarrassed us. "You can't go acting however you want out in public. You're a wild child, Journey, but you'll learn that people don't like to see you step out of line."

And he was right. After years of being kicked in place, I realized that I was just happier when people liked to see me. I hated to think about that. How I'd learned to stand in line and like it. How I'd been numbed.

But was my mother right? Was I . . . was Kayla . . . seeking apples that weren't sweeter than the ones we had?

If being a happy adult meant being thirty-three with a mortgage, husband, tenured job, and loving family and friends, then I'd done that. I was something my family could be proud of, healthy and as happy as I'd expected I could be in my grown mind. Yes, I still had unfulfilled fantasies and got tired of being where I was *being*, but in no story I knew had an adult not felt that way. It seemed that, like my mother said, people were always just chasing something else. Maybe she was right.

The Storyteller

June 23, 2008
Afternoon in the Sky

"Were you pregnant?" Kweku asked, sitting up impatiently. The dignified demeanor he maintained when we boarded the plane at sunrise in Accra had now been reduced to that of a high school girl sitting in the bleachers, listening to the latest gossip. "What happened at the house with Billie and what was going on with that deacon at the restaurant? Did you ask your mother about it again?"

It was early afternoon. And the flight attendants announced that we were halfway to a layover in Amsterdam. Kweku and I eased into our routine as neighbors, chatting and passing snacks and drinks along when the flight attendants did their rounds. The baby a few rows back was crying again, but we'd been in the air for a long time now and Kweku and I joked that she must be wondering why on God's earth her mother still had her on that plane. "Let me off," we joked, translating her cries.

Kweku was a great listener and even though he was a

man, I felt so comfortable sharing even the most intimate things with him—some things that two months ago, I wouldn't have dreamed of uttering to another person beyond Billie. But here I was, not giggling or covering my mouth, but sharing my story like a grown woman and knowing deep down that this was a good thing. I needed to hear my story. To remind myself of how things were before that plane touched down. In this way, I guessed Kweku wasn't a friend or even the guy who was just sitting next to me on the plane. He was an ear. And I really needed someone to listen.

"No, I wasn't pregnant," I said. "Billie and I did all fourteen of those tests and each time we saw a 'negative.' "

Kweku repositioned himself worriedly.

"I wasn't upset," I said, patting his arm. "It was odd, but when I realized I wasn't pregnant, I felt kind of relieved. Like . . . maybe it wasn't meant to be or . . . maybe it wasn't time yet. Evan and I hadn't been trying long and if we really wanted a baby, it would come. God would see to it. I had to trust that."

"Faith is sometimes the only thing that can get you through times like that."

"That and a little uncertainty," I said. "Maybe God knew I needed a little time."

"So what did Ms. Billie have to say about it?" Kweku asked. He seemed to like hearing about her.

"She's my best friend, so she had my back either way. We hugged and she said it would be okay. But really, I think she knew what I was thinking inside about it. Your friends tend to know what you're really feeling—even if they don't say it aloud."

Kweku turned and looked through the sliver of space between our seats at a white man who'd been listening, I was sure, to most of my story. Each time I lowered my voice, I saw him nod forward. And sometimes, when we were laughing, I heard a chuckle come from behind.

"Are you okay?" Kweku asked the man gruffly.

"Yes." He responded and turned his head as if to say he was no longer listening to us, but I knew better.

"Anyway," Kweku went on. "I'm afraid to ask, but what about the deacon?"

"At the time, I just kept thinking of reasons why my mother would be meeting with Deacon Gresham. I mean, it was clear something was going on. My mother was no liar and 'lie' was written all over her face. And then when I got to the house, I ran it past Billie and she reminded me of what Deacon Gresham did for a living."

"What?"

"He's a divorce attorney. One of the biggest in the city. And if my mother was meeting up with him for lunch . . ."

"She was trying to get a divorce?"

"You've already heard—my father wasn't the easiest man to be married to. And with everything she was complaining about at lunch, it had to be so," I said. "And the sad thing was that I was only a little upset. I was more concerned about my mother and that she was obviously going through this on her own. I wished I could be there for her, but she wasn't the kind of woman I could call up and say, 'Are you trying to divorce Daddy?' That would break her heart. She still thought of me as a baby. I had to wait and catch her at the right time."

"I know this. My mother, whenever you say too much she doesn't want to hear, she just stops listening. Like she's deaf. You call her, and she says nothing," Kweku said, and we both laughed . . . along with the man behind me.

"American mothers do the same thing. Just block you out. I think it comes with giving birth."

"So, was your husband sad about your not getting preg-

nant?" Kweku asked, folding back to the start of our conversation.

"I didn't even tell him. Evan and I were having so much fun just being lovers again that I didn't want to ruin it. I figured I'd keep things quiet until he asked. And there was the business of his running for office. The school. The church. We were already dealing with a lot. Mentioning the test would just make the baby thing a race. That's his way."

"Yes, and this Dame fellow," Kweku said and I felt my heart flush its blood out everywhere. "It sounds like that was troubling you, too."

"Yeah," I started and pressed myself back into my seat. "That was another part of the story."

I looked out of the window and saw that the sky was so bright that it seemed it didn't expect that sunset would ever come.

I gasped and tapped at the glass, covering one of the clouds with my fingertips.

Was I ready to tell this part of the story? I wondered in my long pause. Was I ready to remember those good times?

PART TWO

Taste

Chapter Nine

April 29, 2008
Tuscaloosa, AL

Everybody was moving. From here. To there. Over and around. The school was like an ant farm turned upside down. And not just the teachers either. The kids. Girls and boys I hadn't seen in months were posted up in the hallways giggling and holding books in their arms I knew they hadn't seen since the first day of school. I had full attendance in all of my morning classes and even a few students who didn't have my class were trying to get in. And I couldn't say no. The cafeteria was overflowing. From the cafeteria workers to the oldest teachers who knew nothing about Dame or his music, it was apparent that this was the biggest thing that had ever happened at Black Warrior. The most attention we'd gotten from the world in . . . forever. Television crews? A star? In our school? *Our* school? The little old school for black kids that was started in a farmhouse on a plantation that once had slaves? Everyone was beside themselves. But I'd yet to feel the excitement.

I was still uneasy about my role in this whole thing, but a new piano, instruments for the band, and a proper sound system made it easier to accept the check from Dame. "You heard your father at dinner," Evan said, bringing up the topic again one night as we sat out on the lake talking. "That boy has a bad reputation and that could hurt me later on. Those white boys downtown would love to tie me to some rapper when I run for mayor. That's all they need. But if you do it, we can say he was one of your students and that'll be it. Besides, he asked for you."

When fourth period came, and we were all just a few seconds shy of Dame's arrival, I stood in the lobby of the school with my fourth-period students collected in a huddle of excitement behind me. Along with a few other classes, mine was selected to greet Dame at the door for his tour with the camera crews from BET, while the other students waited in the auditorium.

"When he coming?" Opal asked after I'd just managed to calm down my class again. Like a few other girls, she was wearing a T-shirt that read "The Same Dame" across the front and had a picture of Dame with no shirt on, oiled completely and flexing in the middle.

"My cousin say his tour bus just left the Waffle House on McFarland," Devin King, the jokester of the class, said, tucking his cell phone into his pocket.

"What, that fool want his hash browns scattered, covered and smothered or something?" someone said, and everyone laughed.

"Yeah," Opal jumped in, fanning herself. "Get his

order. I want to know what he's eating, so I can make it in the morning."

"Girl, you ain't got to worry about nobody being with you in the morning with those buck teeth you got," Devin said, and the laughter grew louder.

"Okay. Okay. You all calm down or we're going back to the classroom," I threatened, beginning to feel their anxiousness.

The BET camera crew was busy setting up. Men dressed in T-shirts and shorts with equipment hanging from their hips pointed to this and that and recalculated measurements for some other thing. Bright flood lights were perched here and there in the lobby like we were on a real television set. And while I'd opted to do my own makeup, they even had Evan in a folding chair in the bathroom with a stylist. He decided to wear his favorite tan suit with a blue shirt and golden tie. He looked like a regular good ol' frat boy. Just one of the guys.

"Move fast!" I heard one of the crew people say to a man carrying a camera as they ran by. "I want to get a shot of him walking in. Shoot him and then these people standing all around."

"You guys ready?" another crew member asked, standing on a ladder and trying to organize the growing crowd. "Dame's about to come in here and we'll all get a glimpse of him. Let's just remember to be patient."

Having stepped away from my students to stand in a row of teachers who lined the head of the crowd blocking the doorway, I looked up to see Billie's eyes frozen, transfixed on the door. "He's coming," she said breathlessly as she might have at a Bobby Brown concert when we were thirteen. Her brown eyes were opened wide and the flashes from cameras flickered there for a second.

The roar from the lobby came without warning. The crowd pushed forward, the doors came open and all the cameras fell into position as Dame walked into the building. I inched up a bit, leveraging myself with Billie's arm, so I could get a good look. From the door, shaking hands with Evan, he looked different than I expected. Than I remembered. Bigger in some way. He was dressed in a plain white T-shirt that was small enough to show his muscles, blue jeans with designs hop-scotched all over them, and extra-white sneakers. Aside from the crew buzzing around him, he didn't look flashy or out of place. And even from my position, about six feet away, I could tell by the shine in his eyes that he was just as excited as we were.

The man on the ladder signaled for the crowd to quiet down as Dame and Evan shook hands and chatted a bit in front of the cameras. Evan went to put his arm around Dame for one of the photographers who was with the local newspaper. It was a welcoming gesture, like one of the old guys was welcoming a kid made good back to town.

Dame made his way toward me, shaking hands down a line of teachers who'd taught him. I could see that he really had grown up. Puberty or testosterone or something had changed even his skin. I remembered him having a caramel complexion with common cocoa eyes, but now everything in his face was smoky. His brown skin was now a lacquered dark chocolate and his eyes were more mysterious and pointed. Even his hair had changed. Far from the little pointy sticks he used to sit in the back of the classroom and twist as he wrote in his notebook, his locks were now long and feral in a way that warned of enticing danger. Just a bit darker than his skin, it looked clean and soft like pre-spun cashmere rinsed in myrrh. It almost begged to be touched. Looking at the magazine cover I had at the house, I'd thought this was airbrushing or the effect of celebrity lighting, but no, it was the real thing. He smiled and his perfect, white teeth contrasted against his skin, making him shine effortlessly. He looked like a star. And as he walked the greeting line, one by one, the grown-up female teachers turned into grinning girls with crushes. How ridiculous they looked, I thought . . . until it was happening to me, too.

As I watched him move, everything around me grew so loud, but all I could hear was my insides turning. Saliva spinning at the back of my throat. My pulse tickling the insides of my wrists. My breathing going slow, slow, and then the vibration of air tunneling down the center of my chest before an exhale whistled out of my shuddering body. It was like I was at a concert, catching a fever of emotion from everyone circled around me. It was a surprise that I'd felt this way, but I couldn't ignore the energy and pretty soon, the excitement was inside of me. I looked down to see that my right foot had turned coyly toward my left ankle. I was standing there like a little girl. I wondered if anyone had noticed and quickly moved my foot back into position.

"Ms. Cash?" Dame stopped suddenly as he was talking to another teacher a ways down from me. "Say it ain't so," he said, laughing as he strutted toward me with the cameras behind him. "My favorite teacher! Ms. Cash!"

He scooped me up into his arms and spun me around so quickly I had to catch my breath. As he opened his arms and I slid back to my feet, I could feel the muscles in his chest.

"Oh," I said, smiling and telling myself not to look at his arms in front of the camera. "I'm Mrs. DeLong now. I got married," I blathered, and so I flashed my ring in front of the camera as proof.

"What?" Dame looked over at Evan grouped with some other people from the school board. "You married Dr. DeLong?"

"Sure did," I smiled, inadvertently waving my ring again. "And we're so happy to have you here to visit the school you once called home," I said and one of the crew members whispered for me to look at Dame and not at the camera when I spoke.

"I couldn't think of a better place to be," Dame said sincerely. "When my manager said I had some time off before my world tour, I told him to cut me a check and book me a plane ticket home. I had to come see about my people. The Black Warriors."

Benji Young, a boy I used to see writing rhymes in the back of the classroom with Dame, hollered, "Warriors" the way the kids did at pep rallies and other school functions, and the kids replied, "Warriors," and everyone began to clap.

After the greetings and me getting my students settled in the auditorium, I escorted Dame and the crew around the school, so he could show off his old locker, the basketball courts, and the bathroom where he jokingly said he'd almost lost his virginity until the girl's boyfriend walked in. As we walked around the school, Dame had the whole crew laughing, me included, with his memories of Tuscaloosa. While most people would think someone his age didn't care about the place, Dame seemed to remember everything that made Tuscaloosa special and unique and every time he said, "Let me tell y'all about the time . . ." everyone gathered and listened intently.

When we finally made our way to the chorus room, I was beginning to feel like a celebrity myself. Between takes, a woman popped out of nowhere and smoothed my hair, gave me a sip of water and redotted my lips with the gloss I'd given her—I still didn't trust her to touch my makeup.

"This is where it all began," Dame said. He dashed up the steps that led to the back of the room and sat right in the seat he once inhabited. "I used to sit right here and write my rhymes with T-Brill and Benji. We'd be in here bugging out . . . just dreaming of making it big someday." He stood back up and walked down toward my desk where I was standing behind the camera. After everyone shifted around, he looked at me. "And now I'm big . . . and I have you to thank for that."

"You're very welcome," I said.

"I know sometimes you must've felt like you weren't teaching us a damn thing . . . man, we were so damn bad!" He laughed and I nodded in agreement. "But you were teaching us. Just being in here and listening to your music and seeing you do something you loved . . . sometimes that was all we needed to learn. We was coming out the projects and seeing what it was like to have a job where ain't nobody looking to take you out. You know? That's real talk." His eyes grew more serious. "I know that ain't something you can measure on a test, but it saved my life. It gave me a vision that I could do what I loved and not have to answer to anybody. I took that and ran with it. Literally! I ran right out the classroom and ain't never come back." Everyone except Dame and I laughed at his story. We kept our eyes on each other.

"But now I'm here," he said, lowering his voice. "I'm back home."

When Dame and I finally made our way into the school auditorium, it was standing room only. The noise was so loud, Dame had to take the microphone himself to get everyone settled down. I was standing on the stage beside him. Evan and Mr. Williams were a few steps away.

While I'd sung in front of crowds at the church and traveled with the choir to places where audiences were twice as large, knowing so many people were watching and filming made me nervous. Was I standing too close to Dame? Too far away? Was my hair messed up? Should I have let the woman do my makeup? Did I look shiny? Did I sound crazy? And pretty soon, I had so many questions that I just wondered, Why am I on this stage?

"I'm one of you," Dame said when he finally got all the kids to sit down and relax just enough so he could speak. "I'm not from the 'dirty'; I'm from the dirt. Where folks got less than nothing. Got to go outside and eat fruit all day because that's the only thing that grows free in your grandmama's yard. I know some of y'all know what I'm talking about." Their eyes locked on Dame, the students grew quiet. I'd never seen them so focused.

"And when that fruit runs out . . . when them collards run out," he went on, "you're fast to do anything to feed yourself—to feed your family. And you know it's wrong, but you're hungry. Ain't nothing worse than being hungry. I ain't talking about the clothes you wear or the car you drive. Where you live.

I'm talking about being hungry. And when my stomach was empty, I used to dream about someday just doing anything. Anything somebody would let me do. A garbage man. Anything. So I wouldn't have to be hungry no more. But ain't nobody give me a chance, so I went out in the street. And when that ran out, when folks started getting popped and the game got real bloody, I realized I wasn't no street dude. Not really. I realized that I had to hustle to live for myself. So I could be Dame. Not what the world expects me to be."

"We love you, Dame," a girl cried out from the crowd.

"And I love you back," he said and the auditorium filled with the sound of laughter and screaming girls. "And I love you so much that I'm giving this school, my school, a little bit of what I got out of hustling for myself. This money I'm giving is just for you. So you don't have to be hungry in your school. So you don't have to want someone to let you be anything. So you don't have to get in the drug game and lose respect for your community and keep bringing us down."

Led by the teachers, everyone began to clap at his last point and I was honestly surprised by what I was hearing. This wasn't the young man I'd expected. The person who was saying this didn't sound a thing like the Dame I'd seen on *Entertainment Tonight,* in magazines, and even in his songs. Suddenly I was thinking that maybe my father was wrong. Maybe none of us knew who the real Dame was from what we'd seen.

"This check is so you can have a chance at Black Warrior," he added. "A chance to be better than your parents, better than your teachers, better than me.

Because this is your future." He paused and looked off toward the left wing of the stage. "Benji, bring the check out."

Benji, who I'd since learned had become Dame's bodyguard, walked out, carrying a huge, blown-up check like the ones television shows use when people win a million-dollar sweepstakes prize.

He handed the check to Dame and Evan and Mr. Williams came over to stand beside me.

"Would you like to do the honors?" Mr. Williams asked, handing me the microphone.

"Sure," I said. I held up one side of the check and read into the microphone, "A check to Black Warrior High School in the amount of one million dollars, signed by Mr. Damien Mitchell."

Everyone in the room cheered his name and then a few kids were rapping his lyrics and the camera crews were scampering to the front of the stage to get a picture of the two of us holding the check.

"Smile," they said one after the other for so long my cheeks began to hurt. I was smiling and holding one side of that check from the center of the stage to the back of the auditorium, where some cameramen were still waiting to get a good shot.

"That was wonderful," Evan said when we were finally out of the limelight and the circle had dwindled down to just me, Dame, Evan, and Emily, Dame's assistant, who was fussing over Dame's clothes and taking the hidden microphone pack from underneath his shirt.

"Yes, I really think the children got something from your words," I agreed as someone else removed my microphone pack.

"Thanks," Dame said. "I wish I could come speak to them more."

"If only we had more people who thought like you, young man," Evan said. "Hey, I was wondering, what are you doing tonight? Mrs. DeLong and I would like to take you out for dinner. The Cypress Inn? I know it's no Hollywood meal, but we'd be honored to have you join us if you don't already have plans."

I looked at Evan, surprised at his suggestion. He'd said explicitly that he wanted to keep his distance from Dame and now "we'd love to have" him? I didn't recall ever discussing going out with Dame. Perhaps Evan had the fever, too. I looked down to see which way his feet were pointing.

"Man," Dame started and it sounded like he was about to say he was busy, "I can do that. I have to do some signings, but I need to eat, too."

"Wonderful," Evan said, smiling. "I'll have my secretary make reservations for 7 p.m."

Trying to get out of the school was like maneuvering through a herd of traveling cattle. The kids were in a frenzy, running around to try to get to Dame, who'd already slipped out the back door for safety reasons. And the teachers were only blocking the traffic, gathered in bunches where I overheard most of them talking about how handsome Dame had become.

"I need to get me a twenty-three-year-old," Billie said when I finally got outside and found her standing in the parking lot talking to Kayla.

"Yeah, he was something to look at," Kayla agreed. "Did you see his arms? You could swing from them."

"You two should be ashamed of yourselves . . . looking at that young boy," I censured them playfully.

"Please, Mrs. DeeeeeLong, your mouth was salivating, too," Billie said. "And your husband was there, so that makes you even worse."

"Oh, no, you didn't!" I replied, slapping her hand.

"Did you see his butt?" Kayla said all dreamy. "The way it was holding those jeans . . ."

"Even with the sag, you could tell the brother has a nice, rock-hard ass," Billie said. "I wanted to tap that thang." She pretended she was slapping his butt.

"Oh, let me go. I'm not about to stand here and listen to this foolishness," I protested, pulling out my keys. I thought the boy was fine, too, but I didn't think it was appropriate to share that with people. And for some reason, I felt I'd been too close to him to admit I was thinking that way. But he did have a nice butt.

"Stop being a bump on a log, J," Billie said. "Men look at women all the time. What's wrong with us recognizing sunshine sometimes? No one said we were actually trying to sleep with the boy—"

"No, *you* didn't say that," Kayla said, and I had to laugh.

"Now, I want to hear Journey admit it," Billie dug. "Admit that he's fine!"

"What? I don't see how that makes any difference. Why do I have to do it?"

"Because it's a dare." Billie put her hands on her hips like we were kids in the school yard. "I dare you to admit that you found your former student to be an impeccable specimen of a chocolate man." She was always coming up with these ridiculous dares.

"That's stupid."

"Then do it." Billie and Kayla folded their arms expectantly.

"This is ridiculous, and I'm not doing it."

"Hmm . . ." Billie looked at Kayla. "Told you she was stuck-up."

"No, I'm not." She wasn't slick. This was how she'd get me to do things in high school. She'd call me a prude, stuck-up, a lame, Miss Tight-Ass, until I felt so bad I did the dare.

"A straight-up prude." Billie dramatically pursed her lips again and looked at me accusingly. I could almost hear the Old West standoff music playing in the background. "Stuck-up. Miss Tight-Ass herself—"

"I thought he was hot. Happy?" I said quickly, pulling my bag back up on my shoulder and turning to walk to my car.

"Love you, Mrs. DeeeeLong," Billie hollered after me as she laughed with Kayla.

"And did you see his teeth? I love a man with nice teeth." I heard one of them say.

"That and a nice tongue."

"And that hair! Girl, that hair makes you want to just jump rope!"

"Or pull it."

They cackled me all the way to the car.

Chapter Ten

One of the most annoying things about being married to someone who was so involved with community relations was the waiting. Evan was always late. Everywhere we went. Anytime we were supposed to meet up to do anything. If we weren't planning to arrive together, I could expect Evan to be late—at least fifteen minutes late. He was held up in a meeting. Lending a listening ear to some parent in the parking lot. Providing a group of constituents with talking points for future engagements. Or just trying to find a parking spot. Because I'm often late myself, I could understand being a bit late on occasion. However, there were only so many fifteen-minute-meeting carryovers, face-to-face confrontations, planning boards, and full parking lots I could take without feeling like I was playing second fiddle to the rest of the universe. I'd sit forlorn in concert halls, theaters, restaurants, and sometimes at my own dinner table, imagining Evan smiling and charming those around him—not even thinking about where he was supposed to be. What made it worse was that Evan was never late for functions when my father was involved. If we were headed to church or on our way out of town to hear Reverend Jethro Cash speak, Evan would snap into action and sometimes go out and sit in the car early, before I was even ready. And if I had the nerve to be late, he'd shoot his eyes at me and say I needed to be a better planner.

Sitting alone at a table for three in the middle of the dining room floor at the Cypress Inn, one of Tuscaloosa's top restaurants, I was struggling not to be rude or, worse, a nag. I avoided pulling out my phone and asking Evan where he was and when he planned on getting to the restaurant. When he'd invited Dame to dinner, I remembered that Evan already had three meetings scheduled and needed to complete a presentation for the next day. Thinking he was so excited with the idea of meeting with Dame and milking him for more money for the school board's plans—another catalyst of his secret plan to someday run for mayor—I called him hours before the dinner to remind him of this and said it wasn't too late to reschedule or just cancel. "I'll be there, darling," he'd said. "Can't miss it."

Twenty minutes after our early 7 p.m. meeting, the dining room was filling up and it was evident that I'd have to keep Dame company until Evan showed up—if Dame even came.

The Cypress Inn, with its elaborate outdoor gardens, formal dining setting complete with elegant light fixtures, and a 550-gallon fish tank, was a natural destination for the city's elite and newspaper-ready faces. Nestled right along the Black Warrior River, it was the kind of place where dinner served double duty—nourishment of the body and maintenance of social status. Rubbing shoulders, brown-nosing, and just general schmoozing was encouraged as $500 wines were sent to tables like bread baskets and bills were often paid anonymously. The governor, mayor, local celebrities from television, college presidents, and even the University of Alabama's football coach Nick Saban and his wife were regulars.

Even though it was Tuesday night, the place was full by the time 7:30 p.m. rolled around and I decided to text Evan to ask what the holdup was. I was becoming more certain Dame wasn't coming and wanted to leave. But then, there was the matter of Evan's corporate account that the restaurant had on file. I could eat alone . . . on the county.

Squinting in the candlelight at the table, I texted:

WHERE ARE YOU? I THINK DAME ISN'T COMING.

When I looked up from the phone, I saw two, skinny white women walking toward the front of the restaurant.

"He's that rapper," the blond with the too-tight dress said to the other woman.

"With the song . . . 'Get This in You'?" She giggled as they walked arm in arm.

"Yeah, he's outside."

"Outside?" someone else said, and I turned around to see other people nonchalantly, yet clearly inching up and craning their necks toward the door.

"Who is it, Tilda?" the round-faced white man with the exaggerated chin said to the woman across the table from him.

"You, *know* . . ."—she smiled sensuously—"the one *we* listen to when *we're* . . ."

"Oh." He patted his mouth and turned toward the door, too.

The windows of the restaurant were being crowded by onlookers, and all I could think of was how most people around the country would've assumed that Dame wouldn't have been welcomed in such a place in the deep South . . . and years ago, he wouldn't have. But watching Mr. Round-Face and Tilda grin at each other as I supposed they replayed his latest raunchy tune in their heads, it was clear that like the Yankees, rap had arrived in the Old South.

Debating if I should go look at the spectacle with the rest of the grown groupies or call Evan to let him know Dame had arrived, I realized that in a minute all of this attention would be coming my way.

"Mrs. DeLong," a waiter said, approaching me. His voice was dignified and exaggeratedly Southern.

"Yes?"

"We have a table change."

"A table change?"

"Yes . . ." He paused and Tilda and Round-Face looked at me curiously. "Your . . . company prefers to sit in one of our more private seating areas. It's just a security precaution. Please follow me."

I trailed the waiter to a long table that was tucked to the far right of the back of the restaurant. It was where I'd seen Saban and his wife eating. It was an area I'd never been to.

When I turned to take my seat, I saw Dame walking toward the table, flanked on either side by the white women I'd seen rushing to the door to greet him. Benji was just steps behind.

Dame, who was still in the same clothes he'd worn to the school, walked along laughing with the females and I watched the faces of the white men in the room turn from possible excitement to a bit of disdain at how closely the women were glued to his sides.

"So, ladies . . . give me a call and we'll see what we can do," Dame said, spinning the girls around simultaneously and then releasing them. "We've got to get you two fine females in the next video. Fly you out to L.A. and everything." His voice sounded fake and inflated, much more playful than it had at the school, and even though I wanted to be disgusted with his puffed-up playboy rendition, he was obviously toying with these women. Only they had no clue.

"Benji, please make sure I never see them again," Dame said when the women, beaming and blowing kisses, finally departed. "Cocaine ain't good for you."

He and Benji laughed, but I was less enthused. Dame put his arms out to embrace me, but he must've noticed my internal frown.

"Oh . . . cocaine." He laughed lightly. "That don't mean the real thing. I meant fine-ass white broads . . . you know, like slang, Ms. Cash. Don't act like you don't know."

I looked at Benji, who was standing beside him now and he nodded along with Dame.

"Like cocaine, fine-ass white broads," he said pointedly, "make brothers act crazy and give away all their money."

He and Dame burst out laughing and even I had to giggle.

"Finally," Dame said as I inched closer to receive his hug. "I mean, you're a teacher, you have to get metaphor and simile and hyperbole and all of that."

"Yes," I said, "but the cocaine is a stretch."

In a loose and friendly embrace with Dame for

just two seconds I noted again how tight and imposing his chest muscles were. He smelled spicy and clean, like something green in the woods, wild, yet tame enough to tantalize. I pushed away quickly.

"Everything all right?" Benji said to Dame.

"No doubt." They gripped each other like five times. Benji tipped his cap to me and turned to walk out.

"Does he have to approve of all of your guests?" I asked as the waiter pulled out my chair again and we sat down.

"Man, you'd be surprised what fools will do nowadays," Dame said. "I can hold my own, but they be out looking to bring me trouble. Five-ten fools all together. I ain't no punk, but it's too much money on the line for me to get locked up for stomping some fool."

"So you let Benji do it?"

"He has a license to ill and kill . . . like Bond. But for real, I was just happy I could take him along with me on the road. We came up together. I know I can trust him. That's my boy. Whenever you see Benji, know that I'm just two steps behind," he said as the waiter put down the menus and asked what we'd be drinking.

"Really?"

"You can believe it. He has my back."

"That's good to know."

"So, where's Mr. I-Love-the-Kids?" Dame asked after we ordered our drinks.

"Oh . . . Evan's . . ." I paused and looked down at my phone to see I had a new text:

CAN'T MAKE IT. GOV JOHNSON CAME TO MEETING.

RIDING TO HIS LODGE FOR DRINKS. I KNOW YOU CAN HANDLE DAME. GIVE HIM MY BEST.

I took a deep breath and looked back at Dame. ". . . not coming," I finished. I tried not to look disappointed, but I knew I was rolling my eyes. I knew this would happen.

"Okay," he said, unmoved.

"I know he set the whole thing up, but sometimes his schedule just—"

"You don't have to apologize for him," he said, sliding off his hat and setting it on what would've been Evan's seat. "I know all about schedules. And really I didn't feel like *politricking* tonight anyway. I'm home and I just want to relax. None of that star stuff . . ."

"That's not how you looked earlier . . ."

"That wasn't work. That was pleasure. See, those white girls actually buy my CDs. They don't want nothing from me but a little attention. It's all good."

"That's a good way to look at it."

"And the other way I look at it is, I get to break bread with a fine lady I've admired for a long time."

I tried not to blush, despite feeling a little flushed.

"Dame, you never came to my class, and when you did, you just sat in the back, joked around with your friends, and wrote in your notebook," I listed.

"I did," he said, nodding and laughing.

"What's so funny?"

"You don't even know what you did, do you?" The smile on his face washed away quickly. "Look, you never turned me away. You never let me act up in your class. And you always tried to include me in on what y'all was doing."

"Well, it's school. You're supposed to be included. I'm a teacher."

"You think all teachers do that?" he asked.

"I think I'd be naive if I did. But I know most try."

A woman walking by waved at Dame and he smiled back.

"Try? Most pretend they don't see half the kids—the bad ones. Most either treat their students like criminals or ghosts. But not you. . . . Man, you was trying anything to get us to sing that gospel stuff."

"It means a lot to me," I said as the waiter put the drinks we'd ordered on the table.

"And one day, you were dead serious. Got mad because nobody had their handouts from the day before and people were talking. Man, me and T-Brill was cutting a fool in the back of the room and you got up and stood next to that old beat-up piano and was like, 'You all think other schools have pianos like this? You think they have broken computers, rusty water fountains, and outdated biology labs with no biology teachers?' And to be honest, I'd been smoking and I wasn't listening to you before that, but when you said it, I was thinking, man, finally somebody's talking real talk to us. And you said, 'If you don't care about your education, no one else will.' You remember that?"

"Yes, I do." It was one of the worst days of my teaching career. I'd lost complete control of my classroom and felt helpless and useless. When I came to work, I was so excited. We were supposed to be singing "Amazing Grace." I was still a new teacher then, and I thought that the Word needed to be in each song I taught. While other schools weren't teaching gospel music in chorus, our mostly black and Christian faculty and student body insisted upon it. It was the tradition before the government even recognized the school. And, as my first principal told me, we weren't changing until the government came in and stopped us. They'd taken everything else from our little school and we weren't going to let them take the last thing that was sure to teach our students about goodness.

I knew the kids would love the song and prayed all night they'd receive the message of God's good graces. Only it was clear they weren't. The students were so rowdy that day, they wouldn't receive a message if God jumped out of the piano and sang the song Himself.

"When you were standing up there," Dame continued, "I just kept thinking, when I get out of here, I'm gonna make sure we have a new piano, new water fountains, a new biology lab, and some good teachers. Good teachers like Ms. Cash."

"Really?"

"Man, I was sixteen and high"—he laughed—"but I know truth when I see it. And that ain't never leave me. I traveled the world and that ain't never leave me. I knew as soon as I got my money right, I'd bring it home, so other kids don't have to see Hay Court and McKenzie like I did. So they can dream of more than making these white folks happy every day." He looked at the waiter, who was standing nearby, waiting obediently to take our orders. "My mama and my grandmama served these people all they lives and ain't nobody bothered to give them nothing but trouble. Now, I'm giving them the world."

The waiter came and took our orders after we'd heard the specials and Dame joked with him, asking if they had any hash browns covered and smothered. The waiter laughed robustly, but I was sure if it was anyone else, he would've stared them out of the restaurant.

The food, when it finally came, was good but scarce. I'd ordered the grilled salmon with asparagus and mashed potatoes. But what I got looked like a sticky pad, two pencils, and a dab of hand cream. There was so much white space on the plate that I tried to spread the food around to pretend there was more.

"You know, when I dreamed of eating in places like this, I never thought that rich people's food was just like rich people," he said.

"How so?"

"It's skinny," he said, and we laughed together.

"You're quite the comedian," I said.

"Daaaame," a female voice oozed just as I was about to look away. Standing before us was a twenty-ish white girl dressed in a preppy pink sweater with a khaki skirt. Her hair was curled tight and pushed back behind her ears. "I'm sorry to interrupt your dinner, but I'm Mary Kate. I'm your biggest fan."

"Hi, Mary Kate," Dame said coolly. There was an awkward tone at the table. We were sitting there eating and she was standing, hovering above us. It seemed she was going nowhere.

"I downloaded your album and I was so excited when I heard you were coming home to Tuscaloosa," she went on. "Who knew you would come over here to join us for dinner."

"Us?" Dame repeated. "Us who?"

"Oh . . ." she said, taking a breath and turning red immediately. "I didn't mean it like that."

"I'm sure," he said.

"Well, can I have a picture?" She pulled a camera from her purse.

For the first time that day, I saw Dame's face fill with tension. Through all of the screaming kids, flashing lights, and countless directions from the camera crew, he was cool and relaxed, but now he seemed strained.

"No pictures," he said bluntly, even though the girl was already standing there holding the camera up to her eye.

"Excuse me?" she said, her voice cracking in disbelief.

"No pictures. I'm having dinner." His decree was louder this time and the waiter came over to the table.

"But I—" she tried. Her voice was whiny now.

"Is everything okay?" the waiter asked.

"Just clear my bill and have my driver come around, please," Dame said, holding out a black credit card.

"Certainly, sir," the waiter replied. He took the card and turned to Mary Kate, who was still holding her camera. "Ma'am, could you please return to your seat?"

"But I . . ." she repeated.

The waiter nodded his head patiently and directed the sad girl to her seat. People who heard the exchange were looking on now.

"You ready to get out of here?" Dame asked.

"Out of here?"

"Yeah," he said. "I'm hungry. Let's go get some real food. This was an appetizer."

"You don't want to order something else?" I asked.

"Trust me, we don't need to stay here. Once Mary

Kate texts all her friends and says I'm here, things are going to get worse."

"Are you serious?" I asked.

He nodded and signed the bill.

"Now, I was supposed to put that on Evan's tab," I said.

"You can get the next one," he replied.

"Really, I don't think I should." I looked down at my watch. It was nearing 9 p.m. "I need to get home."

"No. . . . You promised me dinner and I'm hungry," Dame teased.

Twenty minutes later, Dame and I were walking into the old Dreamland BBQ, a far cry from the frill Evan had in mind for the dinner. Dreamland was my daddy's favorite restaurant. All they really served was meat and bread, and most people liked it that way. I tried to resist, remembering my diet, but my mouth started salivating the minute I saw the sign from the road. Dame and I were riding in the back of his Bentley. When we exited the Cypress Inn, I saw the silver, shiny car lighting up the front of the restaurant. Peeking through the little curtains hanging from the back windows with a few admirers, I admitted that I'd never been in one and Dame insisted I ride with him. Benji drove my car and I got to feel like royalty riding in the luxurious automobile that seemed more like a rolling, plush couch than a car. I could hardly feel the thing moving and Dame kept laughing as I slid around on the backseat, my dress caressing the soft leather. All this and when I looked over at Dame, he seemed so natural riding there. Like he'd been born riding in Bentleys. And even though he was wearing a white T-shirt and jeans, he made the car look more stylish.

Glancing at him carefully from my seat, I thought of how different he seemed from Evan. Both men were handsome. Both were confident. Both were successful. But Dame had this kind of strut and style that screamed "I'm here." In the school, in the restaurant, it invited all eyes on him, and then dared them to stare. It was mystifying and exciting and it made me wonder what my former student had done and seen to make himself glow in such a way.

When we walked into Dreamland, a few people looked up from their barbecue plates at Dame familiarly, and one girl took out her phone and sneakily snapped a picture, but that was it. The people, most of whom looked like they'd just gotten off work, seemed more inclined to enjoy their own meals and allow Dame to enjoy his than to make a fuss. We sat down and Dame exclaimed happily, "Now, this is *us.*

"You should've gotten that whole chicken," Dame joked after we ordered our food. "This is on Tuscaloosa. We might as well do it up."

"I need to watch my figure," I said, loosening up to him with the promise of BBQ filling my nostrils.

"I've been watching your figure for a long time and I can tell you, it's all good."

I didn't know how to feel about this statement. Sitting there, my first inclination was to be offended that he was admitting that he'd "watched" me. Dame was a kid. He may have grown up now—in a lot of visible ways—but to me, he was still a student. But then, there was another side of me, the side that had spent too much time picking out the dress I was wearing that felt like I looked good when I walked out of the house and was happy that someone noticed—there was nothing worse than when no one noticed. This side wanted to point out how nicely the red wrap dress held up my breasts and accentuated my hips. She wanted to get up and do a runway walk through Dreamland. But instead, I decided to settle her down and calm the odd moment at the table with a bit of comedy. A big girl joke.

"Spare me. No one likes a fat girl," I said, laughing. But Dame didn't budge.

"You have a point. I hate fat girls. I only date big girls," he said.

"What's the difference?" I asked.

"You ever notice how women who say they're 'fat' never seem happy about it? They say it like it's negative—a curse or something. Now, big girls—when they say they're 'big,' they say it with pride and confidence. They know they look good and that's a turn-on," he explained and I was completely intrigued by this idea. "They know what they want and how to get it. Most big girls are like that. And they know how to treat you."

"Oh, you mean you can run all over them because they're big?"

"No, what I mean is, they aren't all worried about silly stuff that doesn't matter—calories and impressing their damn friends with a bunch of labels," he said. "I get enough of that from these industry broads."

"Exactly," I said. "You say you like big girls, but the last time I checked the gossip columns, you were dating Madison Night—that actress from *Moonlight*. She's like ninety pounds."

"See, that's what they want you to think." He smiled. "You can't trust everything you see on television—my publicist makes most of that stuff up and leaks it to people. Really, I was trying to get at Madison's sister. She's like 300 pounds." He pretended to draw the girl's ample shape in the air, but I could tell he was joking.

"I'm sure," I said drily.

"I don't know what's made you think you're anything but bad as hell," Dame said, catching my eyes again. "Half the time we were joking in the back of the classroom, we were talking about how fine you were and placing bets on who'd get with you first."

"Are you kidding?" I asked, surprised. I always imagined I looked goofy from the back of the room. Old and tired to them.

"Hell, no!" he said. "We were just boys then, though. We knew none of us stood a chance. But that was then . . . and this is now."

"What do you mean?"

"I can't tell you all my secrets now."

The waiter slid our plates onto the table like gifts, and Dame and I sat back in a moment of silence, inhaling the tangy scent of BBQ as our eyes began to feast on the spread.

"I's home now, Ms. Celie. I's home," Dame cried playfully.

My father always said that good BBQ tastes like meat and great BBQ tastes like butter. I tasted nothing but butter on my plate. It was dreamlike, and I wondered how Evan and I had managed to stay away from the place for so long. I made a mental note to make him take me there the next week.

"So," Dame started, wiping his mouth, "what do you think of my music?"

"Think?"

"Yeah, that was a direct question." He looked at

me and then threw his hands up in disgust after I said nothing. "You don't listen to it?"

"Oh, I've heard some . . . but . . . I . . . well, I'm not listening to much rap right now," I tried.

"Don't give me that cop-out. That's what lazy people say. They complain that there's no good hip-hop, so they don't listen to it. But really, there's plenty of good stuff out there. You just have to look for it."

"I guess you're right," I said.

"So what made you stop listening to me?"

I looked at him and started chewing at the inside of my lips nervously. I didn't want to offend him.

"Don't be shy," he said. "I'm an artist, not a student. You can't hurt my feelings."

"It's just that all the stuff I heard was about sex and violence and drugs. It seemed like the same old rap music. Nothing new."

"You're right," he mused. "I do write about sex . . . and violence . . . and drugs. And let me say this—"

"You don't have to. You really don't have to explain anything to me. I was just answering your question," I said.

"I'm not explaining what I do. I'm good at it. I know that. And I'm paid very well for it. So there's no need to explain," he said between taking sips of his beer. His voice was tough. Secure. "But I will tell you what I do. Because I respect you."

"Okay."

"I love sex. It's great. It's good. It makes you feel great and I think people should write about it. Sing about it. Rap about it. Paint about it. Take pictures. Videos. Whatever. I bring that up because it seems every other art form in the world has deconstructed, sold, defined, and redefined sex and sexuality. And I ain't learn that in no book. I've been to Florence and seen Botticelli's nude paintings for myself. Now, that was in the 1400s and he was painting naked pictures of the broad he was trying to steal from the dude who was lacing his pockets. That's some pimp shit," he said, laughing. "Man, artists have been doing it ever since—even before then. But as soon as a bunch of young black men talk about how much they like sex . . . and get paid for it . . . people have a problem. Then sex is dirty and nasty, and meanwhile, they're willing to pay millions of dollars to buy a Botticelli. Now, Little Richard and even Ray Charles sang about sex, but ain't nobody talk about them like they talk about us. And I'll tell you why. It was because they were making a whole bunch of white boys rich. And now that I'm stepping up, making sure most of those bills come back to me, suddenly the most human thing a person can do is vulgar. And I'm not even talking about having sex with little girls or making people do stuff they don't want to do. I'm talking about real stuff."

Dame went on, and I learned more about his music. More about him just as a person. He seemed so angry at times. So political and militant. He saw sides of the music industry that I thought were myths. Beyond the dancers, videos, and flashy cars, people were stealing money and labels were rejecting what would be considered positive songs by top artists. He said the worst thing he ever did was make a platinum record. Now everyone had platinum dreams. He had to remind himself every day of who he was and that's what the latest album, *The Same Dame,* was about. Being himself and returning to his roots. So far, the fans got it and all of the people at the label who wished he'd been more raunchy, more aggressive on the release, looked silly when the entire industry agreed it was his best release.

"Don't get me wrong," he said. "I ain't no flower child MC. I ain't rapping for peace or ending homelessness."

"But why not? Don't you think those kids in the school today need to hear that? To know what's going on in the world? You have such a powerful influence on them. You could use it."

"This business is about money first." He ate the last bit of a sandwich he'd made with some rib meat and bread. "You can't forget that. It'll use you and spit you out like you ain't shit. If it's not a hit, it ain't a hit. You're out. I'm in this to make money. That's first. The art is second. And the fans are third. They feel me. You may not feel me. People trying to hate on me may not feel me. But the fans feel me. And that's it."

Dame and I went back and forth about this for an hour before I realized I was talking to a grown man who had his mind made up about what he did and was making millions of dollars doing it. I kept telling him that the kids he was reaching and the art should come first, but he had a point about the hits the industry was expecting. If no one was making money, he wouldn't have any fans and his art would be recorded on a cassette tape in the projects he once lived in. While that seemed like the proper place for someone trying to remain connected to his roots, it was a lot to ask of someone who already starved for most of his life.

It was an interesting debate that was hands-down the best dinner conversation I'd had in years. It wasn't about me or church or family; it was about art, the world, and dreams. And all of this from a former student I'd fully expected to arrive back home as a boy. Now I knew the world had made him a man.

When I got home, Evan was still out, so I climbed into bed alone and called Billie. The news of the evening would no doubt keep us on the phone all night.

Chapter Eleven

"So, what was he like?" Evan asked as we sat on a bench inside the tennis courts at my parents' estate, watching Jr and May finish their match. It was 7:30 a.m. and I was looking up at the brightening sky, praying the sun wouldn't suddenly make its grand appearance once Evan and I got up to play.

"What?" I asked. I'd spent most of the night on the phone going over the dinner with Billie. "Why didn't you call me? I wanted to party like a rock star!" she'd squealed.

"Dinner with Dame—what was he like?" Evan repeated.

"It was fine. I mean, we just ate and . . . that was it."

"Come on, you had dinner with a rapper. I'm sure there were some highlights. Strippers? Moët?" he joked.

Jr was serving balls at May like the Wimbledon trophy was waiting inside on the mantel. He'd hit them hard and fast, even though he knew the woman could hardly play. And then he'd take time-out between obnoxious sighs to point that out.

"If you'd anticipate my hit, you'd see where it was landing," he growled, and she just wiped her brow, hustling to get to the other side of the court.

"He was a little flashy at first," I said to Evan, "but then he warmed up and we just talked."

"What did you talk about?"

"I don't remember, Evan. Music. God. Everything. I wasn't exactly keeping track." This wasn't half the retelling I'd given Billie. But I knew Evan didn't really want to know how it felt to be sitting at a table in a restaurant with someone who drew eyes from everyone walking by. How fun it was to ride in the backseat of that Bentley. And how I'd found Dame's smile endearing. His ideas potent. And his company just plain refreshing.

"Good hit! Great! Good!" Jr hollered, coaching May. Looking ragged but not defeated, she swatted at each ball defiantly and I wondered if she imagined it was Jr's big head.

"Did he say anything about the school?" Evan asked me. "About donating more money?"

"No."

"Well, did you bring it up?"

"I didn't know I was supposed to," I said. "Maybe if you'd come, you could've."

The sun was up now. It was already warm, but by the time Evan and I were midway through our match, it would be near dreadful.

"See, if you'd just anticipate my moves more and really run the court, you'd do better," Jr said as he and May dropped their rackets and walked over to Evan and me. "Your turn," he said to us.

I looked up at the sun and thought about my hair.

"Jr, your game was good. Maybe you should play Evan, so May can see your skills from over here . . . then maybe she can anticipate your moves better," I said, knowing just how to rub my brother's ego to make him insist upon playing again.

"Hmm," he said, pretending to consider my suggestion before responding. "Maybe you're right." He tilted his head and paused reflectively. "Yeah. Let's play, Evan." He pointed to Evan as if he was enlisting him into the Army and picked his racket back up. "And May, you can watch, so you can see me move."

Evan popped up and gathered his racket as well. As May sat down, I rolled my eyes at Jr. If I could count on one thing from him, it was his ego leading to disaster.

"Thanks for saving me from having to sit here arguing with him for another half hour," May said, settling into her seat next to me. "Your brother keeps me in prayer."

"Oh, that was for me," I said. "If my hair feels one more drop of sweat, this mop will be an Afro for sure."

We both chuckled, and when I refocused, I saw Jack Newsome stepping into the gate. He was alone and dressed in some loose-fitting shorts and a Prophet House T-shirt.

"Pastor Newsome," May said.

"Hey, everyone," he said, walking onto the court.

May and I got up and walked over to greet him, meeting Evan and Jr halfway.

"Your father invited me out to play this morning," he said.

"He did?" Jr asked, scowling as if he was ready to bounce Jack off of the court.

"Well, welcome," May said pleasantly. "Let's get you a racket."

Jr mean-mugged Jack for as long as he could before we continued pleasantries and decided to let him play in the next match. He claimed he hadn't played in a while and needed to loosen up. Jr, smelling weakness in his unfortunate opponent, was adamant that he help. In fact, Jr added, he was just about to show everyone his new serve.

Evan, May, and I scrunched up on the small bench and watched the two get into position. The only thing missing was a commentators' table and microphones. Jack had no clue, but this was sure to be the hottest action the courts had seen since the infamous Justin and Jr matches in the nineties.

"I hope your brother doesn't embarrass us. The man's a guest," May whispered, sitting on my left.

"I think that's part of the problem," Evan said on my right.

Jr hit the first ball hard, but Jack, who apparently knew how to "anticipate a play," hit the ball right back at Jr, slamming it at his feet.

"Nasty," I said, watching Jr hustle to get the ball as May had. "Good and nasty."

The ball was up again and the pair hit it side to side, fast and forcefully. It was more like a fight than a match. We could hear them grunting with each hit. And when the ball came down on Jr's side again, he flung his white head band to the ground and started bouncing around on his feet like a fighter.

"They kinda look alike," Evan said, his head moving as we watched the ball.

I looked back and forth between my brother and Jack. Jr was lighter and a bit taller, but from where we were sitting, they did look a lot alike. The same build, way of hitting the ball. Even their profiles favored one another with the sun's shadows.

"Well, you know what they say about people hating each other looking like one another," May offered.

"I thought that was about people who were always together," I said as the ball slammed at Jr's feet again.

This battle went on until my mother called us all into the house to eat. Jr lagged behind, cursing and spitting so much that my mother told him to sit outside and cool down before he came inside the house.

Fortunately, for the sanity of my family, Jack, who was as cool as a politician after the match, had to get back to the church to excuse the children's Bible study academy, so he had to leave. He made his apologies and promised to join us again next time. Only we knew that next time would be more like never once Jr spoke to my father. I volunteered to walk Jack to the car. He was a year older than Jr and lived just blocks away from us growing up, but I never got to know him very well outside of the church. He was an interesting man—dedicated to the church and God. Like my father, he had a strong grasp of the Bible, but he'd taught at the Johnson C. Smith Theological Seminary in North Carolina, so he tended to think of things in the Bible in less conventional ways than my father. He wanted to break things down, ask questions, and explore other texts. This came through in his smart, lecture-like sermons, which attracted a young, more educated population. Unlike other assistant pastors, when the church knew Jack was going to lead a sermon, they showed up in numbers. I thought this was why Jr was so jealous of him.

As we walked to the car, I complimented him on his backhand and apologized for Jr's behavior.

"He'll have to accept it on his own time," Jack said

openly, and I assumed he was talking about his eventual leadership of Prophet House.

"Jr is stubborn. He gets that from our father. I'm sure he'll be okay," I replied.

"I'm happy to hear that."

"You know, I'd like to get to know you better. We never talk that much outside of the church," I admitted.

Jack looked at me meaningfully.

"I'd really like that, too, Journey," he said.

We shared a friendly hug and I walked back inside the house to see everyone assembled at the table.

"So, tell us about that Dame," my mother said as I sat down. "What was he like? And when are you going to be on BET?"

Chapter Twelve

As they did most Mondays, that fourth-period class put a beating on me. No one had their music sheets, every section forgot their notes, and when I tried to get them warmed up by singing "Lift Ev'ry Voice" to get ready for the opening at graduation, anyone listening would've thought not one person in the room had ever heard the song. I'd rolled my eyes and frowned so many times that I was sure if someone walked up behind me and hit me on the back, I'd have a cross-eyed scowl on my face for the rest of my life. I'd had good days teaching, but this unquestionably wasn't one of them. The students were too busy talking about Dame and BET to hear a word from me.

As they hurried out of the room when the bell rang, I tried to remind myself that I only had three weeks to go until it was all over.

"You busy?" Zenobia asked, slowly strolling behind the crowd.

"Well, that depends on if you intend on having a 'Student Death Match' outside my classroom again," I replied. Zenobia had just returned to school the previous week from her suspension for fighting with Patrice.

"No, I ain't fighting, Mrs. DeLong," she said, amused by my comment. "I know I be acting up in your class and stuff, but I ain't no fighter. Patrice stepped to me, so I had to do what I had to do."

"Fine with me. Just do what you have to do someplace else next time. Maybe by the science lab," I said. She sat down in the chair next to my desk. "So what's going on with you?" I pointed to her stomach.

"That's what I wanted to talk to you about." She looked down. "My mama's making me have an abortion. She said we can't afford another baby."

"How do you feel about that? You don't look too happy." I was against abortion, but my personal feelings aside, I also felt Zenobia couldn't afford to have another baby. Not only financially. Psychologically, she was already going through enough. She wasn't even seventeen yet. And if she was going to make anything out of her life, the second baby was about to make it almost impossible.

On the news, people always talk about how there are poor people in Africa and in other far-off places. But there was poverty in Alabama, too. Women like Zenobia had three or four kids they couldn't afford to feed and they worked twenty-four hours a day at the minimum-wage jobs they were lucky to have.

"I ain't happy about it," Zenobia said, answering my question. "I want to keep my baby."

"Zenobia, I'm sure your mother respects your right to choose. But she also wants what's best for you and Mikayla."

"I know she do," she said sadly. "But she just don't understand, you know? She been alone and stuff all the time and she don't know what it's like to love a man like I love Michael. She always saying we ain't gonna be together, but she just mad because she can't find nobody. But I know when I have this baby, Michael gonna help me and we gonna get our own place and everything."

"But I have to ask you again, Zenobia. What about the other baby? How can he do all of this for you and do the same for Patrice's baby?"

She just shrugged her shoulders and kept her head down. I saw a tear fall from her eye and stain her red tank top.

"I can't lose him," she said, sniffling now. "I can't lose Michael."

"Why do you keep saying that?" I remembered her saying that when we first talked about the baby. "You make it sound like your whole life is wrapped up in being with him."

"It's just the way he make me feel when we together. You don't understand. It's like I ain't even alive if I ain't with him," she said, and I could see in her face that she meant it. "And when he be with Mikayla, just holding her, I'm like that's what I wanted from my daddy. Somebody to just hold me and love me. But he was never there for me." She crouched over in the seat and covered her face with her hand.

I moved my seat near her and began to rub her back.

"I do know what love feels like, Zenobia," I said. "And I also know that you won't find the love you're looking for from your father in any other man."

She looked up at me.

"Having another baby isn't going to bring Michael

closer to you," I said as compassionately as I could. "And it's not going to erase the pain you feel for never having a father."

Soon I started crying, too, and Zenobia and I sat there talking and crying until my lunch period was over and the next section of students started filing in.

Before Zenobia left, I embraced her and told her I'd be there for her, whatever the decision was.

I was exhausted. So tired I was sure my feet had divorced my body and whatever stubborn strips of skin that continued to keep the two attached were going to snap the moment I reached my car toward the back of the school parking lot. After missing my lunch break talking to Zenobia, I was on my feet for the rest of the day and every muscle in my body was aching—from my index fingers from pointing, to the very tips of my toes from running around the room. To make matters worse, I'd stayed late, working with a few of the soloists, and it was 6:15 p.m. The sun was still high, though, and it felt like it was sitting right above my forehead. Trying to juggle two heavy bags and a radio I'd carried to work, I thought fainting and rolling under one of the other cars might be a better option than setting my sights on my own car. At least, then, I'd be out of the sun's spotlight.

"Whew," I exhaled, finally making my way to the driver's-side door. Not caring where anything landed, I dropped all of the bags right where I stood and let my shoulders go limp to take a second to catch what little breath of life I had left. When I finally got enough energy to actually bend down to get the keys out of my purse, I noticed that the brightness around me had dulled and thought maybe a cloud had snuck up and covered the sun. If I hustled fast enough and found the keys, I'd be lucky enough to ease into the car before the sun came striking again. No one else was in the teachers' parking lot, so I was sure it would find me again.

"Nice view," I heard someone say.

Still bending down, I turned my head to see that the cloud was actually an old pickup truck.

I straightened up quickly, snapping the found keys into the palm of my hand.

"Oh, I'm . . ." I covered my brow with my hand, so I could see who was sitting in the truck.

"No need to apologize," the person said. "That's exactly what I was looking for."

I stepped forward and squinted a bit more.

It was Dame. He was grinning and leaning out of the truck window with one hand still on the wheel.

"Excuse me?" I asked as I frantically straightened my skirt.

"Oh, I'm sorry. I didn't mean it like that," he said, smiling, yet apologetic. "Well, I meant it like that . . . but I didn't mean to be disrespectful."

A bead of sweat trickling down my forehead, I could see the muscles in his arm tighten and flex as he spoke.

"Thanks . . . I guess," I said, trying to sound unaffected—stern, yet calm and not staring at his biceps. "Can I help you with something?"

"Yes, you could," he said. "I was actually here looking for you. I knew it was late, but you always stay late before graduation."

His statement caught me off guard. I wondered how he'd remember that.

"For what? I mean, what did you want?"

"Well, we could start with you coming a little

closer, so I don't have to scream my business out over this whole parking lot."

"Come over there?" I asked, looking around the lot. It was a simple request. But I still felt inside that I needed to stay where I was. Like walking to the truck was wrong in some way. I felt girlish and ridiculous for thinking all of these things.

"Yes," I said . . . looking at his arm and then away. Closer to the truck, I saw that the old, blue thing really did block out the sun. Maybe it was the steel or just the size, but I felt cooler there. Cooler and smaller somehow.

"I wanted you to hear something." He shifted the gear and put the truck in park. The engine growled and then grunted as if it was threatening to cut off, but then it kept going.

"Hear something?"

"Yeah. Something I think you might like. I'm thinking about putting it on my next album."

"Dame, I told you I don't really listen to music like that. Don't you think you—"

"I'm just trying to get your opinion. That's all. If you like it, you like it. If not, you don't. It's all good."

"Well, I have to . . ." I turned to look at my bags on the ground. "I was on my way home."

"It's just one song, Ms. Cash."

"Mrs. DeLong."

He smirked slyly.

"Mrs. DeLong," he repeated.

"Okay," I said. "I'll listen to the song."

"Good."

I stood there, two inches from the car shaking my head in anticipation. Waiting for him.

"Oh you're waiting to hear it now?" he asked, sounding confused.

"Yes," I said.

"Come on now. You can't be serious."

"What? I said I would listen."

"We got to roll. You don't listen to something like this just anywhere." He was laughing. "We got to roll with it. Drink it in with the breeze."

"But I was about to . . ." I looked back at my pile on the cement again and couldn't think of a thing to say.

Dame helped me get the things into my car and we were driving away from the school in the pickup truck. He plugged his MP3 player into what was clearly a new radio in the old truck, turned the volume all the way down and pushed back in his seat. Looking around as we rode in silence, I noticed that there were no seat belts, the air-conditioning had been torn out, and there was a big hole in the floor beneath the gas pedal. I hadn't been in a pickup truck in years, and this one had to have been old enough to belong to my grandfather. But Dame, who'd looked comfy riding in the back of a chauffeured Bentley days before, seemed just as natural here.

"Do we have to go somewhere to get the song?" I asked.

"No . . . I'm just waiting until you can hear it."

"Hear it?"

"Trust me," he said smoothly. Still handling the truck, he looked over at me and I swore he winked without moving his eye.

I felt I should probably protest, but the heat in the car was getting to me and I just wanted to catch a breeze, so I sat back in my seat like him and held my head toward the window frame, just as I had when I was a little girl riding in my grandfather's truck. I relaxed my neck and let my arms fall to my sides.

As we rolled down University Boulevard and through the middle of downtown, I wondered for a while who might be seeing me riding with Dame. The people from church. From school. My parents. What would they say? We weren't doing anything. Just riding. But I knew they'd say something. I wasn't where I was supposed to be and that was enough. And then I thought of how crazy it would look if we inched up to Evan at a stop sign. He'd look over at me. Open his mouth. Roll down his window. Say my name in a question. I searched the lanes, the parking spots for his silver BMW, but never saw it. And by the time I got tired of looking for the car and recognized that no one—not one single person walking by—even bothered to look, I realized that I'd been riding in silence for over thirty minutes. I'd unbuttoned the top of my shirt and taken out my earrings. The breeze had gotten into me and riding along beneath the steel top, I didn't even feel the heat anymore.

"You ready?" Dame asked, turning the knobs on the radio.

"Sure," I said.

Break out, his voice called through the speakers. *Yeah. Break out.* There was a pause and then a beat came in. Fast and full of a kicking bass that thumped in my chest, it vibrated through the truck, rattling so hard I could feel it in between my toes. It was loud. Loud and making the doors creak. But still the constant waves moving through my body made me remember when I used to ride in the front seat of Billie's car freshman year in college as we listened to UGK, the 69 Boyz, 2 Live Crew, OutKast—all of the rap CDs my father would toss in the garbage had he found them in my room.

Then, just as I began to fall back into memory and nod my head to the beat, I heard something that was unfamiliar in a rap song, but very familiar to me—the unmistakable thunder of a Hammond B3 organ.

"Oh," I said, straightening up, "that's an—"

"No." Dame stopped me. "Just stay relaxed. Feel it."

I unfolded again and listened. Dame came in and rhymed on top of the beat. As I'd heard, his flow was fast and intense. I felt old just trying to make out the words and it was funny because when I stopped trying, I could hear and understand them perfectly.

In the verse, Dame was talking about the music industry and other rappers and how he wanted to break through. Everybody wanted something from him. Everybody wanted to "take" something and try to "remake something" and not give credit. Then he said only God could "take and make," so he was going to take and make and he was going to be God. A god. Any god.

I felt my forehead crinkle. I was used to black men referring to themselves as God, a god, but it sounded ludicrous. The very concept of God was perfection and man, destined to die, was innately ungodly. A maker or not, it wasn't something that could be debated.

"What you think?" he asked, turning the song off before it was over.

"Well, I think it's . . ."

"Be honest. I ain't come all the way to get you to have you blow smoke. I want to know what you think."

We were at a stoplight. I saw two girls from Black

Warrior walking by on the sidewalk on the other side of the truck. They were wearing tight jeans and cut-off T-shirts that showed the muscles in their stomachs. Just before the light changed, one noticed Dame and pointed toward the car.

"Dame!" they both squealed, jumping up and down like kangaroos beside each other. A few other people walking by turned and looked, too. Dame nodded his head coolly as if we were in a music video and smashed his foot on the gas.

"So?" he continued, weaving into the traffic in front of us.

"What does it matter what I think? Obviously, I'm not your target audience."

"Oh, you're starting to sound like *them* now."

"I liked it. I liked the beat. The organ was interesting. It all flowed together."

"What about what I said?" he asked, looking at me quickly.

"The whole thing about breaking through the industry—I got that."

"But?"

"But I just don't know why you had to bring in the stuff about God."

"You have a problem with me saying I'm God?"

"I don't have a problem with it. Like you said the other night, you can say what you want to say. I just don't think it's necessary."

"So, you don't think the black man is God?"

"No. That's crazy. God made man. Man can't be God."

"Spoken like a true Christian."

"I'm not hiding behind my religion here. I don't have to do that," I said. "I'm not some Bible-toting fanatic."

"I was about to say, I did notice that you didn't pray over your food the other night."

"Very funny." I sighed. This was where my beliefs seemed to constantly come under the microscope with people. Like I told Kayla, they all wanted me to be one-dimensional—my faith, my life. But sometimes I didn't pray over meals. And I didn't care. I wasn't even sure that it mattered. Sometimes I didn't want to go to church. And a lot of times I made up silly excuses and flat-out lied to my own parents. I didn't know if that mattered either. I'd never say any of that aloud, but it was true.

"I didn't mean to put you on the spot," Dame said, obviously looking to see if I was affected. And if it had been years ago, I might have been. Then I was overly concerned with how my spiritual path looked to other people—is she saved, isn't she saved. . . . But as I got older and it got harder, I decided that me loving the Lord had to be enough. I couldn't pretend I had the Bible all figured out just because my father's a pastor. He chose that when he got saved after years of running the street. I was still a work in progress and willing to admit it.

"It's not that. I just don't want you to think I'm so small-minded that I can't even consider your idea of man being God," I said. "I do question things sometimes. But I believe in one Creator and that's it."

"Look, I was raised in the church just like every other kid in Tuscaloosa. And I believe in God, but I think, if people are going to say we're made in His image, they may as well accept the responsibility that they're Gods, too. Like, your parents, they made you. So you're a part of each of them. Right?"

"Yes," I answered, noticing that it was getting dark outside and looked at my watch to see that it was already 8:30 p.m. Time was rolling fast beneath the wheels of that truck. Evan had meetings and he probably wasn't home yet. But he'd be looking for me soon. I thought to call, but I was enjoying the conversation and company too much.

"So in a sense, if you're a part of both of them, then you're them."

Dame sounded like a poet reading at one of the poetry readings in the Hay Center at Stillman. Listening to him, it was hard to imagine he was a high school dropout. All of this clearly mattered so much to him.

"I can't say no to any of that," I said.

"Now, if we connect that to man, then man should just accept that he's God and stop claiming he should act 'godly,' and just be a god. I think it's some real bullshit when people say they want to act godly, but they're just men. If you say you're a god, you have no choice. Your word is your bond. You're not the God. You're God's son. Still a god."

I looked at Dame and I knew I was grinning. He was so wrapped up in his ideology, he was now tapping on the steering wheel and getting loud.

"What you laughing at?" he asked, just as I burst out in laughter.

"You're so serious about this," I said. "You should've seen how intent you were."

"Hell yeah. I'm trying to build," he said, laughing now, too.

"Well, that's very *Tupac-narian* of you."

"You know 'Pac?"

"Of course."

"No doubt. That's exactly what I'm talking about. 'Pac had a lot to say about personal responsibility and living up to your potential. That's all a brother's trying to say," he added, his voice mockingly militant. We both raised our fists and continued laughing. "You know, it's crazy. All those years I was away, I just kept thinking what it would be like to come home and kick it with you and now I see, it's cool as hell," he said.

"Oh, now we're kicking it?" I asked.

"You know what I mean. Just like, talking to you like a real person. Not my teacher. Just another person."

"I know what you mean," I admitted. "I didn't think you were as mature as you are. I was expecting you to be cursing every five words and drinking forties. You'd be all gangster and rhyming for no reason." I started moving my arms around like I was an angry rapper prowling a stage.

"Oh, MCs are just like anyone else—at least if they want to survive in this industry. We have to turn it off and on. You can't be all hard all the time. Hip-hop is on *The View . . . Good Morning America.* Now, you can't come at Regis and Kelly like, 'Y' know what I'm say? Know what I'm saying, my nigga?' " We both laughed. "That silliness won't sell any records and this is all about money. Trust me. You're hood in the 'hood, but when you leave, you let that go. Hip-hop done grown up. We sip *champagne when we thirsty* now—that's Biggie."

"I know Biggie Smalls, too. I'm not *that* old," I protested, slapping his arm gingerly.

"I don't know," he said, "with all this stuff about you not liking music."

"I never said I didn't like music. I said I don't listen to much hip-hop."

"Well what about your own music? What's up with that?" he asked, and in his voice it seemed he'd been in the church the other week when I couldn't sing. And I hadn't sung since then. It was a fact that presented an internal dilemma I wasn't ready to consider. So I just stopped talking about it and thinking about it and no one had bothered to bring it up again. But I knew I had to figure something out. I couldn't teach music if I couldn't sing.

"Nothing, I guess," I said, lowering my voice. "I'm just not singing right now."

"Not singing? You've got to be kidding me, right?" He slowed the truck down and pulled into a spot at a Waffle House. "You have to be singing." There was a sense of urgency in his voice. He really couldn't believe it.

"Just not right now. I'm kind of taking a break," I answered.

"We can't have that. Man, if you'd only seen yourself when you sang. I didn't like going to church, but whenever you sang, I'd sit and just shake my head in amazement at how pretty you sounded. Even with my eyes closed and my ears covered, I could hear that voice. And other people could, too. They'd be talking and passing notes throughout the sermon, but when you got up, it was like a light was in the room. People would be like, 'There's that Journey. Y'all listen now.' I was stuck wanting to be a thug, but I'd listen. I'd sit up and listen."

"I'm happy I had that effect."

"It was more than an effect. It was like magic that somebody could sound like that. I was thinking, man, if she goes into the industry, Whitney, Mariah, even Aretha and Patti—they can just hang it up and go on home." He looked at me, and I squinted my eyes to show that I knew I in no way compared to any of the names on that list. I had a church voice. A homegrown church voice that no one outside of Tuscaloosa needed to hear. "I'm serious," he continued. "You never thought of that?"

"I did a few times, but everything I need is right here. Why go out there and deal with the industry you hate so much when I can just sing for the Lord in my daddy's church?"

"Well, you just said you're not singing right now anyway. What are you doing?"

"You know, to be honest, I don't know sometimes. I . . ."

"Just say it," he pushed.

"I . . ." I hesitated again and looked out the window. "Sometimes I think I'm ready to just get out there. I even got this passport I keep in my purse." I tapped my purse. "I thought someday I'd get out and see the world. Maybe sing. Maybe even write some songs. Who knows."

"So, what happened?"

"Well, I don't have any stamps yet. It just never seems like it's the right time. There's always something else going on." I ran my hand over the bulging part of my purse where my empty writing pad was hidden and thought of Evan and the possibility of a baby.

"The world is waiting," Dame said softly.

"What?" I turned to look at him.

"It's just waiting for you to return. Maybe you'll start singing again when you do."

"Maybe," I replied somberly, thinking it sounded silly for me to return to a place I'd hardly ever known or explored. And feeling foolish that it was true.

"Hey," he said, his voice suddenly filled with an enthusiasm to break the mood. "You know where they have some great music tonight?"

"Where?"

"Fat Albert's!"

"You mean that old shack in the woods?"

"There's only one." He smiled at me and it was clear he was inviting me to go over there with him. "It'll cheer you up."

"Oh, I can't do that." I looked at my watch. It was going on 10 p.m. "Evan's home by now. He's got to be waiting for me. And I have to teach in the morning."

"It's early," he said. "And we won't stay long. Just a little while."

"But I need to go. I have work to do and—"

"You need to get out to hear some music." He cut me off. "You need to be close to the art, so you can create it."

"Art at Fat Albert's?" I looked at him cross.

"Look, I'm trying to sell this to you," he said jokingly. "I just want you to come. Be out with me. Aren't you having a good time?" He groaned. "Ain't nothing really going on over there right now anyway."

I looked at my watch again. I probably should've called home, but I knew if I did, Evan would just insist on my not going. It was still a little early. I could listen to some music and be home by 11. I lied to myself.

Fat Albert's was in the back of the forests surrounding Black Warrior River. It was an old, windowless, rickety shack that somebody should've forgotten about in 1930 or something, but people still managed to tiptoe through at night or during the earliest hours of the morning to rub shoulders. And getting there did require some tiptoeing. Either that or a pickup truck, which we weren't at a shortage of in Alabama. The place had actually been built by a black bootlegger named Albert during prohibition in the early twenties. I heard people say he built it so far back in the forest so the police couldn't get their cars there to bust up the party. But my grandfather said no one who wasn't rich really had cars back then and the police had only one car which was always broken. So someone was wrong.

Either way, the place's out-of-the-way location made it a magnet for drunkards and hot-and-heavy adults for decades. It had been a part of the old chitlin' circuit and any black singer or band who wanted to make it in the Deep South had to pass through Fat Albert's. And after all that time, while lots of popular clubs downtown had come and gone, Fat Albert's with its cheap liquor, loose women, and looser rules seemed to be here to stay.

I'd learned all of this listening to other people's conversations. Justin whispering with his buddies when they slipped back in after slipping out after bedtime, my grandfather remembering when so-and-so got cut for speaking to so-and-so's woman, and even my parents, giggling and slapping each other on the hand as they told short, short stories about what they did there before they got saved.

All this, but I'd never actually been inside the place. Billie and I had tried once. It was right after college graduation and I was tired of everybody expecting me to be good and ordering me not to go places I shouldn't be seen. Feeling grown, we climbed into Billie's car because we were going to get down and dirty at Fat Albert's! We drove out there and parked the car and trekked down a winding dirt trail, etched out through the woods until we got to the front door. Billie handed the woman at the front door, who looked like she'd had a bit too much of the grain liquor already, our two dollars to get in and just as we were about to walk inside, another woman, with balding temples and cornrows that started at the back of her head, ran up and said, "Das de passtas doughta."

"Who?" the drunk woman asked as the one with the cornrows pointed to me. "Oh, you can't come in here. Albert, Jr will beat my ass for sure."

I sucked my teeth and looked at Billie, who clearly wanted to go inside. "Why can't I?" I asked the woman.

"Chile, it's Friday night," she said. "Half your deacon board's supposed to be in here. Ain't nobody gonna be able to party right knowing the pastor's daughter's right here."

"Fine," Billie said, reaching for her money.

"Oh, no, girls. No refunds. We take tithes, too!"

We heard them laughing as we followed the little dirt trail back to the car. That was the last I ever saw of Fat Albert's. It wasn't the kind of place where Evan was gambling to be seen.

Dame's big blue pickup truck was hopping through the forest like a rabbit. In the front seat next to Dame, I was holding on to the dashboard, the door, and seat, and sometimes Dame's arm to stay in the car. Dame just laughed and pushed on the gas, following a circus of colorful lights ahead.

"You're a country girl. You can take a ride in a pickup truck," he said after we made the clearing into the small lot in front of Fat Albert's. I could already hear the bass of loud music booming through the walls.

"I'm not that country. I thought the truck was gonna just split in two if we hit one more bump," I said, fixing my hair as he parked.

"Don't fix it," he said.

"What?"

"Your hair." Dame took a soft hold of my hand with his and pulled it down from my head.

"But it's all messed up." I could feel it falling down toward my shoulders, out of the twisted bun I'd made with one bobby pin. The middle was curling up and crinkling from the sweat on my scalp.

"You have beautiful hair. Why do you always hide it in those buns now? You should wear it down. It looks sexy."

"Sexy? I don't think you're supposed to tell your old teacher she looks sexy."

Dame said nothing, but he shot me a brief look with a smirk on his face. He jumped out of the truck, and I was surprised when he actually walked around to open my door and help me out of the truck.

"Now, these are my people," he went on as we walked toward the door before the glances of a few odd couples standing out front. Fat Albert's was the kind of place where people could be seen but not acknowledged. For everybody's protection, what happened back in the woods, stayed back in the woods. "Don't come in here trying to bless folks and stuff," Dame added. "It's bad enough you have on that suit."

"You think I'm overdressed?" I asked, pulling my shirt out from my skirt.

"I was just joking," he said. "You look fine. Half the people in here are gonna have on work clothes . . ."

When we walked in the doors, one of which was hardly holding on, the same two women, I swear, who'd been at the door ten years ago when Billie and I tried to get in, were still there—they looked exactly the same, only it was clear that the years in the back of the woods hadn't been so kind.

"The same Dame!" the drunk one taking the money said, dancing around and shaking when she saw Dame.

"Dame!" The other one came limping over. "Wuh yah bin, baybe?"

"I should've known you were coming in here; Benji been here all night." She pointed over to Benji, who was posted at a table with a group of girls.

They both jumped on Dame and he just grinned and hugged them back, tighter and more sincere, though, than he did the women at the restaurant the other night.

"Ms. Albertina and Ms. Essie!" Dame said. "My people. Damn, I miss y'all." He hugged them both again and then turned back toward me.

"Ladies, I want ya'll to meet my old"—he paused in anticipation—"friend."

He looked directly at me when he said it and I just smiled pleasantly. I didn't know if I wanted to be his "old teacher" in the moment anyway. It was my first time being inside of a place I'd imagined in my mind so many times as a girl.

"Das de passtas doughta," the one with the same old cornrows, which were now gray, said.

I exhaled and waited for them to take my two dollars again.

"And you wit' Dame?" the other one said cheerfully. "Well, that's all right. Go on in, chile. Have some drinks and send one over here for me." She laughed and smacked her hip, but I could tell she was serious. Dame later sent two drinks over.

Inside Fat Albert's, it was dark and only a few spots had dim blue and red lights to show people's feet where they were supposed to go and let the bartender and DJ see their hands. The crowd was a mix of some old people and some young, some couples, and some singles, and a whole heap of people I never expected to see inside. But I did. Only I knew not to say hello. I just nodded and kept on moving; the unstated agreement was, "You didn't see me here."

The DJ was playing a mix of old-school R&B and some hip-hop and every space on the dance floor was occupied. Even in the heat, they danced and danced, sweating until their skin had a slick sheen. After opening two more of the buttons on my shirt and feeling my hair completely curl up, I wondered which dancer would faint first.

"You having fun?" Dame asked, sliding an empty bottle of beer on the table.

"Sure," I said. "The music is wonderful."

I'd been watching Dame and noticed he drank a lot of beer and had on a plain white T-shirt that looked just like the one he'd had on at the school. And this was weird to me. It was so simple and nothing like what I would've expected it would be like to hang out with a rapper. He just seemed really . . . cool. I caught myself smiling with my eyes on him and quickly turned the other way.

"You okay?" he asked.

"I'm fine," I said nervously. "I think I need to go to the bathroom."

"It's to the back."

He pointed across the dark dance floor to a red light hanging over a doorway.

"Great. I'll be right back."

I excused myself through the crowd, seeing more

faces I knew along the way, and sometimes getting caught up in between partners, who moved me from side to side in an effort to make me join in. One man slid his hand around my waist and breathed heavily in my ear before passing me along and another pushed me toward his partner, who stepped closer to me as I fell back into her arms.

"Excuse me," I said, looking at her heavy eyes. Only it wasn't clear if she wanted me to keep going.

"What are you doing here?" I said to my reflection in the cracked and water-stained mirror above the sink in the bathroom. No one else was inside, but I didn't bother to go into one of the stalls. I didn't really have to pee. I just wanted to look at myself and get away from looking at Dame. I pat my hot face with a damp piece of toilet paper—there were no napkins—and dabbed on a bit of lip gloss. "Get it together and tell him to take you home," I sternly demanded of my reflection. I nodded to myself in agreement and picked up my purse to return to the bar with that intention. But when I got to the door, a familiar face met me.

"Kayla?" I said. My body went from hot to cold very quickly. She might as well have been my mother walking in on me—an immediate witness to something I wasn't even sure of. The situation had just gone from merely being odd to dramatically complicated. What could I say to her?

"Journey!" She smiled and opened her arms excitedly as if we were in the hallway at school. "I can't believe you're here."

As we embraced I could smell alcohol on her breath, but when I backed up and looked into her eyes, I could see that she wasn't drunk. Just a little tipsy. She was wearing dark-colored skinny jeans and a form-fitting T-shirt. Her hair was loose and wild, hanging in tendrils down her back. She looked more like a student than a teacher. More like a carefree girl in a nightclub than a sophisticated lady from New York City.

"Richard has been dragging me to this place almost every night since I got here." She giggled like a little girl. "I love it. Makes me feel bad, especially when we get home. Why don't you come have a drink with us?"

"I'm actually leaving now." I pushed my shirt back into my skirt.

"Oh." She stepped back and looked me over as if she was noticing something. "I didn't see . . ." she started slowly.

"Evan's not with me. I'm here for . . . some work thing."

"I see." She looked at me. And without saying a word, it was clear that neither of us needed to say anything else. I hated this gag, how it cloaked my goings-on in a shroud of guilt, but it was what I needed to stop Kayla from pushing.

Another pair came into the bathroom. Their clanking bracelets and laughter broke the silence.

"I'll see you in school tomorrow," Kayla said earnestly.

I just nodded and returned to the maze of the gyrating crowd. The music was different now. It was slow oldies and the couples were closer and some were even standing still in an embrace. I wormed my way through, trying to get out of there. I had to get home.

When I neared the edge of the dance floor, I didn't see Dame standing in the same spot where I'd left him sipping on his third beer.

"Shit," I cursed and looked along all of the crowds lining the rest of the short bar.

"Looking for me?" I heard over my shoulder.

I turned and right in front of me, close enough to kiss me, was Dame. I could smell him, feel his presence swallowing up my space, and as I took a deep breath to settle myself, I felt his breath come into mine. I flinched and forced myself to stand erect.

"Yes, I was looking for you," I stuttered, suddenly feeling all at once the reason I hadn't called Evan at home. I didn't need to be there, but I wanted to. "I need to go home," I said. And I knew it sounded slight. I didn't even believe it.

"I want to dance with you," he said.

"I can't," I whispered.

"Ain't nobody here watching us."

I looked back toward the bathroom door. It was ridiculous that I was even considering dancing with him.

"I just can't."

"Come on," he begged. "One dance and then I'll take you right back to your car at the school." He pushed his face into the mass of curls now crowding the front of my ears and whispered softly, "You ain't gonna make a brother beg, right?"

Whenever I'm nervous or afraid, I feel a need to swallow the saliva gathering at the back of my throat. While I suppose it just goes down easily other times, whenever I'm afraid or nervous, it goes down in an audible swallow that I'd prefer to hide.

Just as I did when Dame walked into the school, I couldn't hide that swallow now on the dance floor. His words, his breath, sent tingles around the back of my ears and I went quickly from being afraid of Dame's closeness to being afraid of what I'd do.

I didn't even say anything. Neither of us did. Dame just pushed his arms around my waist and we moved in a difficult closeness to the slow beat. Playing was this old Prince single I used to like to hear when they played slow songs at night on the radio when I was young. "Adore."

The hypnotic, raunchy beat, Prince's arrestingly sensuous voice, the words, all engaged inside of me, plucking each of the bones up my spine until I unfolded into Dame's chest.

I'll give you my heart.
I'll give you my mind.
I'll give you my body.
I'll give you my time.

Prince crooned and I believed him. He was sexy and strong, whispering and just nearly screaming the most intimate needs I felt deep inside. I could feel my heart racing down in my stomach. I wanted to move, but this was the closest I'd felt to music in so long. I needed it. This honesty. It was controlling me. Reminding me of what music could do. And it wasn't even about Dame. It was about being there and hearing the sound of emotion coming from someone else.

And then, without knowing what I was going to say, I opened my mouth just as the song ended and Dame's hands slid to my lower back.

"Thank you," I whispered into his ear. "Thank you for bringing me here."

Something was happening. At some point between the dance beneath the blue lights at Fat Albert's and Dame and I giggling as if we were drunk as we stumbled out to the truck, I'd lost my barrier. I was laughing at nothing at all. I was just happy to be out in the night air, in the world, feeling and hearing and smelling it all around me. It was as if I'd never been in this part of the world. At least not in a long time. Not like this. And all I really wanted was someone to be there to remind me that this was really happening. And that was funny because nothing had actually happened. Not something someone there could see. But it just was.

The white moon was hanging low in front of the truck. A crescent shaped upward, it looked like a smiley face was bearing down on us.

Sitting in the truck beside Dame as we drove along University Boulevard through downtown's crowds of beer-sipping blondes and frat boys waiting to get lucky, I rolled the window all the way down and sunk low in my seat to let the breeze come in all around me. My neck, my shoulders, around my ears, and through my scalp. I thought to slide off my right shoe and stick my foot out the window and then without considering anything else, I just did it. I just wanted to feel the air press against my foot and dare me to keep on coming toward it.

Dame turned the music up high and leaned to the side in his seat, too, looking over at me and laughing every few minutes. In this dark night, he looked brilliant, exciting, and familiar like the stars above us. Every few feet, someone would look, and then look at him again, and then whisper to the person beside them. It seemed that I noticed each of these heavy stares, but Dame just kept on rolling.

I knew that what was happening to me in that car was also happening to us. And I was happy about it. Happy to have a new friend—I could even call him that now—who could sit so close to me and ask nothing. He seemed to only want to give. And while something inside of me was saying this was dangerous, another side was tired of being afraid of what was dangerous.

"I had a good time," I said, not looking at Dame.

"I knew you would," he said. "Man, ain't nobody allowed to have a bad time at Fat Albert's. That's certified."

"Certified?" I laughed and looked at him.

"Hell yeah. I've been all over the world and I'll tell you, ain't no place that gets down like that. A bunch of old, fat ladies that can outdrink the ex-cons sitting next to them. . . . That's a damn party."

"You're crazy," I said as we both laughed. "And there were no ex-cons in there."

"What? Fat Albert's not even an ex-con. I think that fool is still supposed to be in prison. He escaped the chain gang in like 1901 or something."

"Not true," I said, slapping his hand and feeling it raise slightly, as if he'd wanted me to keep my hand there. I jumped and pulled my leg back into the window.

"You okay?" he asked.

"Yeah, I just, um . . . need to get ready for . . ."

"Oh, Baby Barack," he said as we turned onto the road that led back to the school where my car was parked. "It's not even 1 a.m. Just tell him you were out with your girls."

"Out with my girls? You just made that sound so easy. I can hear it now, 'Hey, I was just out with my girls!' That might work if I had girls and we ever went out."

"You expect me to believe that you don't go out?"

I shook my head.

"Ever?" he added.

"Ever."

"But you're grown and you have a job. And you're married. You deserve to go out and have a good time every once in a while." He looked at me and touched my hair.

"It's not that simple," I said, pulling away.

"It's as simple as you make it."

The light ahead of us turned red and Dame pulled to a stop.

"Like these folk over here, they're out having a good time. Enjoying a fun Friday night in Tuscaloosa," he said jokingly and pointing to a car on the other side of the truck that I couldn't see. "Oh, never mind. It's just a woman by herself. Looking really crazy . . . probably like you do on Friday night."

"Not funny," I said. I pushed up on my knuckles to look to the other side through his window. Right away, I noticed that it was Jethro Jr's old Buick, the car May drove. Both of the windows were rolled all the way down and May was sitting in the driver's seat with both hands tight on the wheel.

"She looks like she's about run a nigga down for something." Dame laughed.

"Shh," I said. "May?" She didn't answer. She just loosened her grip to wipe a tear I saw fall from her eye. "May?" I hollered again.

Just after I called her name the second time, the car scurried up the road and I looked to see that the light in front of us changed.

"You know her?" Dame asked, taking off behind May.

"She's my sister-in-law. Could you catch up?"

Dame sat up in his seat and pushed the gas as we chased the tail of the Buick. May was swerving slightly and then she ran a red light. Dame, without so much as blinking, followed suit, and a block later I was poking my head out the window hollering out, "May!"

If it was anyone else at any other time of day, I might have thought it was better to mind my own business. But May? Something had to be wrong, and whatever it was, May was leading us to it.

"You know where she's going?" Dame asked.

"No clue. It's just not like her," I said as we hit a bump and the seat bounced me up in the air.

"Does she live on the east side?" Dame asked, and I realized that was where we were headed. It was the neighborhood I grew up in. While we'd moved to another side of Tuscaloosa when I was in middle school, we still kept the old, three-bedroom house and Jr rented it out to church members in need of low-cost housing. May turned onto the avenue that led to that house.

"No," I said, cautiously reaching for my cell phone now. "She lives north of the river. . . . I think I need to call my brother. . . . Tell him what's going on."

"I think he's about to find out."

"May!" I screamed out the window again. "Why is she coming here?"

When we turned onto the street that led to the cul-de-sac where the three-bedroom house was that I'd grown up in, I knew why May was headed there.

Jethro Jr's new Buick was sitting in the driveway of the old house. Lights off. No Jr in sight. It was 1:30 a.m.

"That's your—"

"My brother's car," I finished Dame's thought as we pulled up behind May's stopped car in the middle of the cul-de-sac.

"He lives here?"

"No," I whispered as if the night would hear me. I wasn't sure what I'd stumbled upon at that stoplight, but now I was certain it wasn't good.

"Ooooohhhh." Dame gritted his teeth and gave a shrug of innocence.

May's car just sat there silent and dark in the middle of the cul-de-sac. Suddenly, I realized I was somewhere I wasn't supposed to be. But I knew May needed me there.

"Look, I'm going to talk to her," I said to Dame as I gathered my things and slipped on my abandoned shoe. "You can go."

"You sure? What about your car?"

"I'll get home. . . . I just feel like I need to handle this . . . alone. And I can't let them see—"

"No need to explain," Dame said, turning the truck back on. "I'll just catch you in the breeze."

"Sure." I smiled nervously and slid out of the truck.

"May, are you okay?" I asked after approaching the car when Dame had left. "I was in that truck . . . calling you."

"I need to get my husband," she said caustically. Both of her hands were still on the wheel.

"He's in the house? Did you two have a fight?"

"I need to get my husband," she repeated and I noticed that while her voice was cracking not one tear was in her eyes now. Her Bible, the one she always carried with the red leather cover case, was sitting on the seat beside her. It was open.

"May, I can tell you're very upset," I said, feeling my heart begin to race. I wanted to ask her why Jr was in the house again, but I knew I shouldn't. I was afraid of what might happen next. "I think maybe I can go get him from the house. Do you want me to do that?"

She didn't respond. She just nodded and kept her hands on the wheel. It seemed that she was afraid to let go. Afraid of what she might do herself.

"You stay here," I said. "And I'll go get him for you. okay?"

"Yes," she said uneasily.

I backed away from the car and then turned to face the house repeating, "Please don't be doing what I think you're doing" to myself. "Please! Please! Please!"

I kept looking over my shoulder to make sure May wasn't coming up behind me. Whatever it was, May was in no condition to confront Jr.

When I got to the door, the door of the house I grew up in, I didn't know if I should ring the bell or just walk in. I knocked lightly, holding the screen door my father had put up one hot summer back with my foot. There was no answer, so I knocked again, almost a light tap. It had to have been after 1:30 a.m. now and all of the lights were off. I looked back to the car to see that May still hadn't moved.

When the door finally opened, Jr was standing there looking back at me. Neither of us said anything for a second. We just stood there in the awkwardness of the situation, silent and looking at one another.

"Your wife is here," I said.

"Honey," a tired, feminine voice called from behind Jr. "Who's here so late?" The woman's head came poking out. She was a tall, light-skinned woman, who looked a lot like my mother had when she was much younger. I'd seen her at the church before.

"Kim, I told you to stay in bed."

"Who's this?" I looked at the woman. "Who is she?"

"I'm Kim, Journey," the woman said defiantly. "Would you like to come into my home?"

"Kim, I just told you to go back to bed," Jr repeated more forcefully, but she just stood there.

"I ain't going back to bed. I'm tired of hiding. This is your family." She stepped around Jr and came closer to me with her hands folded across her chest. "I'm his fiancée."

"How could you do this to me?" I heard May cry out. I turned and she was right behind me, crying and shaking. "You lied to me!"

"I told you to stay home," Jr shouted at May. "Go home. Journey, get her back in the car." He looked at me.

"Ain't nobody listening to you tonight, so you might as well just tell everybody what's going on. Tell her," Kim demanded, pointing her finger at Jr, and I swear in all my life I'd never heard anyone speak to him in that way. "Tell her now."

I reached back and grabbed May's hand. I hadn't processed what all was going on—how long it had been going on and how long May had been dealing with it—but this was way out there for Jr.

He pushed Kim to the side and came charging out the door, trying to get past me so he could get to May. I stumbled back, but then I jumped and tried to get in front of him.

"No!" May started inching back. "I want to know what's going on."

"Leave her alone," I said, pulling at Jr, who seemed like he was about to hit May.

"You want to know?" he shouted. "You really want to know?"

"Yes," May cried and Jr broke away from me. He was standing right in May's face.

"This is my girlfriend," he said as calmly as he might have had he been ordering a cup of coffee. "You don't make me happy anymore. You've put on all this weight. I'm not attracted to you. I haven't had sex with you in months. We don't have a life. You couldn't even give me a son."

Jr's words were so cold I wasn't sure if it was even my brother. I stood behind him, shocked and waiting for May to say something, but she just stood there. Tears started falling from her eyes and she covered her mouth with her hands.

"Enough," I said to him. "That's enough."

"You wanted to know," he said with his eyes mad and still set on May. "There it is. Everything. So now you can go and get back in your car"—he started pushing her toward the car—"and drive home and wait for me to get there when I'm done."

"Jr," I called, but he didn't stop pushing her.

"No!" May shrieked, and then she just jumped on Jr, wailing and screaming, "No!"

I leaped to try to pull her off Jr and then I felt Kim on my back, trying to pull me off. We all fell to the ground, three women, piled on top of Jr, wrestling and crying.

"You devil," May cried, pounding her fists into Jr so hard that I could hear it when each one landed.

"Get off my man," Kim yelled, pulling at my hair.

And I had one arm around May's belly to try to get her up and another swinging at Kim. And then, just when we all got tired enough, I heard a little voice calling from the door.

"Mommy! Daddy!"

We all froze and looked up. Inside the frame of the door was a little boy, red as Jr, standing there, holding a little blue blanket.

"Jr," Kim said. She hopped off me and ran toward him, fixing her clothes along the way.

My stomach flipped and turned as I struggled to get up. I felt light-headed. Like this was all too much for me. I needed my mother there. My father. Somebody to carry some of this. It was simply too much. And I couldn't imagine what May must've been thinking and feeling at that point.

Jr ran over to the boy and Kim and got on his knees.

"Why did you get out of bed, buddy?" he asked the boy, who couldn't have been more than three years old.

"I heard screaming," he said, and I stepped over just enough to see that he had my mother's honey-colored eyes.

"Hi," he said softly, waving with his little fingers curled a bit.

"Baby," Kim said, "this is the nice woman we always see at the church sitting near Daddy. She came over to say hi to us."

I turned to see May looking at the boy. Heartbreak was spilling out of her eyes. I could see her chest sinking in.

"This is your son?" She looked at Jr with clear contempt, hate in her eyes. "The son you wanted. . . . The son you made me ruin my body for? This is your son?"

"Come on, Jr," Kim said, picking the little boy up and walking into the house. As they headed down the hallway in the direction of my old bedroom, I watched as the boy's blanket hit the floor and he waved at me one last time.

"How could you do this?" May asked. "I haven't done anything to you. This is evil, Jr. Evil."

The light came on next door and I saw Mrs. Matthews, who'd lived next door to us all my life, come outside.

"You kids okay?" she asked.

"Everything's fine," Jr said. "Just had an emergency with the tenant."

"Hmm," she muttered, but it was apparent she knew what had been going on over at the house. I wondered how many other people on the block, at church, in town, had seen Jr's car there and knew what was going on.

"Look, it's clear you two have a lot to talk about," I said. "But this isn't the place for it. Mrs. Matthews is probably calling Mama right now."

"Let's go," May said sadly. "There's nothing here for me."

Every light was on in the house. They shone bright and rude in the middle of the night and I could see them before I even turned onto the driveway in May's car. They looked angry. Almost accusatory. And as May and I parked and walked to the front door, I felt like a teenager returning home to her father after sneaking out.

"Where have you been?" Evan said, pulling the door open with my key still in it. He had on the slacks he'd worn to work that morning, shoes, and his undershirt. His face was bright red. "I've been—" he charged, but then he looked at May, who was standing behind me and then back at me. "What's going on?"

"May and Jr had a fight," I said.

"But I've been calling you all night." He held up his cell phone. "Why didn't you answer?"

"Evan, I apologize," May said softly. "She was just trying to help me. Jethro and I had a fight and luckily Journey was there to help. We're—" May's voice waned and she lowered her head.

"Look, let me get her situated in the guest room and I'll come and talk to you," I tried, both wanting to comfort May and needing more time to think of what I was going to say to Evan. I knew he'd have more questions and I didn't want to lie to him. I hadn't done anything wrong. But I knew that at 3 a.m., the little I said would be acceptable. Even with May there.

Evan closed the door behind us and I patted May's back as we walked slowly to the guest room. She was quiet, but I could tell by how she moved her lips, she was already praying.

"Do you want me to call Jr to come—" Evan called behind me.

"No." I quickly cut him off. "She's fine."

After making May some tea and helping her calm down enough to just lay down, I walked through the house nervously, listening for sound coming from my bedroom. There was silence. Evan was waiting for me.

The last light, the one in the foyer before the front door, led me to my purse. I slid my cell phone out to place it on the charger and looked to see that I had twenty-seven missed calls. All were from Evan. The last two came with alert pages—PLEASE CALL HOME.

"I was worried. Really worried," Evan said when I walked into the bedroom.

Anything I could say sounded flat here, so I waited for him to go on.

"You never stay out that late. I didn't know what happened to you. When I came home and you weren't here, I called and you didn't respond."

"The ringer was off. I had it off since I was at work. I forgot to turn it back on. I didn't know you called." I sat down on the bed, eased my shoes off and began undressing.

"And then John called, saying he saw you joy-riding downtown with some thug," he said, pulling off his undershirt. John was his assistant.

"Some thug?" I was frozen now. The mention of John, joyriding, and downtown made me afraid to move. I'd forgotten about this possibility. That someone had seen me. Someone I didn't see. Of course they had. But they hadn't seen anything. I hadn't done anything. But that was easier to think than say.

"Yes. He said you were driving down University in the front seat of a pickup truck with some thug. But I knew it couldn't have been you," Evan went on. "But he kept insisting—"

Evan was walking around the room and then he stopped to look at me.

"Wait . . ." He came closer. "Was that you?"

"I wasn't joyriding with *some thug*." When I said this, I wished so hard that that was what it was—some drug dealer, a hustler, a pimp who'd kidnapped me. Anyone but Dame, because now I had to explain.

Evan's next question came as no surprise.

"Then who was it?"

I exhaled and thought again that I had nothing to hide.

"It was Dame."

These three words splintered into the room like buckshots. They were loud and fast, ricocheting off the walls and hitting Evan and me so hard that months from now, I'd know that we never recovered from that very moment.

"Dame? What would you be doing in a pickup truck with your former student? Riding down University?" Evan's questions came carefully, but there was confusion attached to each one.

"He came to the school," I started.

"Again?"

"No . . . well . . . yes . . . It was to see me. He wanted me to hear a song he'd written and I just went with him."

"You went with him? Why couldn't he have played the song at the school? Wait . . . and why did he need you to hear it?"

"He's doing some work with the organ and he wanted me to hear it in the truck. He has this whole sound system thing. . . . And I just went with him." I tried to make the situation sound as simple as possible. As simple as it was.

"Why didn't you call home and tell me this?"

"Everything was happening so fast. I was just going to listen to the song and then I lost track of time and then there was the whole thing with May."

"Journey, you're a grown woman. You don't lose track of time. You call your husband. That's the bottom line." Evan's voice was tightening. He started walking around the room again. "And you can't just go riding around with that kid."

"He's not a kid," I said. "And what do you mean, I can't just go riding around?"

"John saw you. Who else do you think saw you?

What do you think people are going to say? This could hurt us," he rattled off.

"Don't you mean hurt *you*? Last week, you said no one was looking at me. You put me in front of him. I didn't even want to do it," I said. "And now you say I need to think." I popped up angry and started taking off my clothes.

"I asked you to pose for some pictures and accept a check, not listen to his music like you're some teenager and parade him through downtown," Evan shouted.

"I wasn't parading."

"I don't want you to see him again," he directed. "You had no relationship before and there's no reason to have one now."

"Don't you think that's a little paranoid?" I asked. "He just wanted me to hear a song."

"I'm not going to say it again. I forbid you." These words rolled from Evan's mouth so easily, it seemed he'd spoken to me in this way all our lives.

"Forbid?"

"I'm not discussing it." He sliced the air with his hand at each word, sealing his point. "And May has to go home in the morning."

"May?"

"Whatever happened between her and Jr needs to stay in their house. That's your brother's wife. Don't turn his fight with her into your fight with him."

"Evan, he's cheating and he might have a—"

"I don't even want to know what's happening in that man's house," he said sternly. "I know what's happening in my house. And I know I don't want someone else's drama coming in here."

I was still putting on my nightgown when Evan

turned the lights out and got into bed. I didn't say anything. I didn't have the energy to fight for May or even for myself.

The moon and I were sleeping with our backs to one another. I couldn't find it outside the windows of the French doors as I lay in bed that night, so I turned and closed my eyes to pretend that nothing had changed. As I tried to rationalize my behavior, I realized that most of what Evan said was right. I should've called my husband. I shouldn't have gotten into that truck. I hated that Evan had the nerve to think he could forbid me to do anything, let alone seeing Dame. He sounded like my father. Like my brother. But then, with the word "forbid" echoing in my mind, I realized I was doing just the opposite. Because I was thinking of Dame. In a secret place inside my mind, one that I was even ashamed to visit, I wondered where he'd gone when he left. What he thought of the time we'd spent together. And if I'd ever see him again.

Chapter Thirteen

"Journey, I'm asking you nicely. Just stay out of it," Jr said. We were standing in the holding area behind the stage after my father's sermon. Jr hardly looked at me throughout the service, keeping his eyes glued on the pulpit and his hand rested on top of his Bible, which he conveniently placed in May's empty seat. She'd gone to stay with her mother in Northport after she left my house and asked me to bring some of her things from her house.

"How can I stay out of it? She's like a sister to me," I said to him angrily. Jr still hadn't even admitted that he'd done anything wrong. He was busy blaming May. I wasn't even sure he'd told our parents why she wasn't in church. It was like he'd expected her to just come back and everything was going to be okay. "How could you do this to her? And is that really your child?"

Jr furiously grabbed my arm and pulled me into a

corner, out of the way of a few people who were walking by.

"That's none of your business." He gritted his teeth.

"None of my business? It's a human life. You can't just pretend he doesn't exist. If he's your son, he's my nephew—Mama and Daddy's grandson," I said.

"You don't know what it's like to be a man, Journey. And to be married to a woman who can't have your child," he said, pointing at me. "I wanted a son."

"You could've adopted. You could've kept trying. There are dozens of things you could've done, Jr. And none include having an affair and letting some . . . some woman lay up in your parents' house."

"That's my house, fair and square, and Dad is in no position to give me any pointers about dealing with my wife."

"What is that supposed to mean?" I asked.

"Oh, please stop the innocent ears routine you play. Just listen to what's going on at the top of this church and you'll see where your father's loyalty lies."

"You mean Jack?" I asked. He looked so angry that it appeared he would spit at any moment. "Look, I'm not going to let you spin this around so you can focus on yourself and whatever little pissing contest you have with Jack. You need to be thinking about your wife for once."

"May ain't gave a damn about how I felt in years. Her head's so stuffed in that Bible, she can't even make love to me."

We both smiled nervously and nodded at two deacons who walked by.

"Maybe you need to be reading your Bible, too," I whispered before walking off.

* * *

Evan was just as harsh as Jr when I told him I needed to go see May after church. As we rode home, he kept repeating how he knew what Jr had done wasn't good, but that he and May were adults and perfectly capable of handling their own business. We were happy and there was no sense messing up our thing with their drama.

"I'm so tired of hearing you say that," I fumed when we pulled into our driveway.

"Say what?"

"About how we're so 'happy' and we shouldn't bother ourselves with other things," I said. "May's family and we can't just pretend this isn't happening. Can you imagine how she feels?"

Listening to Jr and Evan reminded me of how these men saw it as being so easy to put their feelings first. What they wanted. What they needed. It was about survival and at the top of their charts was a great big old picture of one of them. Women found ways to live with pain. But men developed crafty ways of finding comfort. Even in my own doting husband, I knew this was true. The love he gave to me was really love he gave to himself.

"She'll be fine," Evan said. "She'll be fine and she'll go back to Jr. And have you ever thought of what will happen with your relationship with Jr after that? You two will still be fighting because of how you acted and they'll be back together."

"Jr and I have been fighting since I was born. That's nothing new."

"Damn, Journey." Evan hit the steering wheel. "Why do you have to be so flippant? Why can't you just listen to your husband?"

"*Listen* to my husband? You sound like my father."

I opened my own door and turned to get out of the car.

"Wait." He took a hold of my arm before I could get all the way out. "I didn't mean it like that. I just meant that maybe I know best here."

"I hear what you're saying, but I need to be there for May. I'll be back by dinner."

May's mother lived in a cute, white house in the suburbs of Tuscaloosa. Her name was Ms. Sunshine and she was known for baking cakes for local diners. Like her mother and grandmother, she'd never been married and May was her only child. She never even told May who her father was. But in spite of this story, which led to a lot of people saying their blood line had been carrying a curse, she was as sweet as the cakes she made and so lovable that just one smile from her made you want a hug. She wasn't nearly as spiritual as May, though, and had never joined a church. Apparently, May's Christian upbringing came on account of Ms. Sunshine's mother taking May to the old evangelical tent revivals with her when May was a child. The goal was to get May saved, so she could break the curse.

"Hey, baby," Ms. Sunshine said, standing in the doorway of her house as I managed the steps in my church shoes and two bags of clothes hanging from both of my shoulders. I'd rushed over to Jr's house in my church clothes after I left Evan at home. I didn't want to risk running into Jr and fighting with him again. I'd been worn down.

"Hello, Ms. Sunshine," I answered.

"You always look so pretty." She smiled and opened

the door farther, so I could get inside. "Got that good Indian hair from your father's people."

"I guess so." I walked in and immediately dropped the bags on the floor. Ms. Sunshine and I hugged and I could see the kitchen from over her shoulder. Pots were everywhere. She was making Sunday dinner.

"You cooking?" I asked.

"Oh, I was just trying to make some dinner to cheer up my May. She been back there in my mama's old prayer closet for hours this morning. She's finally out. You want a plate?"

"I'll have one before I go," I said. I wasn't hungry. My belly was too full of confusion. But I knew that it was just as rude in Alabama not to feed company on Sunday as it was to turn down a plate. People cooked because they expected company and sometimes, for the poorest families, they'd use the last of their groceries to show their guests how grateful they were to have them. It was an insult to their sacrifice to say no.

"I'll get a plate ready for you." She smiled gleefully. "Even fix some for Evan, too. I know how much he likes my cobbler."

"Thank you. I know he'll love that."

"Well, May's in her room." Her voice turned sad. "She's real sad, you know? And hurt. I've tried to get to her, but something tells me ain't nothing but time gonna help her through this. Jr really done a number on that girl."

I couldn't say anything. I felt almost like it was partially my fault.

"You can go on back there, baby," she said. "I'll bring her things in later."

Pictures of May from the cradle to her wedding

day dotted every table top and surface of the walls in the house. She was smiling in some, praying in others, and sometimes just looking up at the sky.

"Hey, there," I said when I reached May's room at the end of a short hallway. The house was very small and Ms. Sunshine's room was right across the hall. Her TV was on.

May was sitting in the middle of a full-sized bed that seemed to have the same pink, ruffled comforter on it that might have been there when May left for college. A Bible rested in her lap.

"Journey." She smiled awkwardly and reached for me.

"How are you?" I asked, after hugging her and sitting beside her on the bed.

"I'm good. Just been here thinking. Trying to get myself together." Her eyes were red and nearly bulging out of her head.

"I understand."

"How did Jr look at church?"

"Jr's Jr. You know how he is. Have you spoken to him?"

"We were on the phone all last night. He said he wants me to come home."

"Come home?" I dropped my purse to the floor. "After what happened? He has some nerve. I mean, what did he say? Does he love that woman?"

"He said she's just some woman from the church. She's been chasing behind him and he got caught up. He was upset about us not having a baby . . . and she was there."

"That's bullshit. All these years he'd been lying to you . . . to his family because he was upset about not having a baby?"

"Your brother is really sensitive. He struggles with a lot."

May's voice was sad but a little sympathetic in a way I hadn't expected. Here she was, being made a fool of and she was still thinking of Jr's feelings.

"And so do I," I said. "It hasn't been easy for me either living in my family, but I've tried."

"There's a lot of stuff going on that you don't know about. Jr's protected you."

"He's just been lying," I said. "He's a selfish man. Always has been and—"

I stopped myself. I realized I was sounding angry and probably making matters worse. I didn't want to burden May.

"So, what about the baby? Is it his?"

"He thinks it is. Say's he'll take a paternity test if I come home."

I sighed and fought so hard not to curse. Jr had some nerve.

"Do you want to go home?"

May was quiet. She slid the Bible closer to her and closed it.

"I don't know." She paused. "You know, I never thought Jr would even marry me—didn't think anyone would. When I met him, I thought he'd find out who I was and then just dismiss me. Jr's so particular and with my family's past—you know how people can be."

I nodded my head. Even in 2008, after most myths had subsided, a lot of people still secretly believed in these things. They didn't say it, but they thought it.

"But Jr was always so impressed with my walk with the Lord," she went on. "He said I was the kind of woman he needed by his side. In love with the Lord first and him second. I was overjoyed when he even asked me out. Thought maybe the reason I'd gone to church with my grandmother and learned my Bible so well was finally paying off. I had a real good man. Someone who had his faults but loved me and wanted so much to be good. We could make something together. Start our own church even."

"I remember you telling him to do that," I said.

"But he wouldn't leave your father, and he just kept cracking, trying to make your father happy. I knew I lost him when it was obvious I couldn't have babies. Wasn't no shot gonna fix that. It's the Lord's will."

"You can't tell me you believe that stuff," I protested.

"It's in the Word, Journey."

"There ain't nothing in that Bible that says a bunch of stuff that happened before you were born will make you unable to conceive."

"Jr deserves a child."

"And you deserve to be happy. We all do."

"I know that. And sometimes I get so angry at myself. But I can't change this. Jr is my husband."

"So, you're going back?" I couldn't believe Evan was right.

"He doesn't want a divorce."

"But what is he going to do with that woman? And the little boy if you find out it's his? What is he going to keep playing house? And you're supposed to just take it?"

"He said he'll end it with her and if the boy is his, we'll get custody."

"That's crazy," I said. "May, I know you are a decent woman." I reached out to her and held her hand. "And you're always trying to do the right thing. But you deserve better than this. You deserve to be with someone who can love you no matter what. I know you're going to do whatever your heart tells you, but think about that before you sign up to raise someone else's son."

May began to cry, and we sat there, holding hands as she prayed for her marriage and I secretly prayed for myself.

Chapter Fourteen

May's worries followed me from Sunday to Monday under a cloud of sadness. I was moving, but slowly and seemingly waiting for the day to pass. The children came and went, and the day clamored on with the kind of dull repetitiveness that kept me constantly checking my calendar to see what day it was. Only, I felt like I had nothing to look forward to. I was so ready to just let go of everything, to stop carrying the sadness around with me and be happy for a few minutes, that by the time the day ended and I was walking out of the building, I prayed it was Friday and not the beginning of the week. I wanted to relax. To sit down and just talk to someone about everything that was going on.

When I walked out of the building and looked toward the end of the lot where my car was parked, I remembered Dame pulling up behind me the other day when I almost felt the same way leaving work.

How he cheered me up and we just talked about everything. It was an unexpected pleasure. I looked around, hoping I'd see the old pickup sneaking down another aisle, but it wasn't there. Dame was probably long gone now and not thinking about me or our conversation. And that was a good thing. It was best if I forgot whatever I was thinking about him.

"Mrs. DeLong! Mrs. DeLong!" someone screamed. I turned around toward the school to see Ms. Newberry, one of the secretaries from the front office running out the doors to me.

"Mrs. DeLong," she repeated out of breath now and heaving as she caught up to me.

"Calm down," I said. "We don't need you fainting on us."

I walked toward her and extended my hand to pat her on the back.

"Oh, I'm fine," she said. "I just wanted to make sure you got this message."

She opened her hand to reveal a pink message slip with words and a number written on it.

"The person said you needed to get it today," she said, finally catching her breath. "Something about a meeting."

She handed me the message.

"Who is it?" I asked, reading the text above the number: FORMER STUDENT.

"He wouldn't say. Just said to tell you it was about going back to a dream . . . or a dreamland. . . . Something like that."

My heart jumped. Pulsated so quickly, I felt it vibrate down to my knees. Suddenly, Ms. Newberry wasn't standing before me. I wasn't even in the parking lot. It was just me and the pink slip of paper existing in a tunnel where all I could imagine was picking up the phone and dialing that number. It was striking how immediately this need came over me. A moment ago, I wasn't even thinking about this number, but now, it was like water in a desert, and I hadn't had a sip in days.

"Mrs. DeLong?" I heard Ms. Newberry say.

"Yes?" I answered, emerging from the tunnel.

"Who do you think it is?"

"No idea." I widened my eyes comically to portray indifference.

"Hmm . . ." She bounced from one hip to the other and flicked her hand in the air dismissively. "Oh, well. . . . At least I got it to you. Maybe they'll call back. I'll be on the lookout."

"Thank you," I said, jiggling my keys.

"See you later."

I watched Ms. Newberry walk far enough from me so that she wouldn't see me look down at the paper. I felt I had to contemplate it on my own. In secret. When she neared the door leading back into the school, I looked down at the slip and felt my heart flutter again.

I looked around the lot and pulled the paper to my chest.

"Oh, my God," I said. "Oh, my God. Oh, my God. Oh, my God!"

I zipped through the lot, seeking a secret place to look at the note again in the refuge of my car.

What does he want? Why is he calling? Is he here? Is he in the lot?

Questions paraded themselves through my mind as I slid my purse into the backseat and eased into the driver's seat. I didn't even roll down the windows or turn on the air-conditioning. I just sat there with the note held to my chest and weighed what was happening. At first I wanted to ignore my feelings. To pretend that I couldn't understand why he was trying to contact me. But then I realized that that was only because a little part of me was illuminated by the idea that he had. But I was a married woman and he was my former student. Ten years younger than me. I shouldn't be illuminated. I shouldn't even have been sitting there with that note. My husband had said no. And then I thought that maybe that was it. Maybe this note meant nothing to me. And that the only reason I was even thinking about this whole thing was because Evan had acted so pig-headed. Maybe it was because I was just bored with my life and went out and had a good time and now I had a secret I was keeping from my husband. That was it. This was nothing. I looked down at the note again and thought if I should call. Dig myself deeper into this nothingness. Maybe I should've prayed. Called my mother. Went home to my husband. But I dialed.

"Yeah," a voice said on the first ring. I knew who it was. Dreamland.

"Dame," I said quietly, suddenly feeling the heat growing around me in the car.

"You got the message." His voice was strong but still excited. It sounded like my heart felt when Ms. Newberry finally said "dream."

"Yeah." I replied. And then there was silence. It was like all of the things I was thinking before I dialed the number were floating in the air. We weren't saying anything, but somehow we both knew that this phone call wasn't as simple as me listening to another one of his songs. I wanted it not to be true. Wanted then to hang up and drive right home to Evan. But then he spoke.

"I want to see you," he said, the strength in his voice lost in a nervous, short breath.

"You know, I just have so much going on," my mind sent my lips to say. "That thing with my brother and my family. I really need to focus on—"

"Journey," he said. And it was as if no one had ever said my name before. Like I'd never heard it. Not really. And then I realized that I'd never heard him say it.

"Yes."

"I need to see you."

"When?"

"I'm in Miami right now, but I'll be in Atlanta in two days. I want you to come to my show."

"What?"

"I'm sending a car over there for you and I want you to come to my show."

"I can't just go to Atlanta. I'm a . . . Dame, I'm a married woman. I can't just leave. Evan won't have it." I imagined telling Evan I was just going to Atlanta. It would sound absurd. It wasn't far, but I never went to Atlanta. Not even to see Justin. I didn't have the time. And if I did, Evan would come with me.

"Tell him you're coming to see me perform," he said.

"It's not that simple."

Dame sighed deeply.

"Look, I'm going to have a car waiting for you in the parking lot at Dreamland at 9 p.m. on Wednesday," he said. The excitement had surrendered from his voice and I wondered what he looked like right then. "He'll have two tickets to the show. If you don't show up, it's cool."

"Okay," I said. "But there's no way I can do it."

"I really need to see you," he repeated and this time he sounded like he was the one in need of water.

"I'll see what I can do."

I hung up knowing I could do nothing. This was impossible. Dame was making my life sound like some rap video where I could just jump into the back of a Bentley and ride out of town to a concert. I was not young. Not one of the white girls at the Cypress Inn or one of the teenagers stalking him from the curb as we rode down University Boulevard. I was a grown woman and sneaking away like that could rock every surface of my life. What was happening with Jr could possibly be happening with my parents, and Evan concerned about his career, I could not afford to shake anything. The secret had to end there. I crumpled the paper and threw it into a trash can as I pulled out of the school parking lot.

That night, as he had almost every night since my birthday, Evan reached out for me when I climbed into bed. He ran his hand suggestively down my arm and kissed me on the cheek. Before he could move to my lips, I turned away and said I was tired. That fast. I said I was tired and exhaled in show before turning away.

"You sure?" he asked. I could see him raised up on his elbow behind me.

"Yes," I said, my eyes wide as I looked out into the night. "I had a long day."

"Okay." He fell back down, hitting the bed hard and in a huff.

I blew out again, but in relief this time. I just couldn't bring myself to sleep with Evan after I knew I'd been on the phone with Dame. I had to get a hold of my feelings before I could have Evan again. This was all new emotion to me. And I thought that just by touching Evan, I'd be adding more to the secrecy.

As the clouds shifted in the sky, ambling about like tumbleweeds, my thoughts buoyed between not wanting to think about Dame and hearing him call my name. I tried so hard to block it out, but then, when I felt Evan's body loosen and then freeze next to me as he descended into sleep, I heard the silence in the room and realized I was alone again. I could sink into my mind and have my secret to myself.

And then I saw him. The brown skin on his arm as we sat at the table at the Cypress Inn. It was so chocolatey, so smooth, I could hardly see the hairs curling up at his elbow. He moved his arm from the table and then to his chin, where I stroked it as he smiled at me, laughing and saying something I couldn't even hear, because I was looking at his lips, his teeth, the dimples in his cheeks.

In the bed, with this image in my mind, I looked up at the moon and slid my hand between my legs. I thought of Dame until I fell asleep next to Evan.

"Journey!" Evan's voice crashed into my dream. Still between both worlds, I began to open my eyes.

"Huh?"

"Your alarm clock—it went off ten minutes ago. You have to get up to get ready for work."

I rubbed my eyes and looked at Evan, who was

standing in front of me, wet and with a towel wrapped around his waist. He was leaning toward me, his yellow face was so close to mine he looked like a little bobblehead threatening to bash in my brains.

"You must've been really tired," he said, hitting the alarm beside me.

"I guess." I looked around the room quickly.

"What?" Evan asked.

"What?" I was still laying in the same spot.

"Are you going to get up?"

"Yeah," I said, sitting up.

"And what were you dreaming about?" He turned to walk toward his closet. "You kept groaning all night."

Chapter Fifteen

"It was a wet dream?"

"Shh! Don't be so loud," I said to Billie, who was supposed to be in the downward facing dog position. We were in the middle of a class at the yoga studio I sometimes let Billie believe she was dragging me to, talking about the dream I'd had that morning. Billie jumped out of position totally and just sat in Indian style next to me. "And it wasn't a wet dream," I went on. "Only a man can have one of those. It was just a fantasy. Like I used to have when I was younger."

"First off, I have wet dreams all of the time," she whispered.

"Too much information . . ."

The namaste transitioned into the next pose.

"And second, you haven't had one of your freaky fantasies since college."

I flipped over with the rest of the class, but Billie just sat there. A woman in front of us was bending over and I could see her head from between her legs. She rolled her eyes.

"I know," I said. "And that's what was so odd to me. It was just like it came from out of nowhere. It was so real. . . . So hot. I could really feel him touching me. And—"I lowered my voice a bit more—"when I woke up, my"—I looked down between my own legs—"was still . . ."

"Oh, girl, that's some damn dream," Billie said, patting herself with her towel.

The woman in front of Billie rolled her eyes visibly this time and Billie rolled her eyes right back.

"So maybe it's because you and Evan are having more sex right now," Billie added. "Like your sexual life is being reawakened and so is your sexual psychological mind."

"Well, thank you, Dr. Billie Freud."

"It's either that or you're really sexually frustrated about something else." Billie transformed with the rest of the class into the traditional resting position where we laid on our backs with our elbows tucked beside our torsos.

My head cocked toward the ceiling to open my airways. I didn't say a word to respond to her suggestion. I hadn't told her about Dame. About him showing up at the school and us riding around. I also failed to bring up the phone call. I didn't know why. I usually shared everything with her. But this made me feel embarrassed. And gossiping about the situation would only make it more real to me. More like an actual situation and not just some misguided events I needed to forget about.

"So?" Billie called.

"So what?"

I looked over and her head was turned toward me. She jerked back and glared at me.

"You're not saying something," she said finally.

"What?"

"There it is again. Your eyes got wider and you looked away from me."

"What are you talking about?"

"Journey Lynn Cash, I have known you since hup was pup. I know when you're keeping something from me. You get quiet and try to look away," she lectured me.

"I'm not." I sat up alone and looked around. I had to get out of there. I couldn't breathe. I got up and rushed out.

"What's going on?" Billie asked, following me out of the door. She was wearing an electric blue tank top and white biker shorts. She looked like we'd just stepped out of some eighties movie. I was wearing an old black sweat suit that made me look slender and long like the other ladies.

"It's Dame," I said slowly.

"Dame?"

There were a few other women standing in the lobby of the studio, so she pulled me into a corner.

"You're still thinking about him?"

I nodded.

"Don't feel bad about it, Journey. That's natural. Shit, he's fine as hell, young, and rich. Who wouldn't think about him?" she said, waving her hand dismissively. "You did spend a lot of time with him when he came to the school. So, it's only natural for you to have fantasies."

"I guess so." I looked over at the women who were beginning to file out of the classroom, hoping Billie wouldn't ask any more questions.

"You're looking away again." She jabbed me on the shoulder with her fingers. "Wait . . . something happened. Something really happened. Did you see him again? Did you go out with Dame?"

"We didn't go out. We just went—"

"And you didn't tell me? You didn't tell your best friend that you went out with a rapper, who happens to be your former student, who's ten years younger than you, and completely fine and filthy rich?" she said with mock seriousness. "That's completely scandalous. I'm your best friend! That's why I'm here!"

"Billie, there's no scandal. And I didn't tell you because you're so busy running around with Mustafa and there was nothing to tell. He just wanted me to hear his music, so we went for a ride and then we went to listen to some music at Fat Albert's." I tried to sound as cool and nonchalant as possible. If I got excited, Billie was sure to double it.

"You went to Fat Albert's? After all these years, you went to Fat Albert's without me?"

Billie and I went into the locker room and I told the entire story about the time Dame and I spent together. About how I felt when we danced. And how afraid I was to continue to feel this way about him.

"Don't worry about it, Journey," she said after we'd gotten dressed and were standing outside in the parking lot near our cars. "It's just a crush. He's new and exciting and I'm sure married people go through this all the time."

"Well, what am I supposed to do?"

"What do you mean? You can't possibly be thinking of really, really doing anything with him?" She looked at me. "It could never work. It's like that old saying, a dog and a fish can marry, but where will they live?"

"I think that was a bird and a fish."

"You know what I mean. Look, the point is it can't work. Now, you can either pretend it didn't happen until the feeling goes away, or you can try to see Dame for who he really is. A young rapper, who's still trying to figure himself out. He's in no way ready for the things you're doing. He's a kid. Probably doesn't even have a retirement fund in his own name. And I'm sure, once you get past the muscles, and the money, and the fame, and the success, and the car—what kind of car was that again?"

"A Bentley."

"Yes—and the car, and the travel, and that chocolate skin, and those tattoos, and the way he walks, and the—"

"I get your point," I interrupted.

"Then, you'll see that our good old Evan is the one for you. It's like when Diana Ross finally got to see the big, strong, all-powerful Wizard for who he was in *The Wiz*—they pulled back that curtain and there was Richard Pryor looking like every other ashy negro," she said, and we both giggled. "I guess the only problem with this plan is that he's long gone now and there's no way you'll ever see him again, until he comes back to Tuscaloosa anyway."

"Not exactly," I said, looking away from Billie again.

"There's more?" she pleaded. "There's more than Fat Albert's?"

"Yes, he wants to see me again. He invited me to see him perform in Atlanta."

Billie looked like she was about to fall over.

"Okay," she started, pacing back and forth. "We can't panic. This is the perfect opportunity for you to pull back the curtain and see who he really is."

"You're not suggesting I go, are you? Because that's just bad advice. Because I can't go. It's crazy."

She looked at me all wide-eyed.

"You want me to go?" I asked. "But it's tomorrow night. It's impossible."

"Look, all we need is a plan."

If nothing else, Billie knew how to put together a good scheme. She organized schemes like lesson plans, blinding the most suspecting participants. And this time was no different. After convincing me that I had to see Dame again to get over what she kept calling my "little crush" and to stop the dreams, she planned for me to ask Evan to accompany me, her, and Mustafa to see August Wilson's *Fences* in Atlanta on Wednesday night. It was last minute, but she'd just gotten the tickets and wouldn't it be so fun? Now, Evan didn't like Billie, hated plays, and detested Atlanta. No matter how sweetly I said it, he'd say no, and feeling bad he'd tell me to go on my own. It was pure black genius and when I got home and unfolded it to Evan, he bowed out before I even finished my sell.

"Please, I'm not in the mood to go see a play about some man cheating on his wife. You go, and maybe if you're in a good mood when you get back, we can talk about something," he said, sitting beside me on the couch as we watched the news.

"About what?"

"Just your going back to school and working at the church."

"The church? You mean, what Jr keeps talking about?" I clicked off the television and turned to him. "You know how I feel about that. Why would you even bring it up?"

"Well, he's kind of right. You could do better things with your time and the job will pay well," he said nonchalantly, but it sounded as if Jr had listed these things for him. "You're a smart woman."

"I don't need either you or Jr to say how smart I am."

"There you go, trying to argue." Evan moved his arm from around me.

"I'm not arguing. I just don't see how you could even think to ask me about that," I complained.

"Look, I didn't want to talk about this now, but when the baby comes, I need some help around here and your father and I just think things will be easier."

"What does he have to do with how we live?"

Evan looked away and I repeated my question.

"He helped me a little when I got the house," he mumbled.

"Helped you?" I got up. "Helped you how?"

"It's nothing. I just didn't have the money and he helped us out."

"See, I knew we couldn't afford this." I looked around angrily. I didn't like my parents being involved in any of my finances. Even in his best form and intentions, my father used that to control me when I was in college. He chose my major. He said where I could live. He planned everything. When I graduated and started teaching, I immediately started paying my own bills. It was the only way I could claim any independence from them.

"How much, Evan?" I asked. "How much did he give you?"

"He gave us half."

"Half? My father paid for half of this house?"

"He volunteered. Went to the bank himself. I thought it was the best thing to do. This is what you wanted."

"Yes, but not like this," I said. "Damn. . . . That's why Jr's so sure he can get me to come work at the church. He knows I owe my father."

"You don't owe him anything. I just think it'll be a good gesture."

"You don't know him like I do. My father cares. He loves me a lot. I know that, but if I don't pay attention, he'll plan the rest of my life. . . . Sometimes I think he already has."

Chapter Sixteen

The day after Evan told me about the money, Jethro Cash was someplace he seldom frequented. Just as I was about to let my last class go on Wednesday afternoon and consider if I was even going to take the trip to Atlanta, he walked into the classroom.

I was standing in front of the sopranos, going over some notes they'd confused in "Amazing Grace." He came in and excused himself, tiptoed to my desk and took a seat. He was wearing one of his chocolate brown suits and had his old brown hat in his hand.

When we finished and the bell rang, he clapped proudly as they exited more expeditiously than I'd ever seen them. At least seventy-five percent of the kids were raised in Prophet House. "Hey, pastor," they said respectfully, waving as they walked by the desk. "Good job, kids!" he replied. "I'll see you tonight at Bible study."

"Hey, Daddy," I said, walking over to the desk and bending down to kiss him on the cheek.

"How are you?"

"I'm fine. What brings you out here? The last time you came to see me teach was five years ago when I won Teacher of the Year."

"Ah," he began, "don't be so skeptical about your old man. Maybe I just wanted to see my little girl. We don't talk much anymore. Not since you got married."

"I know."

"Speaking of marriage, I spoke to Evan today. He came by the church," he said.

"I knew it had to be something," I hissed and stepped away from him.

"He was concerned. That's all. Wanted to talk."

"Look, Daddy, I don't know what kind of deal you and Evan made, but I don't want any part of it," I said. "We'll pay you back everything."

"You think I care about the money?"

He slid the hat onto the table and stood up.

"I just want you to be happy," he said. "So does Evan. What's so bad about that?"

"No one's saying it's bad. I just want to be financially free from you and Mama," I pleaded as he walked over to me.

"You've been saying that since college and I don't understand it. Do you know how many children wish their parents could give them five hundred thousand dollars to buy a house? How many parents wish they could do that for their kids? It's a blessing."

"You gave him five hundred thousand dollars?"

"It's not about the money, cupcake."

"Yes, it is," I cried. "Gosh, I've been struggling all

these years, all this time to just try to be myself, to be who I am, and all this time everyone is just pulling strings above me. I don't know if I chose any of this or if you just gave it to me."

I started to cry and hid my face to stop the tears.

"I didn't mean to make you cry. You know that hurts me," he said softly.

"It's not just you, Daddy," I said, feeling bad that I'd gone this far with him and raised my voice. My father was who he was, but I was raised to respect him and I believed in that.

"Look, if you want to be financially independent, that's fine with me," he said. "I only did it because I wanted to make you happy. I wanted you and Evan to start out with your dream house instead of waiting fifteen years to get it like me and your mother."

"But that made you stronger."

"It almost tore us apart," he said sadly. "If you want to give the money back, that's fine. I'll put it in a trust for my grandchild and then we'll all be happy. Right?"

He smiled and pinched my cheek.

"Yes," I said vacantly.

"You can't deny me that joy. Because when I get to see my first grandson, I'll be a new man."

Just then I realized Jr still hadn't told him about the little boy.

"Have you spoken to Jr?" I asked cautiously.

"We had some meetings yesterday. Why?"

"I was just wondering if he'd spoken to you about something."

"You mean all the stuff with May?" He turned and walked over to the desk to retrieve his hat. "I told him, he's got to control her."

"Control her?"

"Yes. She can't let her worship come between the two of them. I've seen it happen. Women get so wrapped up in the Lord, they think that's their husband and not the man in bed next to them. They forget the orders from the Bible. The man submits to God and the woman submits to her husband and the Word."

"So, he told you that May went to stay with her mother because she's too wrapped up in the Word?"

"He said she won't talk to him. Won't go anywhere without that Bible," he said. "Why? Is there more?"

My conscience tells me to say that as I drove to Dreamland later that night, I thought of a million reasons not to show up. A million reasons to feel bad and turn that pretty red car around and go home to Evan. Tell him the play was canceled. But really I hadn't. I didn't even come close to ten reasons and the two I was considering seemed just flimsy in the wake of the confrontation with my father. My heart thumping madly, my mind racing as I passed people and cars on the street, I kept thinking that what I was doing was just wrong and that once I left Tuscaloosa physically, mentally there'd be no turning back. I had to admit that to myself. But at the moment, I felt like I wanted to leave Tuscaloosa physically and mentally. I felt like everyone was trying to control me. To have their way. To have me submit. And suddenly in my spirit, I was just now longing to be free of all of it. If only for a little while.

I was thirsty to see Dame. To know the freedom I'd felt when I was with him. To smell him. To have him say just one nice thing to me that I really believed. And it wasn't because I hated Evan or my dad or even

Jr and I was going to leave for good and start some scandalous affair with my former student. That was ridiculous. I just wanted to feel something else inside for a little while. To get away. For me and for May.

When I turned into the lot at Dreamland, the Bentley was parked and the driver, the same, short white man with jet-black hair who'd driven Dame and me to Dreamland the first time, was standing by the door, waiting to open it for me. Billie's empty car was beside it, but I couldn't see if she was in the Bentley because all of the curtains were pulled in place.

I waved at the driver and pulled my car beside Billie's.

I pulled down the visor to see myself in the mirror.

"Okay, Journey," I said to my red reflection. I was excited, but also nervous and it was literally evident on my face. "You're just doing this to get over the Dame thing. It's just a *little crush.* That's it. You're going to see him one last time and then move on with your life."

I looked into my eyes in a pause to see a flash of agreement, something in my reflection that knew this was the right thing to do. I waited.

"What, you getting ready for Glamour Shots at the mall?" I heard Billie yell. I looked and she was standing with half of her body outside of the back of the Bentley. "Come on!"

"Okay," I said, quickly flipping up the mirror. "I'm coming."

I snatched my purse and hopped out of the car.

"Good evening, Ms. Cash," the driver said as I walked up. He extended his arm toward me graciously and opened the door.

"Mrs. De—never mind." I smiled and turned back to my car. Looking at the car was suddenly like looking at Evan's love and just like that, all of the million reasons I needed to turn back set heavy on my heart. This wasn't just crazy. It was *really* crazy. This was beyond rational. I knew better than this.

"We'll need to leave now," the driver said, "if we are to catch the show."

"Yeah," I replied, hearing Billie giggling inside the car.

"Mr. Mitchell is very excited that you're coming," he said then, and I could tell by his voice he knew I was considering turning around. "I've never seen him this excited about . . . a woman."

"Really?"

"I don't get paid to lie," he declared.

"Come on, J," Billie called, but I couldn't see her behind the curtains. "I want everyone in the A to see me in a Phantom. Big time!"

"I guess I'm going to Atlanta," I said uneasily.

"I guess so," he said, smiling.

I bent down to get into the car, and Billie was so close to the door that I knew immediately she was sitting in the middle of the row and that someone must be seated beside her.

"Mustafa?" I said, looking in to see him sitting beside Billie.

"Is it okay?" Billie asked. "He wanted to come see Dame."

I was still standing at the door, and seeing the frown on my face, Billie eased out to talk to me.

"I can't believe you brought him," I said.

"I really wanted him to come. He won't even talk. He's just going to be with me."

"That sounds crazy. How is he not going to talk? And we only have two tickets."

"I already spoke to Mr. Green"—she winked at the

driver—"and he said not to worry. He'll call Benji out to get us. It'll be fine."

I gasped and kicked a bit of dirt at my feet.

"I really can't believe you somehow managed to make this be about you," I said. "We were specifically going here to—" I ground my eyes into Billie because I couldn't say what the plan was in front of the driver.

"I know. I know," she said. "But then I realized that I needed a date if you were going to be alone with—" She said "Dame" with her eyes. "So you can—. And what was Mustafa supposed to do, in my house all night by himself?"

"Watch Barack Obama on CNN like the rest of the world."

"Don't be mean, J. Come on. This'll be fun." She grabbed my arm. "We'll have drinks and hear some music and get you over this—thing with—." We both looked at the driver.

"Fine," I grumbled. "But only because I need to—!"

I was back in high school. Memories of riding in the back of cars with Billie and a boy. She giggled and whispered and every five minutes pretended to care about how I was doing. This was how it went the whole way to Atlanta. Mustafa was quiet all right. But that was only because everything he said was whispered into Billie's ear and most of the time I couldn't even see his mouth, because it was glued to hers. I wanted so badly to hate her. As I rolled my eyes at their cooing, I was desperate to curse her out. But this was just Billie being Billie. And I realized when we were in sixth grade, she only traded my warm tuna fish sandwich with her honey ham because she knew the tuna would make her sick and she'd have to go home—that it was better to learn to live with who she was than to try to change her. Everybody had flaws. At least I got to benefit from her selfish craziness sometimes. And I always knew she'd be on my side. . . . But I was still mad.

I know I'm in Atlanta when I see the lights. Like fireworks blazing in the dark night sky, riding into the city, everything goes from being dull and consistently familiar, to big and bright and inconsistently attractive. And not in the same way that it does when I see the lights in downtown Tuscaloosa or Birmingham. It's like comparing a street lamp to a Vegas sign, and that's no insult to the street lamp because one is more necessary than the other. Like the signs in Vegas, the lights that seem to encircle and hover over Atlanta are meant to dance to the eye. To fill me with excitement and make me believe this city is the biggest in the world. And while I am like every other person in every car being led to the city like fireflies to a porch light, I know this isn't true, but I really want to believe that something brilliant and bright could be born in my South.

Mustafa, Billie, and I, all in one row in the back of the Bentley, became quiet and wide-eyed as the driver pulled off the highway exit and chauffeured us into the city. It wasn't the most spectacular sight that any of us had ever seen, but we all seemed to be waiting for something to happen.

The club where the concert was happening was right off the highway, and when we turned onto the small street that came to a dead end, people were everywhere. In the street. On the sidewalks. Standing on top of cars that checkered both curbs. Just wild and everywhere. Posters of Dame's album cover were tacked to every pole lining the street and some of the cars even had posters taped to the sides.

As Mr. Green made his way through the tangle, I looked at women yelling and laughing, men macking and some rapping in circles. It was more of a party than I expected from a concert. And looking at the faces through the window, mine seemed old and out of place.

"The club must be at capacity," Mr. Green said to us. "I know they've opened the doors."

"Is it normally like this?" I looked down at my slacks, and realizing I hadn't seen one pair in the crowd, I thought of the jeans Kayla had been wearing at Fat Albert's.

"Yeah. The shows get pretty crazy. Mr. Mitchell doesn't like performing in the arenas—he actually enjoys these smaller stages—so he has his manager book the Apache when he's not on tour." He beeped his horn at someone walking in front of the car. "All of the fans know about the shows, so it gets a little nuts. Sometimes he just comes outside and gets on top of one of the cars."

"I guess they think he's in this one," Mustafa said, pointing to a group of girls who were walking beside our slow-moving car and peering inside. One of them put her phone up to the window and took a picture, thinking Mustafa was Dame.

"Oh, my!" Billie jumped at the flash.

Just then another flash went off on my side and a thump came at the back, shaking the car a bit.

"Dame, you in there?" a girl shouted.

"I know my man's inside!"

"You the same Dame! You the same! Get out and show your people some love!"

And then a pair of silicone-filled breasts were exposed right in my face.

"They don't even know if he's in here?" Billie said, pulling my arm.

"Can you imagine what it's like when he is?" Mustafa added.

"I guess we know why he leaves the curtains closed." I drew my curtain even though the breasts were still glued to the tinted glass.

"How did she do that while the car was still moving?" Billie asked.

"Groupie skills," Mustafa answered.

"Okay, guys," Mr. Green said, stopping the car in front of the club. "You're here. Benji's waiting right inside the door and I'll be out here all night. Have fun."

It seemed that they were giving away money inside of the club from the way people acted when Mr. Green let us out of the car. All eyes shifted to us, cameras went flashing, and two brothers with muscles bulging out from their tight shirts pushed everyone back, so we could go right to the door.

"They with me," Benji said, standing inside the doorway beside a woman with a clipboard in her arms. A red, velvet rope was holding us at bay. "All comp."

"Who said? They on the list? I can't let them in if they ain't on the list." She was trying to sound as annoyed and frustrated as possible. She glared at us like we weren't even supposed to be there. "We're already at capacity, Benji."

"Naima, they with me. Dame's people," Benji said.

"Fine," she said, shaking her curly brown hair in disgust. "Let them in."

She pointed to the red rope, as if she wasn't an

inch away and had a hand free, and one of the bouncers undid the rope.

"Who they?" a woman wearing short shorts at the front of the line said. "That ain't fair. We been standing here for an hour. They ain't no stars."

The inside of the club was no bigger than my parents' tennis court. There was a tiny stage hugging the window and probably 100 to 150 people standing in front of it, dancing to music as they waited for Dame to come out. Smoke drifted closely above them and I could even smell the sweet and unmistakable odor of marijuana burning from every direction.

"Dame's in the back," Benji said, knocking people aside as we weaseled behind him. I could hardly breathe; there were so many people pushing in.

"We're going to get a drink," Billie said, pinching my arm.

"But how will I find you?"

"We'll be right here."

She pointed to the bar.

"But—"

"Look, Journey, don't chicken out now. You need to see him."

Another one of Dame's bodyguards was standing in front of the door Benji was leading me to. Benji whispered something in his ear and they both looked at me before the guard moved to let us through.

Benji and I ended up walking outside the back of the club where there was a little outdoor patio set up.

There were only a few groups of people sitting out there. Scantily clad women and rappers whose faces I'd seen in the few music videos I caught by mistake on television.

I saw Dame sitting at a table with a group of these

rappers. He had his foot up on one of the chairs, and they were laughing. Plumes of smoke came rising from most of their hands. Dame's hand was empty.

"Yooooo," Dame said when he saw me. He didn't smile wide like he did at home. Instead, he grinned slyly and nodded in my direction. He got up with an air of careful coolness and came over to me as Benji took his seat at the table.

"Hi," I said, noticing again how handsome he was. Even in the same white T-shirt I'd seen him in every day, he looked brand new. Clean.

"I can't believe you came. I just knew you weren't going to make it."

"Here I am," I said.

"Well, welcome to my world." He raised his arms and looked around. "Lord of the flies."

"I see," I said, watching Benji puff one of the joints.

"What?" Dame turned to look over his shoulder. "Oh, don't pay those fools no mind. They just in the cypher."

"Are you smoking?" I asked and suddenly I regretted it. I sounded like his mother.

"I'm on my best behavior," he said. "None of that for me."

"Oh."

"Dame, we can't wait any longer," Naima said, rushing onto the patio with her clipboard. "The crowd is about to get rowdy."

"I'm good," he said. "My guest is here."

"Wonderful. It's so nice to see your family supporting you," she said disingenuously. She looked me up and down and sneered, as if to say in so many ways she was sure I was Dame's older sister or aunt visiting from wherever. "Nice slacks."

I was growing tired of her nasty routine. I said, "I can't wait to see you onstage, baby," and kissed Dame on the lips.

Her eyes went from tired to tortured. She slammed the clipboard at her side and trotted off in a huff.

"Now, I went from being *a baby* to being *your baby*?" Dame laughed.

"I was just fighting fire with fire."

"Yeah, Naima is one of my promoters. She's never been shy about wanting to come home with me."

"I guess you haven't done that," I pressed.

"Of course I have. Did you see her butt?" he joked playfully.

"See, that's why she was acting crazy." I slapped his arm.

"I'm a man. . . . I'm a man."

Dame's show was fully phenomenal. Just as he'd mesmerized the kids at school, he easily controlled the crowd at the Apache. He had a live band and two backup singers. "This is what I do for fun," he said when he finally managed to get through the crowd and was up on the stage. "Other people go to the mall, go out for dinner, kick it with some broads, but when I'm not selling out arenas around the world, I do this. Up close and personal. Because I'm a real MC and ain't nobody gonna test you like the people in the street." Everyone went insane, hollering praise at him. And by the time I paddled up to the front so I could see just a bit of the show in the packed room, Dame was hopping around the stage, pushing his energy off into the crowd like he'd been performing all his life. He was electric. On fire. Sweating and flexing. Building up so much intensity in the room, so much give and take between him and the crowd that was so close they could touch him, it had almost become sexual. And then he took off his shirt and a girl standing right in front of me nearly fainted into my arms. It was a good thing she had her girlfriend there to help though, because I didn't even move to catch her. Like the other open-mouthed women standing around, I was too busy watching Dame. Beads of sweat dripped over his tattoos. They rolled down slowly as he continued to rhyme about something I couldn't hear, tumbling toward his navel and then around the V-shaped slits his taut pelvic muscles made just above his—

"Journey!" Dame's voice boomed through the microphone. Hearing my name, I shook and refocused my attention away from the V shape to see that it was now right in front of me. "Journey!"

Dazed, I looked to see that all of the women lined up in front of the stage were now looking at me.

"Journey!"

I looked up at Dame.

"Yes?"

"Come on stage," he said, holding the microphone to his side and reaching down to help me up.

"Me?"

"Come on." He beckoned again and I reached for his hand.

"Now y'all know when Dame comes to town, there's always gonna be something real special," he said as one of the band members brought a chair up on stage and instructed me to sit in it. I sat down and looked at Dame, wondering what he was going to do and praying he wasn't about to embarrass me in front of all of these faces I didn't know. "This time, something real special came to me," he went on and

I saw the girls I was just standing beside turn from looking confused to jealous. "I won't bore y'all with the details, so let's just say, this is someone from my past. And I brought her up here tonight because I'm about to drop a rhyme that's going on my next album. Y'all all right with that?"

Excluding the sour-faced women, the crowd cheered and Dame looked at me and smiled.

"And she needs to be up here because the song's about her."

"No," I mouthed to him nervously. I couldn't believe he was putting me on the spot. I looked at him hard, but he just kept smiling and turned back to the audience.

"You know how when MCs be about to spit a rhyme about some personal shit, they usually be like, 'I don't want people to get the wrong idea'? Well, I do want you to get the wrong idea about this one. It's called 'Teacher's Pet.' Yo, drop it."

The band laid down a melodic, upbeat groove. The two singers, who'd stepped away to sip on water bottles placed on a table at the side of the stage, rushed back to their microphones.

"Teacher's pet. Teacher's pet. Everybody wanna be the teacher's pet," the two women sang slowly in unison as he bopped his head to the beat.

Sitting there, I didn't know if I wanted to hear what he was about to say or if I was dying to hear everything he had to say. I looked out to see if I could find Billie's face, but instead, there was just Naima, standing at the foot of the stage with a grimace on her face.

Dame looked back at me and then he started rhyming:

It's like you and me,
And me and you,
I couldn't pass your test
even if I wanted to.

It's like me and you,
And you and me,
I couldn't pass your test
because past you I couldn't see.

His flow was quick enough to keep up with the tempo set by the band but still slow like a poet's, so I could hear each line. A serious and almost longing look on his face, he turned from me to the crowd and stepped up to the edge of the stage.

"Yo, check it," he went on:

I wanted so bad to leave childhood behind,
My childhood crush, I'd leave that at the same time.
Her hair, her scent, her smile just let it go,
But you can never leave your teacher, you can never let her go.

Between the verses, the singers sang the chorus, improvising in the background in call and response fashion when he started to rhyme.

I used to sit in the back with my boys and just chill,
But when she walked into the room, my universe just went still.

She was the sun, the moon, the stars and I was just in orbit,
Do anything to touch her, I'd do anything just for it.

I thought the love would end when I got up and left,
But the real truth is, your face was etched in my chest.
Like a poem, like a song, like a book, like a psalm,
You had the teacher's pet, wrapped up inside your palm.

And it's no mystery now, no secret anymore,
I've been to hell and back and you're the one I long for.
I'm haunted by your beauty, your angelic face,
And then I came home to see that someone took my place.

But it's nothing 'cause I've been at this hustle for a long time.
And if I have to reach you, love, then teacher's pet will have to climb.

Go however, wherever you say it's gonna take,
And tell old boy that even Jesus couldn't stop the Lord's fate.

So,
It's like you and me,
And me and you,
I couldn't pass your test
Even if I wanted to.

It's like me and you,
And you and me,
I couldn't pass your test
Because past you I couldn't see.

Like my heart, the faces before me went from worry to wonder and then froze in amazement.

The friend of the girl who almost fell into my arms mouthed, "Who is she?" And I was thinking the same thing. Because listening to what Dame was saying, I was sure he wasn't talking about me. Yeah, he'd made some passes at me and we'd had some heated moments, but his words were the feelings of a man infatuated, a man with a plan to win someone. And that couldn't be me. Of all the women in the room? Outside the club? Out in the world? That couldn't be me. I was wearing slacks.

When Dame was done, he came over and hugged me amid the crowd's cheers and coos. Only this hug was a bit more uncomfortable than the others: After learning what I'd heard, I felt a need to protect myself. It was one thing for me to toy with having a crush on Dame, but for him to pronounce his desire for me in such a public way—in any way, period—seemed like a development toward something I neither anticipated nor wanted. Yes, it was exciting being up there and having this half-clothed, successful young man pine for me in front of all of those girls who were probably twelve years younger than me, but all I could worry about was what Dame intended to do next. And how I could stop him.

"Thank you," I said, as I rose to walk off the stage. My words were gracious, yet distant. Dame looked at me quickly and the same concern I was feeling was in his eyes. It seemed he might be wondering what I was thinking and worried that maybe he'd gone too far.

Benji helped me off the stage and Dame pushed into what he announced was his last song, switching the mood in the room from tender and open back to the raw and rugged excitement he'd injected before.

As I walked toward the bar where Billie was supposed to be waiting, the crowd went on like nothing had happened and the show would never end. But I was wondering what I'd say to Dame when it did.

"Excuse me," I said, sliding around a couple who was locked in a shameless make-out session in the middle of the floor. When I almost passed, I felt a hand grab my shoulder and turned quickly to be sure it wasn't the lip-locked boy who was literally swallowing the face of his date.

"Journey," Clyde said, "I was trying to get to the stage to you."

"Clyde?" I said as if I hadn't seen the man in decades, which wasn't true, but his face certainly wasn't one I'd expected to see there.

He was smiling wide and when he reached to embrace me, I saw that Ms. Lindsey was standing behind him.

"Hey, Journey," Ms. Lindsey said, waving.

"Karen?" I questioned this time with even less familiarity. "What are you two doing here?"

"This one just had to see Dame perform," Clyde said, "and because he didn't do anything in Tuscaloosa, I agreed to drive her to Atlanta."

"Don't act like it's all me," Ms. Lindsey said playfully. "You were the one talking about how this would be cheaper and we could get out here to have a little fun."

"And I was right, too, because the show is hot! I'm mad it's already over."

Behind us I could hear the crowd cheering Dame off the stage.

Considering the near-impossible odds that I'd run into these two people at that club on that night after Dame just confessed his feelings to me on stage and Billie was floating around somewhere in the club with Mustafa, I thought surely the Lord was . . .

"But forget us. Why are you here?" Ms. Lindsey asked. "We saw you on stage." She pulled my arm knowingly as if we were friends.

"It's not like that. That was just a joke up there. . . .

He's quite a jokester," I said as comically as I could. I even added a chuckle that Clyde and Ms. Lindsey cordially joined in on. "Dame just wanted me to see him perform, so I drove up."

"All this way by yourself?" Ms. Lindsey said, concerned.

"Is Evan—" Clyde tried to ask, but Benji came pushing between us suddenly. Ms. Lindsey rolled her eyes at his large frame like she'd come up against him in a fight in another life.

"Dame wants you to come backstage," Benji ordered more ardently than usual. He didn't even look sideways at Ms. Lindsey and Clyde. "Come with me."

"Oookay," I said at his abruptness. "I'll see you two tomorrow?" I looked back at Clyde and Ms. Lindsey.

"Sure," they agreed, smiling again, but I could tell they still had questions floating in their minds.

Benji took my arm, and we pushed through the crowd that had now turned into a full after-party. I looked around for Billie and Mustafa, but I still couldn't see them. The club was so small and we were just a few feet from the bar. I was hoping they hadn't snuck off somewhere. It was time to go and I didn't want to risk having them run into Clyde and Ms. Lindsey. It was enough that they'd seen me. And I knew it would be a few hours before I had to worry about folks at the school chattering if Ms. Lindsey went and shared the news. And if I knew her like I thought I did, there was no "if" involved. But there was nothing I could do to stop things at that point. I just needed to get out of there.

"So, did you like the show?" Dame asked. He was sitting on a furry red couch that someone had obviously moved from inside the club. I sat down next to him, but left a clear space between us. I didn't want Ms. Lindsey or Clyde or anyone else to walk up and get the wrong idea about us. But even with that space and the rawness of the confession in his lyrics still in my mind, I felt an energy pulling me toward Dame. There was a stimulating shine in his eyes and even though a towel now hung over half of his sweaty, naked chest, it was hard not to notice how solid and flat his pecs were—like cutting boards and the tattoos there had been etched with some sharp knife. The beads of sweat looked like drops of thick honey and like all the other women buzzing around Dame, it was hard not to look and wonder what it tasted like.

"It was okay," I said, giving my best effort at looking away. This was about getting over my crush, not getting closer. The only progress I'd made so far was getting caught.

"You okay? You seem nervous," Dame said.

"I'm—"

"No," he cut me off. "You don't need to explain. I know what it is. I put you on the spot. Right?" A few of the guys he'd been sitting with came over. "No doubt! Tell that nigga to call me, so we can get up in the studio," Dame said after they had a brief exchange.

"Well, it's that—" I tried when they moved on, but Dame cut me off again.

"I know," he said. "But I had to get it off my chest."

"What do you mean?" I saw a few ladies from the crowd who'd managed to slip onto the enclosed patio stroll by slowly in front of us, but Dame looked right past them.

"I'm feeling you, Journey."

Hearing him say my name again, the way he did,

all smooth and new, made me feel like lightning was bolting through my body. I was shaken off my axis. And while I didn't realize it then, suddenly, I'd forgotten all about Clyde and Ms. Lindsey and whatever else was waiting outside.

"What?"

"Man, I used to think it was a crush or just an old thing I had for someone in my past, but it's not going away," he said as openly as if we were sitting in a café and not surrounded by dozens of fans and industry folks who were trying to get hold of his attention. "I'm feeling you. I'm fucking crazy about you. And don't laugh at me, but a part of me thought that when I went home, you'd be all old and married with kids and just wrinkly . . . but you're more beautiful now than you were then."

"D-D-D-Dame," I stuttered, "I don't think this is the place or time to discuss that."

"So, you're saying you don't feel the same way, too?" He reached for my hand and pulled me toward him. "Look at me. Tell me you don't feel the same way. That you're not at all interested. Because I heard it in your voice the other day on the phone."

"Dame, I'm a married woman," I whispered even though no one could possibly hear me over the chatter. "And I'm ten years older than you."

"You're not happy."

"What?"

"I can see how you look at him. You want more and he can't give it to you."

"That's ridiculous," I said, looking away from him.

"Did you tell him where you were going tonight?"

"I don't need to answer that."

"Exactly."

A nondescript white man dressed haphazardly with two cameras hanging in different directions from his neck came and stood in front of us.

"Let me get a shot," he said, pulling a third camera from behind. Dame moved closer toward me and smiled and, quickly, the camera flashed and the man disappeared into the crowd.

"So what are we going to do?" Dame asked.

"About what?" I asked with my eyes still blinking from the flash.

"About our feelings. About us."

"I just told you . . ."

"You told me what you have to say. You told me what you think you should say. I want to know what you feel." Dame paused and smiled for a few other people waiting to take his picture. "Look, I'm not trying to ruin your marriage or change your life. I understand that's who you are and that's fine. I just want to know if maybe"—he looked into my eyes and it was like everyone in the room just disappeared or stopped talking; there was only us—"maybe I could have some time . . . just breathe the same air as you and talk to you, so I can be reminded in the middle of all of this crazy shit in my life what beautiful really looks like?" His voice was as genuine and true as someone saying a prayer. As cocky and cool as he seemed to everyone else there, he was naked and open to me. And while this might have seemed like a good thing, in a way, it made me feel like I'd led Dame on in some way by coming to see him. Looking at him and knowing what it was like to be with him, I wanted to believe that what he was asking for could be—that we could just talk, just have our little conversations about nothing and everything and be happy. But right then, listening to his request, I knew it couldn't work. Even in the room that had gone still, sitting there surrounded by drooling women and bottles of champagne and sweet burning cigarettes, grown men in basketball jerseys and Dame with no shirt and tattoos all over his body, it was clear that we were a world apart. Billie was right. I had mine and he had his. There was nowhere we could go.

"I can't do that," I said. "It's just not the right time. We live different lives."

"That's still more of what you think you have to say."

"Well, what about you? How could you be so sure about everything?" I asked, trying to shift the focus from me. "This isn't some romance novel where you can fall head over heels without having any reservations."

"I'm not the type of man that works with reservations," he said. "I know what I want and I chase it. This feeling has been with me for too long to play games."

"Dame," one of his assistants barked, nearly skidding into the couch with her BlackBerry in her hand, "I need you for some interviews and Naima wants to know when you're ready."

"Thanks, Emily."

She pressed the phone back to her ear and rushed over to Benji.

"I guess you didn't count on leaving with me," I said snidely. I knew Naima had a reason for looking at me sideways earlier.

"Naima?" Dame said. "No, she arranges my exit. That's it."

"I bet," I said.

"I don't want to go, but I have to do these interviews or they'll just start making stuff up," Dame said. "Can I call you?"

"Dame, I just told you, I can't," I said, watching Benji and the girl walk back over to us.

"I'm gonna call," Dame said.

"Don't."

"You ready, man?" Benji asked.

"He's ready," I answered.

When I went back into the front, the place was just as packed with sweaty men and scantily clad women as it had been when Dame was on stage. A DJ had replaced the band and it seemed no one wanted to go home. I did, though. My toes were starting to burn and even though I didn't have to drive back to Alabama, thinking of the trip made me wonder if I'd be able to open my eyes and get to work when the sun came up.

Once again, hoping luck would find me and my toes, I headed back toward the bar where Billie promised she'd wait at the beginning of the night, but I still didn't see her there. So I started toward the door, praying she'd gone to the car, but then I noticed a small crowd gathered at the far end of the bar. Even in the darkness, I noticed the tall silhouette of a dark man standing in the middle of the group and as I got nearer, I saw that it was Mustafa and heard angry voices rising a bit above the music.

Many of the people, holding drinks and dance partners in their hands, stopped moving to the beat and just turned and looked toward the center of the crowd that seemed to grow more agitated with each step I took.

"You got some nerve," I heard Billie protest even though I couldn't see her. Instead, all I could see was her hand pointed accusingly at someone standing in front of Mustafa, who I couldn't see either, but I certainly knew who it was. I quickened my steps then, weaving around the clumps of people that separated me from Billie's voice.

"Nerve? I can go wherever I want," Clyde said to Billie when I finally pushed my way past a tight circle of onlookers. He was standing beside Ms. Lindsey.

"What's going on?" I asked, coming between Clyde and Billie, but no one answered.

"This isn't about you being here; it's about you having that two-bit skank, slut, bitch next to you," Billie blustered, looking at Ms. Lindsey so harshly that I was sure she was about to spit. The circle, of course, highlighted this moment with a refrain of support.

"Slut?" Ms. Lindsey charged, trying to get to Billie. "Who you calling a slut?"

"Calm down, baby," Clyde said, holding Ms. Lindsey back from Billie, but from looking at his loose hold, it was evident that wasn't a hard task because Ms. Lindsey in no way intended to ever really reach Billie.

"Y'all stop it!" I snatched Billie's arm. "Hold her," I said to Mustafa, who was standing there, looking as if he was waiting in a crowd of strangers. And while he was, for the most part, I at least expected him to try to protect and control Billie.

"That's right," Clyde said venomously, "Tell him to handle her crazy ass."

"Crazy?" Billie repeated and I turned from Clyde

to her in what seemed liked slow motion at the time. I'd been involved in many Clyde and Billie fights in my life and what I'd learned, and Clyde knew, was that the best way to fully upset Billie was to call her "crazy." More specifically, if it was anyone else, she might have laughed, but from Clyde, it was a fighting word—and with Ms. Lindsey standing there. . . . I'd never experienced it, but I knew it would be bad. Horrible. At that moment, she may as well have been Zenobia in the hallway and Clyde and Ms. Lindsey were Michael and Patrice.

"You're going to call me crazy after all these fucking years?" Billie said, her face contorting into an evil war mask. "I got your crazy!" She raised her arm as if she was about to swing a punch at Clyde.

"No," I hollered, going for her, but it was too late, her purse was already up in the air and by the time I got a hold of her arms, that book bag–sized, leather heavy hitter had bopped both Clyde and Ms. Lindsey. And even after I had the best hold I could get and Mustafa had lifted Billie up and was pulling her toward the exit, she was still swinging and hitting Clyde and Ms. Lindsey and anyone else who happened to get caught. Along the way, security caught us and one big, bald man with hands the size of car tires pulled me off Billie and in what felt like a snap of his wrist, threw me out of the club and onto the sidewalk.

My face inches from the dirty pavement, my hands splayed out in front of me to break my fall, I first looked down at my body to make sure I hadn't been hurt and then over to see that both Billie and Mustafa were on the ground next to me.

"What the hell?" I screamed, and a boy who was standing nearby and looking on with a bunch of other people waiting outside came and helped me up.

"You okay, ma'am?" he asked, and I just looked at him. I was too angry to answer. "I was just trying to help." He held up his hands defensively and backed away. By then, Billie and Mustafa were up, too, and arguing again.

"I didn't sign up for this," Mustafa said, only his African accent was gone now and he sounded more like the guys standing around us.

"Don't be a damn punk. Nothing happened to you," Billie said dismissively.

"Nothing? That nigga was about to swing on me if you didn't come between us," he said. "Look, just give me my money for tonight, so I can go home."

"Money?" I said, looking at Billie. "What is he talking about?"

"Don't be a bitch, Jerome," Billie said, holding out her hand for me to be quiet. "I told you he was gonna be here. All you were supposed to do was to be cute and shut your damn mouth. No one told you to kiss me."

"You said to act! I'm an actor, and I felt like that was what my character was supposed to do at the moment!"

"Act? What the hell?" I tried again.

"Oh, please, negro. You ain't been in a damn thing, past your best friend's wedding video, and you managed to mess that up, too," Billie said. "You know what?" She reached into her purse and pulled out a thick envelope. "As a matter of fact, you can take your damn money. And go somewhere and take some acting classes or something." She threw the envelope at him and he caught it just before it hit the ground in front of him.

"What's that?" I asked and Billie grabbed my arm.

"Let's go," she said, pulling me.

As we searched for the car and Mr. Green, Billie explained the intricate and ridiculous plot she'd organized to somehow make the exchange between her and Mustafa possible, who she'd confirmed was actually Jerome Jenkins from Jasper, Georgia. Apparently, Billie had grown so desperate to get back at Clyde for dating Ms. Lindsey that she'd hired some help. In an attempt to get over Clyde, she did try Internet dating for a while, but that didn't work and somehow she stumbled onto a male escort Web site. Jerome was listed as an escort for hire, who happened to have acting experience. His "ad," Billie said, which featured shots of him in a tuxedo and in a thong, actually said he was the perfect, discreet accompaniment for high-class, high-powered single ladies not wishing to attend another business function, family dinner, or class reunion alone. He could play a long-lost love or boyfriend and leave a lasting impression on every person he encountered. His talents included international accents, dancing, and massage. Assuring me that she didn't sleep with him, Billie said after looking at Jerome's ad a few dozen nights in a row, it came to her that she could use his services to make her own lasting impression on Clyde. In all the years that they'd been breaking up and making up, never once had Clyde been forced to suffer seeing Billie in the arms of another man. And she thought Jerome/Mustafa would be the reality check he'd need. Handsome, smart, and international, he was sure to make Clyde rethink his decision and, she'd hoped, come crawling back to Billie's door. She just needed to make sure Clyde saw the two of them together. She paid Jerome to stay in Tuscaloosa for a few days and after that he just drove back and forth from Atlanta. But there was no success. Not until another teacher told her Clyde and Ms. Lindsey were going to the very same show in Atlanta she'd agreed to attend with me.

"Why didn't you tell me?" I pleaded when we were in the car and already headed home.

"There's no way I could've told you," she said. "You had to go along with everything for it to be real. You would've stopped me."

"Exactly. And I would've stopped you because none of this makes any sense," I said, searching for sanity in my friend's eyes. "I love you to death and I've been through a lot with you, but this is just . . . it's past crazy. It's the type of stuff people do in movies. It's not real. It's not . . . it's not what people do in real life." I was ranting, but this, even for Billie with her ways and love for Clyde, was beyond being a bit too much.

"I know it doesn't make any sense," Billie said. "But I was tired."

"Tired of what? Clyde? I'm your best friend. You could've come to me."

"You don't understand."

"Understand what?" I asked.

"I'm thirty-three and single in a town where everyone expects you to get married right out of college," she said. "Late is thirty. Thirty-three . . . I may as well be a senior citizen."

"I got married at thirty-two!"

"Everyone knew you were going to marry Evan. And he's been begging you to get married since high school. I don't have anyone but Clyde. You don't know what that's like."

"So the answer to that is hiring some actor to come to town to pretend he was your boyfriend?" I asked and I didn't mean for it to sound that simple, but it just was. "Don't you think that's a stretch? Pretty soon, you were going to run out of money . . . or someone would find out. And why get everyone else involved?"

"When it all came out that Clyde was with Karen it was just like everyone was laughing at me. . . . Like I was a fool. Everybody knows how long I've been with Clyde and everything we've been through . . . all the crap I've put up with. Everyone knows," she said, and I could do nothing but nod along in agreement. "And when everything came out—that he was really dating some little girl that's more than ten years younger than me—I know everyone was laughing."

"No, they're not," I said.

"Yes they are. And you know why? Because he's probably going to marry her," she said so sadly that I began to cry at the thought. Not because I wanted Clyde and Billie to be together, but really because I knew if that happened, Billie simply wouldn't survive it. "Men never marry the women they go through all the crap me and Clyde went through. They just look for the next one in line. And here she is." Billie began to sob on my shoulder, and I looked out the window of the car at the empty highway. "I just wanted him to feel as hurt as I do. Even if it's a lie."

"You don't know that he's going to marry her," I

tried. And there was nothing left to say. It would have been easy to tell her to just get over it. But she had to get past it first. We just sat there for a while crying.

"What happened with Dame?" Billie asked weakly, still resting her head on my shoulder. "Did you talk to him?"

"Yes," I said.

"Are you over him now? Did it work?"

"Yes," I said. "I think it did."

Chapter Seventeen

The impulse for forcing myself out of bed and getting into my car to get to school only hours after I returned home was "damage control." I suffered through all of Evan's questions about the night over breakfast, making up careful yet interesting lies that I was sure I'd be able to recall should he bring them up again, thinking in the back of my mind that I had to get to school to somehow intercept Ms. Lindsey before she intrigued the school with her story about Billie and seeing me at the club. I knew I didn't have to worry about Clyde or Billie telling anyone, but Ms. Lindsey probably went straight to the school from the club to share the news. I had no idea how I'd stop her, but I had to try. If Evan found out about Dame and the club and me being on stage, he'd never understand why I went. And even with the situation with my father and the money still keeping me at odds with Evan, I didn't want him to lose trust in me.

While I could honestly look back at the events at the club and admit that my attendance was completely suspect and had more to do with me wanting to see him than needing to get over him, it was my hope to work through both of these complicated desires alone and without damaging my marriage or Evan.

While Ms. Lindsey and I hadn't spoken much since she joined the staff at the beginning of the school year, and even less after she was caught in the janitor's closet with my best friend's boyfriend, I ran into her twice each day. Along with most of the other teachers at school, her first stop in the morning was in the teachers' lounge where there was always hot coffee and mailers for special announcements. There, I'd usually see her looking over her lesson plan or chatting over coffee with some of the other rookie teachers. And the second time we normally found each other was at the copy machine after lunch. Along with a group of five or so teachers, Ms. Lindsey and I discovered that the copy machine in the main office was usually free right after lunch. To avoid the long lines and fights over paper and toner replacement that occurred in the morning, it was best to hold any copies to this hour in the day when most teachers were still out trying to forget the morning's drama and prepare for what was ahead.

While Evan's inquisition about the "play" and my still-numb feet led to me being late to work and missing Ms. Lindsey's morning coffee, I ended up finding her standing alone in an unusually empty and quiet main office. When I walked in, two of Angie Martin's ghouls were walking out with stacks of paper in their arms. They were whispering and looking over their shoulders at Ms. Lindsey. In fact, when they saw me, they were so busy cackling that neither made enough time to roll their eyes and say something nasty.

Although Ms. Lindsey's back was to me as she leaned over the copier, I knew it was her, and to my surprise, she'd actually taken time to go home to change clothes before she came to work to ruin my life. Then I thought maybe she'd already started to spread the word about the club and wondered if that was why the ghouls had been whispering.

"Karen," I called softly, unsure of what I'd say when she turned around. "Excuse me?"

Without answering, Ms. Lindsey turned slowly, and when my eyes met her face, I found a deep purple shiner over her left eye.

"Ewww," I said, bracing myself at the sight.

"I know—it's awful," she said. "Clyde put ice on it, but that only made it worse."

"That's from the purse?"

"What do you think?" she asked, annoyed.

"Oh, I'm so sorry," I said. "I know she didn't mean to do all of that."

Ms. Lindsey stood there unmoved by my explanation.

"What do you want?" she asked coldly.

"Well, it's about last night," I started and trying not to look at her eye to figure out just what part of the bag slammed into it, I knew there was no way she'd ever agree to keep the night a secret. I was lucky she hadn't pressed charges and held a news conference. It was the biggest shiner I'd ever seen and I could almost make out a Gucci symbol over her eyebrow.

"What about last night? You want to talk about how that crazy bitch assaulted me?"

"Really, I wasn't coming to talk about Billie," I said. "It's about me."

"You?" She turned and picked up her finished copies from the machine.

"I need you to . . . I need you to—"

"Just come out with it," she cut me off. "My left ear is ringing."

"I was just wondering if you could not mention that you saw me at the club," I said finally.

"Not mention?"

Ms. Newberry and another administrator walked into the office laughing loudly. They excused themselves when they noticed us at the copier and I saw Ms. Newberry look at Ms. Lindsey and say something to the other woman. They both nodded and separated as they went to their desks with their eyes still on Ms. Lindsey.

"As in, not ever tell anyone I was there," I whispered, pulling her to the side of the copier where there was a little wall separating us from the pool of desks where the assistants sat.

"And why would I do that?" Ms. Lindsey asked.

"Because I don't want people to know. I was just there trying to support Dame, and you know how people are around here; they'll try to make more of it than what it is."

"Well, what is it?" she asked.

"It's nothing."

"It didn't look like nothing."

"Karen, could you please just help me," I said, trying to find some sympathy in her. "I can't have that kind of gossip going around about me. With Evan's career and the church . . . I just—"

"Stop it," she said, rolling her eyes and pausing.

"Look, I don't have any beef with you, so I'm not running to tell everybody."

"Thank you."

"If anyone in this school knows what a bitch gossip can be, I do," she said. "Ever since I walked in that door, people have been calling me a whore and a slut . . . and for what? Because I'm dating a man who asked me out?"

"Well, you know there's more to it," I said.

"Really, there's not. Clyde can do whatever he wants. He's not married and he wasn't in a committed relationship, and unlike everyone else here, I don't think anyone can belong to someone else just because they've been linked to one another for a hundred years. I knew I was getting involved in a sticky situation when I agreed to date Clyde. He obviously still loves her."

"He said that?" I asked.

"I tried to call the police after last night but Clyde took my cell phone and said his mother would kick his ass if Billie went to jail because of him."

"I don't understand, then, Karen," I said. "If you know he loves her, then why would you keep seeing him?"

"I'm twenty-one. I just want to have fun. And Clyde just wants to have fun, too. He's right here in Tuscaloosa and it's not like I'm trying to marry the man. Clyde's too old for me," she scoffed. "I'm seeing someone else anyway and that's why I wanted to go to the club to see Dame."

"The club? You're trying to date Dame?" I asked.

"No," she said, grinning. "I'm trying to get back with my ex-boyfriend—Benji. You know, Dame's bodyguard that came over when you were talking to me and Clyde at the club?"

"Oh, that's why he seemed so angry and rushed." I recalled the furious look on Benji's face when he saw me with Clyde and Ms. Lindsey.

"Yeah, he's the jealous type, and I thought if he saw me with Clyde, he'd get upset and want me back. He's been tripping off all those groupies ever since he's been on tour with Dame. But I keep telling him when it's all over, he'll be looking for me. I know it sounds insane. But I love him. . . . You know how love can make you do crazy things."

"I'm learning that," I said.

"Anyway," Ms. Lindsey said, looking at her watch, "I only have fifteen minutes before my monsters come back from lunch." She looked at me. "Don't worry about your secret. Just keep your friend away from me."

"I'll do that," I said, and we walked out of the office together. "Ms. Lindsey," I called when she turned to walk back toward her classroom.

"Yes?"

"Did you tell Clyde you're not serious about him?" I asked.

"No," she said. "He knows I'm just having fun."

"No. . . . He's a little older than the 'just having fun' age," I said. "I think you should tell him. Make sure you two are on the same page."

"Gotcha," she said, winking her good eye like she was breaking in a flag football game. "I'll think about it."

Watching her walk down the hall, I noticed that on one of the benches in the lobby sat Zenobia. Even though this was her normal resting place between classes, I didn't expect to see her there because she hadn't been to my class. I was sure she skipped other classes, but for most of my students, music was at least tolerable if they were in the building. She was slumped over with her head resting, cheek down on the tops of her knees. Her arms were hidden somewhere, folded into her lap.

"Ms. Hamilton?"

I stepped toward her. She didn't look up, move, or shrug her shoulders to acknowledge that I'd called her name.

"Zenobia?" I called again. Nothing. "Zenobia?"

I tapped her on the shoulder.

She moved slowly to lift her head, looked at me, and averted her eyes. They were dry but red and puckered.

"Everything all right?"

"No," she said blankly.

I sat down beside her and pushed my body close to hers, easing down to rest my elbows on my knees to be head to head with her. We sat there for a minute, not saying a word. Zenobia just stared out toward some of the students rushing to their classes, and some of my own even walked by en route to my classroom, but I felt I needed to wait there with Zenobia.

"Ha, ha, you ain't gonna make the cheerleading squad next year," one girl teased another. "You dance like you got two left feet, Calaya!" The two laughed and popped their gum as they followed the crowd down the hallway. A single tear slipped from Zenobia's left eye and she wiped it away quickly with one of her fists.

"You want to go to the office?" I asked.

"No." She looked at me for the first time. "I went today."

"To have the operation?"

"Yes." She looked away again.

"Well, why are you here? Shouldn't you be at home resting?"

The bell rang.

"Mrs. DeLong, everything all right out here?" Ms. Newberry asked, poking her head out of the office in front of us.

"Yes. . . . Actually, could you go down to my classroom for a minute until I get there?" I put my arm around Zenobia.

"Sure," she answered quickly.

"Let it out," I said to Zenobia when Ms. Newberry left. "It's okay to feel sad. You just did something very adult. You just have to be strong now. You hear me?" I lifted her head with my hand so she could see my face.

"I didn't do it," she mumbled.

"What?"

"I couldn't do it. I went and my mama left me because she had to go to work and I waited and waited and I just left."

She started crying openly then; tears were coming from her eyes faster than she could wipe them away.

"Oh, Zenobia," I said, and she went to rest her head back on her knees.

"I can't kill my baby," she said and her voice was both angry and sad. "I won't do it. It's my baby. I won't kill it."

"It's okay," I said. "Just let it out. No one's going to make you do anything."

"Mrs. DeLong," she said, "I don't know what I'm going to do. I keep thinking that—that I don't know what I'm going to do. But I have to figure it out because I can't kill my baby."

"So, this is really what you want?" I asked.

"Yes."

"I can't lie to you. It's going to be hard. Really hard. And there will be a lot of sacrifices. But if you pray and really keep God first, you can make it."

"You believe that?" she asked tearfully, and in the eyes of this girl who'd fought me so many times and complained and turned her back on me, I saw for the first time that she really needed to hear my opinion of her and that it mattered.

"You can do anything you put your mind to, Zenobia," I said. "You're a strong girl. You're passionate. You're bright. You're smart. If you use all those skills—skills that God gave you—you'll be blessed."

She shook her head, and I could see that she hadn't heard these things about herself before. But I meant each of them. As feisty as Zenobia was, her passion always shined through. Similar to most of the kids like her, she just had to focus this energy on a goal. And now, she had one.

Chapter Eighteen

As desperate as things seemed to be getting in my marriage, in my family—in my personal life in general since my thirty-third birthday, there were moments like the one with Zenobia that day out in the lobby of the school at the beginning of sixth period that brought some clarity. The days following, I remembered what my mother said about taking stock of my life and I realized that while I wasn't clear at all on the direction anything was going to take—at that point I was willing to admit that—I had to begin to trust myself. As I told Zenobia, who was now having to take stock of her life and start planning a path that even I couldn't imagine how dark it was going to get, I had to believe in myself. That only *I* knew if *I* wasn't happy. That *I* knew if *I* was happy. And that soon, I'd have to make a decision about everything and trust, like I'd told Zenobia, it would be okay. Now, this was just a tested theory in my mind at the time. While I'd tried to seem confident and all-knowing like adults did whenever they shared advice with children like Zenobia, I was preparing myself to take baby steps to get to wherever I was going. So when Evan came to me each night when the moon was high and he wanted me to make good on my promise to start a family, I kept a secret to myself and just said I was tired. But the truth was I needed time to think. Time to make a decision to stay and move forward. To fall back in love with my life and having him in it. Or time to plan a way out. To just walk away from everything and leave my past behind and Evan with it. And then I'd think about Dame and how he'd left and went out into the world even before anyone said he should. Just like me, everyone had plans for him, but he had plans for himself.

At church on Sunday, it was as if I wasn't even there. I was sitting in my seat beside Evan and next to May and Jr, but I wasn't there. I couldn't hear the sermon or focus on one song that was sung. I was praying. Not in a formal way. Not with my hands lifted or my head bowed. In fact, if anyone found my face in the row, they'd think I was just listening. But I was in my mind. Meditating and thinking of the better me. The better Journey I wanted to be. The things about myself that I hadn't said to myself in a long time. My wants. My desires. My strengths. The things that Dame had said to me that tickled my ears like the lightest feather.

Evan rested his hand on my lap and laughed at something my father was saying. It was a big laugh—one that let me know that Evan was just in his world while I was in mine. As he was static, I was racing. As he was staying the same, I was changing. And then I looked out over the congregation and suddenly all I could see was moving parts. Everyone was the same.

The way my mother looked at my father—even when she was angry with him. The way Jr rolled his eyes when Jack Newsome stood up. Mrs. Alice sitting in the third seat from the aisle in the fifth row. The choir in the loft. They were all the same as they'd always been. The same grudges. The same fears. The same happiness. The same sadness. The same praise in the same place I'd been every Sunday of my life. And for the first time, I thought maybe I wasn't even there. It was like I was watching a movie. I wasn't even there. Just in it. Participating as expected and playing a role, saying lines when cued. After this, Evan and I would walk to the car, talk about the sermon, and head to my parents' house for dinner. There, my father would press me about children. May would be quiet. Jr would say something mean and I'd sit and wait for it to be over. The act was the same and I'd be there for the entire thing until I went to bed and lay in my space in the bed where the moon looked down on me to see that once again, I was exactly where I was supposed to be. This list turned into a tornado in my mind. It was spinning and kicking up dust all around. Forever—forever. I was breathless just thinking about it. Just wondering how I could do it all and come out okay on the other side. Could I still be me each night when I went to bed? Could I be my best? Or was I someone else?

I looked up into the rows in the second and then third balcony to try to find something still to stop the spinning—to focus on. Six faces I counted—all laughing, all smiling at the same thing. Seven. A door swinging open. A man with his back to me. He was walking outside the doors, but even from my seat I could see his size, his gait, how he carried himself in the loose fitting jeans and buttoned-up shirt he was wearing.

"Benji?" I said, and hearing Dame say in my mind, "Whenever you see Benji, know that I'm just two steps behind," my heart immediately began to palpitate.

"What'd you say, honey?" Evan asked, leaning toward me.

"Nothing," I answered, but there was something. Like a rope was tied from my navel to Benji's waist, I was being tugged somehow from my seat. "I have to go," I said next and I didn't know where I was going or what excuse I was about to use to get out of that church. But I just had to. I had to see.

"Go where?" Evan looked at me.

"My head . . . it hurts." I massaged my forehead. "I need to go home."

"Well, let's go," he said, moving to get up.

"No." I put my hand out to stop him. "You don't have to come with me. . . . I don't want you to miss the rest of the sermon. You were enjoying it. I'll just go home and rest up a bit and come meet you at my parents' for dinner. I'll take the car and you can catch a ride with Jr and May."

"You sure?" he asked.

"Yeah," I said. "I just need some rest. Some quiet."

He handed me the car keys.

"I'll see you later," he said, kissing me on the cheek.

"Yeah."

"Wait! Wait!" I hollered at Benji's back. I'd run—not in an inconspicuous trot, but in a full dash as if the very air I was breathing depended upon it—out the doors by my seat, down the stairs, through the lobby, and out into the parking lot to catch him. I was out of breath and sweating, my hair had come loose and I realized I'd left my purse in my seat, but I was still running.

Benji stopped.

"Wait," I said, reaching out to grab him as I fought to keep my breath. "Wait."

He turned to me.

"Is . . . he . . . here?" I managed. "Dame?"

"He's waiting for you," he said, "by the river."

They called it Princess Pale Moon's Throat. A secluded, untouched corner of the Black Warrior River where a gentle stream created by rolling hills beneath the fall line separating the upper part of the river from the lower part ran beneath canopies of maple, sweet gum, and poplar trees. Behind the trees, a mixture of sand, gravel, and mud that washed up from the floor of the stream when the river ran high created a path that was just wide enough for a car to come winding down to get up close to the stream so that someone could get out and walk over to enjoy its beauty. For years, this path was known as "the Throat," a road that led lovers to the most beautiful face Alabama had to offer—Princess Pale Moon, a Choctaw beauty who was said to be loved by more men than Mataoaka, known to most people as Pocahontas. It was the most secret place in Tuscaloosa every lover, old and young, knew about. Unlike other parts of the river, which were now largely rerouted for navigation and big business with the coal from the basin, nothing was ever built there or left along the edge of the path to let anyone know it had been discovered. And we liked it that way. So much so that if anyone arrived in a car with their lover, hoping to park and be alone in the world for a little while, and there was already another car there, the new arrivals would quickly shift into reverse and head back out onto the main road. The face was to be enjoyed alone. The secret of the place had to be kept.

When Benji said Dame was waiting by the river, I knew where to go, where to head off the main road and catch the start of the throat to lead myself to the sweet gum trees. In the clearing, where the throat turned for the last time and then a straight path led to the stream, I saw the old pickup truck. It was up on the side of the path and the driver's-side door was open. I pulled up behind the truck and turned off my engine. All around outside was silent when I got out of the car, but then a yellowhammer flitted off the top of the stream and flew up into the sky. I watched the bird disappear and then looked back at the quiet truck. I couldn't see Dame.

"You're scaring off all of the birds," he said behind me. I didn't turn. I just laughed and shook my head.

"Maybe he's going to tell his friends I'm here," I said.

"And maybe he already knew you'd be here, but he was too scared to approach you face to face."

"Scared?" I turned around as I laughed. But Dame wasn't there.

"Got ya!" He poked me on the shoulder and I turned again and there he was—brown and beautiful again.

"What are you doing here?" I asked.

"I don't know. I haven't been out here since I was in high school," he said, and we started walking toward the stream.

"Not at the Throat," I said. "I mean, why are you in Alabama? I saw Benji at the church."

"I know. I sent him there."

"For what?"

"What do you think?" he asked. "I told him to go there and just see what happened. If you saw him and asked about me, then he'd tell you I was here, and if not . . . it wasn't meant to be."

"But there are thousands of people in the church. How could you know I'd see him?"

"In a room full of a million people, if there's one thing you want, you'll see it."

"Oh, you're so sure of yourself."

"I have reason to be."

"Why?" I asked.

"I am who I am."

"You're . . ." I shook my head, trying to remember where I'd heard that quote in the Bible. "Exodus—"

"3:14." He grinned, knowing I didn't expect him to know where that came from.

"That's blasphemy!" I couldn't help but grin back as I said this.

"What?"

"You're too cocky."

"I should be cocky. I'm a black man."

"Here we go again."

"No. No. No." He reached out for me, placing his hand between my arm and torso. "You want to know why I'm really cocky today?"

"Why?"

"Because I'm here with you."

I looked away, knowing my cheeks revealed my excitement at hearing that.

He pulled me closer to the side of the stream where a big, flat rock sat right in the middle.

"Let's sit down." He pointed to the rock, but there was a little pool of water between the dirt where we were standing and the rock.

"I'll never make it in these shoes," I said, looking at my heels.

"Okay," he said, putting out his arms to pick me up.

"Oh no, you can't pick me up. I'm too big," I said. "I'll just take off my shoes and—ohh!"

I was up in the air. Before I could finish my statement, Dame picked me up and hopped onto the rock light and assured like it was a lily pad. He let me down slowly and easily as if he could hold me for another five hours and I felt so light. So impossibly light and just manageable. After easing down to my feet with his arms still held at my sides, I realized I had no clue how big or small I was right then. It didn't matter. In front of him I purely felt like a woman. A graceful, precious, feminine woman who was okay . . . *as is.* My diet was permanently over.

"I know you said you didn't want to see me again, but I can't do that again. I just can't stop thinking about you," he said after we sat down. "Since you came to Atlanta, it seems like everything else in my world is just dead."

"I've been thinking the same thing, too," I said.

"I can't go back to that. I can't pretend anymore."

"But I—"

"Wait, before you say that, let me say something," he said, pulling me down to sit on the rock beside him. "I don't care about my image, my fans, the industry—I don't give a damn what anyone in that club the other night thought about what I had to say about how I feel about you. I'm open and I'm not going to hide it anymore." He paused and looked at me. "Now, all I want to hear from you right now is what you really feel—not what you believe you should feel or should say. I want to know what you really feel about me because that's all I'm giving you. I'm not hiding anything."

He pitched a rock he'd picked up out into the stream, and the yellowhammer appeared again, flying from a branch along the canopy. Another followed behind it.

"You make me feel like I'm ten years younger—and not like I did when I really was ten years younger—with duties and promises—my life set out in front of me like a map I couldn't change. Maybe like I should've felt then. Like I could do anything. Go anywhere. And that's something because before, I was so comfortable, and now . . . well, I've never been so afraid in my life. Afraid somebody might find out. But that fear—that rush—has made me see everything differently. Like what I would do if I could just pick up that map and tear it up and walk away . . . just leave everybody," I said, looking at him. "And when I think about walking away—even though I know I can't—I think about you. About your energy. Your kindness. How everyone just looks when you walk into a room. It's like you're electric. You own yourself and you don't care what people think. And no matter how old you are, that's the most manly thing I've ever seen. In fact, it's beautiful."

"Thank you," Dame said, sliding his hand between my legs. He handed me a rock and I pitched it this time . . . way out into the middle of the water where the ripples would take some time to reach us.

Chapter Nineteen

I met Dame out there the next morning. Just like we'd planned, a bit before dawn, I drove along the throat to where the bottom of the trees were as black as tar and the dirt was so soft it felt like peat moss. I did this . . . not once . . . but every "just before dawn" that week before graduation. And every time I got there, Dame's Bentley would already be at the foot of the trees, sleepy and quiet, seeming to wait for me to knock on the window to wake it up. He had Mr. Green drive him to Tuscaloosa from Atlanta each night after he left a show or the studio. He'd sleep the whole way during the drive and wake just in time for me. Then Dame would get out or I'd get in and we'd talk a bit and giggle and sometimes hold hands and walk out into the water to watch the sun rise. I'd let go of telling myself this was all nothing on the first day with the yellowhammer. And by the second, I knew it was something I wanted so badly that I'd wake up long before the moon went to bed and the roosters came out to post. It was a rush that kept me feeling more alive than I could recall, just tingling up the middle of my back and happy just because. It was like I was a fish and Dame was the lake. I had to get to it. To hear his stories, his radical and sometimes visionary ideas. To have him listen to mine . . . really listen to mine and encourage me and remind me of what it felt like to really believe I was brilliant.

By day four, when I packed my gym bag and reminded a heavy-eyed Evan I was exercising before I went to work, I remembered what Kayla and Billie said about crazy love that night at Wilhagens. About the crazy, headless chicken, Bobby and Whitney, Luther and those love songs he sang. How love was supposed to make you feel something. Passion. Sick. Crazy. Walking out of the house to meet Dame, I thought maybe this was me now. I felt sick, out of breath, and suffocating whenever I wasn't with him. And when I knew it was almost time for us to meet again, when I was just about to fall into a deeper sleep in my bed, passion would find me and like a headless chicken, I'd jump up out of bed and race to get to the river. None of this sounded comforting, but it felt so good. Like hot cookies right out of the oven, cooled by my lips, and then in my mouth. It was warm and cozy and something else I couldn't describe, but anyone else who'd had that cookie before just knew. When I pulled up next to the Bentley, I remembered Billie and Kayla high-fiving over the table, oozing and agreeing about this feeling. Now, in my mind, I was high-fiving and oozing and agreeing with them. I knew this crazy feeling, the secret of the hot cookie. What Zenobia knew. What Ms. Lindsey knew. But back then, I had no real launching pad. And, I knew it was dangerous to compare Evan to Dame in this way. If I were a fish, Evan was another fish swimming in the lake beside me. That's how we'd learned to love each other. For me, it wasn't about longing or passion. It was about loving that he'd always swim beside me and was a fish just like me. This had been enough—I'd been taught this was enough—for me forever. But by day five, when the week had ended and I'd been late for work every day but still arrived with a smile stapled to my face, I wondered if forever was enough.

"You gonna tell us yet why you been smiling so much now, Mrs. DeLong?" Devin King said just before the fourth-period bell rang and I was still greeting the students as they walked into the room.

"Excuse me?" I asked, trying now not to smile so brightly, but knowing it probably had the reverse effect—the smile was even bigger.

"There it is—big, old Kool-Aid smile!" Opal said, pointing at me, and the other students started laughing.

"Well, can't your teacher just be happy?" I asked.

"I ain't never seen no grown person looking that happy," Devin said. "Not unless they drunk or high."

"Okay, that's enough," I said, realizing that maybe I felt both drunk and high inside. Dame surprised me that morning with a recording of himself performing the song he'd written for me. Only this time, it was without a background. No music. No singing. He said when he got into the studio to record it, he felt like the music and the background singers were only hiding his words. That he wanted his feelings to be loud and clear, nude and unmistakable. He opened all of the windows and doors and turned the sound all the way up and played the song out loud to the whole forest. His love for me, how he saw me, echoed all around me. The birds knew. The squirrels knew. The trees knew. The lake knew. And now I knew, too. Not my big white house. Not my pretty red car, or even any gift my father or Evan had ever given me could amount to this. It was the biggest, most honest gesture I'd known. And unlike the house and car and jewels, no one could ever see these words. And then Dame promised that no one would ever hear them either. He wasn't going to use the song on the next album. Not as long as I was with Evan.

"Your husband must've gotten you something nice," Zenobia said. She smiled and eased back into her seat. "Some diamonds or platinum." In just two weeks, she had swollen to the size of a woman who was about to deliver. It seemed like she was carrying all of her love, all of her needs, right there in front of her. Only I knew that wouldn't come out with the baby in six months. Fat or skinny, it would always be there until Zenobia learned to fulfill those needs herself.

"Maybe he got her a new car!" Opal added and another student ran to the window to look out at the lot.

"Sit down, silly," I said, laughing. "There's no new car."

"Then what is it?" someone asked.

"I am just happy." I walked over toward the organ to sit down to begin our warm-up. "Just happy."

After we finished warming up and we'd sung through the Negro anthem, to my satisfaction I was met with groans and rolling eyes when I played the first chords of "Swing Low, Sweet Chariot." The music sheets were long gone and now we were supposed to be confident, singing with our bodies erect, faces up, and mouths wide, but I had none of this in front of me. They were slouching and looking down and not at all prepared to sing.

"Come on, folks," I said, getting up from the organ. "We only have a week until graduation. We can't afford to look like this."

"We tired," Opal acknowledged.

"Tired of what?" I asked. "You all are too young to be tired."

"Not tired like that," she answered.

"We tired of singing this old people song," Devin said, and they all chuckled just light enough not to offend me.

"It's not an old people; it's your song," I said. "Our song."

"We know all that. We know everything you told us about the slaves and how it's supposed to be about hope, but really, to us, it don't sound like hope," Kim Davis, one of the lead sopranos, said. "People sing this song at funerals."

"That's because it feels like death. Like we dying or something . . . and *we don't want massa to hit us over the head with no shackle when we running off to freedom,*" Devin added and his voice mimicked that of a stereotypical slave. The chuckle in the room went to a full laugh this time.

"Look, I understand," I started, and the little yet grown-looking, faces around me went to looking like they'd never heard me say I understood them before. "It does sound old. And sometimes it does sound sad . . . but . . ." I tried, but I couldn't think of any encouragement I hadn't already said. Yes, there was hope. Yes, there was history. Yes, there was tradition. But sometimes, even those things needed a face-lift.

If the children weren't feeling anything . . . they weren't feeling anything. Maybe they needed something else.

I paused and gazed out the windows. I saw the trees out by the edge of the parking lot, looking tall and smart. They knew what to say. They knew all of the secrets. Caught every echo we'd ever uttered.

"Let's try something different," I said, turning back to the class. "You say it sounds old. You say it feels like death. Let's take the sound away." I walked past the organ and right to the middle of the floor. "Let's take the sound away. And give it our own sound and our feeling."

"You mean, sing it a cappella?" Kim asked.

"Yes."

"But you said the music is just as important as the song," she added. "It's the tradition."

"Why hide behind the music?" I asked rhetorically. "If we want people to feel the words, let's give them something they can feel . . . our voices."

"You joking, right?" Zenobia asked.

"No. Let's do it." I clapped and went to hit the key, so they could remember the pitch. "When I raise my hands—just like I do with the music—you guys just start on this chord." I hit the key a few times so they could hear it.

Each on their own time, they straightened up at this new challenge. Listened to the note and watched eagerly for me to begin. I'd seen them, time and again, at their best, but with this experiment, they seemed better than their best—they were interested. They had to depend upon one another to hear where they were to go to next. The sopranos looked at one another. The tenors stood more closely together. And the altos turned their ears to the center of the crowd. And while we had some bumps and struggles along the way and had to begin again a few times, what I heard and what they heard, what the trees outside heard, was beautiful.

Without the music, the youth in their voices could be heard. The song was reborn with new life.

"We really gonna get to sing the song like that at graduation?" Opal asked after class had ended.

"I don't know," I answered.

"But it was good. It sounded real good. Don't you think?"

"It did. But it would need a lot of practice to be ready to present to everyone. It's not easy to sing a cappella. Especially not out in a field in front of a thousand people who are used to hearing it a different way."

"But what if we practice every day and get better?"

"We only have five more days to practice next week," I said. "And half of you already refuse to come after school."

"Please!" she begged, grabbing my arm. "It'll be the bomb."

"Oh, girl, calm down," I said. "I'll think about it and let you know. But I'll tell you right now, we may be able to do a new arrangement, but we'll probably need accompaniment. People are used to hearing it that way at our graduation. It's all about tradition."

"Okay!" She grinned, straightened up and darted out of the classroom with the rest of her friends.

"She might be onto something," Kayla said, coming into the classroom.

"Hey there," I said.

"You all sound great."

"Thanks. We were just trying something different

today. It's hard to keep them interested. Especially so late in the year."

"They sounded interested to me," she said. "Usually, I can't hear them above the music. But today, they were quite a force."

"What are you doing back here?" I asked. The math and science classes were in a whole different wing. Nothing was at the back of the hallway by the chorus room, except one of the janitor's closets and a door that led to the parking lot.

"Richard." She grinned, and I saw hot cookies all over her smile. "He sneaks up here before fourth period and we have a soda together."

"A soda? You sound like you're in high school."

"That's what it feels like," she said. "And I love it."

"That's sweet," I said.

"What about you?" she asked nonchalantly. "You seem a little sweet, too, lately. Got everyone talking about how happy you look. Some of the students say you're pregnant."

"Me?" I laughed. "Oh, no. I'm not pregnant. I'm just . . . I'm . . ."

"What?" she pushed to break my nervous pause.

"I'm happy."

"Happy," she repeated, smiling. "Well, that's good. Because you deserve to be happy. We all do."

"You know," I said, "I've been thinking about that for a while now. And I think, what if that happiness makes everyone around you sad? Like, and I don't want you to take this the wrong way—"

"I won't."

"Don't you ever think of Richard's wife. How sad she might be. . . . Of course you guys are happy together. But someone else is suffering."

"No one should have to be with someone that isn't in love with them—someone who's just staying because of time and obligation, and rings, and other people's expectations. That's not marriage. That's a lie. They were both suffering, putting everything they had into a relationship that was dead," she said. "Now, I know everything I did wasn't perfect. But at least now, that woman stands a chance of finding someone else. Of finding the love she deserves."

"I see," I replied carefully.

"I hope you do," Kayla said. "Because, as I said, you deserve the same thing."

Chapter Twenty

"When are you going to kiss me?" Dame asked softly. He was lying beside me underneath a cover on the floor of the black limousine he'd been coming to see me in since Monday. When Mr. Green opened the door to let me in, he'd whispered, "He's still asleep," and handed me a blanket from the trunk. I crawled up beside Dame and covered him with the blanket. While he usually woke up, he didn't say a word. Half asleep and awake, he just opened his arms for me to lie with him.

"Kiss?" I repeated. I didn't know Dame had woken up. I was still laying in his arms, my face up toward the glass roof where the moon was still holding on to Tuesday night.

"Yeah."

"Dame," I started, turning to him, "we both know I can't do that. I'm married. . . . I mean, I know I'm doing this . . . thing . . . with you. But I'm not trying to have an affair."

"And this isn't an affair?"

"You know what I mean. I'm already starting to feel guilty about meeting you here. I'm terrified that someone will find out about this. That someone saw me in Atlanta or is watching us right now. And that I'll get caught. And then what?" I said frantically. "I can't go any farther—add anything else—because that'll only make things more complicated in my mind."

This was exactly what I'd grown terrified of over the weekend while Dame was away in New York meeting with studio executives. He'd called and called, mostly just leaving long messages where he wanted to talk about everything that was happening, but I couldn't ever sneak away to answer. Evan didn't have any meetings and slipping off to chat on the phone for even ten minutes would look suspicious. So I was forced to face Evan and get back to the custom of my marriage. We'd been arm in arm to two dinner parties, smiled and traded kisses as we watched a movie with his mother and when we went to church, sitting next to May and Jr, behind my mother and father, we just seemed like the same old us. Not sad or angry. Just us. I looked at May and knowing how angry she must've been at Jr, yet still she'd decided to stay with him to see it through until they found out if the baby was his, I thought that Kayla had to have been wrong in my office that Friday. It didn't matter what I thought I was feeling, I didn't want to make Evan suffer the way May was suffering. The way my mother had. They all deserved better. I told myself that maybe I should stop meeting with Dame. Maybe I should let it go and just focus on my life and being happy with what I'd had. Happy the way my mother told me to be—not the way Kayla explained. But when the sun went down on Sunday and I was just a few hours away from my 5 a.m. departure for the gym, I knew neither happiness would come easily.

"Look," I said, "I'm not saying I don't want to kiss you. I'm saying, I can't. We both know what will happen if we kiss. And I'm not that kind of woman. . . . I mean, I didn't think I was the kind of woman that would be doing what I'm doing right now, but I know I'm not the kind of woman that has sex outside of her marriage. And if you thought I was, then I'm sorry." I sat up and pushed the cover off me.

"You think I've been sitting in this car every day for six hours going back and forth between the studio in Atlanta and Tuscaloosa to have sex with you?" Dame asked as I turned around to him. He was still laying down and had his arms behind his head. "When I walked out of the studio last night, there were two girls, one who was on the cover of *Vogue* last month, waiting for me."

"Why are you telling me that? Am I supposed to feel bad that you had to miss that?" I imagined these beautiful, thin, and young women waiting outside the door for Dame, and immediately I felt jealous.

"I don't need sex, Journey. I have good girls—great girls with careers and cars just like mine waiting to have sex with me. But that's not what I need. That's not what I want. I need and I want you." He sat up.

"When I was in New York, man"—he laughed a bit and looked out the window at the river—"I felt like one of those fish out there that jumped out the river. Like I had to get back to you or I'd die." Dame inched closer to me and it was like he was reading my mind. Like he had been for weeks and knew exactly how I was feeling for him, how I felt with him, because he'd been feeling the same way, too. "This isn't a sex thing. This is a love thing," he said, inching a bit closer and leaning his head toward mine. His lips were now just a kiss away. His brown eyes were locked and longing on mine. I felt something in my stomach flutter and then pound so restlessly that my ears began to ring. But I didn't move. I opened my mouth and closed my eyes, feeling Dame's breath enter into mine. And then everything, just in the one second it took for his lips to brush up against mine, became perfect. Like we'd both found a lake and were swimming deep, deep down to the bottom. His tongue stroked mine with so much passion and force that the pounding inside of me went to heat and then exploded. I felt my body pushing toward his, my mouth opening wider, begging him for just one more second in the water, to go one inch deeper. He grabbed my neck and began caressing me lightly. I just didn't want it to stop. But then the sun, or something just as bright, pulled me up from the bottom of the lake to the surface.

On the inside of my eyelids danced spots of orange that burned so bright that I had to squint and then open my eyes to see if maybe the sun had somehow fallen into the back of the limousine.

"What's that?" I asked after Dame had pulled away from me and was looking out of the window. I could hear a car engine rattling.

"Someone's high beams," he said, shielding his eyes with his hand at the window.

"A car?" I went to the window with him, but because the lights were so bright, we couldn't see the car. Just Mr. Green's back.

"Yes, my wife," the voice of a man said angrily. "Get out of my way."

"Evan!" I said, putting my hand over my mouth and looking at Dame. "It's Evan."

"Oh, shit," Dame said.

"Shit," I said, reaching for my purse.

"Where are you going?"

"I have to get out. He knows I'm in here. My car's right outside."

Dame grabbed my arm and pulled me.

"Let me talk to him," he said forcefully.

"Look, I don't need that kind of thing. No fighting. Evan isn't like that. Please don't get out of the car and start something. Let me handle this." The pounding inside of me was fear now. Dame didn't say anything. He went to one door to open it and I went to the other.

Evan was pushing Mr. Green out of his way and walking toward the limousine when I opened the door and got out.

"Journey, what the hell is this? Who is this?" Evan said, coming to me.

"I'm—" I tried so hard, but I couldn't lie. Everything was right there for him to see. Dame came from the other side of the limousine and stood behind me.

"Dame?" Evan looked from me to Dame and then back at me. "What is this?"

"I—"

"She's here with me," Dame said.

His admission immediately paralyzed me. I was aching. Everything I didn't want to happen was now happening. I closed my eyes and prayed it wasn't real.

"Journey . . . Journey, look at me," Evan said, coming closer and reaching for me.

"Don't fucking touch her," Dame said. He pushed himself between me and Evan.

"Dame, don't do that," I said, stepping back. "Evan, I'm sorry. I was just here talking and . . ."

"I don't care what you were doing. You shouldn't be here. I told you never to see him again."

"She's a grown woman. She can see whoever she wants."

Evan didn't even respond to Dame. His faced turned red with pain, he just looked at me confused, bruised, and angry. I'd never seen him like that. I'd prayed I never would.

"Let's go," Evan demanded. "Come get in my car and we're going home."

"She's not leaving," Dame said, pushing Evan away from me. The two tussled, pushing back and forth before Mr. Green and I broke them up.

"Stop it, both of you," I cried. My heels were digging into the loose dirt. "Just stop." I held my arms out between them. Mr. Green managed to get Dame up against the car and I stood in front of Evan.

"Fuck this gay-ass nigga," Dame hollered. "Journey, tell him. Tell him you're not leaving with him. That you want to be with me."

"Come on, Mr. Mitchell, don't do this. We don't need to get in trouble down here," Mr. Green said to calm Dame down and stop him from charging after Evan again.

"What's he talking about?"

"Let's just go," I whispered as tears filled up the corners of my eyes.

"No, I want to know. How long have you been meeting him here?" Evan's face just broke into desperation.

"Tell him," Dame said.

"It's nothing," I said. "I don't want to hurt you. I'm so sorry." I felt a tear hit my cheek and roll down to my mouth. Dame was still hollering out to me, but Evan wasn't saying anything. He just stood there and looked at me the same way May had looked at Jr that night at the old house. I could see his chest heave and then he turned and walked to his car. I looked back at Dame and wiped away one of my tears.

"Don't do this," Dame shouted, trying to push Mr. Green off him. "Don't leave. You know you don't want to be with him. Come with me." I began to step away, and right before Dame stopped fighting with Mr. Green, he called my name again.

"Journey," he shouted and his voice sounded so broken and rushed, like he was fighting for me to keep my life, that everyone just froze where they were. I turned back to him. "You said I was electric."

I nodded.

"You got it, too. You got that same spark in you. You just got to being afraid to show it. You said you wanted to know what life would be like if you just tore up the map and went anywhere . . . just left all of this behind." Dame walked toward me and then he was right in front of me. Mr. Green was behind him and Evan was standing behind me. "We can do that together," Dame said, and even though I saw not one tear in his eyes, there was a sadness, a desperation there. "We can go wherever you want. We can leave everything and start something new. Just you and me. But you have to come with me."

Face to face with Dame, my heart was steadily breaking. I trembled in the absoluteness of my aching. While I'd just realized it then, the man I'd fallen in love with was in front of me. But still, the man I'd always loved was behind me. It was an impossible moment for me to manage with any clarity.

I smiled at Dame remembering my words, my dreams. He was so right, and I wanted so much to just believe in this idea we'd shared. But I just knew it wasn't right. It couldn't be right like this. With my whole life just out in the road being tortured. There had to be another way.

My eyes brimming with tears I cupped his face with my hands so gently, just to feel him.

"I can't," I said.

Chapter Twenty-one

When I was a little girl and I got what my brothers and I called "in trouble," and my parents came like a jury to my bedroom to convict and sentence me, "trouble" almost always came out to be easier than I'd expected . . . or could remember. While I was afraid and shaking with dread, the older I got, the less painful and disturbing my parents' whippings and rants seemed. In fact, after a while, "trouble" became an acceptable consequence to something I fully intended to do in spite of the possibility of getting caught. I'd wear my mother's pearl earrings to school, sneak the cordless phone into my bedroom after bedtime to talk to Billie all night about some boy who had a crush on her, or read one of my naughty romance books, thinking every second how I was sure to get "in trouble" and be prosecuted to the fullest extent of the law.

The trouble I was in with Evan after I followed him

back to our house from the Throat was so much easier than any trouble I'd ever been in that it was somehow the worst.

Evan headed to the house with ease. He'd been wearing one of his gym suits, the one that was on the chair beside our bed when I woke up, and when he got out of the car, I saw that he'd zipped up the jacket and had his hands in the pockets. He looked cool. As if he was coming home from a jog and heading to the shower. He said not one word. Kept his stride and didn't turn to be sure I was following him.

The moon was gone now and the sun was awake. I looked up at the orange thing that was still fighting with some clouds and searched for some kind of strength. Some kind of energy. But it only sat there. Just stared down at me and threatened to come out soon to burn me. I was in the dark just a few minutes ago, but now the light wasn't pretending to play games. It was time to get up.

In the house, Evan was moving fast. He was packing his bag for work. He had laid out his suit on the bed and then he started to take the sweats off to get in the shower. I just sat on the bed unmoving and in fear like a child. His silence was deafening.

"You need to get ready for work," he directed me. "You're already late. You can't miss work."

"Yes," I said. I looked around the room contemplating how I could get moving like Evan. Get ready. Evan kept zipping past me. In his towel. He got his cufflinks. His watch. His socks. Where could I start? In this room now, my room, I felt like a stranger, a prisoner, an intruder all at once. It was like I didn't belong anymore, but I had to stay. And I had no one else to blame for this feeling. I'd done it. I'd broken this place. I needed Evan to at least recognize this. What I'd done. I started crying, weeping, wailing. But Evan kept preparing.

"Say something to me," I sobbed.

"Get ready."

"No," I said.

He walked toward the bathroom and stood right in the doorframe in front of me. He stopped then and turned around to me.

"What are you crying for?" he asked. "You did this. You fucking did this and now you're crying?" He came closer to me and I held myself in fear. "I'm not going to hurt you. I'm going to keep moving, Journey, because I assume this is what you want. Right? For me to just pretend this isn't happening. Let you do whatever you want to do."

"No," I said, choking on my saliva, "this is not what I want. I'm so sorry. . . . I'm just so sorry."

"You're not sorry," he said. "I told you . . . I warned you to stay away from him. I knew this was going to happen."

"You knew?"

"The way you looked at him that day at the school," he shouted, grabbing my chin hard with his hand. "It was all over your face. You fucking measured us up against each other. And I didn't know what to think about it. I thought you were stronger than that. That there was no way you'd be so stupid. But when I asked you about him at your parents' house . . . I knew . . . I knew what was coming."

He released my chin in disgust and stepped back with his hand over his mouth.

"How could you risk everything we have to be with that boy?" he asked. "Don't you know how this is going to end? He's a kid. He's going to get tired of you and throw you out into the street like some groupie."

"He's not like that."

"You don't know a damn thing about him. Does he have any diseases? Does he have a criminal record? Does he have a fucking bank account? Can he count any of that money he has?"

I didn't know the answers to any of these questions.

"He's a fucking high school dropout!" Evan bellowed as I cried. He closed his eyes and winced as if he was trying to control his anger. Carefully, he came and sat next to me on the bed.

"Did you have sex with him?"

"Evan—"

"Don't talk to me. I just want an answer."

"No," I said and I actually saw a weight fall from his body.

"Did he touch you? Kiss you?"

I paused and closed my eyes.

"No," I lied.

Evan sat there and shook his head as if he was weighing this thing.

"I need you to decide what you're going to do," he said. "I'm your husband and I'll always be your husband and I want you to be with me. But you have to decide if you want to be with me. You have to decide if you want this to work . . . and move past this." I didn't look at Evan, but I could tell by his voice he was crying. "Because I'm willing to let it go. To start back where we were if you want to. To start our family. I can do that." He slid his hand behind my back and after we sat there for a while, I leaned into him. I rested my head on his shoulder and just stayed there. Neither of us went to work.

Chapter Twenty-two

"I'm so sorry, Journey," Billie said. We were sitting in her car outside the yoga studio. After Evan and I lay in bed for a few hours, I said I wanted to go to yoga. He looked at me like I was crazy, like I'd shot myself in the foot, but I said I needed some air. Just to go somewhere to relax. "Okay," he said, reaching for my car keys. "I'll drive you."

"Don't be sorry," I said to Billie. We'd already done the class and were waiting in her car for Evan to come get me.

"No, I feel like I did this somehow . . . with my bad advice. I didn't know how serious you were about the thing with Dame. I didn't think it would go this far."

"It was bad advice," I said, laughing, "but really, if I didn't want to go, there was no way any advice could've gotten me there. It was up to me in the end. I was just looking for someone to give me permission to do what I already wanted to do. Maybe it didn't even matter what you said."

"How did Evan catch you? How did he know you were going to be at the Throat?"

"He said he saw that I left my gym bag and he ran out of the house with it right when I pulled out of the driveway," I explained. "He didn't want me to get all the way to the gym and realize I didn't have it, so he jumped in his car—my caring husband. He was able to follow me for most of the way, but then he lost me. . . . Only, I was going in a completely different direction than the gym. He said he sat in the car, just driving around for a little while, thinking which direction I might've gone in . . . and then he ended up at the Throat."

"Coincidence is a bitch sometimes," Billie said.

"I'm not silly enough to believe in coincidences," I said, hearing Dame in my head. "If you want to find one face in a crowd of a million, eventually you'll find it."

Billie nodded.

"So what are you going to do?"

"I'm going to try to make it work with Evan. . . . Both of you were right. I don't know anything about Dame. It was a childish thing in the first place. Maybe just some country, desperate wife drama. I got bored."

"Bored in Tuscaloosa? I couldn't imagine," Billie joked.

"As exciting as my life is here," I said, laughing, "what I did wasn't fair to Evan or Dame, so I'm moving on. I'm growing up and I'm going to accept my life the way it is. I'm lucky. What other husband in the world would put up with all this?"

"One you met on the Internet!"

"Exactly," I said, watching Evan pull into the parking lot behind us.

"Now, don't think this is crazy, but as your best friend, I have to ask," Billie said.

"What?"

"I had your back when you got married. I had your back a little while ago when you announced that you wanted to have a baby . . ."

"I know . . . I know."

"And even though I wasn't sure if you really wanted to do either thing, I didn't say anything because I didn't want to be all up in your business."

"What is it?"

"Are you sure this is what you want?"

Evan eased up beside us and just sat there in his car.

"No," I admitted quietly. "But I don't think I can know what I want right now."

Every year on the Saturday night before graduation, Evan and I dressed up to attend the senior prom. He'd pull out his tuxedo and I'd go shopping for a blush-colored dress—the same color I'd worn when it was our prom and we'd been crowned class king and queen, and he'd arrive at the house just in time to pick me up, with a corsage in his hand and I'd have a pink rose to pin to his lapel. It was a silly tradition we'd enjoyed every year since I'd started teaching, and it wasn't only because we were able to put on our black-tie best and dance beneath soft light, but somehow, going to the prom always helped us to reconnect. The silly night when my seniors got ready to enjoy their first recognized evening of true freedom, we were remembering how long it had been since we'd been the couple leading the pack, looking back at no one and dreaming, like only young people can about what our future together would be like.

When I got home from work on Friday evening, after going over the songs the chorus was to sing at the graduation for hours after school, and walked into the bedroom, I was surprised to see that Evan had pulled his tuxedo out of the closet. It was hanging behind the bathroom door in a fresh plastic covering from the cleaners. While I'd seen the flyers all around the school and a couple of people had asked if we were attending, I didn't think to ask him to go. With everything going on, the drama with Dame just two days behind us, I thought he'd want to stay home. But when I saw the suit, I was actually happy. A bit relieved. If Evan could see himself going to the dance with me, surely he was serious about forgiving me. Maybe we could move on from what happened. Maybe this could be our new start.

And the next evening, just as he had for years, Evan picked me up at 7:30 p.m. He'd left the house earlier, so I could get ready on my own. When I came outside, dressed in the same blush gown I'd worn the year before, he was standing in front of his open car door holding a pink corsage in his hand. His legs spread a bit apart, his shoulders up straight, he looked dignified and handsome. While none of our parents were there waiting on the steps to see us off, beneath the setting sun, he seemed like a teenage boy who was courting his love for the first time. It was an uneasy moment to say the least, but still, even in our stress, I appreciated his sweetness.

When I was in front of him, Evan got down on his knee and slid the corsage on my hand.

"I don't have a boutonniere for you," I said with a slight grin.

"I picked up one," he said, pulling one from his jacket pocket. "I figured you'd forgetten."

"Oh, Evan," I said.

"There's been a lot going on." He got up and stood in front of me. "A lot of mess. But let's just let tonight be beautiful. Let's let it be our new start."

"I was thinking the same thing."

As wild and out there as we all claimed our students were, on prom night they always proved us wrong. These kids had style and panache; they were creative and bold. And each year, walking into the prom, this was put center stage. The girls looked like movie stars. Hair was everywhere and their dresses, most of which they'd designed themselves and had someone sew, made them look beautiful and so grown up. And while they were usually underdressed, on prom night, the boys came to be seen. They were clean from head to toe. Some in all white and others with silly top hats, coat tails, and canes.

While we didn't have the money to rent a space or go to a catering hall, the students did a fine job of turning the school gym into an underground Atlantis, blanketed in colorful nets and seashells that shimmered with glitter. All of the students looked so proud in their moment, and having worked with most of them for four years straight, I was able to remember the hard times when some of them had left school temporarily or didn't look like they'd ever make it through. But here they were, beating the statistical odds and moving up in the world. For some of them, this would be the last stop, but others would see many more black-tie balls, and even with all of the stress, I was happy to have been an usher along the way.

As Evan and I danced in the middle of the floor, where no other teacher could come up to try to grab him to get more information about how the school was going to divvy up the million dollars, I thought of Zenobia and prayed she'd someday make it to the prom. After I'd spoken to her, I walked her to the school psychologist's office, and together we got her mother to the school and she told her about the baby. It was hard for both of them at first, but once Zenobia's mother realized that the girl was serious, she agreed to come up with a plan so they could all just survive. I knew it was no solution and that there'd be many more days I'd find Zenobia crying, but it was a start.

"What are you thinking about?" Evan asked.

"Just one of my students," I answered. "What about you?"

"What I always think about," he said. "You."

I smiled and rested my head on his shoulder.

"Do you remember what happened the week before our prom?"

"Oh, no, don't bring that up again," I said.

"No, tonight is about reminiscing." He laughed.

"You got hives," I said reluctantly.

"Yep. My father was adding a new room to our house, and I fell on the insulation and got hives all over my body."

"It was gross," I added.

"My face was red as a strawberry, and the doctor said there was no way I'd be able to make it to the prom."

"You didn't come to school the whole week," I remembered.

"And you cried. You called my mama and you cried so hard about how you didn't want to go to the prom alone that I could hear you through the phone."

"I was not that loud," I protested playfully.

"Yes, you were," he went on. "And she was in the kitchen on the phone, so you know that was loud."

"Well, who wants to go to the prom alone?"

"Not my Journey," he said, holding me tighter. "And I felt so bad—"

"You swallowed half the bottle of antihistamine the doctor gave your mama!"

"Almost died. Mama had to rush me to the hospital," he said, and we both laughed. "But then I got better . . . and the next day, by the time they sent me home from the hospital—"

"The rash was gone."

"That's right."

Evan kissed me on the forehead, and we danced slower for a few minutes until the next song came on.

"I always try to think what in the world would make me do that," Evan said. "And then I remember your smile . . . the way you looked when I got to your house and you came outside in your dress."

"After my father lectured you for half an hour."

"That's right. And it was worth it. Because you just had this look on your face, this brightness, that made everything okay—even getting my stomach pumped."

"Tell your mother that. I still don't think she's forgiven—"

"I'm sorry, Journey," he said suddenly.

"Sorry for what?" I asked, looking up at him.

"I stopped doing stuff like that for you after we got married. I let my work take over, going to all these meetings, and working nonstop. I thought I was doing all of it for you, but maybe you've been lonely."

"Don't do that, Evan," I said. "Don't blame yourself for what happened."

"If we're going to move on, to really move on, then something has to change. We have to work harder to understand each other. Maybe I need to be home more."

"And give up your dream? It's not like you're out there meeting with a bowling team. You're getting ready to run for office," I said. "I support you."

"But what about you? What about your dreams?"

"I . . . I don't know."

"When are you going to start singing again?" he asked.

"I don't know," I said and I realized I hadn't even thought of singing in weeks.

"We have to get you back to singing," Evan declared. "Maybe we could find a studio where you can write your own songs and everything. You could do a CD."

"Really? You think that would be a good idea?"

"Of course," he said. "I'll look into it Monday. The summer's starting. You have nothing but free time on your hands."

"Wow," I said. "I never thought I'd hear you say that."

"Well, you'll be hearing a lot of stuff like that from me from now on. I really want this to work."

We kissed on the lips. Evan closed his eyes, but I kept mine open. I had to see him. To see who he was and remind myself of who I was with him. I loved Evan dearly and if he was willing to work so hard to make me happy, I was signing up, too.

* * *

"I was about to come over there to throw some of this punch on you two," Billie said. We were standing at the punch bowl, watching the students dance. Evan had gone to our table and was chatting with Principal Williams and his wife.

"Yeah, I don't know what's come over Evan. He's all Mr. Nice Guy right now."

"So he really meant what he said about working things out?"

"I guess so." I took a sip of my blood-red punch and looked around the room. "Where's Clyde?"

"Ain't seen him; ain't trying to see him!"

"I suppose that's a good thing," I said, waving at some of my students walking by.

"He's been calling me all day," she said.

"About what?"

"I don't know. I'm not answering. I don't want to hear another word about him or Ms. Lindsey. I just want to move on now. I have a clean slate. No more drama in my life."

"Good for you," I said, slapping her a high five. Billie and I stood in silence, people-watching and sometimes giggling at the few fashion mistakes and mishaps walking by. And then, out of the corner of my eye, I saw a man walk into the room in a sweat suit. I turned quickly to see that it was Clyde. Unshaven and underdressed, he made heads turn in waves as he walked through the tables set up behind the dance floors. "Billie?" I called, noticing that he was headed to us. She was looking in the other direction.

"What?" She turned and because she had her punch to her mouth when she saw Clyde, she nearly choked. "What the hell?" she managed, clearing her throat.

"I need to talk to you," Clyde said, almost running her down.

"Yeah, I gathered that," Billie said nastily.

"Look, Billie, I'm not trying to fight with you tonight," he said. "I just need to talk to you."

"About what?"

"Outside," he said.

Billie looked at me, and I put my hands up to say I was staying out of it.

"Can you hold my purse?" she asked, handing it to me.

"Sure," I said.

I watched Billie follow Clyde charging back through the crowd. Everyone watched, but only the students looked surprised. For us, it was just things going back to normal.

"What was that?" Evan asked, coming up beside me and picking up a full cup of punch.

"He said he wanted to talk to her," I said. "Looked pretty crazy, too."

"Hmm," Evan said, and I could tell by the look on his face that he was thinking something.

"What?" I asked. "Do you know something?"

"When I was at the mall today getting your corsage, I saw him fighting with Ms. Lindsey."

"Really?" I looked at the door to see if Billie had come back inside.

"Yeah, I didn't want to get involved, but he looked so torn up when she stormed off that I asked him if he was okay and he said she broke up with him. Said she was in love with her ex and wasn't coming back to Black Warrior next year. I didn't say anything because I figured Billie would tell you."

"She doesn't know," I said. "But I wonder what their breaking up has to do with Billie."

"Who knows with those two," Evan said, and then Billie came rushing back into the room.

At first I thought she was angry, but then she flicked her hand up in the air and screamed so loud that I could hear her even over the music, "I'm engaged!"

"What?" Evan asked.

"I'm engaged!" Billie said to every face she passed in the crowd. Clyde was behind her, standing tall and proud, smiling at everyone as they congratulated them. Everyone was clapping and then Billie was standing right in front of me with the ring on her finger and Clyde at her side.

"Congrats, man," Evan said to Clyde.

"Can you believe it?" Billie said, hugging me. "He just asked me outside." She looked down at the sparkling ring and then back at me. "Can you, Journey? Can you believe it?"

"No," I said, and seeing how happy my friend looked, I didn't have the heart then to say what I was really thinking—that Clyde had done this because Ms. Lindsey was leaving to find Benji. I hugged Billie again and kissed her on the cheek.

After that, the prom became a kind of engagement party for Clyde and Billie. They led the electric slide and when the king and queen went up on stage to claim their royal crowns, they handed them off to Clyde and Billie. I was so happy to see her getting what she wanted for once. And then I thought maybe I was wrong. Maybe Clyde did want to marry Billie and Ms. Lindsey's leaving only helped him see it. I knew he loved her. And I knew she loved him. I couldn't see myself bursting Billie's bubble. Not then.

Chapter Twenty-three

It was the close of the 7:30 service at the church. Tired and sleepy-eyed, I'd inched out of bed that morning to follow our old ritual of going to church right after the prom and before the graduation ceremony. When I was in high school, I thought it was so absurd that they'd have the prom on Saturday night when most of us had to be in church the next day and we'd also have graduation right after that. But the older I got, the more it made sense. If kids knew they had to be in church at the early service the next day in order to make graduation in the afternoon, they were less likely to be out in the street too long after the prom. While this didn't keep them from breaking even their extended curfews, it gave the adults something to laugh at as the kids crept miserably to their seats at church, some just an hour or so after getting home from wherever. Nana Jessie said that the church service between prom and graduation was once considered a send-off, the last time many of the kids would congregate in their church as official members before leaving for college. Back then, she'd said, some of them were going a long way. They were catching rides all the way up to Wilberforce in Ohio, Howard in Washington, D.C., and Hampton in Virginia. Many of these routes still weren't safe for them. And transportation and lodging were few and far between. The church gathered to bless them. To lay hands on them before they headed out into the world.

My father was in the pulpit. Dressed in a kente cloth robe one of the African church members had specially made for him, he was pensively looking out into the seats as the choir sang "Grateful" together with him at the lead.

"*Flowing from my heat are the issues of my heart./Is gratefulness,*" they sang as my father embellished with "hallelujah" in his tenor voice.

Grateful
Grateful
Grateful

The tenors roared.

Grateful
Grateful
Grateful

The altos chanted.

And just before the sopranos began to cry out, I was on my feet shouting.

Grateful
Grateful
Grateful

I joined in, praying for God's mercy over my actions

as I lifted my hands, my palms facing upward for just one touch from God.

"I'm not a perfect man. Never have been," my father said as the choir began to hum softly behind him. "I've tried. Lord knows, I've tried." I looked to see my mother's eyes transfixed on him. She moved not once. Just kept her hands on the Bible. "But I learned long ago that there are no perfect men. Just us all down here striving to be. Just to be. *Be.* And we fall. And sometimes we stay there. But you know, church—" Taking my seat, I watched as he paused and took a sip of the water sitting beside his Bible. "I've never been surprised to see a man fall. What surprises me is what he does when he falls down. Who he talks to. Goes to. Chats with. And, church, that's because it seems that when most men are down, they go to everyone and everything else but their Creator to get fixed. We self-medicate. We drink. We smoke. We cheat." A humbling silence unfolded around my seat and almost visibly swam around to my brother and rolled up to my father's feet. "We pay thousands of dollars to sit in a chair and talk to some other man who has problems of his own. And I'll never know why we do this. Why we don't go to the Maker, take it to the altar."

The organist hit a chord and the entire congregation, even the tired and reluctant kids who'd been forced out of bed after the prom, began to make indistinct sounds in agreement.

"When your car is broken, you don't take it to the dry cleaner's. You don't take it to the grocery store. No. You take it to the fix-it man. Someone who has experience fixing that particular item."

"Yes, pastor," someone called out, springing to her feet. "Tell it now."

"And if you're really smart, you'll bypass the fix-it man altogether. Yes, he has experience with that particular item, but he didn't make it. You realize that if you really want to get that thing fixed the right way—"

The choir continued to hum and the organist struck another chord to carry my father's break.

"If you really want it done right . . . you take it to the maker." He balled his hand into a fist and brought it to his mouth briefly before going on. "And that's good news. Because if you know that, then you must know that when something is wrong with you. When you're out searching for help to get back on your feet. When something has come into your life that was so hard that it rocked your very foundation and made you question everything that you thought you were—"

My eyes filled with tears, I looked up into the section by the door where I'd seen Benji standing the other week. I wanted so hard not to see him there again. Not to find him in a crowd of a million and have him lead me to Dame. I wanted a clean heart. A clean mind. A clean spirit. I prayed and clutched Evan's hand as I closed my eyes and turned my head away.

"There's only one God—your Creator—who can fix that. And, church, I'm so grateful," he went on as the choir became louder again. "I'm so grateful that our Creator is so merciful. So present. His doors are always open. Mr. Fix-It. The people who made your car. They might all be closed. But God, your Creator, never closes. Never turns away. Never forgets you. God is there in the midst of the storm, waiting to hold your hand and pull you out of the water. And for this, we should forever be grateful."

The organist replayed the melody leading to the chorus and we all stood up as one church to sing along. May holding my left hand and Evan holding my right, we sang about how grateful we were to God for life, for stability, for redemption. And I felt every word.

The air outside was much too cool for it to be a May day in Alabama. While we were in church, the dew was supposed to lift from the grass and the sun was to dry the tips of the trees. But as Evan noted when we got into the car to head to the school for the graduation ceremony, it was nearly chilly. And that was a good thing.

We let the top on the car down. We wanted to possibly catch the last of good breezes that would surely stop when June came. Riding along, I thought of everything my father said about going to the Maker. About redemption and being grateful for the second chance that God was willing to give. I thought of my father and how many times he'd hurt my mother, and how my brother was now doing the same thing to May and I'd almost done it to Evan. We all seemed so ungrateful for what was standing right in front of us. Like my mother and like May, Evan wasn't a perfect man. But he loved me. And I had to find a way to love him back. I had to feel for him the way I'd convinced myself I was feeling for Dame.

"You really think Billie is going to marry Clyde?" Evan asked when we pulled into the parking lot at the school.

"I don't know," I said. "I thought if anyone was

sure, you'd be sure. You're always talking about how much they can't live without each other."

"I know," he agreed. "But sometimes, I think maybe I just want for them what I have with you."

I looked at him as we pulled into a spot.

"What do we have?" I asked, not knowing I'd even had the question in my mind.

"After twenty-five years you have to ask that?" Evan laughed in disbelief. "Don't be silly, Journey."

"You say twenty-five years like we're so old. Like this is just it for us. We're only thirty-three."

"This isn't it?" he said, taking my hand. "Because I thought it was. Just you and me. Growing old on the porch together." He looked into my eyes playfully.

"So you don't ever think that maybe there's someone else out there for you? Like another life or something."

"Damn, girl! Where are these questions coming from?"

"I don't know . . . I just—Forget it." I took off my seat belt and got out of the car with Evan.

"Look," I went on. "I'm going to the chorus room to get the choir together. I guess I'll meet you back at the car."

Evan walked around the car and took me into his arms.

"Okay," he said, kissing me on the forehead and stopping to look into my eyes again.

"What?" I asked as he just stood there and stared.

"There's no one else for me. No other life I want to have. This is it," he said earnestly.

"That's good to know," I said. "Really good to know."

* * *

The was no room left in the bleachers on the football field. Not one space. And the grass surrounding the seats that had been set up before the stage for the graduates was covered with people—old and young, in baby strollers and leaning on walkers, men and women, from here and everywhere, waiting to get a glimpse at Black Warrior's class of 2008. This was how it always was. Homecoming and graduation at Black Warrior pulled people out from all over. Some knew graduates; some didn't. Some went to Black Warrior; some hadn't. But they were all there. Packed in like this was the social event of the year. And it had been at one time. And this year, after that million-dollar check, it definitely was. Everyone wanted to claim the alma mater. To finally say how proud they were of Black Warrior. And my kids in the choir, who'd only heard bad things about their school up until all of the attention that came with the check, were beaming as we lined up in the rows to the right of the stage set aside for the choir.

"All these people here to see the seniors?" Opal asked as she walked past to get to her seat with the sopranos.

"They sure are," I said proudly.

"I hope they come out like this when it's my turn," she added.

When everyone was in position and the graduates had finally marched in to their processional, I led the choir singing "Lift Ev'ry Voice and Sing" and then Mr. Williams gave his opening remarks. Afterward, he invited Evan to the stage to speak on behalf of the school board, and as Evan stood at the podium, I watched and noticed how natural he seemed speaking in front of our community. People listened and bent forward as he thanked—without belittling anyone—the community for working with him to build a better school for our children. He thanked them for supporting him, lifting him up and letting him lead the school. He said he knew this was not easy, as so many others had led them in wrong directions in the past. Listening, I realized I'd forgotten how passionately Evan felt about what he did. This was easy to forget day to day as he tried to climb up the political ladder. Then, he seemed so determined to just be on top of everything that it looked like he didn't care who was at the bottom. But now, surrounded by our friends and family, I saw a glimpse of the man I knew in my heart he was.

I looked out into the audience and thought of how lucky I was to have him. How many women out there would be happy to actually have Evan. He was a blessing I was fortunate enough to receive early on in my life and at that moment, I was grateful for it.

"Now," Mr. Williams said back up at the podium, "we'll have the choir sing a song that's always been sung during the graduation ceremony here at Black Warrior, 'Swing Low, Sweet Chariot.' "

I got up and turned, raising my hands to signal for the choir to get on their feet. I stood there, looking at them, moving my eyes from face to face, feeling their excitement about what we were about to do. As they must've been, I was nervous but equally energized and ready to show everyone our new composition. Smiling at Opal and then Zenobia and then Devin who was leading the tenors and another boy, Trent, whose sister was in the graduating class, I winked to let them know that whether the audience liked it or not, we did and that was all that mattered.

And then, when I was about to gesture for the pianist to begin the music, I lowered my hand. I thought, right then that if I wanted the audience to really hear the beauty of our new arrangement, it should be unaccompanied. Zenobia was right. We should sing it the way we had in the classroom. Just us letting the words vibrate around us.

I shook my head to the pianist and stepped toward the choir.

"A cappella," I whispered. Their eyes widened and then I witnessed smiles curling up on faces sporadically. Zenobia winked back at me and smiled, too.

"Watch for my hand and then come in just as you did in practice," I added.

They straightened up and I could feel the crowd growing restless behind us.

I closed my eyes briefly and took a deep breath. I opened them, counted to three, and raised my hand in front of my chest to begin conducting the song.

Nana Jessie used to have this saying. When I came off the altar after singing a solo, she'd pull me to her breasts and whisper in my ear, "Sounds like the flapping of angels' wings." And that's how my students sounded on the first notes. They hit "Swing low, sweet chariot" crisp and clean, so defined and so articulate that I was sure everyone in the whole outdoors could hear them. Standing in front of them, their voices made me quiver through and through and I hardly had to direct. I don't know if it was the crowd or the occasion, but these young people poked out their chests and stood tall and proud, hitting notes as if they were a professional gospel choir. From stanza to stanza, some looked at me, their eyes alert and clear, as if they too were surprised at how melodious their voices sounded as they met the open air. It was a moment of chance confidence, of reverence to the blood that had no doubt been shed beneath our feet. And suddenly, the reason we sang that song, year after year, for so many years, left me full as they sang:

If I get there before you do
Coming for to carry me home
I'll cut a hole and pull you through
Coming for to carry me home

This wasn't a song about dying. It was about living. About getting free and starting a new life. Being reborn. Not as a slave to man and his rules. But free of sin and washed clean in the river. They sang:

If you get there before I do
Coming for to carry me home
Tell all my friends I'm coming, too
Coming for to carry me home

And I started crying. For our past and the students who'd come through Black Warrior by the river for which the school was named, for which Tuscaloosa was even named—"the Black Warrior" in Choctaw. And out of this place those students, the sons and daughters of slaves, for generations went on to become great. To become what they dared them not to. And then I cried for my students. Who it seemed time had turned its back on. Zenobia and Opal. And the others. Who had endless talent—all of them—but nothing seemed to be tapping into it. They needed a sweet chariot right now. And their voices were calling for it to just swing low to catch them from falling.

Everyone was silent when the last note was sung and the song had ended. But I wasn't nervous. I just stood there looking at my children and smiled, not bothering to wipe my tears. I'd performed enough to know what this kind of silence meant. And even with my back turned to the crowd, I knew then that they'd felt what I was feeling. They remembered. And they wanted more. It was like in church when my father signaled for the pianist to keep on going. Play the chorus again. People were fired up and the Spirit was turned loose in the crowd. And if the choir didn't keep it going, then somebody else, Nana Jessie or one of the other church mothers, would just stand up and start her own song, lead the praise until we were all full.

And then, as if she was thinking just what I was thinking and had forgotten we were at the high school graduation and not Prophet House, Zenobia just started the song again altogether. Alone. In the sweetest, most peaceful voice I'd ever heard, she sang, with tears in her eyes, "Swing low, sweet chariot."

Then I raised my hands and the choir joined in behind her. But what happened next was what moved me the most. I felt sound hit the back of my head, as if it was coming from booming speakers. The audience, I turned to see, was on its feet, singing now, too. The same notes, the same lyrics, the same cadence, as if they'd learned to sing that same song at Black Warrior. Even the graduates and the guests and stakeholders on the stage joined in and we were one choir in praise.

It was the most touching thing I'd ever experienced at Black Warrior. And when we were done, the crowd cheered the choir on so lovingly that Mr.

Williams joked he was putting all of the million dollars the school got into the music department. That would've been nice.

As I walked back to the car to meet Evan to head to my parents' house for their annual postgraduation barbecue, people stopped me every two steps I took.

"Great job!"

"That was amazing!"

"I hope you get the million dollars for real!"

"We need more teachers like you!" Everyone had something positive to say in my ear. And I couldn't help but to remember how nervous I'd been about the new arrangement and singing the song a cappella. If only the one person who'd inspired me to do that could've been there.

"Not too bad, music teacher," Angie Martin said when I walked past her car. And I insisted I was going to just keep walking as I normally did, but filled with pep, I stopped.

I tossed my hip to the side and put my hand on my waist like Billie always did when she was about to tell someone off.

"Well, the way you watch me, you should know," I said, rolling my eyes and giving her as much cattiness in my one line as I could to make up for the years I'd just walked by. I was tired.

"Okay," she said. She dropped her keys and looked completely stunned.

"And by the way," I started (I was on a roll), "why don't you try worrying about your own life—about your own students and what you can do for them—and stop sweating me!" Not bothering to wait for a response. I dropped my hand from my waist and sashayed the rest of the way to the car.

I was about to drop my purse and hightail it when I saw a certain somebody standing with his back to me between Billie and Evan at the car. It was the silhouette of a body I'd looked at thousands of times as I played babysitter and kept his head from hitting the hard edges of the wooden pews as he toddled around at church.

"Justin!" I hollered, extending my arms before he could even turn around to see me.

"Big sister!" He turned and ran toward me, ready to embrace.

I stood there, locked in my baby brother's arms for at least a minute before I would let loose. I hadn't seen him since Christmas when he and my father got into a huge fight after my father asked why he wasn't married yet and what in the hell was he doing with his life in Atlanta anyway. He was almost accusing Justin of being gay, and for once I just wished he'd come out and say it. Just say it and stop allowing the whispers and secrets to make him lie about who he really was to everyone he knew and loved most. But Justin stormed out, and just as he did almost every holiday, he swore he'd never come back to my father's house again.

He looked good. He'd clearly been putting on some weight in his hips, but he looked good. Like a younger and more strikingly handsome version of my father and Jr, Justin had a strong, almost Anglo angle to his jaw line, high cheekbones and a dimple in his chin that made him look like he belonged on a runway in Paris. In fact, when he was a little boy, his features were so pure and almost pretty that everyone thought he was a little girl. My mother, who doted over Justin hopelessly, always connected his handsome genes with her grandfather, a full-blooded Choctaw, who married her white grandmother.

"Baby brother," I said, welling up again. "I can't believe you made it."

"You know I had to come home to see the baddest choir in the land!"

"And they did sound like that today, too," Billie jumped in, coming over to hug me as well.

"They were good," I added. "I was so proud."

"You worked hard enough," Evan said.

"And then when everyone started singing," I said, "that was amazing." I wouldn't let go of Justin. It was like I was afraid he'd just disappear. I had so much to tell him. So much to share about what had been going on with me.

"Yeah, Mama was crying," Justin said.

"Where are they?" I asked. "Mama and Daddy?"

"They went back to the house, so they could make sure Ms. Cobb and Fanny had everything laid out like they like it," Justin answered, referring to the two cooks my mother always hired when we were expecting guests at the house for a barbecue. They knew how to cook, but my mother liked things organized a certain way and my father was pretty particular about his barbecue. He seasoned everything himself the night before and insisted on working the grill. "I told them I'd hitch a ride with you."

"I guess we'd better head over there, then," I said. "I'm starving."

"Actually," Billie said, frowning, "I was coming over to say I wasn't going to make it over to your parents'. I'm going to Clyde's family barbecue."

"Wait a second, guys." I excused myself from Evan

and Justin and pulled Billie to the side. I couldn't believe she was obviously still considering marrying Clyde. After the prom, I finally got the nerve to tell her everything Evan said about seeing Ms. Lindsey and Clyde fighting at the mall. This had to matter in her decision.

"Are you still going to do this?" I asked. "I mean, after everything he's put you through?"

"I love him," she replied.

"I know you love him, but it's just not right. He's not going to change just because he asked you to marry him. He's still the same Clyde."

"And I'm still the same Billie and I don't know how to love anyone else. So I'm going to take this chance and see what he's talking about. After all that's happened, that's the least I can do."

"But you can do better than be with a man who only wants to be with you because he thought you were with someone else . . . someone you hired," I whispered so Evan and Justin couldn't hear me. "Do you really want that to be how your marriage begins? That he came to you because of that and because Karen left him?"

"I don't even know anymore," she said. "I just know I have to try. You don't know what it's like to want someone to love you like this for so long and then to finally get it. I know it's not all right, but it's just . . . what I got. And I have to know if it'll work."

"I got your back," I mouthed.

"Good or bad?"

"Good or bad."

We hugged and Billie looked down at her ring.

"Now if I could only get this fool to give me a mansion, we're onto something," she said. "That and my red drop top!"

As Billie headed to her car and I rejoined Evan and Justin, I said a prayer that she finally got what she wanted from Clyde all these years—true love. And while I knew it was a shot in the dark, if she was strong enough to still have hope, I had to hope, too.

"Okay, I guess that leaves us three," I said, linking back up with Justin.

"More bad news," Justin said.

"What?"

"I'm going to hitch a ride with John," Evan said. "He's swinging over here now to get me." He looked down at his watch. "Said he has something to show me."

"Are you serious?" I protested. "But it's a family day."

"He's said it's really serious. I'll have him drop me by your parents' if we end early."

"Work. Work. Work," I repeated. I moved over to hug Evan good-bye. "Will I really get to see you later?" I asked, feeling the happiness of the moment.

"Sure, sweetheart." He kissed me and when he moved to step away, I saw in Evan's eyes a trace of worry.

"Everything okay?" I asked as he opened the car door for me.

"Everything's fine. You guys go ahead. I'm sure I'll be over shortly."

He closed the door and stepped up to the curb beside the car.

"So, Ms. Thing, what is going on?" Justin said when we finally pulled out.

I kept my eyes on Evan in the rearview mirror. When we got across the parking lot, I saw John's car pull up and Evan got in.

"What do you mean?" I shifted the mirror.

"Jr's acting all crazy. May was reading scripture in the dining room when I left to come here. And Mama and Daddy hardly said two words to each other."

"It's a lot of stuff," I said, telling Justin all about Jr's affair and how I'd run into his live-in mistress at our old house. He and May were still awaiting the paternity results and she swore she was going to stick by her husband's side.

"Well, that explains the Bible being everywhere," Justin said.

"I don't know why she'd even try to put herself through more of Jr's garbage, but she's prepping herself for the role of her lifetime."

"Speaking of preacher's wives, what's up with Mama and Daddy?"

"I don't know, Justin," I said. "I had lunch with Mama a few weeks ago and she claimed she was upset with Daddy because he's expanding the church, but then I saw her speaking to Deacon Gresham."

"From the church?" he asked.

"Yeah. And you know he's a divorce attorney."

"Just because Mama was talking to a divorce attorney doesn't mean she's leaving Daddy," Justin reasoned. "She'd never do that."

"I don't know. She could just be fed up. Anyway, I'm just waiting for the first shoe to drop, so I can know what's going on with her. But you know Mama; she'll never talk about herself," I said. "But what's up with you, Atlanta Man? I'm sure you're making it happen in the big city. I see you're putting on a little weight. Must be eating good."

"I actually wanted to talk to you about that."

"About putting on weight?"

"Not that directly," Justin started, and I could feel

the uneasiness in his voice. Turning onto my parents' street, I slowed down the car a bit and rolled the windows up so I could hear him. "But more about the reason I came home. I think it's time I told all of you about my life." He paused. "This is really hard for me." His voice weakened.

"Justin," I said, pulling into my parents' driveway, "you don't have to tell me anything. I know about your sexuality and I want you to know that I will always accept you. I'm your big sister and I'll always love you."

"Do you really mean that?"

"Of course I do. And you know, they'll have to accept it, too. I know it will be hard, but it's time for us all to stop living these lies. I've gone through some things recently myself. And I just realized how lucky I am. I just want us all to be happy."

Justin placed his hand on top of mine on the gearshift between our seats and gripped it tightly.

"You don't know how much it means to me to hear that from you. I've been living a lie for a long, long time. And it's time for my family to know who I really am."

"It's a tough job, but somebody's got to do it!"

"I hear ya." He let my hand go, and we got out of the car and walked to the door in silence.

"Wait," I said when he went to open the door.

"What?"

"Before we go inside, I have something else I want to say to you. And it's that I'm so proud of you. That you left and made your life on your own terms. I always told you, you were the lucky one. And I really believe that. You didn't let this place numb you. Take away your vision. That makes you more than lucky; that makes you free. More free than I'll ever be."

"Big sister, you're talking like you're eighty years old. If you want to change your life, just go out and do it," he said, sounding like Kayla.

"It's not that simple—I have Evan; I have—"

"It is that simple. If there's one thing I've learned on my own, it's that when you're numb, you pinch yourself," he said passionately. "When you ain't free, you get free. There are no other options. We only get to do this once."

"Thank you," I said. "Now let's go in here and get something to eat before you make me cry for the third time today!"

Justin opened the front door for me. As I walked by, I saw a glint of light shimmering from his eyelid. I turned to him and blinked.

"A sparkle," I said.

"What?"

"You have a sparkle on your eyelid." I reached over and plucked it off. "Probably from my eye shadow."

"Probably."

"Excuse me," a voice called from behind Justin. We both turned to see a woman standing at the foot of the steps. It was Kim.

"Can we help you?" Justin asked.

"Yes, you can," she answered slyly.

"Oh." I laughed uneasily to hide my confusion. Justin didn't know who she was and the last thing I wanted was for him to get loud and lead everyone in the house to the door. "This is my friend from work, Kim. I'll handle this."

"You sure?" Justin looked at me oddly, I guessed hearing the tension in my voice.

"Yeah, we just need to handle something with the

choir," I managed, daring Kim to say anything to the contrary with my eyes.

"Okay," Justin said. He looked from her to me and squinted his eyes. "Don't take too long. You know the natives get restless when someone's holding up dinner."

"I won't," I replied as Justin walked away slowly.

"She won't." Kim tried to step up to see inside, but I came outside quickly and shut the door behind me.

"You have some nerve coming here," I said. "This is my parents' house. Whatever drama you have with Jr needs to be handled somewhere else."

"Oh, I plan on handling my 'drama' all right," Kim said, puckering her painted red lips. A black car was parked beside mine and I could see the little boy's face pressed against the back window. "I just needed to give Jr something."

"What?"

She reached into her purse and pulled out an envelope.

"His results." She handed the envelope to me and folded her arms. "It's still sealed. I ain't need to open it. Jr knows damn well that's his son."

"Mama," he cried.

"Look, I have to go," Kim said. "My problem's not with you. Just give Jr the results and tell him he needs to take care of his fucking responsibilities. We ain't going nowhere. This boy needs to know his family. He's a Cash."

"I'll give this to him. You just leave," I said. Kim rolled her eyes and walked toward the car. "And don't you worry," I looked at the boy's face, "if he's a Cash, we'll know him soon enough."

After watching Kim pull away in the car to make

sure she'd actually left, I walked into the house with the envelope in my hand.

"What's that?" May asked, standing right inside the door.

"Just a note," I lied. I'd already decided to keep the envelope to myself until after dinner. Then I'd give it to Jr.

"I already saw her, Journey. It's the results."

"She asked me to give it to Jr."

May put out her hand.

"May, I think it's best he looks first and then you two talk. . . . I don't want to get in the middle of it."

"You already are," she said. Her hand was still extended. "Just give it to me."

"May, just promise you'll wait until after dinner. Justin just came home and this is supposed to be a celebration. You know—"

"Give it to me!" May's voice splintered with an anger and sadness that broke me. I handed her the envelope.

Outside, everywhere was brightness. My mother was telling some story about how when we were younger, Jr almost put Justin's eye out with a firecracker. Justin cried for three days and couldn't hear in his left ear. Everyone was laughing—my parents, Jr, Justin, and even Nana Jessie. Everyone but me and May. Sitting right across from each other, we avoided eye contact and every time she went to whisper to Jr, I was sure she was about to say something about the little envelope. After she took it, she ran to the bathroom and didn't come out until it was time to eat, so I was sure she knew the results. And while everyone was laughing, there still seemed to be an ominous air hovering over the picnic table we shared. I could see the smoke from the grill drifting by, but I knew there was more than a promise of barbecue. Something wicked was on its way.

"Well, family," Justin started as everyone tried to recall a part of the firecracker story.

"No," I said, tugging at his pants leg. He was sitting next to me, and I didn't want him to share his secret. I knew now wasn't the time.

"What?" he said to me.

"Just don't do it now," I murmured. "Let's wait. Now isn't the time."

"But what about what you said in the car?" he whispered. "I'm tired of hiding."

"Just wait," I demanded.

"What's that, Journey?" my father called from the head of the table, stroking his new beard.

"Nothing. I was just telling Justin how happy I am that he's home with us." I smiled.

Everyone smiled and Nana Jessie, who was seated on the other side of Justin, kissed him on the cheek.

"Thanks, Nana," Justin said to her. "I hope everyone will still feel that way, because I have an announcement."

I grabbed Justin's arm, but he just brushed me off with a resolute stare.

"This is really hard for me, everyone, but it's time for me to stop lying to you about who I am," Justin said, pushing himself up in his seat to command everyone's attention. I shifted away from him to the other side of my chair and rested my face in the palm of my hand.

"No, Journey, don't be scared." He tapped my shoulder.

"Scared of what?" my father asked, straightening

up in his seat, too. Like everyone else at the table, he seemed to know what Justin was about to reveal. "What do you have to say, boy?"

"No, Jethro," my mother said from her end of the table beside Nana Jessie. "You won't intimidate him. Go ahead, baby. You tell us. But before you say anything, I just want you to know I already know and I love you. I'm willing to accept that you're gay."

"Oh, hell, no," Jr chided.

"No, let's stop pretending," my mother went on worriedly. "We all know. Let's just let it go and move on."

"No, we won't, not in this house," my father declared.

"Gay?" Nana Jessie repeated, looking at Justin. "You're gay?"

"Oh, no," I sighed.

"But that's not it, Mama," Justin said and I turned to look at him.

"What?" I asked.

"I mean, I am gay," he went on.

"That's it; stop it!" My father banged his fist on the table and we all jumped.

"No, Dad, you stop. I've been living this stupid lie all of these years because of you. And I'm not going to hide anymore."

My father, shocked by Justin's unusual defiance, fell back in his chair and glared at my mother.

"Do you all want to know why I haven't been coming home?" Justin began. "I've been hiding myself in Atlanta because I've been living as a woman for two years."

For the first time since I sat down, I looked directly across the table at May. I had to see—to see if someone else had heard what I'd heard. Because all there was now was silence. But looking at May, it was clear this was because they all indeed had witnessed the same thing. And then my mother groaned.

"Oh, no, Justin," she said, her voice emptied of confidence.

Next to him, Nana Jessie's face flattened.

"Boy, you stop it!" my father shouted.

"I'm going through my changes right now," Justin said, continuing his revelation in the din of our objections.

"Changes?" my mother asked.

"Surgically. I'm having sexual reassignment surgery."

"Sexual reassign . . . what?" Nana Jessie asked, holding her ear out.

"I'm getting a sex change."

I looked at Justin and realized that the weight I thought he'd put on at the school was actually a bust line and even though he was sitting, on his little frame, exactly the opposite of my father's and Jr's, his hips had widened.

"Are you serious?" I asked, still putting the whole thing together in my mind.

"Baby brother," Jr said, chuckling cruelly. "I always knew you were a sissy. Now, I know you were always a girl."

"Fuck you," Justin shot back.

"Oh, now you're talking like a girl, too . . . wonderful."

"You two stop it," my mother jumped and I could hear in her voice she was crying. "You stop and Justin, you go and just—" Her voice cracked and she began crying into a napkin she was holding.

"Mama," Justin said, getting up and going to my mother, "I'm not trying to hurt you. This is who I am.

It's who I've always been." He massaged her shoulders and tried to wipe her tears, but there was no consoling her.

"You let go of my wife!" my father hollered. "You've done enough in this house."

"Your wife?" Justin looked at my father like he was looking at a stranger. "She's my mother."

"Not anymore," my father said. "You get your things and get the hell out."

"Daddy, that's not necessary," I tried.

"This is not a house of sin and what I say goes," my father said so harshly it came out in a whisper and I knew not to say another word. I just looked at Justin standing there alone to let him know I was feeling his hurt. "Go!"

"So, you don't want me here?" Justin said and now he was crying, too.

"If I get up from my seat, so help me Jesus, I will remove you from this house myself." My father slowly backed up his seat, and I sat stunned, knowing this was more anger coming from him than any of us had known. His eyes were already red and I could see the veins bulging in his neck.

"Fine," Justin said. "I'll go. But I'm still a member of this family and some day you will all have to face who I am. Do you think you're the first family to go through this? Well, you're not. And you won't be the last. None of this changes who I am. Don't let it change you."

"Justin," I called, getting up, when he turned to leave but my father banged his fist so hard on the table this time that I flinched.

"Don't you dare follow him," he ordered me and at once, I realized I was in my father's house. "No one moves."

Justin looked at me and I looked back sympathetically. I could hear our mother crying. I was too overwhelmed with the pain at both sides of the table to choose a side to fight for. I loved my brother and he was hurting. But I also loved my father and I knew, even in his anger, he was hurting, too.

Justin walked into the house. And no one moved.

"What are we going to do, Jethro?" my mother asked. "We can't just let the boy leave like that. He's too upset."

"Let him go." Jr shrugged. Then, smiling maniacally as if nothing had happened, he reached past May and picked up a corn cob and began to chew on it. "Anybody hungry?" he asked.

"Don't be a jerk, Jr," I said, pushing my plate away from me.

"One less brother in this family for me to worry about," he said. "Yeah. . . . That's two girls and one boy now. Right, Dad? Or is it more?"

"Don't say that," I said, not understanding how Jr could be so cruel to everyone. "Daddy has nothing to do with this."

"Hush, Jr," my mother pleaded.

"Oh, that old man doesn't scare me anymore," Jr managed between bites of his corn. "If he wasn't so busy running around out in the street with his other son, maybe this one wouldn't be so fucking soft. You know?" Jr looked at me with ice in his eyes.

"What do you mean?" I asked.

"Stop it, Jr," my mother demanded. "That's enough."

I looked at my father on the other end of the table and he was sitting back and staring at Jr.

"I don't know, Journey," Jr went on and pointed his half-eaten cob at my father. "Ask your father about his other son. About how all these years, he's been lying to us."

"What is he talking about, Daddy?"

"You shut your mouth," my father said venomously.

"No, you shut your mouth," Jr snapped, slamming down the cob. "I don't have time for this shit anymore. I'm tired of this family's crap." He leaned in toward the middle of the table. "Old Jethro here has had his very own secret family right under our noses. Right at the church. Right in the pulpit."

"Jr, stop it," May tried now, but Jr only pulled away from her.

"It appears," Jr went on, "that Jack Newsome isn't a Newsome at all. He's a Cash. The oldest of the Reverend Doctor Cash's sons. And the next in line to the throne." He laughed.

"Oh, Jr," my mother said. "Why couldn't you just shut up?"

"Jack Newsome? He's what?" I looked at my father again for a sign of dissension.

"He's *your* brother," Jr said, and with the last word it sounded as if he'd finally felt some vindication in his exposure.

"No," I said, but my father did not move or object.

"Daddy, say it's not real," I implored him, bracing myself.

I watched a tear form in the corner of his eye.

"Can't even say anything to your family, can you?" Jr said. "After all these years of supporting Jack and his mother—taking them on vacations and making sure Jack got into your alma mater—I heard you even went to the parents' weekend with his mother—of doing the right thing by them and you can't do the right thing by your own family and just tell us the truth? From your own mouth?"

My father gnawed at his lip and got up from the table with a kind of sad resolve that let me know he'd never admit anything Jr was saying.

"That's right," Jr spat to his back as he walked away. "Just leave us and go about your business of doing good in the community. Make sure you stop by Jack's!"

"Oh, no," Nana Jessie said, getting up to follow my father.

"How could you treat your father like that?" my mother cried.

"No," Jr said. "How could he treat *us* like that?"

I felt ill—like I was about to vomit what little food that was in my stomach onto the table. I couldn't take it anymore. And then I remembered that this wasn't even what I'd feared when I sat down at the table.

"Evil is as evil sees," May uttered hard-heartedly.

"What?" Jr asked, and we all looked to her.

"You heard me," she said. "You should know about treating people wrong." She pulled the envelope from beneath the table and I felt my tonsils quiver as she flung it to the center.

"What's that?" my mother asked.

"Now who needs to tell?" May said to Jr. "Who needs to man up to his family now?" Her voice grew to a scream.

"You don't have to make me man up to a damn thing," Jr announced boldly. "I know exactly what it is."

"What?" my mother pressed.

"It's about my son."

"Your son? What? What are you talking about?"

"I have a son, Mama. His name is Jethro III and he's going to be coming to live with me," Jr said proudly.

"A son with who?" My mother looked at May.

"He's not your son, you jackass," May said.

"What?" Jr asked.

"Look at the letter. That boy ain't no more your son than he's mine."

"What?" I said, reaching for the envelope, which had fallen closer to me at the table. I pulled out the letter and opened the results.

"What does it say?" Jr asked.

"You're not the father." I read the results and they plainly said that there was less than a five-percent chance that Jr could be the father of Kim's child.

"I'm not?" Jr's expression quickly shrank. I tossed the results to him. "It can't be true. He looks just like me. He's mine."

"It is true, Jr," May said. "You lay down with a whore and now you have whore problems. . . . Let that woman lay up in your father's house and paid her off all these years . . . and for some child that's not even yours."

"You let a woman live where?" my mother asked.

"It can't be true," Jr repeated, looking over the letter again and again. "I was there when he was born."

"Well, evidently, you weren't there when he was conceived," May said. "And you know what else? I want a divorce."

"May, don't say something you'll regret," Jr said passively.

"All these years, I thought you were leading me and that I needed you for something. That I had to be here because nobody else would want me. But you know, after reading those results, I realized that all these years I've been letting a fool lead me around. And only a fool lets another fool lead."

May threw her napkin on the table. She got up from her seat and nodded to me.

"I'm thinking about myself now," she said. "And I'm not going to be a fool anymore."

"May, don't leave," my mother said, but this was only to May's back as she walked away from the table without looking back.

Jr just sat there with a vacant carelessness in his eyes.

"See what you did?" my mother cried to him as she got up from her seat, too. "You see?"

"I didn't do anything, Mama," he said flatly. "I was just being my father's son." He looked at her. "Maybe you should try looking at him for a change, because he made us how we are . . . all of us." He looked at me and through the corner of my eyes I saw my mother walk slowly from the table.

"You didn't have to do this," I said to Jr. "Not like this." I started crying and looked around the table to see that we were alone. Everything had changed. Justin had started it by saying he wasn't who we thought he was . . . and now I wasn't sure who any of us were . . . not really.

In the house, I found my mother sitting in her tea chair in the living room. It was where she always sat when she wanted to think and be alone, to plan, to pray.

"Your brother," she said as I sat in the chair beside her, "he took his bag. I should've stopped him. . . . Should've said something. He can't drive like that."

"He'll be fine, Mama," I said, still parsing out what

he'd told us. And it was strange because I wasn't really that surprised. Yes, I wondered what had led him to make such a big decision, but in a way, I was happy for him. He looked happy. He looked good. But it would be a long time before any of us truly accepted him. "Justin knows how to take care of himself."

"He was always a good boy. Never asked for anything. And the one time he does, I let your father just throw him out." She was holding a napkin in her hand, but she'd stopped crying. Instead of sadness, I saw anger in her eyes now.

"Was what Jr said about Daddy true?" I asked carefully. She didn't look at me. "Oh, God. How could he? How could he lie to us like that? All that stuff about what we can and can't do in this house . . . in our lives . . . and he was lying all along."

"He wasn't lying."

"What?"

"I knew. What do you think, I'm blind?" My mother looked at me quizzically. "I always knew about him and Iris Newsome. Always. And when Jack was born . . . just months before I was due with Jr, I just knew."

"Why didn't you say anything? Why didn't you leave him, Mama?"

"Leave? *You don't just leave.* Your father and I had plans," she said with her voice demanding and grim. "I knew what we could be together. What we could build. And that he loved me. He always loved me more than he loved any of them. Just like Jr, your father's just the kind of man who needs an audience. If he doesn't have a crowd of people following him, he feels empty. One person isn't enough. That's just his way. I can't leave him for that."

"But what about the divorce?"

"Divorce?"

"Yeah, when I saw you talking to Deacon Gresham when we had lunch," I said. "He's a divorce attorney. . . . I thought maybe you were thinking of leaving Daddy."

My mother looked off in a way that churned the bile in my stomach again.

"No, Mama," I said. "I know that's not it. Don't tell me that's it. Not that . . ."

"Timothy came to me when I had no one to go to."

"No, Mama," I cried. "But you can't. Not with everything you've said to me about marriage and love and accepting who I was and where I'm at . . ."

"Marriage is hard, Journey," she said. "It's very hard. And you have to work at it to stay. To keep it together. Nothing is perfect. You need to learn that."

"So working at it means you just pretend nothing's wrong and act like your blind while everyone is just . . . doing whatever?"

"It's not that simple . . . not the way you make it sound."

"I used to think that, too," I said. "But . . . now I think it should be."

In that room, the last promise holding my family together withered like an old rose petal orphaned at the bottom of a vase. If this was who we were, then who was I? What was I? What life was I living? Whose life was I living?

"You told me everything would be okay," I said and I wasn't sure if I was talking about her marriage or mine. "You sold this to me. You wanted all of this for me? Knowing what it was like?"

"So your life hasn't been good? I haven't protected you? Helped you make the right choices? You have a good husband. Don't throw it away because of what's happening in this house. Don't be a fool."

"No, Mama," I said, getting up. "My life hasn't been good. . . . It's not working . . . and maybe if you and everyone else hadn't been protecting me all these years, I wouldn't feel like I've been just . . . just . . . sleepwalking around in my life. Mama, I'm thirty-three years old and I feel like I haven't ever left home. Like I'm stuck here. And now I see that all of you are. And I'm just like you . . . just like you, and Daddy and Jr. . . . I'm stuck."

I just wanted to get home. To get into my house, up the stairs, and into my bed where I could be alone and stop the noise in my head from rumbling. It seemed that just when I thought I had a hold on one thing in my life, had figured things out and how to just be happy, everything else was unrecognizable. My parents. My brothers. My marriage. Even Billie and Clyde. My whole world that just one month ago was quiet and forgivably imperfect was now screaming and ruined. And I knew that the things that had just been said, the things that had been done, couldn't be changed or taken back now. We'd never be silent again.

Evan's car was pulled closer to the front door than usual and the door was wide open. I thought maybe he'd come out and walked around the back for something, but when I entered the house, I saw Evan sitting in the living with colored pieces of paper scattered everywhere around him.

"Evan?"

I walked over to him. His shirt was pulled out of

his pants and crumpled. His tie was gone. I could tell he'd been crying.

"What's wrong? What happened?" I walked closer and looked around at the papers. They were glossy pages from a magazine. My heart thumped hard and I felt my throat swell.

"Where did you go when you went to Atlanta?" Evan's voice was so low that it was frightening. He looked at me and the redness in his eyes seemed to infiltrate even his irises.

"What?" I asked, peeking at the pages he was still holding in his hand.

"Where were you?" he growled.

"I . . . Billie and I—"

"Don't lie to me!" Evan jumped up from his seat and pushed me in the center of my stomach until I was up against the wall next to the fireplace. "Don't fucking lie to me, Journey!"

"What? What is it?" I cried. "Tell me. Tell me what it is."

"You tell me where you were. You look at this and then you tell me where the fuck you were!" He handed me a page and in between two columns was a picture of me and Dame sitting on a furry red couch at the Apache. His arm was around me and at the bottom of the page was the date and a caption: "Dame chills with mystery beauty at concert in Atlanta."

I dropped the page and felt the last bit of air I had coming through my throat squeeze out. I crouched over and started coughing.

"You tell me," Evan screamed, spittle flying everywhere. "You tell me how my wife is in *People* magazine with a rapper when she told me"—he came over to me and banged me against the wall again—"she was going to see a play."

"I can explain," I tried. "It was—"

"I told you not to see him anymore. I told you not to see him anymore and you just went and did it. You did it. Why were you there? What were you doing?"

"He invited me and I just went."

"No! No! Don't lie to me. Because you could've told me that. You could've told me." He let me go and turned his back, knocking over a lamp as he walked away. "Are you sleeping with him?"

"No. . . . I wouldn't do that. You know that. . . . I just—we were just—"

"Then what is it?" He turned back to me. "Then why would you lie to me? I know something's going on. You won't even let me touch you anymore. Stopped talking about the baby. And I couldn't figure out why, but I knew something was going on with you."

"It was just a crush," I said. "Just a crush, but it's over now. I swear. I told him never to contact me again."

"He's a kid. He's a fucking kid."

"I tried not to . . ." I said, sitting down on the couch. "I tried to let it go, but he's just—"

"Just what?" Evan picked up some of the pages from the floor and threw them at me. "He can take you to parties and have you in magazines? Is that what you mean? He can take you out of this boring old house and away from your boring husband?" He came over to me. "What do you want? What do you want, Journey?" He bent down on his knee in front of me. "Because I swear to God I've been trying to give you what you want all my damn life and I can't seem to do it right. I give you everything." His head dropped and tears fell, salting the carpet between us. "My life. My whole fucking life and it's never enough."

"It is enough, Evan." I tried to touch him, but he pulled away.

"No, it's not." Evan looked back up at me and I saw in his eyes that he was broken. Broken inside. Past the tears, his eyes were shallow and empty like something had died. And then, just then, everything I was doing and how it must've affected him became so real. This wasn't sneaking around. This was pain. And if I never wanted to hurt anyone, to make anyone feel pain, it was Evan.

"I'm so sorry," I whimpered, wiping his tears. "I'm so so sorry."

"Do you love him?" he asked, stopping my hand on his cheek. And while my first instinct was to say no, I couldn't. I just couldn't. I hadn't even been sure if anything I was feeling for Dame was real until that moment, but then, it just was. And I couldn't lie about it.

I dropped my hand slowly and looked cautiously into Evan's eyes.

"Tell me," he blurted out, his voice cracking as tears poured down his cheeks again.

"I'm sorry," I whispered.

Evan fell back and began to weep.

"I'm sorry."

And I couldn't take it back. Seeing Evan, my best friend, my love for my whole life, crying on the floor for what had just been lost, I wanted so badly to take it back, but I couldn't. I was screaming inside and I couldn't stop it.

I stood up and tried my best to wipe my tears, but

I was shaking so hard that I couldn't hold my hand to my face.

"Where are you going?" Evan called when I reached the hallway. And I didn't know where I was going. I just knew I had to leave. I had to go somewhere quiet.

"Don't leave me," he said. And I turned to see him up and coming toward me.

"I'm not leaving you. I just . . . I need to go," I cried, picking up my purse.

"You can't leave me, Journey. We can work it out. We can try to make this work." He was stuttering and heaving.

"I have to go," I said. "I can't pretend anymore. We can't pretend anymore."

"No . . . no . . . no," he protested, grabbing the purse from my hand.

"Evan, we can't go back. We can't just go back and pretend anymore. I need to go and be alone, so I can figure this out."

"You're my wife," Evan blared.

"I'm in love with another man," I said and the words stabbed me so hard in the gut that they went through me. Through me and then through Evan.

He stepped back from me and dropped the purse.

"He can't love you like I can," he said. "There's no one in this world who's gonna love you like I can."

"But I have to find out. I have to go out in the world and find that out for myself."

The Listener

June 23, 2008
Sunset in the Sky

"Where were you going?" the white man seated behind me on the plane asked sympathetically. His name was Pete. He was an architect from Philadelphia who'd gone to Ghana to finalize a new contract for his company. Kweku and I gave up on locking him out of our conversation when we could actually hear him groaning in disagreement at my decision to go see Dame at the Apache. Then, we just stood up and leaned over the seats like teenagers on an overseas end-of-the-year school trip—chatting, laughing, and, me, sometimes crying.

The sky was growing calm with the setting of the sun. It wasn't gray yet. Just dull with streaks of pink and disappearing white clouds beneath us. The flight attendants announced that we'd soon be approaching our layover in Amsterdam.

"I didn't know where I was going—not for a long, long time," I said. "Once I got out of that house and was in my car, all of the big talk had folded up inside of me and I was

just driving. At first, I was on my way to see Dame in Atlanta, but then I realized how nuts that sounded. He wasn't expecting me; I'd just turned my back on him to be with Evan and I'd deleted every number I'd had for him from my phone. I was going nowhere."

Kweku's face had gone from displaying a measure of inquisitiveness and concern to empathy. His suit jacket was off. His knees were digging into the seat of his chair, and he rested his chin contemplatively in the palm of his hand.

"So for a long time I was driving in circles," I continued, "wound up on this idea that I was free anyway and I didn't care where I was going. I was just free. And I didn't know what I was free from . . . It was like all this time I'd been riding up on the edges of my life with training wheels. And suddenly, I felt like someone had kicked them off. Kicked them off and kicked me down and dared me to ride again without them. It felt kind of good. And then—"

"That feeling ran out?" Kweku asked.

"Either that or you were out of gas," Pete said.

"It was a little bit of both. I was on 20, headed east. My cell phone was in my hand and so many times I wanted to just call someone, but every person I thought I could call . . . I just didn't want to speak to anyone. I needed to be alone."

Kweku stood up and went to sit in the empty seat beside Pete.

"After an hour, I ran out of gas, so I stopped at a little out-of-the-way gas station off the highway. There were two pumps and no credit card slots on the machines, so I had to go inside," I said. "There was this old Hispanic woman working the register and after she swiped my card, she looked up at me and in the most surprising Southern voice said, 'Too late for you to be on the road, hon.' I looked at my watch. It was only a bit after eleven. 'We don't have no place for you to stay here, but if you go about ten miles up the road, they got some fancy hotels where you can rest for

the night. Cost you about thirty-five dollars,' she added. 'No, thanks, ma'am,' I said sweetly at the idea of a fancy hotel costing only thirty-five dollars a night. 'I'm just passing through.' I took the card, pumped my gas and got back on the highway. By this time I'd decided maybe I was going to see Justin. I could call him when I got into the city in the morning and go by his place to make sure he was all right after the blowup at the house. Then, when the lights on the highway went from dull and sparse to bright and frequent, I started seeing these fancy hotels the old woman was speaking of. It was a clump of two-star inns with light that shone onto the highway. I thought of maybe stopping and as I tried to decide which one was the fanciest—the one advertising free Internet or the other with HBO—I wondered when the big hotels would come charging down 20 into Tuscaloosa. And then I remembered something."

"What?" Kweku asked.

"A conversation Dame and I had once where he admitted he'd spent nearly a million in the past year at the Ritz-Carlton in downtown Atlanta. He had a big, fifteen-bedroom mansion with a pool, movie theater, and basketball court out in the suburbs of Atlanta, but he only stayed there when he had company. Otherwise, he said the house always seemed lonely and just too big. So, he spent most of his time in the penthouse at the Ritz-Carlton. It was in the middle of everything, the place was never quiet and it came with maid service."

"I wish I had that kind of money," Pete said. "I'd let my wife have the house and go live at the Days Inn!"

"Did you go to the Ritz?" Kweku asked as we chuckled at Pete's remark.

"I sure did. But by the time I got into Atlanta and the time change switched from Central to Eastern, it was after two in the morning."

"What happened?" Pete asked.

"I called the hotel for directions and after getting lost a few times, I ended up asking people on the street for help. And then when I pulled up outside of the place, my heart was beating so fast that I was sure I was about to go into cardiac arrest. The thought of him being so close, and me being so far and unable to touch him, made me ill. I was so nervous, so on edge. . . . I didn't even get out of the car. I sat there for hours, thinking of what he'd say when he saw me—if he'd see me at all. If he cared. If I'd just walked out on my life for nothing. Then the sun came up and I was sitting in my car half-asleep and half-awake trying to decide what I was going to do next." I wiped a tear from my cheek.

"The street sweepers came and went. People started walking up and down the sidewalks on their way to work. A couple of cop cars went by," I remembered. "I realized then that everything was still changing. I'd been in that car for hours, stuck in this limbo in my mind—not knowing if I should move forward or turn back—but the rest of the world was still going. Even after everything had changed for me, the rest of the world was still moving. And I had to as well."

"You left?" Peter sighed. It was as if we were both watching the same sad movie.

"No," I said with a slight grin. "I got out of the car."

Both Peter and Kweku were silent now. The two looked up at me leaning over the seat as if I was a film unfolding to the climax. Their eyes were wide and shiny. Their mouths just cracked open a little.

"I went into the lobby, sure I was going to be turned away, knowing there was no way the staff would just let me go up to the penthouse suite or even admit that Dame was staying there. But I had to see. At least try. I walked to the front desk, trying to remember my story—I was Damien Mitchell's sister, visiting from Alabama. I wanted to see him. I was still wearing a pink church dress and heels from

the graduation, so this was a believable tale. I didn't exactly resemble one of the groupies from the club. 'Can I help you?' one of the receptionists asked cheerfully. 'Yeah, I need—' I started, but at my side, I saw a familiar profile trudge to the counter."

"It was Dame!" Pete said triumphantly.

"No," I said. "It was Naima. Her hair was everywhere and she looked like she'd just crawled out of bed. I was happy to see someone that could connect me to Dame and tell me I was in the right place, but then I realized it was Naima, a woman I knew wanted to be with Dame at his hotel at six in the morning. My mind leaped into suspicion. The Wiz Billie had talked about was already being uncovered. Naima stood there, fumbling with her purse. It was as if she couldn't see me standing beside her. Or didn't care to. 'Naima?' I said. She looked at me, grinned emptily and said nothing. But I could tell she knew who I was. 'I'm looking for Dame,' I added. 'He's gone,' she said and then she looked at the receptionist. 'I need a cab.' Naima locked her eyes on the woman, dismissing me. 'Look,' I said, laboring not to sound defeated, 'I don't know what kind of relationship you and Dame have, but I was just wondering. . . . I just needed to see him.' Naima grunted and looked at me. 'There's no relationship. I pretended I was drunk and couldn't drive home last night from the club, but he made my ass sleep on the couch.' She exhaled and looked down at her nails pensively. 'Of course I tried. . . . But once again, all he could talk about was you. . . . Journey! Journey! Journey! Jesus!' she added drily. 'Really?' I asked. 'I thought he hated me . . . that maybe he'd moved on.' Naima looked back up at me. 'You try telling that to all of the women he's been cutting off lately. It's like a graveyard around here.'

"Naima and I walked out of the hotel together. And while she was still working overtime to convey that she had no desire to be in my company, I could tell now that she was just

a woman trying to get the attention of a man. I was learning that was how it could be sometimes. But I wasn't going to let that faze me. And after melting Naima's ice away, I was able to charm her into giving me Dame's cell number. After telling me it was pointless to call because I'd probably already missed Dame, because he, Benji, and one of his assistants left to go to the airport at 5 a.m., she made it a point to warn me never to tell anyone about her Southern hospitality that morning. 'I don't make it a habit to help strangers,' she said. 'This is a cutthroat business and you get hurt if you don't watch your back. But Dame's a good guy. The most real I've met in the business, so you can consider this a favor to him—not you. If I can't get what I want . . . someone should. Tell him I said good-bye.' "

"Naima is a good enemy," Kweku said, getting up and coming back to our row. "You need those."

The flight attendants instructed us to return to our seats and buckle up in preparation for landing.

"So how did you end up in Ghana?" Peter asked, comically pushing his face between our seats.

"That's the best part of the story," I said. "It was an unexpected arrival and departure."

PART THREE

See

Chapter Twenty-four

My senses just wouldn't connect. They were scattered everywhere around me, trying to process every sensation and what the impression meant in my mind, but it was all just happening too fast for the rationale of my mind and body to keep up with the passion of my heart and soul. In there, in my heart and soul, was fluttering and bursting and amazement and all I could do was try not to let the sensations overwhelm me.

Naima was wrong. It wasn't too late to call Dame. I knew this because I'd been listening to his voice on the phone for a while now as it led me to the airport and terminal where I could find him. And while I was just as excited to hear him speaking to me, sounding as if maybe his heart and soul were fluttering and bursting, too, this sound was nothing more than a rattling reminder of what I needed, what I wanted to see, to feel, to smell, to even taste. It was like a hungry person smelling food. Until I had the thing within me, the aroma was nothing but a reminder of what was to come.

I ran from my parked car into the terminal with the phone held loosely to my ear.

Inside of the terminal, there was ringing and talking, some laughing and chatter. The sweet smell of cinnamon buns from a bakery window in a corner of the circular waiting area wafted out to me. I could see people walking, holding hands, hugging, and saying hello and good-bye. I rushed from these circles, around and underneath to find my own, listening to Dame's instructions along the way.

"I'm right over by the big palm trees in the middle of the waiting area," he said. "I'm looking around for you. Are you over here yet?" I didn't answer. I just kept looking and soon my eyes found the now familiar smiles of teenage girls. I followed their faces, one by one, along a line where they stood with their arms outstretched, holding cameras and rolled-up pieces of paper with pens clutched in the center. At the front of this jumbled line was Benji, big and menacing, meeting worthy adversaries in these young girls as he struggled to keep them at bay. I craned my neck a bit so I could see where their eyes were batting, yet Benji's protection also guarded my view.

"You see me?" Dame asked.

"No," I said.

"Wait." I heard scrambling and what sounded like steps. "I'm getting up on a chair, so you can see me."

The line of girls shifted back, and high up behind Benji rose Dame. His back was to me.

"Do you see me?"

"Yes!" I dropped the phone and rushed past Benji and the girls, who'd become more excited by Dame's leap on the chair, and now other people were standing up and looking on.

"Well, where? Where are you?" Dame looked around and then, just as I arrived at the foot of the brown leather seat where he was standing, he looked down and saw me. Throwing away all caution, I followed the racing of my heart and jumped up on the chair next to him.

Without saying anything, we embraced and the world inside the airport lobby went into a panoramic slow spin around us. Nothing else mattered. All I could feel was my heart finally resting against his and his strong arms holding me close. Oddly, it was the most familiar feeling I'd ever known. And while the embrace was just fast enough for the starry-eyed girls to take only one or two pictures, it filled my spirit so much that it felt like forever. Through the corner of my eye, I saw a police officer running toward us.

"Why are you in Georgia?" Dame asked, looking at me.

"I'm going to have to ask you two to get down from there!" the police officer barked, now standing at the foot of the chair next to Benji and the girls, who were cooing and calling out for Dame.

"I left. Evan found out about everything and I left."

"To come—"

"To you," I said, finishing Dame's statement, and quickly, his eyes flashed from being endeared to distant. "I know you're probably still mad at me," I tried, "and I'm sorry for what happened. You don't have to forgive me, but I had to see you . . . to let you know that—"

"Sir, ma'am," the officer called, but neither Dame nor I looked at him.

"Give them a second," I heard Benji say.

"To let me know what?" Dame asked me, his eyes still far away.

"That I—" I looked down at the girls and the officer, who were standing there as quietly as Dame now, waiting for my answer. "I . . ." And I didn't know quite what to say . . . what to add . . . how to express what I was feeling all inside of myself, and with each second the massive room seemed to grow more quiet with expectation. "I . . . shit." My eyes wide open, I wrapped my hands around the back of Dame's head, pulled his face down to mine, and pushed his lips apart with my own, delivering a passionate and impetuous kiss that I led without reservation or care of what was going on or who was looking. I held my breath and pulled Dame's into mine again, working his tongue so aggressively that I felt his body go limp. The sparks exploding between us were rivaled only by the flickers of cameras around the lobby.

"Damn," I heard one of the girls say, and then there was the sound of cheering. When I finally let go of Dame—and it was I who had to let go—I looked down to see that the police officer and two others behind him were clapping and nodding along with everyone else. Behind them were men holding bigger cameras than the ones I saw before and the men looked less like travelers and more like paparazzi in their sweat suits and sneakers.

"You know this is going to be all over the news tomorrow," Dame whispered under the noise as we continued to hold each other.

"Yes," I said,

* * *

After Dame and I finally decided to get off the chairs after risking our lives messing with airport security, we were escorted to a private waiting area on the second floor of the lobby. Pushing through the crowd and past the photographers, I'd lost an earring and learned very quickly that the paparazzi's flashing cameras are much closer than they appear on *Entertainment Tonight.*

Dame and I sat in a pair of seats before a huge one-way window that showed the floor of the lobby and I told him all about the *People* magazine picture and what happened with Evan. He kept apologizing for not telling me the pictures people took of him could end up anywhere and that he never intended to harm my marriage. But for me, the picture, while untimely and hurtful, represented the truth and I was old enough to know that at some point, the truth would have to expose itself. Just right then, I was happy it had. I couldn't worry about tomorrow.

"Dame, we have to get to the gate; the flight's about to start boarding shortly," Emily said, coming toward us with her BlackBerry in her hand. She'd been standing next to Benji at the door.

"Shit," Dame said.

"Where are you going?" I asked him, suddenly reminded that we were in an airport.

"Ghana," Emily said before clicking on the phone to take a call.

"Ghana?" I repeated.

"Yeah," Dame said. "I'm doing some studio work out there with a label. And I kind of needed a real break before I go on tour."

"For how long?" I felt my heart cracking into bits

like Dame and I had been together for years and he was suddenly leaving me.

"A month."

"A month? You're going away for a whole month?"

"Yeah . . . Well, I requested more time and I'm working through some things with the label," Dame said. "Hey, you can"—he looked at Emily and then back at me—"you can come with me."

"Come?" I asked. "But I don't. . . . I can't go to Ghana."

"Why not? You can come with me." Dame's eyes started dancing like we were being served a fat bowl of ice cream.

"I don't have a ticket," I complained, and he frowned.

"I can buy out the entire cabin if I want," Dame said.

"Well, I don't know anything about Ghana. I was just driving here to see you. I don't even have my things."

"Emily, I need you to get another ticket. Journey's coming to Ghana with us," Dame said and Emily looked at him like he was crazy.

"Really?" she asked, clicking the phone off.

"Wait," I jumped in. "I can't just go."

"Yes, you can."

"No," Emily said. "She needs a visa and her shots to even get into the country."

"You handle the visa," Dame said. "Just call the ambassador in D.C. He owes me a favor after that benefit we did last summer."

"Ooookay," Emily answered, clearly weighing Dame's order in her head. "Well, I'm sure I can get him on the phone. . . . But we might have to wait and get a later flight."

"I don't care," Dame said, looking at me.

"And then we can handle the shots at the layover in Amsterdam." Emily produced a pad and started writing this down.

"Shots?" I asked.

"You have to get a few shots to get into the country . . . yellow fever . . . all this stuff. Wait, what am I talking about—" She slapped herself on the forehead.

"What?" Dame and I asked.

"The shots and the visa won't matter if you don't have your passport—not nowadays. There's no way around that. They can't even rush it."

"Oh." Dame sighed, and we all traded looks. She was right. There was no way around the passport thing. I sighed and felt an itch at my hip.

"Wait!"

"What?" Emily and Dame looked at me.

"My passport!" I pulled my purse off my shoulder and pried it open.

"Yes. . . . Yes! Your passport," Dame said so loudly that Benji turned to us.

"I keep it in my purse. I have it. I have it!" The way I said this, it sounded as if the passport carried all of the winnings of a lotto ticket. But then, it was priceless. It had gone unused and without reason within my purse for months and now, suddenly my ridiculous New Year's resolution made perfect sense.

"You keep your passport in your purse?" Emily asked as I pulled it out.

"It's a long story," I said. "I figured I'd need it one day for something real special."

As expected, it took Emily more than an hour to get to Dame's contact at the Ghanaian embassy in

Washington, but the fact that it was even an option proved how powerful celebrity could be. My father had a certain amount of power in the South and certainly in Alabama, but Dame's connections were reaching over oceans and the fact that people seemed to want to help was both exhilarating and exciting. The ambassador himself demanded to chat with Dame and I was sure it was supposed to be official business, but when Emily handed Dame the phone he just laughed, exchanged a few words, and in minutes, Emily announced that he would handle it.

"Just when I think you're amazing, you do something else to impress me," I said to Dame after listening to him chattering with the ambassador as if they'd gone to Princeton together.

"Well, that's a big surprise."

"Why?"

"I never knew I impressed you at all."

After we missed the initial flight and changed airlines, Dame and I walked through security, huddled together under Benji and Emily's jackets as photographers and fans who no doubt got word that Dame was in the airport followed along. I was being pushed and pulled and questioned. There was so much going on, but nothing mattered more than who I was with.

I held Dame's arm tight and didn't let go until we were on the plane and up in the air. And even then, we started to hold on to each other, staring straight into each other's soul with so much desire, the flight seemed like a short hop over a puddle on a pogo stick. Yes, it was funny—time, between two people who had found each other, melted like butter in a hot skillet. First we were laughing and then smiling and before I knew it, we'd passed through Amsterdam and were on our way to Africa.

Chapter Twenty-five

The day I die, I always imagine myself lying in a bed, surrounded by family—my children, my grandchildren, cousins, nieces and nephews, and anyone else who'd come into my heart by that inevitable date. And as I lie just hours, minutes from closing my eyes forever, I will tell the story of my life. Not everything. Just highlights. The day Justin almost died drowning in the ocean at Mobile. It was the first time I'd seen my father cry. When Billie and I stripped naked and jumped into the lake in the back of the old church and we both came up with leeches all over our bodies. But we were afraid to go home and tell what had happened, so we somehow got the idea to burn them all off with matches. We had burns all over our bodies for weeks. The day I was strong enough to walk away from the only man I was sure I would ever love, without knowing what would come next. And now, to this list, I had to add the day I arrived in Africa.

Dame was asleep. He'd been snoring and grunting like a big old baby for hours and only moved once to lay his head on my shoulder. Seated beside the window, I leaned away from him, so he could have my whole shoulder. Resting my head against a pillow placed on the closed window shade, I looked at him quizzically. How could such a big, bold man sleep so serenely in a metal box zipping through the skies? He seemed so vulnerable and tender leaning against me. I could watch him like this forever.

"Something about the sky," one of the flight attendants said, leaning on the chair in front of Dame. "Just lulls men to sleep."

"He's been like this for hours."

"Enjoy it," she said, smiling wickedly. She turned to walk away, but then stopped suddenly. "May want to put your shade up. Some pretty stuff passing by."

"Oh, sure," I said, easing up in my seat. Dame felt my rustle and turned sleepily to his other side without so much as wrinkling an eyelid. I set the pillow between us and pushed up the shade with my left hand. As it came up, the sun, which I'd last seen many hours ago, came stalking in fast. It was bright. Like we were just inches away, floating in the sky. And I wondered if maybe it seemed so big because I hadn't seen light in so many hours, but when I peeked out the window, I saw that it was true. The sun was so close that I felt I could break through the glass of the window and just push my hand into it. Grab it and think that it felt like what orange juice tastes like—waking and friendly.

When my eyes adjusted to the rays, I leaned into the window a bit farther and turned my head to look down at the surface below the plane. See what the flight attendant, Shola, was speaking of.

What was there was an impossibly big blanket of tan. Everywhere. Sometimes it looked like waves, like an ocean of land, ripples riding for miles. And then somewhere, out of nowhere, a tree would push up and green leaves, dotted sparsely like dollar bills hanging from a birthday girl's shirt, gave a bit of color in the middle. Then there were spirals of different tans with some brown and blue black mixed together. The plane dipped lower and then I saw that one of these spirals was unraveling into what I could see was a river trail. It opened and sprang big like the trunk of a tree, going like this for miles until it just divided again and began to branch out into so many limbs. It was past beautiful. Simple and quietly alive.

"Makes you want to jump out there and swim in the sand, don't it," Dame said lazily, pulling his chair up after the flight attendants announced that we were preparing for landing.

"It's brilliant," I replied, but I didn't think he could hear me.

Seeing all of that quiet openness for so many miles in no way prepared me for the hectic hubbub of Accra. From the edge of the city, I watched the sand roll into rivers and led to trees, and then forests, and then roads, and then the tops of homes packed so tight that I could hardly see the ground anymore. I kept trying to connect this vision to something I had seen before, but there was nothing else like it. It was suffocating and hypnotizing. And that was just from the plane.

When Dame and I exited the plane, I didn't know if I'd arrived in Ghana or if it had arrived in me. Standing at the top of the steps that led to the tarmac with other passengers who'd deboarded and were gathering at the bottom, I immediately felt the heat.

It was quick, merciless. Steamy and almost visible, opening my pores like I'd just stepped into a sauna. Growing up in Alabama, I knew what the hottest days of summer felt like and had learned to live with them, but I instantly knew this was different. My hair immediately surrendered at its roots and beads of sweat gathered at my temples.

Dame grabbed my hand and looked back at me before walking down the steps.

"You feel that heat?"

I nodded.

"You'll get used to it. You'll like it soon."

There was a group of three short and stout Ghanaian women standing by the entrance of the airport. Singing and welcoming each passerby, they looked like they were in their late fifties and were wearing colorful native clothes that matched just enough to appear as costumes. Their heads were wrapped in white linen, and beaded earrings, the color of the sand waves, hung from their ears. A sign above them read "Akwaaba." I'd learn later that this meant "Welcome" in their native language.

"Akwaaba," the one in the middle, whose cheeks were striped with cuts, said when Dame and I appeared in front of them.

And then she did something I hadn't seen her do to anyone else. She opened her arms and came to me smiling.

"Welcome home," she said into my ear as she hugged me. She backed up and looked into my eyes while holding my cheeks as if I were her own child. "We've missed you sorely."

"Thank you," was all I could say, but that's not nearly what I'd felt. In her eyes I saw the faces of every mother and sister at the church who'd kissed me in this same way when I was a child. She looked nothing like them. We'd been so mixed over in our history that even the darkest one of us didn't look as unaffected as the face in front of me. But in her eyes, I could still see them. It was an undeniable reflection of our connection. And no matter how far we'd come, looking there, into her eyes, I knew it was true; this was where we were from.

While it was completely spontaneous going to Ghana meant a lot to me, probably more than I'd told Dame when he asked me to come, but I didn't expect to feel all this so quickly. I didn't want it to be the cliché experience of black people who stepped off the plane, kissed the ground, and did a happy dance that they'd returned to "Mother Africa." But really, inside, I was dancing. I was hopping, dancing, screaming, and crying. Because the woman, who was probably just doing her job and had kissed every black woman who walked off the plane for the same response, was right. I was returning home.

Dame hadn't lied. He kept the same driver in every city. When we left the airport, Benji was already out front, helping the driver pack their bags into a little minivan. Dame greeted the driver like he was an old friend and slid a few bills into his hand. "Brother Kofi," he said, and they went on talking and laughing about something that had happened the last time Dame was in Ghana. "No trouble this time, Brother Sisi," Kofi said, calling Dame by his Akan name that Kofi later explained simply told what day Dame was born on—Sunday. My name, Kofi added, was "Adowa" because I was born on a Tuesday.

As I'd seen from the sky, the streets of Accra were

tight. Cars clogged the sometimes dirt and sometimes paved roads like taxi cabs in Times Square. And in between each car was a man, moving about from driver to driver, selling anything, sometimes stopping for a long time and other times just nodding and moving on. Like we did in Alabama, when they wanted to chat for a while, the traffic just kind of stopped as people waited for the meeting to move on.

Women and children crowded the sidewalks. Some walking and others sitting and selling things like the men in the road. The most beautiful thing to see was the way the women held their babies so close to them as they worked. The babies' little brown heads were popping out of the sides of the women's backs where ample cloth was used to hold the children snug and in place as they hung in a kind of simple sling that seemed so tight that it left little room for the baby to cry or wiggle around. Instead, they either slept as the mother moved, or observed the goings-on like a grown person.

"No, no, no," Brother Kofi said to me when I tried using Dame's camera to snap a quick picture of one of the women carrying her baby. "You must ask the mother first. Never take a picture until you have consent . . . or give a dash."

"A dash?"

"That's a tip," Dame said, laughing with Benji at Brother Kofi's honesty. "Everyone dashes in Ghana. These are your people."

After three days in Ghana, I knew that Dame was right—these were my people. I could tell by how they communicated with one another in loud tones and expressive faces. The women all seemed so proud and unapologetically complicated, and the men, they always had something charming to say and a smile that meant more than one thing. Yeah, I was far from home, but these were definitely my people.

I learned that Accra had a way of making repose a state of mind. The heat or something in the crowded air eased my mind into a constant state of relaxation and even if I wanted to worry about something, the need quickly drifted away in the breeze.

"Am I gonna have to leave you here when I go home?" Dame asked one morning when he was getting ready to go to the studio for one of his daily sessions. I was still in bed. He'd been spending most of his mornings working on his music and sometimes meeting with local artists and visitors, but I mostly stayed behind, walking around the parts of the city that seemed safe and having Brother Kofi drive me to others. I was wearing a full wardrobe of African dresses I bought at the craft market, and decorated our hotel room with beaded masks and Ashanti stools, where Dame and I were sleeping in separate beds.

"I am Mother Africa," I joked, pulling my hair off my face. Drenched in sweat, it refused to be straightened even after I washed it each morning. So I'd let it curl up into a loose Afro.

"Okay, Mother Africa," Dame said, pulling clothes from his bag. "Just don't forget who your real mother is. I'm sure she's already pulled a switch for you from the backyard."

"Oh, don't bring that up again." I rolled over in the bed and pulled the sheets over my head. I'd told him about what happened with my family the first evening.

"You're gonna have to face her soon. Just call, so she knows everything's okay. You've been gone a few days." He pulled the sheets off me.

"I'll call!" I said, looking at Dame.

"Today?" he asked.

"Today!"

"You promise?" He sat down next to me on my bed.

"Yes."

"Hey, why don't you come down to the studio later this afternoon?"

"I can't," I said. "Brother Kofi is taking me to the slave dungeon again."

"Again?"

"Yes," I said.

"I don't know why you went in the first place."

"You never went?"

"No," he said quickly. "Slavery happened. I know that. I don't need a damn reminder. I was raised in the United States—in the South. I've had reminders all my life. All I need to know now is that we're not slaves anymore."

"It was still something to see where it all began," I said, remembering the feeling of closure I had when I stood in the female slave dungeons and saw the shackles that had been used to bind these women together. It was sad. It was heartbreaking, but somehow I felt that my return after hundreds of years to pay my respect to these women and men and attempt to remember what happened to them made the bitter feeling dissolve just a bit.

"Africa's about more than just slavery," Dame said.

"There's a whole big continent of people out there right now trying to make money and enter into the world market. We have to let them outlive that past."

"Preach, Brother Malcolm," I joked, shaking one of my beaded necklaces at him.

"Oh, you got jokes?" Dame laughed at me. He got up and slid the undershirt he was wearing right off and threw it over onto the floor. "We'll see how many jokes you have when I come in here tonight."

He looked at me suggestively and just stood there. With the new shine the African sun cast on his already dark skin, he'd become spectacular to look at. I was salivating. Worse, in our small hotel room, he'd taken to dressing and undressing right in front of me. It was beyond tempting, but still, I didn't know what to do with him. We'd kissed, we'd hugged, and even fallen asleep beside each other on the beach, but I was still married to another man and had never been so close to anyone but him. I knew Dame, who now had unimaginably gorgeous African women throwing themselves at him right in front of me, must have been frustrated by this coquettish behavior, but he never pushed the subject. It seemed we were both just waiting for passion to overtake reason.

The phone call to my mother might have been better if I'd made it the morning Dame tried to put it in my mind, but I wasn't ready to face her yet. So I waited three more days before I even looked at the phone and then two more before I picked it up. I wasn't sure what I was afraid of, but I knew what I was avoiding. By now, there was no way she didn't know where I was and who I was with. The camera crews on the ground in Atlanta had arrived in Accra and

Dame could hardly leave the hotel without a reporter or photographer spying his every move. Apparently, there was more to the trip than he'd let on. Dame's label troubles were growing and gossip was spreading that he was in Africa to escape some of his contractual duties. Between journalists trying to get a few quotes about this and Dame's Ghanaian fans, who greeted him in the street like the crying European fans at the Michael Jackson concerts in the eighties, I was sure someone had taken my picture and sent it over the airwaves. The only good thing was that no one seemed to know my name. I was still "the mystery woman." But not to the Southern woman who'd just picked up the phone.

"Mama," I said after she answered. "It's me."

"Journey Lynn?" I heard her toss about a bit and then I realized it was very early in the morning there and that she was probably in bed next to my father. "What are you doing there? In Africa? With that boy!"

"Okay! Nice to hear your voice, too," I said.

"It's all over the newspaper," she whispered, ignoring me, and I could tell she was sneaking out of bed. "Everyone down here knows it's you. They're all talking about it. Everyone."

"I know, Mama. I'm just—"

"They're saying you're having an affair with that boy. Is that true?" she asked.

"Well, we're—"

"Poor Evan. The man is sick. Just walking around here like a ghost. It's embarrassing really."

"Evan knows," I said. "I told him."

"You told him what? That you're a grown woman who's running around behaving like she's a child?"

"I'm not a child," I said.

"Precisely. You're a married woman. A woman of God. I didn't raise you to be running around God knows where with some boy—"

"You didn't raise me to do a lot of things," I said, looking out onto the street from the hotel room window.

"Don't you sass me, girl. Even with everything that happened over here, I'm still your mother."

"Mama, I didn't mean to upset you. I just . . . I really like him." What should've felt like lead in my throat instead came out like song lyrics. It was the most sincere thing I'd said to my mother in years.

"He's a child. And you're a damn fool if you think he'll be more of a man for you than Evan. Mark my words. I've been on this earth long enough to know the start of something bad. He'll only bring you down. What do you even know about him?"

"Oh, Mama, why can't you just be happy for me?" I pleaded.

"The way you run off out of here like a scared child? Abandoned your family when we needed you most? How could I be happy about that?" She started to cry. "It's like I have no control over you anymore. No say."

"That's just it, Mama," I said. "I felt like I had no control over me anymore. No say. I'm just trying to get that back."

"And you had to go over to another continent to do it?" she asked, and there was silence.

"Yes," I said finally. "I guess I did."

"Well, when are you coming home? Your father is sick of everyone talking about this thing," she said, and I could hear the real worry in her voice, but I hadn't decided if I was supposed to care about his feelings again. He was part of the reason I'd left in the first place. "He's afraid someone's gonna go telling the press who you are and then folks are gonna start coming down to the church."

"Mama, no one's coming to Tuscaloosa. Believe me," I said. "Look, I'll come home soon. I just need to do what I'm doing here . . . whatever it is. And then I'll come home. I promise." I expected my mother to argue, but she didn't. I guessed she just heard the finality in my voice and accepted my position. It was the strongest I'd ever felt in her presence. "I love you, Mama," I said. "And I'm sorry about everything that happened."

"I love you, too," she said, resigned. "And I'm sorry . . . about what happened."

The studio Dame was always working at was more like a glamorized hut with shoddy music equipment. I hadn't seen nearly as many studios as Dame, but even I could see this when I arrived there after the long phone call with my mother. The place was mediocre at best, and it made me wonder why Dame would really travel so far from the comfort and familiarity of the choice of studios he had in the States for this. It didn't make sense. Maybe the gossip was true. The room, which was just a few feet larger than a standard-sized bedroom back home, was at the back of a single-story building that looked like it used to be a community center.

When I walked in, I saw dozens of women, dressed in skintight spandex and outdated club gear, all beautiful and clearly awaiting one of the men in the studio. I recognized some of their faces from the hotel lobby and while I tried to smile, few returned my glance long enough for any communication, leading me to understand that the man they were waiting for was Dame. They clicked their tongues and I was sure what they were sharing wasn't far from the disdain the women in Atlanta expressed in my presence. These were different faces with the same goal. This made me feel both powerful and jealous at the same time. I was powerful because, as Naima said at the hotel, I had Dame's eyes, but jealous because as I looked at these women, I wondered just how long I could keep his eyes. I was almost fifteen years older than many of these girls and I knew I wasn't willing to do half of the things they probably had promised Dame in whispers in his ears. Looking at their perfect brown skin and flawless bodies, I knew some probably had gotten past the promise and provided.

"You came?" Benji said, walking out of the back room. His skin had tanned, too, and he was now sporting a little face towel over his bald head to block out the sun. He came over and hugged me as the other women looked on disappointed.

"Yes," I said. "I was getting bored at the hotel."

"Well, let me take you back there. Dame will be happy to see you," he said, and I heard one of the women groan in disgust.

In the studio, Dame presented a picture of what people expected a real artist to look like when he was working. While his body was in the room and he was communicating with the people around him, his mind was gone. It was off somewhere creating a masterpiece that was being ushered to sonic reality. He was focused and intentional and in his eyes, I saw love for music that changed, once again, what I'd thought of him. What listeners heard on the radio—the rhymes set to beats—was only a piece of what Dame was in the studio to develop.

"Whoa?" Dame hollered into the microphone when he finally looked up to see me sitting on the other side of a piece of glass that separated him from the man working the soundboard. "What are you doing here?" A smile washed over his face and he pulled off his headset.

"I see the fans are in full effect," I said, nodding toward the women pressed up against the window once he came over to me.

He kissed me on the cheek and smiled. "Don't be all jealous. That's just the industry," he said. "I told you that."

"Yeah, you did. I just didn't think they'd be here, too."

"They're everywhere."

A woman with breasts double the size of mine and a waist that could fit into a bracelet waved at Dame, and he smiled back.

I couldn't hide my annoyance. I rolled my eyes and crossed my arms over my not-so-ample breasts.

"See, that's why I was a little nervous about you coming."

"Coming where?" I asked. "To Ghana? You asked me to come."

"Yeah, but I just kept thinking maybe this would be too much of a peek into my world. I don't want you to get the wrong impression."

The woman slid her finger into her mouth seductively and started sucking it like a baby with a lollipop. Even Benji stopped to stare; his mouth was hanging open like Dame's.

"Oh, I have the impression," I said.

"Let's get out of here," Dame said, turning back to me. "Maybe we need to leave Accra."

* * *

Over lunch, after we left the studio, Dame admitted that the gossip was correct. He was planning to leave his record label. Apparently, he hadn't been happy there for a long while, felt they were controlling his sound and not allowing him to grow into an individual artist who couldn't be compared to others on a list. So he wanted to start something from scratch with a new label. He explained that one of his friends who'd worked with world music with an international label was transferring to lead a new imprint. Dame was switching over there as soon as his contract was up. They were trying to create a new, international sound.

"World music?" I asked, hearing drums and other primitive beats in my head.

"It's not as crazy as it sounds. It'll reinvent the sound and add a more developed edge to the music. Like what jazz did for the blues and hip-hop did for jazz. It's the next level," Dame said passionately.

"You sound like a chef."

"I am a chef," he said, sitting back in his seat and looking out into the road with me at trucks passing by. "They're trying to turn me from a man into a slave. But I'm not having it. I want to do all of the production and the business," he protested. "Like James Brown, I'm going to own my shit when I leave here."

"All of the contracts and endorsement deals you have, you already own your work," I said.

"Yeah, but they still have a say when it comes to my art. I want all mouths to close when I'm doing what I do. I do the wax and I do the deals. After this imprint, I'm opening my own distribution and everything. That's where the real power is. I can do it on my own."

"That's a big undertaking."

"I have big shoulders. . . . My granddaddy gave them to me." With his eyes, he followed a blue truck passing by. "That's what happens when you work on a plantation all your life. You get big shoulders . . . pass them down. Anyway, enough about me. So how was the phone call with your mother? How did it go?"

"It went." I shrugged my shoulders. There was nothing to tell him that wouldn't complicate the situation.

"She hates that you're here. She hates me. She wants you to come home."

"That about sums it up," I said, laughing with Dame. "I don't know. I just wish she could understand."

"Understand what?"

"What I feel." I looked at him "When I'm with you. When we're together."

"And what's that?"

"Like I'm free and this is all I need. Just you . . . and my freedom."

"You need more than that," he said. "You need something for yourself."

I looked down and then back out at the street. A mother was crossing with a baby tied to her back.

"I don't know what that is yet," I said, watching the baby sleep peacefully.

"You've got to find out. Everybody has to have their thing."

Chapter Twenty-six

The streets of the Gold Coast weren't paved with gold. Just lots of golden earth, for as long as the eye could see. If I squinted, just when the sun hit it as I rode along during the highest part of the afternoon, the earth looked like gold and sometimes glints of what could actually be small pieces of gold, so tiny the eye could only see them from far away, sparkled like stars.

Dame and I rode along one of these golden roads in a car he'd gotten from Brother Kofi. After days of visiting him in the studio and running out of things to do with myself and ways to impress the crowd of ladies waiting to catch Dame's eye, I insisted we take a break from everything and go on a vacation from his working vacation. I wanted Dame and Ghana to myself. To get farther away from the world.

"Kumasi isn't too far," Dame said when we set out. "Just make sure you don't have to go to the bathroom. There won't be one for miles."

I watched golden roads and sparkles the entire way to Kumasi, wondering what was ahead for Dame and me there and happy that we'd finally be alone. No driver. No Benji. No Emily with her BlackBerry. Just us.

"Now, this is a beach," I said when we'd unpacked our things and slipped out of the front door of our hotel room. The water was so blue it mixed in with the sky, and the sand, as white as flour, was without a footprint or reminder of the world beyond our eyes.

"It's just for us," Dame said.

"A private beach?" I asked.

"You wanted privacy," he came up behind me in the doorway. "You got privacy. You wanted me to yourself. . . . You've got me to yourself." He kissed me softly on the neck and shockwaves went quivering through me, but I still felt I had to resist.

"Yes," I said, stepping forward and away from him.

"How long are you going to play this game?" he asked.

"Game?" I turned to him.

"What are you trying to avoid?"

"I . . ."

"I can wait," he said. "But I'm a grown man. And you're definitely a grown woman." He looked at my hips, which were poking through the flat shape of the African sundress I was wearing.

Dame stepped closer again and started kissing my neck. I could feel his body grow and harden. He pulled me into the room and we slid behind the door as he continued to caress me.

"Housekeeping," a small, soft voice called from the other side of the door. Dame and I jumped as if it was old Roscoe opening the door to the janitor's closet at the school. "Anyone here?" She knocked.

"Yes, we're here," Dame said, smiling at me and walking out from behind the door. I eased out slowly, too.

"Oh," the woman said, putting her hand over her eyes when she saw Dame and me. "The door was open, so I thought I'd—"

"No need to apologize," I said. "We were just making sure the lock worked."

"Sure," she said, placating my assurance, but also making it clear she believed not one word I was saying. "I'm Farrah. I'll be keeping your room for you. If you need anything, just ask. For it is my pleasure."

"Thank you," Dame said, giving her a dash from his pocket. "In fact, you could be of help to us right now. We're going out dancing tonight and my . . . lady"—I watched as she looked at my hand and saw my wedding band and then back at Dame's bare hand—"needs a nice dress. Know where we can get one?"

"Certainly, sir," she said. "I know the perfect place."

Downtown Kumasi was a little quieter than Accra. There were shops and lots of people, but it had the slow, peaceful tone of any beach town in the States. There were lots of tour buses, and Dame, who visited the city whenever he was in Ghana, explained that mostly Europeans came there to see the slave dungeons and buy kente cloth from the original knitters. Just then, as we rode along through the sandy Kumasi streets, I realized that I might have seen ten or so white people the whole time I'd been in Accra. In two weeks, I'd conducted business, had moving interactions, and even disagreements with only black people. It seemed like a small point, but to many people, even my own people, that would've sounded impossible.

After walking through dozens of craft tents in what seemed to be a spontaneous flea market, Dame and I managed to find the shop Farrah told us about. It was owned by her daughter, Akosua, a woman as short and adorable as Farrah. Hung up on wires and along the length of a table were Akosua's dresses. A mix between the African dresses I'd been wearing and some I'd seen back home, they were sexy and revealing, yet also unique and ethnic. Akosua, Farrah told us, was twenty-two and wanted to go to Paris to study fashion; she'd already been accepted, but couldn't afford the expensive airfare and a year's boarding. She was designing her own clothes now to sell them, so she could save enough money to go.

"You have a beautiful body," Akosua said, touching my hips. "It is a blessing to be shaped like this. That's what I try to show in my clothes."

"That's what I try to tell her," Dame said, repositioning a ball cap on his head. He'd been wearing it everywhere we went, hoping no one would notice him.

"Thank you," I said. "Both of you." I looked over the table and saw a few special patterns I recognized from the shops in Accra. One of the tailors there told me each pattern was once used to represent a different tribe. As I looked the dresses over, trying to imagine which ones were different from the ones I already had and would look nice on my body for the special evening Dame announced, a red dress hanging on the last wire caught my eye. It was a simple red wrap dress with an open chest and African-styled skirt. It was gorgeous and without putting it on, I knew it would fit over my body like a second skin.

"I want that one," I said to Akosua.

"That dress?" Dame pointed to the sexy dress.

"Yeah."

"You like that dress?" He looked at me with a grin on his face.

"Yes."

"That isn't an African dress. That's a red dress."

Akosua and I laughed at Dame.

"I know what color it is," I said.

"Just so you know."

"Know what?" I asked.

"That's a red dress. And it ain't only red. Against your skin . . . with those hips . . . that's a dangerous dress . . ."

"A dress like this," Akosua said, jumping in, "can make a man do bad things."

"Things he doesn't want to do," Dame added.

"Maybe I want you to do bad things," I said and without blinking, Dame pointed to the dress.

"Take that one down and put it in a bag," he said to Akosua.

"Certainly," she answered, retrieving the dress.

"How much is it?" I asked.

"No," Dame said before Akosua could answer. "How much is a plane ticket to Paris running these days? That and a bedroom in one of those student dorms by the Eiffel Tower?"

Akosua stood there looking at Dame like he'd just told the girl her darkest secret.

"Excuse me, sir?" she asked, her voice suddenly formal.

"How much is all of that?" he asked again.

"How do you know that?" Tears were coming to her eyes.

"Your mother, Farrah, from the hotel, she told me you're trying to save money to go to school," Dame said.

"Yes," she answered. "I've been accepted, but we have no money to pay."

"Well you just sold your last dress in the marketplace, so I guess you have the money now."

I looked at Dame. He was reaching into his pocket.

"Call this number later this evening; it's my assistant's and she'll be expecting your call. Tell her how much all of that stuff is," he said, handing her a card. "We'll get that handled for you."

"No," she cried loud enough that the woman at the next stand came over and tried to comfort her. "You can't be serious. Never have I dreamed this would happen. Never." Akosua jumped into Dame's arms and held him tightly. Now I was crying, too, and standing there was a crowd of people who'd gathered around them to share in the news.

By "night out," Dame really meant "night out"—outside and beneath the stars. What I guessed could be called a nightclub was actually a bonfire on the beach with a DJ and a crowd of dancing men. Few women could be spotted on the sand and those that I could see were obviously prostitutes or the girlfriends of married men. When we first got there, Dame and I sat by the bar, listening to the music as they played hip-hop and a little reggae. The dancers, who seemed to all be starring in their own videos where they spent more time proclaiming each word of the songs than actually dancing, pounded their chests and looked up at the sky.

"Want another beer?" the waitress asked, picking up the empty bottle in front of me.

"Yes," I said.

"Wait—" Dame stopped her. "Do you have any palm wine?"

"Yes."

"We'll have two."

"You sure?" She looked at Dame curiously and so did I.

"Yes," he said.

"Okay." Her voice was a mix of warning and fear, the kind of gesture a bartender made when he was sure he'd just given a drunk patron one drink too many.

"What's palm wine?" I asked, concerned when the woman left us.

"It's a local wine made of palm leaves," Dame explained.

"Oh, that doesn't sound too bad," I said. "She looked so afraid."

"Yeah, it's like moonshine. Just made from palm leaves."

"Sounds great," I said, overhearing the music shift from its slow reggae vibe to a more polyrhythmic African beat.

"Two palm wines," the waitress said, returning and putting label-less bottles of liquor in front of us.

"Great," I said, picking up my bottle. "To us," I added, tapping Dame's bottle.

"To us."

Like moonshine, the wine was bitter and burning at first, but after the first five sips, it went down smooth and cooled my insides. I didn't know if this was because it was already taking effect, or if I was getting used to the taste, but looking into the emptying bottle, I decided I'd ask for another.

"You look so nice tonight," I said to Dame, who was looking into the crowd and bopping his head. Now most of the men out there had a partner and they were grinding heavily into each other.

"Thank you," Dame said, turning to me. He was just wearing a pair of loose-fitting khaki shorts and a button-up linen shirt, but it was such a shift from his usual T-shirt and jeans that it might as well have been a tuxedo—one I wanted to see him out of. He'd twisted his hair and tucked it into a bun. "I know I already told you that you looked amazing in that red dress a dozen times at the hotel, but let me get another look." Dame stepped back and watched as I poked out my butt in the dress. As I imagined, it was a perfect fit and somehow Akosua made the bust just tight enough that my breasts were held in perfect position. They were even perky.

I threw my head back and took another swig of the wine.

"Whoa!" Dame took the bottle and held it next to his. He was still at the top neck and mine was almost at the middle. "Slow down. This is strong stuff."

"Really?" I said and I heard that my voice was louder than usual. "I don't feel anything. I just feel good. Like loose." I got up and started dancing a bit to show Dame how loose I felt.

"Oh, shit," Dame said, laughing. "That's the work of palm wine. You feel good."

"I sure do," I said, suddenly feeling the beat from the speakers coming up into my feet. It was as if there was a drum right under the sand beneath my feet. It was pounding and pushing its way up my body. I jumped forward and felt my chest bow toward the sand.

"Let's dance, baby," I said, looking at Dame. "I want you to feel what I'm feeling." The drums were now at my hips and building toward my stomach.

"Okay." He took a long sip from his bottle and took mine from me. "I don't think you need any more of this."

"What?" I reached for the bottle playfully. "I need my wine. My palm wine." I laughed at how my words swayed into each other and then the next memory I had was of Dame and I in the middle of the crowd by the bonfire, our chests knocking into one another as the drum took over our bodies. My hands were up over my head toward the moon above and I touched everyone around me just to feel the vibrations.

"You all right?" Dame asked, holding me up in his strong arms.

"I'm in love," I said. "Love."

"With?" He grinned.

"Y-O-U," I spelled out, trying to tap Dame on the nose with each letter, but always missing.

"You don't mean that," Dame said. "In the morning, when the wine wears off, you'll be back to being the teacher I've been chasing forever." He pulled my body closer to his and we stopped dancing. "The teacher I've always loved." He kissed me on the lips and then looked into my eyes so deeply, even in my fuzzy mind, I knew he meant every word he was saying. "Even if you don't love me in the morning, I'll always love you."

Dame kissed me again. The next thing I felt was his tongue on my breast as my dress hit the floor in the hotel room. I didn't move. I couldn't. I just let my body feel his. His teeth around my nipples, his hands as they pulled my body closer to him. I felt like one of those palms being pressed for the sweet, intoxicating wine. I grabbed his arms and shuddered as he backed up to the bed. There, he stopped and looked at me but I was ready to move on. I pushed him onto the mattress. I got on top and bent down to him.

"I want you," I said into his ear, pulling his hair. "I want you inside of me."

I was in charge then, but Dame was a tease. Before he even took my request, he massaged every muscle in my body with such intensity I knew he'd been planning this for a long while. He made my body feel beautiful and delicate, even in the bright light the moon shone over the bed. As I moaned from his touch, he sighed with a tone of release that built the closer he got to my middle.

"You ready?" he asked, pulling his shorts off.

"Yes."

Chapter Twenty-seven

I placed my wedding band on the nightstand when I got up that morning. Waking with the sun and long before Dame, I put it there because I knew that chapter in my life was now really, really over. It had gone past words and now into action. I had to let go. And I wasn't sad, I said to myself, putting on my sarong and a pair of flip-flops. I wasn't happy either. Instead, I was just wondering what all of this meant. What I really meant when I said I loved Dame. I'd loved Evan, too. But it wasn't like this. I hadn't felt like this. Not as moving. Not as encompassing. I looked at Dame, brown and asleep in the middle of the bed with his arms wide open as if he thought I was still on top of him. This was something more. This was something I could feel.

We're dying for love.

That's what I wrote on the first page of the empty pad that I'd taken from my purse when I went to go sit on the beach. I looked out onto the water.

We're dying for someone to love us.

I thought of Zenobia and Billie . . . Ms. Lindsey . . . Naima . . .

Just to feel that feeling
And know that we're not dying at all.

I thought of Kayla and Richard and then May and Jr.

To imagine that someone could be dreaming
What we're dreaming.
Hoping what we're hoping.

And then there was my mother and father, Jack, and Justin.

And praying what we're praying, too.
We're dying for love.
We're dying for someone to love us.
Just to feel that feeling
And know that we're not dying at all.

I thought of Evan.

That they're wishing what we're wishing,
And willing like we're willing,
To take the fall.

I thought of Dame. I thought of me.

* * *

These words came so effortlessly with each wave in front of me. They rolled up on me with memories of my life and with melody; they were coordinating everything I'd seen into meaning—love. Everyone was just trying to be loved. To be accepted and wanted. Desired by those they desired most. We all just wanted the same thing. Some knew what it was. Others were on a quest to find it. But the feeling was the same. The need was consistent. We wanted to be loved for who and what we were.

Sitting there out on the beach with my words, I was filled with the most spiritual emotions I'd ever felt. It was like I was right next to God, feeling something no church could ever give me—an understanding of the utterly complicated, brilliant, and amazing reality of love. And that was all God was. In fact, the ocean, the sand, the waves, the sky, the sun, that was the church, the Bible, and God. And, as May said, now I knew it was inside of me.

I sang the song to Dame over breakfast. With tears in his eyes, he hugged me and insisted I share it with Farrah. She didn't hold back her tears. She went and got some of the other maids and then, right at the little restaurant in the hotel, I was singing my first song. The melody was somewhat improvised and most times I was just going off of feeling, but the result was the same. Everyone knew what I was calling upon. They understood the urgency of the desire and by the time I was done, they were all crying into each other's arms as if the restaurant had been transformed into a concert hall and then their own hearts.

"They love you," Dame said to me, coming up and standing beside me in front of the small crowd. He was clapping along with them and asking that I sing the song for the tenth time for a new group of people that had shown up.

"Later," I said graciously. "Tonight. After we get back from dinner. I promise."

"Look at you," Dame pointed out. "You're becoming a celebrity already."

"No, I'm not," I said, laughing. "I just don't want to overdo it. I'm still learning the song myself. It's a work in progress."

"Well I'm proud either way." He kissed me on the cheek. "You took a risk and really put yourself out there."

Instead of singing, after dinner Dame and I finished our nightly walk along the beach and decided to go out for some more palm wine. Grinning and giggling about the events of the previous night, Dame teased that I was the cheapest date he'd ever had. He'd spent only three dollars on the wine.

"So, I'm cheap now?" I asked. We were in the hotel room, changing clothes.

"Oh, no," he said. "Not last night. You were more like a pro."

"You stop it," I said, laughing.

"You see, I'm trying to get some more of that palm wine in you!" Dame joked, opening his bag. He pulled out a little box and opened it. Inside was a cluster of sparkles.

"What's that?"

"Some watch the label sent me," he said, taking out the shiny thing and holding it up. "I think they know I'm about to leave, so they keep sending me these little nigga tokens."

"Don't say that. This thing looks pretty expensive," I said.

"It's nothing in comparison to how much I've made them. It's just a carrot they're dangling to keep their nigga in line. They think all we care about is shiny shit and cars and that all they have to do to keep us coming and in line is flash a little candy."

"So you don't like candy?" I asked. "I see you're putting the watch on. Why not just send it back?"

"I'm bigger than this bullshit," he said. "I'm not letting anyone predict my actions or control my mind."

"Not even me?" I laughed, but Dame was quiet.

"No one controls my mind," he said seriously. "Only a dumb man confuses his heart with his mind. My heart is yours, but the mind stays."

Sure most of everything downtown was already closed, Dame and I stopped at a bar along the road. There weren't many cars outside and a few stray goats and chickens played in the street, but we could hear the music from the outside and saw a few people shuffling in and out.

"Does this look like a good place?" I asked Dame.

"Sure," he said, opening my door. "As long as they have wine and music, I'm good."

"I bet." I grinned at him as we crossed the street.

"Hold up," Dame said. "You go on inside. I'm going to get something out of the trunk."

"You sure?" I asked.

"Yeah. I'll be right in."

The Singer

June 23, 2008
Amsterdam

"By the time that man came and sat at our table," I said to Pete and Kweku, who were sitting beside me at a bar in the airport in Amsterdam, "Dame and I were good and drunk. We were laughing about something and I remember that Dame's hand was on my leg underneath the table."

"Were there many people there?" Pete asked, seemingly setting up the scene in his mind.

"A handful. Ten. Twenty," I answered. "We were having so much fun, I wasn't paying attention. Men were coming in and out. I could tell the man knew a lot of them by how the others looked on, but I wasn't counting. It's funny the things you don't remember after situations like this."

"Well, the conversation didn't start off badly, did it?" Kweku asked, taking a sip of his Heineken.

"No." I swiveled my stool around and looked at the soloist, who was sitting at the piano, singing an old Liza

Minnelli show tune. The man was obviously Dutch and his voice needed a lot of work to be near Minnelli's. "He kept us laughing. Greeted us like tourists. Asked what hotel we were staying at. Made some suggestions of places we should go visit. He said we looked nice together. Asked how much older Dame was."

"He was selling himself on you," Pete declared.

"He didn't need to. We'd already made him a friend. It wasn't until the gun came out that I even imagined anything else. The jubilant feeling from the alcohol went fast. I don't think I even heard what he said to us—something about the watch . . . and us not leaving. I wanted to look at Dame, but I was too scared. I just kept my eyes on the gun and then from the corner of my eye I saw Dame jump up. Almost on instinct, I did, too. And so did the man. And then, there was a bang. Everything went still. I looked to see if the gun was still on the table. It was. The man fell to the floor and I went over. I knew he was dead."

I was crying when I started singing my song in the bar in Amsterdam. It was an accidental crowd of tourists and workers. Some were just biding their time and others looked like this was their regular hangout. But I didn't care. I'd grown tired of talking or explaining. I wanted to sing. To make people feel what I was feeling. The soloist seemed surprised when I walked over and asked if I could sing. But I supposed he saw the pain in my eyes and he quickly got up and handed me the microphone and after keying a few notes, the final melody to "Dying" was born. I sang it through without the pad and then even added a few verses between the chorus. It was the only way I could sum up how I was feeling, escaping the sadness that engulfed me like flood water.

* * *

We walked back to our gate in silence. Kweku held my hand and Pete hung his head low. I wasn't crying anymore, but the reliving, the telling, had drained me.

"You can't tell a man," Pete said when we got back to our seats. Kweku and I looked at him quietly, waiting for him to finish his statement. "That's it," he added. "You can't tell a man."

"Tell him what?" I asked.

"There's no 'what' to it. It's anything. Everything. You just can't tell. When he's got his mind made up about a thing, you can't tell him. Not a real man, anyway," he said. "Now, you're upset that this happened. And I understand. A life was lost there. But I'll say this: how do you know for sure that the life that could've been lost wasn't your own?"

"I guess I don't," I said.

"You don't. But can you imagine what that man with you *was thinking when all this was going on? Because I'll tell you now, if he's a country boy, he knew before that gun came out where the story was going. He knew how many men were in that room and what that man intended to do to you." Pete nodded with Kweku. "See, when you were just figuring it out when the gun came out, for a real man, that was working time. You can't ever tell what was in his mind other than that he had to protect you. And you'd better be glad he did. It only shows that he loves you probably more than he loves himself. His heart was working on his mind right there. He had only one shot to get that right at that table. If he missed, if there was another gun in the room, it was coming at him next. That wasn't no Applebee's stickup. That was a showdown. Make of it what you want. But remember, you can't tell a man. Not a real one."*

With Pete's words in my ears, I tried to play that scene in the bar over and over in my head through the night on that plane. I couldn't sleep; I couldn't rest. I just kept trying to see in my memory how Dame might have known what was happening. Where he'd prepared himself. But I couldn't. My eyes were on the stranger, on the wine, on Dame's hand on my leg. I wasn't looking for anything but a good time.

"So what do you think about what he said . . . about Dame and not judging him?" I said to Kweku after turning to see that Pete was asleep.

"He had his points, you know? But then, I guess the only people who can say how you should or could feel are the people who were there."

"I guess I'll never know, then," I said.

"You know. Listen to your heart. Do you think this man is a killer or a man in love? I think that's what Pete was saying. I think that's what you have to decide."

"But that still doesn't answer why he left me alone. He said he regretted bringing me there. He said it was a mistake," I reminded Kweku as I started to cry again.

"Wait," he said, patting my shoulder. "You missed some of what Pete said. The biggest part."

"What?"

"No man wants to feel vulnerable. We try all of our lives to be cowboys, separating our hearts from our minds, and when you pushed Dame over the edge, you reminded him that his heart will always win out. No man wants to remember that. That's female territory."

"I guess you're right."

"Never listen to a man when he's angry—in a rage. You ought to listen to him when he's resting. When he thinks no one else is listening and you'll discover, without fail, what's in his heart."

Hearing this, I could finally rest. While I hadn't solved what happened, I knew that Dame loved me. If I never saw him again, I knew that, at least.

* * *

I was awakened from my nap by an announcement that the plane was preparing for landing in Atlanta.

"Ooooooh," I said, stretching and looking out of the window at the sun. "How long was I sleeping?"

"Quite a while," Kweku said. "Long enough for me to get through the last of the contracts." He pointed to the empty tray table where the contracts had been.

"Wow," I said. "I guess I was good luck."

"You certainly are." Kweku took a pen from his jacket and reached for my pad. I was holding it in my hand. "I want to give you my number—at the office. I work in the music industry and I think maybe you should come to our office." He wrote down his number on a blank page. "I can't promise anything, but I can put you in front of the right people."

"Are you serious?" I asked, looking at the Georgia number.

"After hearing what I heard last night, I know I can't leave that voice in Alabama," Kweku said. "It's time for the whole world to hear it. Give me a call."

I took the pad from Kweku and slid it back into my purse. After I promised him a dozen times I'd call, the voice over the speaker asked that we buckle our seat belts for arrival. I was home.

PART FOUR

Taste

Chapter Twenty-eight

June 24, 2008
Tuscaloosa, AL

I could hear my mother's screams from outside the house. After driving the three hours home from the airport in Atlanta in silence, I pulled into the oval-shaped driveway that came right up to the doorway at my parents' house not knowing what to expect. Either they'd be angry at me and force me to suffer as they listed everything I'd ever done wrong, or miss me so much the fact that I'd run off didn't matter anymore. Either way, this was the only place in the world I had to go and the only place I could begin to get back into what I'd left unburned in my life. My home with my things in it wasn't but a handful of miles away, but I wasn't ready to face what was waiting there yet. I wasn't ready to face who was waiting there.

When I opened the car door to get out, I heard my mother screaming, saw the front door fling open and her body come shooting out as if seeing me from a distance had in some way shaved twenty years off her age.

"Oh, my Jesus, Jesus, Jesus," she cried, wrapping her arms around me and holding me so close I couldn't move. One of my legs was still halfway in the car and I was twisting out, but this didn't matter. In a second, I was crying and holding my mother, too. Shaking and rocking as if we hadn't seen each other in years. And even though it had really been only a few weeks, the way I'd left, the way things were, made it feel like an eternity. Yet, here was my mother, in my arms, smelling like the raw cinnamon she kept in dishes around the house and the summer Alabama breeze. Everything. Everything that had happened before I'd left and while I was gone came through my tears in an outpouring of emotion. I'd tried so hard to stand on my own as an adult. To believe that my solitude could prove something about who I was, but in my mother's arms, I was still a little girl—longing to have her family back together, wishing everything would be okay.

"Mama, I missed you," I cried. "I'm sorry. I'm so sorry."

I opened my eyes and saw that around us was everyone—my entire family, standing there and looking at me. They were arm in arm in a bunch behind my mother. May was crying. My father's arm was around Jr. And Justin . . . Justin was standing there with his hands pressed to his mouth. That's when I saw it. In his eyes was more than a look of anticipation. It was fear. I went back along the stares of everyone else and saw this there, too. They weren't simply looking at a Journey they'd missed. They seemed to be looking at a ghost.

"My baby's home," my mother said, holding my face delicately with both hands. "Praise God!"

"What is it, Mama?" I asked. "Why are you all looking at me like that?"

"We been praying all morning," my father said, "that you'd come home."

"We thought you were dead," May added with her voice cracking.

"Dead?" I repeated.

"The TV," my mother said. "It's all over the TV . . . in the newspapers . . . the Internet."

"We've been trying to get information since last night, but no one knew where you were . . . if you were alive," my father said, stepping up next to my mother.

"But what are they saying? What?"

"Dame," Justin started, "he turned himself in."

All afternoon long, as my mother sat on the phone and called everyone to tell them I was all right and at home, I sat on the couch beside Justin flipping between news stations to piece together what people knew of the situation in Kumasi and what happened since I'd left Ghana. The reports ranged from local sources revealing that Dame and I had actually tried to rob the man to our being involved in a drug transaction gone bad. All statements described a yellow woman with light eyes and wild hair. Some said she'd been killed along with the African man and others told of a possible kidnapping. It was both amazing and disturbing how the stories were so distant from anything resembling the truth. They made what happened sound so sensational. So far away. So unreal. Like Dame and I were some characters in a rap video who'd only gone overseas in search of trouble. And even the man who was killed, whose name hadn't been mentioned one time, seemed like a simple pawn in the thing. Africa was a backdrop and he was just another character in the concocted adventure story.

I had to work to ensure my father that none of this was true. And while he seemed a bit softer than he had when I left, he appeared more happy to see me home and alive than to hear my story. But then, I thought, maybe I was the one who needed to hear it again.

"Here it is," May said, turning up the TV when a grainy image of Dame being escorted into what looked like a police station by a bevy of military-looking police officers. Behind the looping image, the reporter announced that Dame had turned himself into the authorities for the murder of an African man in a Kumasi bar. His attorneys had no comment and there was no word yet on the charges he would face.

"You okay?" my mother asked, handing me a napkin to wipe my tears.

"Yes, Mama," I said.

"I know you're upset about that boy but we're just happy to have you home."

I felt a hand on my shoulder and looked up to see that it was Jr.

Chapter Twenty-nine

"What a month," May said, pulling the covers back for me on the bed in one of my parents' guest rooms. We'd eaten dinner and after a few awkward hugs, Jr left to go back to his house and May stayed in her seat beside me on the couch.

"Yeah. It's been pretty crazy," I agreed. I didn't know how I'd be able to find any sleep during the night, but the rest for my bones sounded very inviting.

"But it's kinda nice to see everyone back in the house. For a while, I thought this would never be possible again."

I slid off my shoes and sat down on the bed.

"I'm sorry," I said, "for everything that happened with Jr. He had no right saying the things he said."

"Don't feel sorry for me. And don't apologize for your brother." She turned and smiled weakly. "As mean as he was, as harsh as his words came out, he made us all finally face the truth and that's the best thing that could've happened, really. I feel like I have a whole new life. It hurts a lot. Sometimes I really miss Jr—I won't lie. But I have to protect myself first now. And I'm seeing more and more that I'm worth protecting."

"Wow," I said. "You certainly don't sound like the same May I left crying on the bed at her mother's house with the Bible in her lap."

"That's because my Bible is in here now," she said, placing her hand over her heart. "And no one can manipulate the meaning there."

"So what else has been going on since I left?" I asked after changing into an old nightgown my mother left on the chair beside the bed for me.

"Nothing," she said, laughing a little. "You know, it's funny. When you left, everyone just went their separate ways. No one was talking and it was like we were just going through the motions, but not really saying what was on our minds. I moved out. Justin left. Your parents—they just went back to pretending nothing happened. And then when the news broke about what happened—"

"In Kumasi?"

"Yeah." She looked off. "We all ended up coming together here again. One behind the other, the cars showed up in the driveway. We sat around the TV and your parents had Justin looking up stuff on the Internet and it was like we had to really see each other again for the first time because we had to depend on each other for support. And while we were still quiet, the apologies were in our eyes. In our silent prayers. In our wishes that the last thing that made us a family would be returned to us unharmed."

"I didn't mean to just leave like that," I said. "But I had to go."

"Did you love him?"

"I *do* love him."

When May finally left me alone in the room, I lay in the darkness in the center of the bed for a long while. I didn't expect to find rest or hear the silence in the room. My mind was too busy tossing around images of where I'd been. Some were sad and some were happy. And I could hear things, too. My singing. Dame's laughing. The gun going off. The thump of the man's head on the floor. The sound of the plane taking off as I departed. Kweku inviting me to talk. These sights and sounds played in no specific order in my mind until they became a foreboding dream. Where I was happy, there was this ominous blanket covering me. Where I was sad, I knew that soon I'd hear the blasts again and this would all end. Even in my unexpected sleep, I knew these images were real and as I fought each second to change what had happened, everything was replayed just the same.

"I guess you ain't dead," I heard a voice calling over my shoulder. I was already awake and laying on my side, looking at the clear Alabama sunshine alive outside the window.

I was about to turn over and then I realized the voice was Billie's. I smiled and decided to stay on my side.

"You know you hear me, heifer," she said and I heard her step into the room. "I know you ain't sleep no more! Leaving me to sneak off with some ashy negro. Got some nerve."

I was truly laughing now and fighting to keep my squeals contained.

"The least you could've done was taken me with you. Then I could've found me a real Mustafa. All those single brothers they got in Africa. I know one got to have love for a schoolteacher. Did you bring one back for me in your suitcase? Let me check."

"You keep your filthy hands off my suitcase," I demanded, turning to Billie. "There's nothing in there for you!"

"See, I knew you were awake," Billie cheered, jumping into the bed and embracing me.

"Yes, I am," I said.

"It's you! My best buddy. How are you?"

"I'm fine," I said as Billie made herself comfortable in front of me on an empty space in the bed. "I've been through hell, but I'm fine."

"Hell?"

"Real hell."

As I told Billie everything that had happened, we laid in the bed just looking up at the ceiling like we'd imagined the whole tale unraveling on the white surface like a movie. In true Billie fashion, sometimes, like the time Dame and I first made love, she made me retell certain sections and others, she balked and threw her shoe up in the air.

"Do you think you'll ever see him again?" she asked, bringing up a question I'd been trying to erase from my thoughts.

"He left me," I said. "It's over. I think we've pretty much discovered where the bird and fish can live . . . nowhere."

"What about Evan?"

"I don't know. Have you seen him?"

"He's been around, laying pretty low. After all the stuff came out about you and Dame in the local papers, I think he was embarrassed," Billie said.

"I never meant to hurt him," I said. "I just wanted to try to make sense of what I was feeling, you know? I couldn't keep lying to him like that. It wasn't right. Either way, it wasn't right."

"Well, we can't be right all of the time. Half the battle of life is counting the time when you're right and when you're wrong."

"Hmm." I paused and looked over at Billie. "So what's up with the wedding."

She didn't look back at me. She just frowned and shook her head.

"I gave the ring back." She held her naked left hand up toward the ceiling. "I didn't like it."

"Stop playing," I said, slapping her hand down.

"Ohhhh." She exhaled and turned her head to look at me. "I was busy planning the wedding. I signed up for all these Internet sites and started ordering things. I was just so excited. And then, one of the sites declined my credit card, so I had to go look at the account to see what happened to my balance. I'd given that fool Jerome Jenkins from Jasper over one thousand dollars in all those weeks."

"One thousand dollars? Are you kidding me?"

"Nope. And I just kept thinking how sad that was. How I did something that stupid to get something that I wasn't even sure was mine." She paused and turned back to the ceiling. A tear rolled from the side of her eye and down to the pillow beneath her head. "I know Clyde loves me, but I don't think his love or even my love is enough for us to survive what we've been through. I need to move on. So . . ." She wiped a second tear and sat up suddenly, smiling wide as ever.

"What?" I asked nervously.

"I'm . . . moving."

"What?"

"I'm moving."

"Moving? From Tuscaloosa?"

"That's right. There are no men here, so I have to go where the boys are."

"Oh, no," I said. "Here you go with your ideas again."

"No, Journey," she said. "I'm serious. I already quit my job."

"What?" I sat up, too.

"I have to leave if I'm going to move on. It's not just about Clyde. It's about everything. My life. My youth. I spent my whole twenties chasing behind someone and I didn't do anything for myself. Now I want to live."

"Well, where? Where are you going to go?" I felt excited for Billie and I could see in her eyes that she was serious, but I also thought immediately that I didn't know how I'd be able to live and just be in Tuscaloosa without her.

"Well, at first I thought Atlanta would be a good stop for me . . . but then I remembered that Justin has been enjoying a vibrant sex life there," she said, and I laughed, slapping her hand again. "And I don't think we should be dating in the same pool of applicants, if you know what I mean."

"Yes, I get it," I said. "Leave my baby brother alone."

"And then I looked a little farther north to Charlotte and then Virginia and then D.C. . . . Philly. And then . . . I looked at New York City. The Big Apple."

"No. You're moving to New York?"

"Kayla already set up my lease to sublet her apartment. If she could find love down here, maybe I could find love up there. Oh, yeah, she and Richard got married at the courthouse last week."

"Oh, my God! Oh, my God! Oh, my God!" I screamed, using the Lord's name in vain too many times and I didn't care who heard me. "I'm so happy for her . . . and you! You! New York City? This is huge!" I hugged Billie and every drop of selfishness I'd just felt dissipated. I thought I'd done something bold. Billie was redefining the word.

"I can't believe you're really going to leave."

"Well, as Langston Hughes said, 'I don't give a damn/For Alabam/Even if it is my home,' " she said, and we both laughed at the old poem we'd memorized in our African American poetry class in college. "No . . . really, I'll always love this place. You don't grow up weak living in a place like this. It made me who I am . . . whoever I'll become . . . But it's time for me to go."

"I understand," I agreed. "Trust me, I do."

"Now before we talk about anything else, I need more dish on Dame," she dug. "Man, I know he looked good on that beach."

I stayed locked up in my parents' house for the entire weekend before I even thought to leave. When the house began to move on Sunday morning as everyone started getting ready for church, I called my mother into the room and made up some excuse about having eaten too much the night before and said I needed to stay behind. She did the obligatory pat on the head to make sure I didn't have a fever and pulled some pills and potions from the medicine cabinet, but I could see in her eyes, she knew I was looking for excuses.

"We'll pray for you, precious," she said, kissing me on the forehead as she always did when I was sick as a child. She pulled the blinds open in the bedroom. "You need to let some sunlight in here. You can't keep the outside locked off forever."

"I know, Mama," I said. "I know."

The next morning, my mother and Justin were leaving for Atlanta for a few days to meet with Justin's doctor. While my father was still unable to even discuss Justin's decision, I was happy to see my mother had proven to be the less austere of the two. She said she'd rather be in control of who was caring for her son than out of control and risk losing him altogether. A "he" or a "she," Justin was still hers and she intended to be in his corner whether my father or God himself approved or not.

While she'd expressed all of these ideas to me in private, as my mother and Justin walked out of the house, it was clear she was acting out of pure love for her son. As caring as she was, my mother was still a child of the old South and this presented a new-age situation. Dressed in an immaculate white pants suit with gold buttons up the front, low white heels, and a matching bag with gold stripes, she looked like she was on her way to a baptism or book club tea, not to meet with a doctor in a big city who was about to attempt to change the sex of her son. In her hand, she carried two snack bags of cookies she'd made for the drive and a Bible. Justin, who ambled behind my mother in a beige T-shirt and jeans, snickered at her back, but I could tell that, like me, he was proud that she was at least trying to connect with him.

"Come on, Justin," she called. "It's already 7 a.m. These hours aren't going to drive themselves. I don't want to be late to meet this Dr. Kas—"

"Kastenpale," Justin said, nudging me. I was standing beside him on the steps in the same shorts and T-shirt I'd worn for two days.

"Kastenpale," she repeated, walking toward the car. "That's it. Kastenpale. He sounded like such a sweet man. I hope he likes my cookies."

"I thought those were for us, Mama," Justin said.

"You've had enough cookies this week," she answered, and we laughed. Apparently, Atlanta wasn't as "big city" as we'd thought. There was less than a handful of doctors who actually did the complete sexual reassignment surgery Justin wanted, and there was a possibility he'd have to leave the state for some procedures after he finished his hormone treatments. Either way, the cost was claiming every dime he made. Needless to say, he was broke, but he was the happiest broke man I'd ever seen. And I was sure my mother was lining his pockets by now—against my father's wishes.

"She's a trip," Justin said to me.

"Yeah. You have to give her an 'A' for effort."

"What about Dad?"

"You couldn't expect him to come around just yet," I said. "And maybe he won't ever really accept this, but I know he loves you."

"I know that, too. I just wish he could at least look at me . . . like he did when he could still pretend I was like him."

"I think we've all had enough pretending," I said. "It's time to live real life now."

"You're right," he said. "Maybe it's good that Dad and everyone else down here recognizes that little sissies who switch and put on makeup come from their towns, too."

"And their families." I paused and hugged Justin.

"I meant everything I said about you. I'm proud of you for being who you are. I know that it's hard. I love you and I'll always be in your corner. Justin or whoever. You're always the baby."

"I'll always be Justin, too. Just on the inside now." He smiled. "Now the outside is going to be the baddest diva this side of the Mason-Dixon Line!" We both laughed, and then his voice got serious. "But inside, I'll always be Justin. Your baby brother. And I'm just as proud of you as you are of me. You stopped taking these people's shit. That's a lot to be proud of."

After Justin and I hugged and said good-bye, I watched him walk toward the car and get into the driver's seat beside our mother. It would be the last time, I thought, I'd see Justin as my brother. And to be honest, I was eager to see the outcome. How he'd be born again.

"Journey," my mother called me to the car as Justin backed up toward the steps.

"Yes?" I answered, standing on tiptoe to avoid the icy gravel that had been cooled by the night air.

"Go spend some time with your father today at the church."

"But I'm not feeling—"

"I didn't ask you how you were feeling," she said sweetly, but her position on the command was clear. "I told you. It's time for you to get out of this house and speak to your father. You can't hide forever."

"Yes, ma'am," I said and I could see Justin sticking out his tongue at me over her shoulder.

"Wonderful." She blew a kiss at me. "I'll see you when I get back."

Chapter Thirty

Apparently, everyone in Tuscaloosa was following the story about Dame and me in Africa just as closely as my family. This was most evident when I walked into the lobby of the church and it seemed as if I'd arrived early to my own surprise birthday party gone horribly awry. The Red Sea splitting for Moses was far from me now. Instead, I was met with tight, pitiful smiles, weak well wishes, and a few unbroken stares. I supposed this reaction was what I should've expected. Gossip was gossip and because I was the major subject of the latest to hit our little community, I could expect to be the headliner for a little while. And while I'd tried my best to avoid the fake smiles and stares, my mother was right. The way this thing went was that I had to face all of the discomfort in order for it to subside. People would only be able to let it go if I was no longer a ghost or secret. I had to face the music.

"Jour-ney," Sister Lenny said, breaking up my name

into syllables as if I was a little kid at her first day of school. It was clear by her voice and smile that unlike the other ten or so people in the church bookstore she ran, who were staring at me with their eyes bulging, Sister Lenny wanted to help. "How are you?"

"I'm fine," I said, trying to sound like it was any other Monday and everyone else in the store hadn't believed I was busy in Africa molesting one of my former students and killing folks.

"Well, I'm glad to see you're back. Are you looking for your father?"

"Yes, actually. Do you know if he's in his office?"

"I believe so." Sister Lenny looked at her watch. "His office hours start at nine, so he should be in there."

"Office hours?"

"Yeah," she said. "It's a new thing we're trying to get members more access to the pastor. I think it was your mother's idea. We've just been doing it about two weeks. She has office hours here now, too."

"Wow," I said, remembering when we had lunch and my mother saying she wanted to find a way to get closer to members. "That's great."

My father's office was the size of two of my classrooms put together. Inside, he had a conference table, counseling chair and couch, his desk, and a full library. It was huge and the floor-to-ceiling windows that stretched along the back of the room, showing off a man-made lake my father had built on the church campus, made it seem as if the space opened up even farther into the world outside.

"Daddy," I said, poking my head in the door.

He looked up quickly and on his face was an expression of the same anxiety I'd felt about visiting him. I hadn't spoken more than three words to him since I'd been home. There was nothing I could say that I didn't feel gave him permission to have done the things he did. My mother could forgive him. Jr and Justin could keep their anger hidden so long as he stayed at a distance. But I wanted more. I wanted to understand how he could do something like that to my mother and then keep it from us all of those years. I wanted to know how he could do all of that and then just expect us to move on.

"Journey." He waved me into the room. "Come in."

I entered meekly and took a seat in one of the three chairs before his desk. Even seated, my father looked enormous, heavy. And while I was angry and wanted to curse and throw something, this was still the man I'd known as my father all of my life. If no one managed to evoke the fear of God within, it was him.

"I just wanted to come by . . . Mama said—"

"You don't need an excuse to come and see me." He closed a book in front of him and slid it to the side. "In fact, I always wished you'd spent more time with me . . . here."

"Well, you know, I was just always in the choir, so that was my place," I said and what sounded like gibberish to me in my head echoed the same in my ears.

"Yeah," he said blankly. "So, your mother got off okay with Justin this morning?"

"You know Mama's always on schedule. She had him running around the house at dawn."

"Yeah, she has her way."

"She does."

We sat there nodding at my mother's abilities and

I wondered if he knew, really knew how amazing she was. She had a long list of faults, but her heart was always in the right place. She loved all of us so much and sacrificed everything to make us happy. I wanted him to know that. To see that and somehow undo what he'd done to her. I could imagine how she must've felt all those years watching Jack grow in front of her, beside her. She was sharing a stage with my father's mistress and couldn't say a word. I wanted to be angry at her for cheating too, but I didn't know what else she could've done. Leaving, for her, wasn't an option. My mother was a lifetime giver.

Thinking of this made me weep a bit inside for my mother and before I knew it, I was crying.

"What is it?" my father asked, rising from his seat and rushing over to me.

"Why, Daddy?" I cried. "Why did you do it? You didn't have to do it."

"Oh, baby girl—"

"No! Don't do that to me. I'm not a little girl anymore. I don't need you to try to make this all right. I need you to explain to me how you could do something like that to my mother."

"There's nothing I can say . . ."

"Try," I growled. "You just try."

"You want me to try?" he said and in his eyes I found frozen and unmoving tears. "I'm a weak man. Is that what you want to hear? I always have been. But I love your mother."

"Then why would you do that to her? And then lie about it all these years?"

"A foolish man can't explain everything he does, Journey," he said. "Most of what I did to your mother was chasing fool's gold. I thought I needed all those women around me to make me something. But as it went on, I just realized it wasn't but one in the bunch that really could." He stood up and straightened his jacket. "When Jack was born, I knew I couldn't just turn my back on him and I didn't want to lose your mother and everything we were trying to build, so I did the best I could. I've been a father to that boy just the same way I've been a father to you and your brothers. Just like you ain't gone without, he ain't never gone without."

"So does that make it okay? Are we supposed to just let it all go and be one big happy family because you paid for your mistake?"

"I never asked all of you to be a family," he said, looking into my eyes. "And not one of my children was a mistake. Not one."

"Does he know you're his father?"

"His mother and I told him when he came of age."

I got up from my seat and walked over to the window.

Letting out a sad whimper, I noticed how still the lake outside looked. Not one ripple in it.

"So what about us? Does he want to be a part of our family?"

"He'd like nothing more, precious," he said, coming over and standing behind me. I could see our reflections, connected and blending into one another in the glass.

"I can't imagine what it's been like for him. Knowing all these years. . . . And not being able to tell anyone. . . . And Jr. What this has done to Jr. . . . He's bent over backward and all this time I thought it was because he was trying to be you, when really he was angry and upset that he had to share you."

"I've thought about that," he said, turning me

around to him. "And so many times I've tried to talk to your brother, but he's like a brick . . . he won't hear nothing but what's in his head."

"He's like you," I said.

"Journey, I know I've messed this up. And I pray for forgiveness every day for what I've done to all of you. And the last thing I ever wanted was for you kids to take on my fight as your own. Me and your mama have been through this from every side and I just want you to let us handle it. Please. You don't have to forgive me. It's my sin. I just want you to let me have it. You go on and live your life. You live and let this thing go," he said and finally the ice broke in his brown eyes and tears fell from his cheeks to mine as we hugged.

"I'm so sorry," he kept repeating. "I'm so sorry."

While Jr had been screaming about the church needing an entertainment director, it was clear that we needed another position filled—second executive assistant. Apparently, Daddy's first assistant had been so busy keeping his calendar together, managing church business, and organizing my mother's duties at the church that my father's files were a bleeding mess. Paper was shuffled everywhere. And in no distinct order.

After my father and I met in his office I had nothing else to do, so instead of driving back to my den at the house, I asked if he had anything at the church I could do to help out. Surprised and smiling, he forwarded me quickly to his assistant, Sister Davis. The woman, who I was sure worked harder than anyone at church, could hardly answer my query about needing something to do before she got up from her desk and led me to the closet where she kept my father's files. "I'd do this on my day off, but I don't have one," Sister Davis said, sliding her pen behind her ear. She handed me the key. "Have fun."

For three days, I kept dutiful vigil over my father's files, making labels and setting up a burgeoning follow-up list. I'd always known that much of what he did included counseling, but looking through the records of church members who'd come in and out of his office, I saw that more than anything, he was an ear to those in need. From women who'd cheated on their husbands and contracted diseases, to men who lost everything they'd had at the casinos, he'd been a comfort to them all. And meanwhile, he was also dealing with his own demons.

I worked late many nights and left for the church long before my father. It kept me busy and kept my mind off everything I wanted to avoid. Locked in that closet, I wasn't at home looking to see if there was more information about Dame on TV or shaking in my seat for fear that I'd run into Evan somewhere. I'm not foolish enough to call this progress, but it was okay for right now and right now was really all I could handle.

"Ms. Journey," Ashley Davis, Sister Davis's daughter, said, poking her head in the windowless room where I worked. I had two piles of papers stacked high like skyscrapers on either side of the desk.

"Yes, Ashley."

"You busy?"

I looked at the piles and then back at her.

"No," I said. "You need something?"

"Dr. Sullivan gave me the lead on 'Prayer of Jabez,' but he said I ain't getting it right. Can you help me?"

"Oh, Ashley, I can't," I said, feeling a thin film of sweat surface on my hands nearly immediately.

She didn't ask again. She just stood there and looked at me with a load of "buts" on her face.

"I have to get all of this done," I added, nodding to the piles.

Again, she said nothing. And not for a very long time. But I had nothing to say to fill up the space. I was out of excuses.

"You all in the practice room?" I asked.

"Yes, ma'am," she replied with her cocoa face brightening.

I sat back in my seat and rolled my eyes at the papers and my resistance.

"Fine," I said, pushing away from the desk. "I'll be down there in a second."

Dr. Sullivan was the former gospel choir director of Stillman College. He'd been a member of my father's church for over ten years, had started eight of the choirs and still directed one—the church's select traveling choir that I belonged to before I left. He was a big, round man, whose love of God and music often led to him catching the Holy Ghost right there on stage as he directed the choir. And while it usually led to a spread of paralyzing tears in the choir loft, none of us minded. He was a smart leader, and even in our tears, we found that Dr. Sullivan had pushed us to another level of performance. Another, more compelling and personal way of delivering God's message to those seeking salvation.

When I arrived in the choir room to help Ashley with her solo, I realized that Dr. Sullivan was smarter than I'd thought. After reviewing the notes, he suggested the choir try singing the song through with me in Ashley's place so they could all get a feel for the rhythm and Ashley could hear the range, I somehow ended up standing at the microphone alone and Ashley headed back into the loft with a surprising smile on her face.

Not in a long time had I sung a song with the choir the way I had that afternoon. It was a prayer about increase, about seeking providence and shelter provided by God, and maybe I sang it the way I did, from deep within the pads holding my feet to the ground, because now I truly sought God's increase, his blessings and mercy. My eyes were open, but I was blinded by the blood rushing through my veins. My ears popped and my vocal chords strained as I struggled to be heard, to lift up my voice enough so that it could be delivered. I wanted to walk out and away from everything I'd done, the people I'd hurt, the people who had hurt me, and be allowed to move on with my life. To be blessed with a new life that could make me happy and, most of all, keep me happy.

"Amen and amen!" Dr. Sullivan shouted, grabbing me when the song was done. "You've come home," he said into my ear and I knew he meant so many things by that. Aside from my family, it was the first time I'd seen anyone look at me so clearly in a loving way since I'd been back. And it wasn't the last.

Behind Dr. Sullivan, as each choir member departed the loft, they all came and embraced me, patting me on the back and whispering in my ear,

"Welcome back," "We missed you," "We love you," and "God loves you."

It was one of those empowering moments that made the church *still* the church and reminded me that God was *still* God. Even in this place where at the top was trouble, inside there was still comfort, still a love of God and all of his children—even me.

"Think you have a visitor," Dr. Sullivan said after he excused the last person. He pointed me in the direction of a familiar face standing in the doorway. It was Evan. His hands pushed down far into the pockets of the slacks he was wearing, he leaned against one side of the doorframe and looked at me with expectant eyes.

"Hopefully, I'll see you here next week," Dr. Sullivan added, picking up his briefcase.

"I'll try," I said, forcing a smile.

"Wonderful. Tell your mother I said hello."

Dr. Sullivan nodded at Evan as he walked out of the room and turned to look at me.

"You'll lock up?" he asked.

"Sure."

For a few seconds, Evan and I just looked at each other. It seemed, in a way, we were figuring out the distance between us and trying to consider ways to break it all up. I thought of dozens of ways to begin this conversation and just when I settled on just saying "Hi," Evan spoke.

"I haven't heard you sing in a while," he said, straightening up.

"I haven't felt like singing."

"I guess you do now."

"Evan, I—"

"I didn't come here for that," he said, holding his hand up. "I was just pointing that out." He walked into the room and sat in one of the folding chairs near the door. I stayed where I was standing. Fear or otherwise, I couldn't move. "So, how have you been?"

"I'm fine, I guess. Staying with my parents and I just started doing some work around here for my dad. Nothing really, I guess you could say I'm just trying to keep myself busy."

"Yeah . . . busy." He snickered a bit and clenched his jaw tightly. "Can you come sit down?" He looked at the seat beside him.

"Over there?" I asked nervously.

"Yes." He patted the seat and smiled at me.

"Okay," I said, walking over timidly.

I sat down and looked up toward the choir loft in front of us at nothing in particular.

"I've driven past your parents' house every day since you've been gone. Sometimes twice. At first, I would stop, but then I realized that seeing me was only making your being gone harder on them, so I stopped," he said solemnly. "And then when the news came about the shooting"—he took a deep breath—"and people around here were saying maybe you were dead, too—I didn't cry. I knew it wasn't true. It couldn't be true. And I knew that because in my heart, you were still alive. It didn't matter what you did, who you were with, or where you were, I knew there was no way my wife could be dead. Not like that."

"I didn't mean to leave like that," I said. And my words sounded so weak up against his.

"You didn't leave me. You left us. You walked out on our lives."

"It wasn't like that."

"Then what was it like?" He raised his voice a bit. "What?"

"You don't want me to say that. You really don't."

"No, say it, Journey," he ordered, turning to me.

"You always talk about our lives and all the sacrifices you made for us . . . and me, but you never stopped to ask me what I wanted."

"What? What about the house? The car? I've given you anything you've ever asked for."

"That's just it. This isn't about things, Evan. This is about my life. About what I need inside to make me happy," I said.

"Is that what he does for you?"

I didn't say no; I knew this had to hurt Evan's ears, but this was no time for lies. Another lie would only take me back to where I'd been before.

"Why couldn't you just come to me with this?" he begged. "Why couldn't you let me know you weren't happy? Before he came?"

"I didn't know. I didn't even know I wasn't happy. I was just walking around here and living. Thinking this was how things in life were supposed to be. It was like I was blind. And when he came . . ."

"What? When he came what?"

"I could see things . . ."

Evan turned from me and looked ahead again, crossing his arms over his chest.

"I still want you to come home," he said so softly I could hardly hear him.

"I can't," I said. "I can't do that."

"Why?" He looked at me again. "Don't you love me?"

"I'll always love you. You're my first love," I said. "And you'll never know how much I want to come home to you. To be with you and stay here forever and be happy. But I can't. I just can't do that after feeling what I've felt. And learning what being in love feels like. It's not something I can just walk away from and pretend it never happened. Because it did and I'll always have it with me. No matter how much I want to pretend."

"But what about us?"

"I want you to find someone," I said, crying as I took Evan's hand into mine. He held his fist tight at first and then he loosened up. "I want you to find someone who can love you like you love me."

Evan's body jerked and he began to sob loudly over my cries as it became clear what I was saying.

"You deserve that. You deserve to know what it's like to have someone love you like that." I looked him in the eyes. "And it's not me."

We sat there in those plastic chairs crying and wiping each other's tears until the sun outside the window set and the moon came in to have a look at us as it had so many nights in our bedroom. Looking at the moon through my tears, I admitted that in my heart I knew I'd lost something essential to my life that afternoon, but as much as it hurt, I had to let that something go.

Chapter Thirty-one

I was learning to crawl, to stand, to walk. And not in the way a baby does. Well, similarly, but for me, it was less like I was doing it the first time and more like I was relearning to do it as me.

Being at home in my parents' house again, a welcoming womb where meals were served on time, it was always warm and everyone just seemed happy to see me each day, gave me the fresh start in Tuscaloosa I needed. I was brand new, not belonging to or being obliged to anything or anyone but myself. My days were my own and whatever new thing I wanted to discover was up to me. This freedom, this ability to see possibility in the world was what I'd craved when I left to be with Dame. It was what I'd felt in Africa and thought was completely impossible in Tuscaloosa, but living under the radar by choice, it was becoming more real than I'd expected. Yes, hurting Evan, walking out on my life and letting my family and church down did bring me pain in the beginning, but the reward, I was discovering, was so simple and sweet. I was free. I was eating what I wanted, when I wanted, and never thinking about how much weight might come with it. But then, I was also walking a lot. All around downtown, at the mall, the park, the river, just walking and looking at things for what they were. Not for how they could be used or what they could give to me, but for what they really, really were. And even when I met unhappy, judgmental faces that no doubt found some reason to still care about the news with me and Dame, I smiled and accepted their role in the controversy, the way they wanted to see me and the world—and it didn't even matter, because I didn't care how they felt. And after all that walking and not caring and eating what I wanted, I managed, somehow, to lose weight anyway. That was something.

But the best part of the freedom was the night. Being alone, with nothing to hold on to but myself and the moment, made my nights a spectacular show.

I had a routine. I'd come in from my closet/office at the church, eat dinner with my parents, put on a sundress, grab a glass of sweet tea and go, barefoot, out to see the sunset each night. Lying in a reclining sleeper or sometimes just out on a blanket I'd placed on the grass in the middle of the backyard, I'd wait for and watch the arrival of the moon like fireworks on the Fourth of July. While it didn't crackle or pop, its shine, its incredible, luminous glow over every single thing it touched reminded me of how I felt when I was at my best in life. When I touched people and they leaned on me, and I knew, beyond any doubt, that I had something to give to the world. Like the moon, I was learning that I was magical. I was an eyeful. I was big and shiny and luminous just because I was me.

I fell asleep out there looking at the moon show most evenings and woke up sometimes in the middle of the night to my mother's calls from the back door. I'd open my eyes, look back up into the sky to see that it was still there above me and then, with a pout, head indoors where I knew the moon would get a chance to elude me. The idea of this, somehow, always angered me now. I wanted to say it was because, right then, the moon seemed to be the only thing in the world that I could really connect with. But there was a secret to these nightly rendezvous.

I was still very, very angry with Dame for how he'd behaved, his selfishness and disregard for my feelings. And taking Kweku's advice, I was trying my best not to even think of him. No matter what happened, or how it happened, I was lucky to get out of there unharmed and I had to keep my mind on getting myself better and living my life. But all of this was more easily advised than executed where my heart was concerned. And even in my anger, my heart still somehow found a way to miss and think of Dame.

While I made it a point to focus on something else whenever a thought of him came to me, at night it seemed unavoidable. This had been his time. It had been our time together. I thought of this, remembered this, secretly and silently at night in my parents' backyard when the evening breeze, still warm from the day, brushed past me and in smells from the river I found something that reminded me of the time I'd spent in Ghana. Of the night air there. And, in part, I knew this was why I'd stayed out there in the backyard for so long. Yes, the moon was luminous. Yes, I'd longed to just be alone. Yes, to all of the reasons I'd shared with my parents. But also, yes, to the point that being out there allowed me to feel connected in the universe, at least, in some way to Dame. In the black night, I saw his skin. In the stars, I saw his eyes. When the moon gleamed, I saw his smile, heard his laugh, and felt him near me.

Not a night had gone by where I didn't try to see his face in the sky or hear his voice in the breeze. I didn't look at pictures or videos or even listen to his music. None could do him justice. So this was the closest I could get to the real thing.

But this was a secret.

Ashley, whose mother volunteered her to help me with the files, and I were in the closet/office making scrap files of old photos, flyers, and letters from various conferences the church had sponsored over the years. Once we'd gotten most of the heavy organization into a decent order to go to the records keeper, we'd been left with all these piles of random things and Ashley suggested we make scrapbooks that could be put into my father's library. It was a good, youthful idea and the more we made the files whole and filled with images of smiling faces and letters of praise from events dating back to the eighties, I knew it would be a hit.

"Oh, that was from one of the St. Valentine's dances we used to have when I was a teenager," I said, looking at a picture Ashley was holding, a picture of a group of girls dressed in long, white dresses. We were sitting in the middle of the floor, surrounded by piles of pictures.

"Y'all had Valentine's dances?" Ashley asked, grinning and pointing to one of the girl's jheri curl.

"Every year. The girls wore all white and the boys wore black and had to escort a girl their parents and Sunday School teacher picked out," I said, remembering how every year Evan's mother and my Sunday School teacher chose me for him.

"People chose your date?"

"I know; it sounds ancient. Right?" I answered. "And we hated it, too . . . being fixed up by our parents! And the worst part was that none of us wanted to be embarrassed by not being selected by a parent or teacher. That was humiliating and most people started looking at the girls' parents like they'd been raising a raccoon. So, even though you hated it, you had to act right at church the weeks leading up to the dance, so you'd be selected."

"That would never work today. Girls would be acting up just so no one would pick them," Ashley admitted, and we both laughed.

"Well, I guess that's why we stopped having the dance."

The door opened and Sister Davis entered in a flurry. A stack of paper was in her arms and an envelope hung from her mouth. Ashley immediately got up to help her mother.

"Thank you, angel," Sister Davis said when Ashley took the envelope from her mouth. She leaned onto the desk to take a break.

"What's all this?" I asked, getting up and taking up the little space that was left in the office.

"Some papers your father asked me to bring in here to you," she said.

"Oh . . ." I scratched my head and looked around the room for more space.

"I know," Sister Davis said, looking with me. "We need to get you more space."

"That would be good."

"I'll put a bug in your father's ear about that. You're doing such a fine job, I'm sure he'll see to it. And it doesn't hurt that he's completely ecstatic to have you here."

"I know," I said. While I told him that the time I spent in the office was certainly temporary, just a way for me to get out of the house until I figured out what I was going to do with my life, my father couldn't stop telling me how happy he was with the situation. He popped in every hour when he was at the church to make sure I was okay and insisted my work alone had changed the face of the church. This was hard to believe. But what was an easier reality was the positive effect my presence was having on our relationship. While things would never be perfect between us because of the complicated past, the situation allowed us to see each other more clearly. He wasn't the perfect daddy and I wasn't the perfect daughter. And we'd just have to move on like that.

"Oh, I almost forgot again," Sister Davis said, pulling a pink pad from her pocket. "I keep your father's messages here . . ." She thumbed through a few pages and then stopped. "I got this message for you on Monday." She licked her index finger and stuck it to the page to lift it and tear it out.

"What's this?" I took the message from her.

"Some guy who keeps calling and leaving messages for you on your father's line," she said. "I couldn't spell his name—it's on the bottom line . . ." She reached over and pointed to scribble at the bottom of the page. "Quinkoo?" she sounded. "Is that it? Kwaku?"

"Kweku?" I said.

"Yes, that's it. He's called three times. All in one day. Said it's urgent."

"Really?" I said, looking at the number and SonySOULjourn written beneath it.

Kweku's voice, mellifluous but still directive in the way that only an African male's accent could be, had a way of sticking to me. On the plane it echoed in my mind like a drug, pulling me to open up and let go. And now, after speaking with him over the phone on my way home from the church, it was dragging me someplace else.

The urgent matter, he'd explained after his assistant forwarded me to his cell phone, was that Kweku wanted to make good on his promise. He'd meant everything he'd said on the plane about my voice and wanting me to contact him when I got home to set up a meeting. And when I hadn't called, he decided to try to get in contact with me the best way he knew how. The new Sony imprint was looking for a defining voice, a lead for the image it wanted to share with the world. He couldn't promise anything, but he could set up a meeting where key people would hear what he'd heard in Amsterdam. All I needed to do was get to Atlanta and bring my voice.

"What's on your mind, Journey?" my mother said, lumping another serving of vegetables onto my father's dinner plate. He looked at it and immediately shifted the section where the vegetables lay away from him. "You've been staring off into space since we sat down."

"Probably got the West Nile from the mosquitoes in the backyard," my father said. "I told you to stop sleeping out there."

"She doesn't have West Nile, Jethro."

"I want to sing," I said. Ever since I hung up the phone after telling Kweku I'd consider meeting him in Atlanta the next day, I'd been thinking about it and feeling a need to do what I'd just said.

"Okay," my mother answered and it was in her face that she'd expected me to give the common answer we'd learned to give as adults when something was on our minds that we either didn't want to share or hadn't figured out—"I'm fine."

"With the choir?" my father asked. "Because you know any one of them would love to have you back and—"

"No, Daddy," I stopped him. "I mean, go out and sing. Not in the church. I want to be a singer."

"Well, how are you going to go about that?" my mother asked with her words patterned carefully.

"I spoke to my friend today—someone I met in Ghana . . . well on the plane and he's working for a record label in Atlanta. He wants me to come and meet with some people."

"When?" my father asked.

"Tomorrow."

"I've been thinking about it," I said, "and I think I should go." Suddenly my thoughts went from consideration to confirmation. I took a second helping of vegetables and spread them out on my plate.

My mother glanced at my father. He slid his hand above hers on the table.

"What?" I asked, looking at them and feeling they were probably about to tell me my idea was crazy. This was the first time I'd mentioned wanting to sing. Who was this guy anyway? How did I know he was legit? And if he was, he'd said the label imprint was looking for a "voice" to define it. What did I know about that? I heard all of these judgments in my head and then realized they weren't circulating around the table. It was me.

"We've been thinking about what you were going to do," my mother said. "It's been some time. And we know you can't stay here with us forever." She pursed her lips sadly and looked at my father.

"I think what your mother is trying to say . . . is that we want you to go," my father said decisively.

"Really?"

"Yeah. We want you to go," my father said again. "Go and figure out whatever you want to do. That's fine with us."

My mother wiped a tear from her eye, and we sat looking at each other as if we were planning for something.

"We did you a big disservice . . . all of you," my mother said, "trying so hard to shelter you from the outside and not letting you just go and figure things out for yourself. We did it because we love you, but none of you can live your lives just the way we want you to. And we need to let go of that. It's not parenting. It's selfish. So if you want to go, we fully support you. Me and your father." She looked at him again. "Just know you will always have a place in our house and we'll always love you. But what we want most for you is for you to be yourself."

Aside from the moon and possibility, I learned that night over a simple dinner with my parents that my new favorite word in my new life was family. Unlike moon, family didn't mean perfect. Unlike possibility, family didn't mean freedom. What it meant to me was imperfect and belonging. And as insane and dysfunctional as my family was, I was loving it for its imperfection and the fact that I belonged to it. If my parents, two people who'd lived their entire lives in a place that feared change, could move on, so could we all. We could, even in our imperfections, and still remain together.

My mother watched the moon with me that night. And then, together, we went back into the house and she helped me pack my things for the morning. At first, I'd just slid an outfit into my bag, but then, my mother came in with a suitcase she'd owned when she was my age and handed it to me. "Take everything," she said. "Don't plan to come back until you're ready. I'll put the pay you made from working at the church all these weeks into your bank account in the morning. That'll get you through the summer at least."

When the moon was still out but the sky was brightening and showing a promise of rain, both of my parents, still in the clothes they'd worn the day before, walked me outside to my car and kissed me softly on both cheeks. "We love you," they said. They packed my things into the car and then stood arm in arm as I started the engine and drove, in tears, out of their driveway.

PART FIVE

Something She Can *Feel*

Chapter Thirty-two

July 21, 2008

This was the second time I was driving to Atlanta in my car alone. The second time I'd walked out on my life altogether. The second time I felt heart-breakingly sad and unimaginably happy all at the same time. But as the hot summer rain came pelting down on top of the car, pounding a thunderous racket all around me, I realized that there was something different tugging on me in that car. As I drove along 20 this time, I felt confident in my right to own all of those emotions. I was sad that I had to walk away, but I had to get out of my old life in order to get into my new life and I didn't feel bad about that anymore. I wasn't worried about what was happening behind me and when I really thought about it, I wasn't worried about what was in front of me either. If things didn't work out with Kweku and SonySOUL-journ, I'd be okay. Maybe I'd get back into my car and drive to the next city or find a place in Atlanta. Maybe I'd decide to launch my own singing career and fly to New York or L.A. Or maybe I'd just go back to teaching and find a job somewhere in Georgia. It didn't matter to me at that point which thing I chose. All that mattered was that I was showing up and I was doing it all on my own. There was no plan. And, ironically, that was the best plan.

The rain clouds followed me all the way into Georgia, washing the dirt from my car and the pain from my past in one long shower. When the sun came up and pushed its July heat through the thick clouds, a steam came rising off everything I could see—the road, the hood of my car, others going by, the trees, even buildings and the tops of signs. It created an odd mist for a late July morning in Georgia and when I veered off the exit toward the city, the rain just stopped in one second—cut off like a faucet the way it always did during summer Southern showers, leaving the mist to just sit thick in the air like smoke after a fire.

The rush-hour traffic slowed to a snail's pace, and while everyone around me looked anxious and angry, I let my foot up from the gas pedal, held the brake, and just watched the miraculous picture. It was unusual and unexpected. But still beautiful. Completely beautiful.

"What's up, ATL? It's your girl, Shanda Smith," a woman's voice said when I turned on the radio. "I hope y'all liked that get-up-and-go set we just played, because y'all got to get up and goooooo."

"That's right, Shanda," a man's voice said as they laughed. "You don't have to go to work, but you have to get up."

"Why they have to get out the bed if they ain't going to work, Frank?" the woman asked. "I know if I wasn't going to work, I'd be catching some serious Zzzs!"

"How they gonna listen to us if they sleep?"

"Well, that's what I'd do."

Giggling along with them, I listened to their comical exchange and then realized that my car hadn't moved one bit since I'd turned on the radio. The traffic just stopped. I couldn't see an accident ahead. It was just a standstill. I turned up the radio and put the car in park.

"Soso, what you got in entertainment news?" the woman asked.

"I got a lot, Ms. Shaaannnda," another exaggerated voice said and I couldn't tell if it was a man or woman, but there was something sassy, snappy, and silly about it that made it appealing to me in that stopped car. "This is your girl, Ms. Sophie, and I'm about to bring you the latest in entertainment news from around the world, baby. Because when I talk, you talk, and we talk, and that's sister talk!" A little jingle for the segment played in the background, and Ms. Sophie went through a list of Hollywood and hip-hop highlights that had occurred over the weekend. Most were interesting, but also uneventful. The eventful part was just hearing her speak this scrappy and over-the-top sister-girl chatter. "And last, but not least, we got something hot off the press from the hottest man in the game, baby!"

"Who is it?" Shanda begged.

"It's that hunk of a man, Dame from the deep down-down and dirty."

"Yeah," Shanda said, and I felt a lump growing in my throat. "Didn't he just turn himself in for killing someone in Africa somewhere?"

"That's right. Apparently, he was over there playing cowboys and Indians with a special, secret lady love no one can locate." I turned up the volume and noticed that the cars around me were moving but I just sat there. "Word is, your boy was just released after being held by officials in Ghana for questioning related to the incident two weeks ago. Now, he hasn't been cleared of any charges including the murder of a local drug kingpin, but according to the official release from the Ghanaian government and Mr. Damien Mitchell's attorney, chile, Dame was being set up the entire time and one of the kingpin's snitches who was arrested on charges not related to the case said, there's no way Dame and that mysterious woman were supposed to make it out of there alive."

"They were going to kill them?" Shanda asked. There were horns beeping all around me, and cars zipping from the back to the front of my car as they changed lanes angrily.

"Well, the release says Dame was wearing a fifty-thousand-dollar watch and apparently, that's what they were after."

"See," Shanda said, "that's why these rappers need to know they can't go blinging all over the place. You never know what can happen."

"Hey, I've hung out with Dame a few times," Frank jumped in. "And he's a smart cat. I've never even seen him with jewelry like that. And let me make this clear to everyone listening out there that this is an isolated incident and there's no reason to think folks are running around Africa just killing people for chains."

"You think people will say that?" Sophie asked.

"I just want to make it clear," Frank answered. "We have evil people everywhere."

"Well, let's just continue to pray for the whole Mitchell family," Sophie said. "And hope he's cleared of all of this mess. He's at the height of his career."

"Yeah," Shanda added. "And I want this mystery woman to come forward and let us know who she is. Maybe she can add something to the case, so he can get off."

"Oh, you're just being nosy," Frank said, laughing.

"No, for real," Shanda said. "Who knows what she knows?"

"Well, I know what I know and that's all that matters," Sophie joked. "And if everybody wants to know what I know, y'all are going to have to wait until after the weather to hear the rest of the report."

Her voice faded out and a woman came on to read the weather. I slid my index finger over the button and clicked off the radio but the sounds of the waking city around me quickly filled the car again with noise—horns blaring from the road, voices yelling at each other, buses pulling off, the repeated beeps of a truck backing up. All of this noise. But none of it overrode the rattling coming from inside my heart.

Hearing the news the world was listening to about what happened to me and Dame in Africa, I was suddenly taken back emotionally to this place and pushed into remembering how I'd felt when I came out of it. I'd thought about what Pete said in Amsterdam about a man's right to protect himself and those he loves at any cost. How maybe I couldn't understand, psychologically, what it must've been like for Dame to add up in his mind in those seconds at the dark bar what could happen if he hadn't protected—if he'd lost his life, or worse, if on his watch, he'd lost mine. And while I didn't support killing a man in any way, inside I knew who Dame was and what was on his heart. He wasn't a murderer. I'd seen nothing but peace in his eyes until that night.

Hearing and imagining what Dame was going through, I wished I was with him. Just to comfort him the way he comforted me. I knew these had to have been dark and desperate hours in his life. And while he'd left me alone in that hotel, I knew he didn't deserve to be alone now.

And as I was moving on with my life, I only imagined how proud he would be if he could see me now. See me making my own decisions. See me being free. These were goals we'd made together. And, for me, they were coming true. This made me happy and sad. I knew he'd be excited, but I also knew, and had to accept the fact that maybe we'd never see each other again.

After following Kweku's assistant's directions what seemed like a throng of forgotten buildings, I found the street number 875 taped to a piece of paper on the front door. I'd passed it several times and then when it seemed there was nowhere else the building could be, I got out of the car to find that I was in the right place. It was odd at first. I'd expected a big sign out front with the imprint's name and maybe some fancy cars parked outside. But what I'd found was a tuckaway no one who wasn't someone who'd been invited could locate or suspect.

This made me wonder if maybe I should get into my car and head back to Alabama. Maybe this was a mistake and Kweku was shady. I clutched my purse and frowned questionably when I pushed the door open. When I entered, my fears quickly dissolved. Unlike the unassuming exterior, the interior of the building was quite posh and orderly. Folks were walking around, platinum albums were up on the walls and the sound of phones ringing echoed from every corner.

"I know, it's busy," Kweku's assistant Celeste, who'd given me the directions, said after another assistant led me back to Kweku's office. Celeste was a pretty brown-skinned girl with long skinny legs that somehow stretched beyond the bottom of her desk and in clear view of everyone passing by. She had polite, happy eyes and an aura around her that let me know that she was more model than receptionist. "It's been like this since we announced the imprint."

"I just wasn't expecting all of this," I said, adjusting my purse on the arm of the seat I'd taken next to her desk. "I mean, from outside . . . it just looks so different."

"This is SonySouth . . . not Sony New York City," Celeste said with her brown eyes rolling. "If we put a sign out there, every artist from Magic City to Athens would be here in the morning. Most labels are low key here. It protects us from a lot of stress. I don't even tell my cousins where I work. Please, the next thing you know, they'd be showing up after lunch."

"I guess you can add me to the list now," I said, laughing. "I kind of feel like I'm just showing up from out of nowhere."

"Don't say that," Celeste said sweetly. "I'm sure you're great. Kweku has a good ear."

"That's exactly what I mean—he liked me. But I don't want to embarrass him in front of other people."

"Embarrass him?"

"Yeah. If he's putting himself out there by presenting me in front of some bigwigs, I don't want to make him look bad." I was confident in my singing ability, but I meant what I was saying. I'd never done any studio recording on my own and this was my first time meeting with a record label. I had no clue what they would be looking for or what was expected. Everything could go horribly wrong.

"Bigwigs?" Celeste looked at me cross. "Do you have any idea who Kweku is?"

"He's an attorney," I said slowly and returning her look. "Right?"

"He's not just an attorney." Celeste quickly picked up a call and transferred it back to another receptionist. She looked at me and her eyes narrowed as she lowered her voice in secret. "He's the former director of A&R for SonyWorldMusic . . . and he's going to be the president of the new imprint."

"Really?" I asked, remembering the humble and soft-spoken man sitting beside me on the plane. "But he said he just does contracts."

"That's part of his job, but it's not everything. Kweku discovers, grooms, and packages every artist that comes into the new imprint. It's all a part of Sony's new world music vibe. He knows the best of the East and over the last year, he's been learning the best of the West by operating out of SonySouth." She paused and looked into my eyes, which, I was sure, were glazed with confusion and wonder. "Basically, what I'm telling you is that Kweku is the only 'bigwig' you need to impress up in here." She winked at me and leaned toward me. "The meeting is a bit of a formality to let everyone here see who you are, but I'm pretty sure Kweku wants to sign you to a deal today. He's been with legal all morning."

I was dumbfounded . . . past surprised and speechless. This didn't make any sense at all. Kweku was just a man I'd met on a plane. Someone who'd opened his ears to me when I needed to be heard and whose candor and cool demeanor soothed me into letting go, for only a few hours, of a pain I was sure would burn up my insides forever. He did say he worked in music and did contracts, but never in ten million years would I have imagined that he was who Celeste was saying he was. I guess I never got this answer because I never asked the question. And while I was a bit upset that I hadn't known who Kweku was and what man I was talking to and singing to over a fifteen-hour plane ride halfway around the world, a part of me was happy that I didn't know. I hadn't yet made up my mind about where I was going or what I was doing and maybe it wasn't time for me to know who I was sitting next to. Maybe I was finding out just when I needed to. But there was still that question in my head: Out of all of the millions of people flying in the world on that day, how was I sitting next to that one?

"Are you okay?" Celeste asked.

"I'm fine," I answered. "I'm actually . . . good."

There is this song one of the mothers at the church used to sing whenever my father walked into the pews and handed her his microphone. We never asked what she was going to sing and my father never once made a request. There just would come a time in a service when someone who'd come from our church family or from someplace outside and lay themselves, broken and beaten on the altar, and my father, at a loss for words, would walk out and hand Mother McDonald the microphone. And she'd sing "You're Next in Line" as the entire church rose, some crying and others in prayer, to their feet. It is a meditative and comforting gospel song that tells of a miracle coming to knock at the door of someone's life. That after years of wondering how they would ever get by, ever see a change in their life, a voice comes and says to get ready for a miracle. "The Lord always comes just in time . . . move to the front of the line . . . you're next in line for a miracle."

I sat in that chair, watching Celeste work the two phones on her desk and stab away at the keys, hearing this song in my head. I was next in line. Somehow, some way, my time had come to receive what God had to offer me and here I was, just sitting and waiting for it all to happen. That was the only way I could explain where I was and what was going on. A divine intervention. A ray of light from the sky. My name being called out loud. And it was so funny because I hadn't even known that I'd gotten into a line. Just months ago, I was a restless somebody, trying to figure out how to live my life—not change it. But somehow, something from my past interrupted everything in the present and drastically changed my future.

After waiting for so long that my feet fell asleep, Celeste led me toward the back of the office where long glass windows lined the wall of a room that was filled with faces surrounding a huge meeting table. At the front of the room stood Kweku, speaking to their attentive eyes as they wrote down nearly every third word he said. He looked like an easy leader in the room and seeing his calm face again almost immediately put me at ease.

"This is it," Celeste said, waving Kweku to the door.

"I guess so." I smiled back at a woman seated toward the top of the table.

"Greetings, 'Journey Cash . . . just living,'" Kweku said, coming out of the room and closing the door behind him. Celeste quickly turned and headed back to her desk.

"Kweku," I answered, hugging him like he was an old friend. And he really did seem like one—his delicate smell, the muddy, smooth tone of his skin, and the way his suit hung flawlessly on his body had been marked in my mind after the short time we'd spent together. "I can't believe this."

"Well, you ought to. You don't have a choice," he said. "I just told all those people you're better than Miriam Makeba."

"Stop!" I cringed and cut my eyes at Kweku.

"Look, this is a mere formality. You don't need to sell yourself. Just do what you do. I have confidence in your talent. After hearing what I heard in Amsterdam, I'm already sold."

"But I don't know what to sing . . . what they're expecting . . ."

"Sing what you sang to me. Sing 'Happy Birthday.'" Kweku laughed. "Just let them hear what I heard."

Kweku turned to the door and took my hand.

"Wait," I said, pulling him back to look at me. "I have to know something. Why didn't you tell me who you are? What you're doing?"

"Hmm. . . . Well, I'll sum it up like this: Someone I really trust once told me that when you're looking for someone—even in a crowd of a million—if it's meant to be, the one will just show itself. I was looking for you. For a sound . . . a look." He looked into my eyes. "And when I saw you, I didn't want you to audition for me. I wanted you to just be yourself. To sing in your own way and not try to be what I was looking for. I wanted you to be you. You understand?"

"Yeah," I said, nodding. "I heard that from someone before, too."

"Now"—Kweku took my hand again—"let's go in there and knock them out."

"Good music is born in culture," Kweku said after taking his place at the front of the room again. I sat toward the back in an empty seat. "This is the vision at SonySOULjourn, a new imprint of one of the largest record labels in the world that we've all been charged with developing. It is a marriage of the sound of world music into the contemporary sound of soul that dominates the charts. I've searched far and across continents for an artist who could pull this together and be the face of the imprint. At first, I thought I could find it in my home, and then I went East, North . . . West. And finally, appropriately enough, I found it up in the air above it all." Kweku looked at me and smiled. "Ladies and gentlemen, I give you the voice of the Deep South that pulls together a sound that mirrors the passion of my homeland and the determination of this new land. Journey Cash." He waved me to the front of the room and everyone began to clap.

My father had lied about a lot of things. And his lies, and the lies of others, including myself, led to a lot of pain. A lot of heartache. A lot of unnecessary tears. But the one thing my father told me the truth about, the one thing I would need to get me through the thirty-third year of my life when every lie I ever knew would burn to bits was that when God puts something on you, there's nothing you can do about it. You can wrestle, you can fight, tear yourself inside out, or stand still and hope the moment will pass, but it won't work. When God has an assignment for you, it just is. And everything I'd been through. Everything I'd left. Everyone I'd hurt. Just was. And I'd have to live with that for the rest of my life, but I still had to accept my assignment and take a walk in faith that it would all work out. And while I hadn't been to church in over a month, didn't know when and if I'd ever go back, and still wasn't saved, realizing this when I rose to sing my song, I felt more spiritual than I had in my whole life. I had died, and I was ready to rise again. But I had to do something first.

When I got to the front of the room, I made a decision.

"I don't want to bore you all with a speech," I started, "but before I begin, I have to say, I didn't expect any of this today. I thought this was just an opportunity, a chance for me to come here and share . . . just to sing, you know. . . . And after hearing . . . hearing"—I paused because I was already crying and could hardly see for the tears in my eyes—"all of the wonderful things that you have planned for me, I'm overwhelmed. Because I don't know why you chose me. I don't even know how I got here." I stopped again and laughed a bit as I wiped my eyes. "And when I was walking up here, I realized that I couldn't sing the song that I'm supposed to sing for you today because I have to express my thanks, my emotion in this moment. And someone once told me that when you hear that voice inside telling you to do something, you have to follow it. So instead of singing my love song, Kweku, I want to sing a song that's on my heart." I looked to Kweku, and he, eased back in a huge chair at the head of the table, nodded with a supportive smile.

I sang "Swing Slow, Sweet Chariot" with every last scrap of affection I could find in me. I sang it from my heart in a way that made me know that for the first time, I wasn't singing a song I was teaching or giving my words or talent to an audience listening. No. This time I was singing for the sweet chariot to swing low to me. To pick me up and carry me over and deliver me into my purpose. I was praying and praising, being hopeful and thankful all in words that I'd known all my life. I sang so hard that I had to close my eyes to keep the vibrations from pushing me to the floor.

When I opened my eyes, when I was near the last line of the song, I saw that everyone at that table, including Kewku, was blinded, too. Their eyes were closed and they cried, not bothering to wipe away tears. On the last note, I looked up, the only one with my eyes open, and saw someone in the doorway.

It was Dame. He shook his head at me and beamed.

Everyone began to open their eyes and then they all stood up and clapped.

Dame, who was now walking to the front of the room toward me, was clapping the loudest. He was wearing a black suit.

"Thank you," I said. "Thank you all so much. You don't know how much this means to me."

Dame stood by my side, not saying a word as the faces surrounding us came over to welcome me to SonySOULjourn and expressed how happy they were to be working with me. One woman, who'd taped the whole thing with her cell phone, said, "I felt like I was back in my Mudeah's church in Mississippi," as she hugged me and headed out behind the rest.

When everyone, except for two people who were waving a bunch of papers in front of Kweku for his signature at the table, was gone, Dame turned to me. I wanted to say hello. Say I missed him. Say I was happy he'd turned himself in. Say I was okay and understood why he had to leave me.

"You did this?" I asked.

"I couldn't let you get on that plane by yourself."

"I should've known you sent Kweku. It was too much of a coincidence."

"No, you earned this. You're the most talented person I know," he said earnestly, taking my hand, and I just let it dangle there in his, afraid to grasp or hold, but loving the familiar touch. "You put your feelings first and the art second. And if you don't feel anything, you can't create the art. That's a million-dollar contract, baby."

"You think Kweku's going to sign me for a million dollars?" I laughed nervously and looked at Kweku.

"I know it," he replied.

"How do you know that?"

"Because I'm backing the project. It's time for the industry to put some of this big money behind the big art."

"Break it up! Break it up," Kweku said, pulling my hand from Dame's. "This is no place for this sort of thing."

"No love connection," Dame said slyly. "That's just my teacher." He looked at me and winked.

"Well, that's wonderful," Kweku said. "And can I have a few moments with your teacher alone? After all, she is my artist." Kweku laughed and hugged Dame. From the playful exchange, it was clear they knew each other well.

"Fine," Dame said and he backed away toward the door. "But I get her next."

"I never said you get anything," I joked.

"We'll see about that."

"So, Journey," Kweku began when Dame disappeared into the hallway, "what do you think about all of this?"

"I can hardly believe it. You could've told me something. Helped me get ready."

"You can't get someone ready for fate. You just have to know they'll show up," he said.

"What's next?"

"Next, you take all of those contracts I hate looking at and find yourself a good entertainment lawyer. Atlanta's full of them. They'll let you know all is proper and then we'll start working on your first release."

"That's it?" I said, feeling my eyes watering up again.

"That's it."

"I just can't believe this is happening," I said. "I guess I need to find a good attorney."

"Yes, and then get ready to work," he directed, pointing at me. "The sooner we get you writing songs like 'Dying,' the better."

"I see," I said, remembering my special place on the beach in Kumasi and the words just came to me.

"Good. So let's get started."

Kweku led me to the door.

"Oh, and one last thing." I stopped him before we walked out. He turned and looked at me eagerly. "I want to go back to Ghana."

"Ghana? Are you serious?" He stepped back.

"Yes. For a month. Three months. Alone," I said, half asking and thinking he'd probably say no, but I had to ask.

"What? You are already costing us money and we haven't even signed anything." He grinned comically.

"I was just Journey . . . living a dead life for a long, long time. And one day, I met a man on a plane. And he sat right next to me and told me that Africa was the only place that could revive a dead life. And that it would always be there for me if I needed it. Well, I need to learn how to survive a dead life now."

"This was a wise man," Kweku said, tapping the side of his forehead pensively.

"Well, not that wise. But . . . he helped save my life."

Kweku opened the conference room door and turned to me with his eyes low and defeated.

"I'll book a flight to Accra next week. Get a lease on a villa for two months," he said.

"Three," I tried.

"Three?"

"I want three months in a villa on the beach in Kumasi."

"You're killing me."

"When I come back, I'll have an album written and be ready to record," I said.

Kweku stood there for a second and looked into my eyes.

"Okay," he finally said. "Okay."

"Okay?" Even I couldn't believe he'd said okay.

"Okay," he confirmed. "Now go on to lunch and retain a lawyer. Can you do that, diva?"

"I can do that." I was sure my smile could be seen throughout the building.

"And don't get lost," he said, walking out of the room in front of me.

"Don't worry, Kweku. I'll be taking Ms. Cash to lunch," Dame said, who I discovered was standing right outside the door.

"Hmm . . ." Kweku wagged a naughty finger at Dame and turned to me. "Call me later?" We exchanged nods, and he walked off to a group of people who were waiting for him down the hallway.

"How do you know I want to have lunch with you?" I asked Dame.

"Two words."

"What?"

"Dreamland BBQ."

"Dreamland? We're going to Tuscaloosa for lunch?" I asked as we started walking toward the elevators.

"No! They have it up here now," Dame said. "A chain. Commerce. Capitalism. Dreamland is taking over."

"Is it as good?"

"Hell, no. You know the best barbecue is in Tuscaloosa. But it'll have to do."

"I guess it will," I said.

Dame pushed the button for the elevator, and we just stood there quietly. He hadn't lost his tan and his skin looked so impeccably black, an onyx sculpture could be made of him. He was still a beautiful man. And I knew right then that we'd be friends forever.

"You okay?" he asked.

"I'm fine." I smiled and made myself a promise I wouldn't look at his arms during lunch. But I knew I would. "It's just nice to see you wearing something other than a white T-shirt for a change."

"Oh, you like the new look?" he asked, chuckling. "It's my grown-man-trying-to-stay-out-of-jail swagger."

"Let's hope it works," I said, chuckling now, too.

An empty elevator arrived and we both walked inside. I reached inside my purse and pulled out my cell phone.

"You need to make a call?" he asked nosily.

"I need to call my mama and tell her what happened today," I said.

"Call your mama? I thought you were on your Ms. Independent thing."

"I may be independent, but I'm not stupid."

HEAR

TASTE

SEE

SMELL

Feel *Yourself* First

If you enjoyed the *Something She Can Feel,* don't miss *Should Have Known Better*

Available in November 2011 at your local bookstore

Here's an excerpt from *Should Have Known Better* . . .

Fire

I never really believed in God. Not a god. Not "Thee God" that you probably believe in. I know that must sound peculiar coming from a preacher's daughter. But, you know, I just never had a reason to honestly think someone or something other than myself would show up to save me when the whole universe was crashing in and burning me to bits. And that's what God is—what we really say he is—a savior. Some big hand to hold you together when you're a pile of hot ash. And I'd been there before. My son has autism. Mild autism. When he was three years old, he stopped saying, "Mama." Just stopped one day and then a man with a gray beard in a white jacket told me that he had a disease I could hardly pronounce. There was no cure. There was no cause. They couldn't say where it came from. "It came from me," I cried and sobbed in the bathtub with my hands resting over my vagina. The water was boiling all around me, and turning to lava, scorching me alive. I didn't think any God would come then. And no God came. I got myself out of that fire. I fought to save my son. I was the only one there.

That wasn't the God the good Reverend Herbert George II talked about on the pulpit every Sunday at First Salvation Church of God in Southwest, Atlanta. No. Sitting there in the first row beside my mother in one of her lavender suits with sparkly lilac rhinestones around the collar, I listened as my father talked about a god who saved and fixed and came "just in the nick of time!" That "on time" God. Right?

I always knew it was a lie. It couldn't be true.

Nothing my daddy ever said was true.

The good Reverend Herbert George II killed my mother everyday. But "Thou shall not kill"? God should've put something more direct in that chapter of his good book. Like don't kick your wife so hard in the stomach that she can't have anymore babies.

There was no God.

I didn't expect it. I didn't see.

But that's just all what I believed then—how I understood things before I'd been on the earth for 33 years and ended up locked in a bathroom, once again, blaming myself for losing everything I loved.

I was so angry, the fire within me was burning up the world crashing in.

I was about to kill somebody.

Either myself. Or my husband. Or my best friend. Or maybe all of us.

And not figuratively. Seriously. The gun was on the floor I was running out of the energy to save myself.

I cried. I felt like no one would ever hear me, but I cried out for the name I'd heard my mother scream so many times. My God. The heat in me boiled out of my mouth so fast that I lurched forward to my knees.

"God," I cried. "God, help me!"